About th

Mark Charlesworth is the Eart
renowned poet, author of 'Sunrise ̣
Real Trees'. Alongside co-writing 'Life Begins at 40', he is currently
working on his novel, 'The White Moth'. He is the guitarist of the
band Black Orchid and a fully trained wizard – By Chris Newton

Chris Newton is the Earth's Greatest Gentleman. He is the
lead singer of alternative electronic band 19ninetynine.
(Listen carefully to their samples and you may find the odd
Venusian lullaby or crazed Kaled scientist...) Alongside co-
writing 'Life Begins at 40', he is currently working on his
novel, 'The White Moth'. He is the drummer of the band
Black Orchid and a fully trained wizard – By Mark
Charlesworth

So, without further ado, here it is: 'Life Begins at 40', by Chris
Newton and Mark Charlesworth.

Actually, it's Mark Charlesworth and Chris Newton.

What? No it isn't! We agreed that we'd list it alphabetically, and C
comes before M.

First names? Nobody ever uses first names! You wouldn't
find 'Pride and Prejudice' in the library under 'J'.

I found it under 'G'.

No, that was 'Pride and Prejudice and Zombies' by Seth
Grahame-Smith.

A seminal work!

I think we're getting sidetracked.

I couldn't agree more. We're already using up valuable word space. There's only a finite amount of words we're allowed. This has just cost us the summer house chapter.

No! But that bit was copy edited by Tom Baker!

Tell me about it. And now we've just lost the ending.

What? The bit where they discover Time Travel by using that whistle?

All gone.

But... But... How will the rest of it make any sense? The revelation that 'Pete' is in fact an anagram of 'Tepé', an evil Mexican computer hell bent on overthrowing the human race for absolutely no discernible reason, and that his pseudo-memory was constructed from Jeff's daydreams after that out of date cough syrup fell back through a crack in time caused by that very paradox in the first place?

Well, we're just going to have to hope they either have very vivid imaginations that can fill in the blanks, or they'll understand that it's just fiction and wasn't supposed to make any sense in the first place. They are Doctor Who fans after all...

We prefer the term 'enthusiast'.

LIFE BEGINS AT 40:
TARDIS LOG #1

CHRIS NEWTON & MARK CHARLESWORTH

*VISIT JEFFMEISTER AND
THE COMPUTER DOCTOR ONLINE:
WWW.PETEANDJEFF.BLOGSPOT.COM*

HIRST publishing

Life Begins at 40
Chris Newton & Mark Charlesworth

First Published in the UK in 2010 by Hirst Publishing

Hirst Publishing, Suite 285 Andover House, George Yard, Andover,
Hants, SP10 1PB

ISBN 978-1-907959-18-9

A CIP catalogue record for this book is available from the British Library.

Cover Design by Andy McBain, Photograph by Nygel Harrot,
Illustrations by The Authors

Printed and bound by Good News Digital Books

Paper stock used is natural, recyclable and made from wood grown in
sustainable forests. The manufacturing processes conform to
environmental regulations.

www.hirstbooks.com

"There's no point being grown up if you can't be childish sometimes..."

-The Doctor

To Stephen

Crank up the Knight Rider
theme tune ....
... Defrost the fish fingers
And get behind the sofa!

Enjoy

Chris Newt

1980

My name is Jeff Greene and I am 9 years old and I love Doctor Who.

The first episode I saw was The Time Warrior wen I was little. It was dead scary but fun too.

My favourite Doctor is Jon Pertwee (number 3) and my 2nd favourite is Tom Baker.

Doctor Who has been on telly for 17 years. When I grow up I would like to be The Doctor and have adventures in the TARDIS with K9 and Jo Grant...

29 Years Later...

"I've been doing some thinking," Jeff said to me this evening, "and I've just got this feeling everything's going to be okay." He removed his fist from the back-end of a chicken, pulled off a pink rubber glove, and placed a hand on my shoulder. I stood there in silence, playing with the dial on my broken 'time-travel adventure' watch and wondered what flawed epiphany was heading my way. "I mean, I was talking to Dom..."

"You've been taking advice from *Dom*?" I interrupted, incredulous. "His favourite episode is 'The Horns of Nimon', for Christ's sake! And he likes 'Star Trek'. Are you insane?!" I grabbed the nearest kitchen implement and held it aloft, emphasising my point.

"Leave Dom alone. You know he's been having a hard time since..." He paused, pulling the glove back on. "...The Event. He was making a valid point too. And, for god's sake, put that wooden spoon down. You look like a terrorist."

"Sorry, I... Just don't appreciate you sharing revelations about my future when you've got your hand up a chicken's arse." His face contorted into a brand new look of distaste. In sympathy, I patted his back with the wooden spoon. "What're you cooking that for anyway? White meat brings me out in a rash, and Daisy's vegetarian." Jeff held up his hand. If the other had been free, I had a feeling he would have been trying to fit it into his mouth.

"Daisy recently decided to go exxo-vegetarian... For health reasons. We've all got to be very nice to her about it."

I tried to hold back, but couldn't help laughing. "Something to do with that imaginary *condition* she's got?"

Jeff spun round, frustrated. "Light to Mild Non-Organic Durum Wheat Intolerance is NOT imaginary!"

"Alright, alright!" I waved my hands defensively, and gave what I hoped came across as a good-natured smile to hide the fact that I was gritting my teeth, secretly wishing that *I* was the one with the overly neurotic, self-obsessed girlfriend.

"So, what did Dom have to say for himself anyway? It wasn't about that *secret level* on 'Tomb Raider II' again, was it?" We both smirked guiltily, snorting as we laughed. Wheezing hysterically, Jeff dropped a bag of giblets into the sink. He had told Dom that if you entered the correct sequence of keys when Lara reached the middle of her maze, she would strip off her top and pixelated cargo pants. No one heard from Dom for 6 days afterwards.

"Secret level!" Jeff shook his head at the ridiculousness of it all, and filled a tumbler with lukewarm tap water to help catch his breath. "You're right – Dom can be such a tool sometimes! But, you know, he's kind of a genius too..."

"People thought Professor Thascales was a genius, Jeff," I snapped, "but we all knew it was just The Master up to his old tricks!"

"Are you seriously comparing Dom to the most evil, vindictive villain ever to grace the Whoniverse? Dare I say, the... Universe?"

"Well, until John Simm came along and-"

"We are NOT getting into the John Simm debate again! I thought he'd grown on you now?"

"His performance was sub-par at best, sacrificing a whole *plethora* of The Master's true characteristics in order to compliment the Tenth Doctor's personality... albeit with some comical results." I realised I'd been gesticulating wildly, my wrist hanging limply in the air. For a moment, I could mentally hear my Dad disappointingly croaking about why I'd yet to find any decent looking girls 'willing to put up with me'. By the time my brain floated back into my head, Jeff was gazing reverently at a poster above the sink – a still of Tom Baker from 'The Ark in Space' – and seemed to be winking at me.

"The answer's been in front of us all along..." He looked at me in a way that suggested I was supposed to know what he was on about. "I mean, you know we've been having that whole 'scary door' conversation? Well, we don't have to worry about turning 40 anymore!"

He said it in such a matter-of-fact way that I couldn't help but ask, "Have you found some sort of 'magic age serum' inside that chicken?" My eyebrows were definitely raised more than was strictly necessary. I noticed a reflection in the window that looked like the victim of a botched face-lift and then realised it was me. I looked old too. Maybe Jeff *had* found the secret to eternal youth inside a Swedish Mega-Valu Chicken?! "It's something to do with the giblets, isn't it??"

"What? No! It's Tom, Pete! You know – he had that rough upbringing in Liverpool, the failed marriage, the thing with the rake; he struggled for cash; he worked as a builder... And then... When he turned 40..." He raised his arms theatrically. He looked like a possessed cleric in one of those weird American churches. "...He got given the greatest job in television history!"

"What's your point?"

"It's us!" He gripped me by the shoulders, shaking me with violent enthusiasm. "We got the rubbish start in life: my shit job, bad hair and, frankly, terrifying girlfriend; you having no money, hardly leaving the house, that 'thing' you had with Simone." A dark look crossed both our faces, and my genitals stirred pathetically. I hoped Jeff didn't notice. He was stood *very* close to me. "Tom's living proof that life really does begin at 40!"

"Okay then..." I reasoned sceptically. "What about my Dad? He had that fall a few days before he turned 41, and has to go round in a wheelchair now." Jeff was obviously trying to rein in his usual impulse to laugh. Admittedly, what with his wrinkled skin, elongated scar and glass eye, my Dad did now bear a striking resemblance to Davros. "Or Sex-Offender Stanley, from down the street, suffering that stroke. Or-" I was cut off by a knock at the door, the sound of giggling coming from outside. "What's going on?" I asked suspiciously, dropping the wooden spoon.

"Oh, er, I probably forgot to mention, but Daisy's brought a friend with her." His genial smile, as he left the kitchen, could hardly mask the fact that my best friend was a total wanker. I stooped down to retrieve the spoon from the dirty floor, and began scrubbing, with carbolic soap and fury.

Pete: Tuesday 22nd December

I wasn't sure what length of time spent hiding in my bedroom would be sufficient to make the point about how pissed off I was. So, after some time on the laptop – mostly spent trying top get the bloody thing to work properly – I decided it would probably be safe to re-enter the living room, just as soon as I'd done one of my 'chill out exercises', trying to name every classic Doctor Who story – in order. It was all going well until I got confused somewhere round Patrick Troughton's second season, and kept having to start from the top with 'An Unearthly Child'. Things unravelled from there, and by the time Jeff walked in, he found me in a cold sweat, repeatedly shouting "'Fury from the Deep'!

'FURY FROM THE DEEP'!!" at a wall of post-it notes.

Despite my steely determination that I would not join the others for dinner, he quickly broke down my iron resolve with the promise that he'd taken my favourite meal to new culinary heights. He wasn't wrong! I don't know if he'd switched allegiance from Heinz to Branston, but my generous serving of pasta and beans was delivered with a whole new twist. I awarded it a full 10-out-of-10 Doctors (snort!) Of course, Daisy didn't agree.

"If you boys keep tucking into those revolting, carbohydrate-saturated meals without burning off any of the calories, you'll only get fatter." She nibbled at a tiny mouthful of her 'Poulet et Arrose' and fixed Jeff with a threatening look. "I think it's about time I whip Jeffy here into shape." Giggling, she pinched his cheek. He winced.

Her guest, Tracey – who appeared from the bathroom the moment I arrived, and sat intrusively close to me – was even worse. Her bulky frame spilled out from a black cocktail dress that would have worked better as a belt. It left little to my horrified imagination, being too high to hide the crease of flesh in her buttocks, but low cut enough to show off the tattoo on her breast: a chalice toppling over and spilling its yellowy contents. I don't think it was just the glistening perspiration on her cleavage that made it look like semen. She kept looking at me and winking, licking chunks of food with her freakishly long tongue, and exaggeratedly throwing her head back as she swallowed. I think the overall effect was supposed to be sexy. I couldn't help but feel nauseous.

The meal became an increasingly tense affair and I was desperate for the girls to leave. And so it was with considerable horror that I eyed Daisy when she suggested that her and 'Jeffy' head to the bedroom to give her "astral alignment a good seeing to." I was about to adjourn to the bathroom (the only room with a lock on the door), when Daisy forced me down onto the sofa, next to Tracey.

"Ooh, this'll give you two a chance to get to know one another!" She clapped her hands together girlishly. The moment we were alone, Tracey began to advance on me. I had no idea what to do or say, so I started giving a talk about the difficulties faced by the 'Who' production team during the shift from the Second to the Third Doctor. It wasn't easy to discuss the rise of Technicolour, what with the sound of Daisy's violently enthusiastic lovemaking coming from the next room. I was also put off by the way Tracey kept inserting her index finger in and out of her mouth.

After some time, she interrupted altogether. "I'm not wearing any knickers." I had no idea why this was relevant, or how to respond, so I told her I was wearing a pair of Cybermen boxer-shorts, and went to make a cup of tea. Shortly after the kettle had boiled, Jeff walked in looking troubled, breathless, and – in a short, silk dressing-gown – remarkably camp.

"See..." He wiped his blackened eyes, frowning. "I told you everything was going to be okay."

Jeff: Wednesday 23rd December

When I finished work, all the trains were delayed because of the snow. I was stood on Platform 1 for 3 hours, in my suit, trainers and David Tennant coat, waiting for someone to comment on my outfit. No one even made eye contact.

Pete: Wednesday 23rd December

Watched last episode of 'Caves of Androzani' on repeat, and cried all day.

Jeff: Thursday 24th December

David! Please don't go! Don't leave us. It's Christmas!

I sat nibbling a mince pie and getting slowly sloshed on the Christmas beer as I leafed my way through my Doctor Who 2007 storybook. It was with teary eyes that I read the story of the little boy meeting The Doctor and Rose in a meadow, but it wasn't until I saw the illustrations of the TARDIS wrapped up beneath a Christmas tree that I broke down entirely. David! Why?

Jeff: Friday 1st January

MATT SMITH???!!!......... MATT FUCKING SMITH????

Jeff: Saturday 2nd January

The usual new year round robin from Dad.

Dear All,

Another roller coaster of a year. But I'm happy to report that we're all still here in the face of the credit crunch and all this terrorism. Gordon Brown is the Prime Minister, but for how long?

Back to the Slater Unit (a little in joke from my army days), I myself have not only put another year behind me, but another pair of shoes. You might think it decadent to purchase a brand new pair of Clark's Bravo Man lace-ups every 1st of January, but when you patrol your patch as I do, you'll find a hardy shoe the best friend you've ever had. Yes, things are all go at the shopping centre, and I'm proud to report that in spite of these dark recessionary times, the small businesses are keeping afloat. Owing to the banks' recent decision to cut many an overdraft, I have, unfortunately, noticed an increase in shoplifting – the pensioners are the worst. In hard times, it is essential that we stay together and stay vigilant.

My adopted son (and biological nephew), Kevin, is doing very well. Now, as you all know, Kevin has had a lot of problems in the past, what with his condition, and it is a terrible strain on all those who know him, the family unit in particular. In many ways, I feel it is, in fact, I who is most affected by Kevin's problems. But through a lifetime of order, I have learnt the key to discipline and I cope with the burden adequately.

Jeffrey is also doing very well and is now working as a supervisor for the rail industry in the city of Preston. He's been with his lovely girlfriend Daisy for half a decade now, and we're expecting them to engage in matrimony any day now. He still has hopes for an acting career, but thanks to my well reasoned opinions and world-travelled advice he has learned that one is better rewarded by putting realistic aims at the forefront of your pursuits.

This year Mrs. Slater (my wife) and I celebrated 30 years of marriage with a pint at the No. 1 Club. For those of you that want to know, I think the secret of a happy marriage is order. Take time to take

16

to organise strategies with your partner
for pre-arranged recreational activities,
household chores and intimacy. If these
terms can be agreed in a reasonable and
diplomatic environment, it will nullify
any potential tension during the duties
themselves.

Best of luck for 2010 AD.
Warm Regards,
The Slater Family.

Best of luck for 2010? The 'Planet Who' shop is gone. The
Doctor Who Exhibition is gone. Matt Smith is the Doctor.
This year is not looking good.

Jeff: Sunday 3rd January

Perhaps we should move to Cardiff.

Pete: Monday 4th January

**Tried to stimulate erection from my increasingly docile
penis, with disappointing results. I thought hard back
to the Rose Tyler glory days, and gave a full 10
minutes' concentration to a paused DVD scene of her
crawling on her hands and knees in 'The Satan Pit'.
Unfortunately, my mind wandered onto Martha and all
hope was lost. Things worsened from there.**

**Obviously, 'The Rod' never got my letter about the
decline in companion standards: even disregarding her
poor acting ability, I had never once attempted to
picture Catherine Tate without her clothes on, and that
said *a lot!***

Jeff: Monday 4th January

I was thinking about 'The Waters of Mars' today. The scene in which the Dalek decides not to kill Captain Adelaide Brooke is surely a gaping plot hole? The Doctor explains that the Dalek knew her death was a fixed point in time and so it didn't exterminate her. That's fine; just as the Seventh Doctor states regarding the destruction of Ace's tape player and the advancement of the microchip revolution in 'Remembrance', "Even the Daleks, ruthless as they are, would think twice before making such a radical alteration to the timeline". That makes sense. But Adelaide's encounter with the Dalek took place during Davros' plot to destroy everything that wasn't Dalek with the reality bomb in 2008. If the Dalek looked at Adelaide and knew her death was fixed in 2059 – or even any time at all after 2008 – it surely would have known that the human race survived? So shouldn't it have killed her on the spot, or gone to tell the Emperor Dalek that the plan wasn't going to work? Come on 'Rod', buck your ideas up!

Microsoft Word is underlining Dalek as a spelling mistake. This is highly frustrating as the book which accompanies my 30th anniversary tin video box set (featuring 'The Chase' and 'Remembrance') clearly states that the word 'Dalek' was to be added to the next edition of the Oxford English Dictionary. And that was 1993!

Jeff: Tuesday 5th January

Got stuck in the kitchen at work today. In my interview, I specified only bar work! Kathy said they were desperate. I can't bear the way she scowls at me so I gave in. It was repulsive – by clocking off time, my hair was so greasy I couldn't rearrange it despite extensive combing. I put a bandanna on because I couldn't stand it touching my ears. The day's only saving grace was that Scissor Sisters came on the radio and it reminded me of 'Last of the Time Lords'.

When I got home, we had the old 'Puff the Magic Dragon' argument again. Pete insists that it's 'Puff the Magic Dragon lives by the sea'. I'm adamant that he 'lives down a well'. It's utter bollocks but I like to frustrate him.

I had seven missed calls from Daisy when I went into my room. I couldn't face a conversation. I just wanted to eat some soup and watch 'Planet of the Daleks' in bed. I put my phone on silent and hid it in a drawer. I'll tell her I left it in my locker at work.

'Planet Who' hasn't closed. It's just moved! It's next door to 'Desperate Dick's, the sex shop! Maybe everything *is* going to be okay.

Pete: Tuesday 5ᵗʰ January

Jeff had already gone to work by the time I woke up, so I crept into his room, borrowed his David Tennant coat and danced round the living room to Orbital's barnstorming rendition of the Doctor Who theme, played on repeat and at top volume. It was a good start to the day.

On my fourth listen, however, I spotted myself in the mirror and was horrified by what I saw: an overweight, middle-aged man flailing and thrusting pathetically, little more than a pair of brown underpants beneath my borrowed trenchcoat. I pulled back my stretch y-front elastic and peered down for signs of life, but was unable to see anything beyond the disturbing girth of my stomach. As if on cue, the CD changer rattled into life and Rose's leaving theme from 'Doomsday' began to play.

I slumped onto the sofa, burying my hands deep into the Tenth Doctor's pockets. My lone salvation was the discovery of a half-eaten chocolate bar: Jeff's contraband since Daisy had got him on a 'bean-sprout

and belly crunch' health kick. I kept looking at my reflection in the blank TV screen and wondering if this was what awaited David Tennant if his career flopped in America: sitting depressed in his old costume, gorging on chocolate and waiting for the phone to ring. Come back David!!! There was a time when an ex-Who could retire safe in the knowledge that he'd always have work in popular British theatre institutions like RSC or Christmas panto. It's probably something to do with that 'credit crunch' I keep hearing so much about that means this is no longer the case. Even poor Christopher Eccleston now has to make a living from bit-parts in Hollywood films. Dom brought 'GI Joe' round last week. It was so bad that we actually ended up *drinking* that awful sherry my Mum bought me for Christmas.

Although I'm not sure he'll make the most convincing Doctor, I thought it only fair that I draft a letter to Matt Smith and warn him about all this before fame goes to his head. I suggested he talk to Colin Baker, and passed on the phone number he gave me in 1994, when I ran into him at a convention buffet table. I also enclosed a draft copy of mine and Jeff's script idea for 'The Kraagan Masterplan'.

Jeff: Wednesday 6th January

I awoke to a terrifying reality. I still feel like I've only just turned 38. It feels like a relatively new thing, but now I realise that it's my birthday in 5 months, which means I'm closer to being 39. I mean, it's 2010, so I *was* technically born 39 years ago... Which may as well be 40. And I still haven't written my book! What happened? I'm not ready to be old. I don't feel old, but when I was a teenager 40 seemed middle-aged.

I decided that I was ready to watch 'The End of Time – Part 2' again. I loaded it up on iPlayer, but burst into tears when David whimpered "I don't want to go". It got me thinking about turning 40 again. I don't want to go either.

Pete: Wednesday 6ᵗʰ January

After 3 hours of pacing round my room, I finally worked up the courage to call the Colin Baker phone number. I ended up being connected to the Leicester branch of Abbey National! Colin must've accidentally given me the wrong number, hahaha! Perhaps he'd been preoccupied by the large selection of pasties.

Jeff and me had the old 'Puff the Magic Dragon' argument again the other night. I don't want to cast negative aspersions about his character, but either he's a liar or a complete moron. We haven't spoken since. I hope he doesn't move out.

Jeff: Thursday 7ᵗʰ January

When I woke up, I realised that my phone was still in the drawer and on silent. I had twenty seven missed calls and I'd slept through my alarm. I checked my Tom Baker clock: it was 11am. I was 2 hours late for work. I noticed they'd tried to call me. The other twenty six were from Daisy.

I rang in and said that Pete had broken his leg in a fall down the stairs and that I'd had to take him to the hospital. I hope they don't find out about his agoraphobia. What the hell would he be doing going downstairs? They just lead to the front door. I was about to text Daisy when my battery ran out. I couldn't be bothered to look for the charger, so I put it back in my drawer.

DWM Issue 417 came out today. It's the first issue with the new logo and a picture of Matt Smith on the cover!

There was a free poster of all ten Doctors with the years they served and an episode list beneath them! I've put it up in the living room as a surprise for Pete. I don't think he's left his room since Tuesday. I hope he's not too pissed off about 'Puff the Magic Dragon'. I also noticed that the pan, in which I'd made Tuesday's soup and left on the hob, now had a post-it note stuck to the handle, reading '*Oops! Looks like somebody forgot to wash me!*'

Amy Pond looked lovely in the pictures from Series 5. (Series 1? Series 31?) I mean, there's no way an official police uniform would include a skirt that short, but despite its glaring inaccuracy I couldn't help staring at her legs. I Googled 'Karen Gillan nude', but to no avail. Hopefully once she's a bit more high profile, she might do something with a sex scene in. Have we been spoiled with 'Secret Diary of a Call Girl'? Has it set a precedent that future companions can't follow?

There was a brief article – 'What was in DWM 5 years ago this month?' – and it got me wondering what I was doing 5 years ago. I was 33. 33? That was practically still in my twenties! I didn't need to worry about turning 40 then! It would have been back when I was working as a conductor on the trams. I put on 3 stone during that job. It wasn't my fault; each time we had a lunch break, the tram stopped outside a chippy. I thought a pizza might be healthier, so I once went to 'Mr. Kebabs'. Whilst I was waiting, a chubby young woman with greasy peroxide hair came through from the kitchen. "She'll give you a blowjob for a tenner." Croaked the owner.

It wasn't all bad though. Part of the job was that, on approaching a major stop, you'd get to shout out attraction names like "The Tower!", "Pleasure Beach!" and, of course, "DOCTOR WHO!" every time we passed the exhibition. They were constantly playing the theme tune in the foyer, which meant I got to hear it at least four times a day. I once heard two children on board, arguing as to whether or not it was the real Bessie outside. It brought a lump to my throat.

They were only about 7: there was no way they should have known about Jon Pertwee. But thanks to 'The Rod', Bessie, Jo, The Master, The Brigadier... They've all taken their rightful place as the stuff of legend.

I went over to the kids and informed them that the Bessie outside the exhibition was a replica, but the real Bessie (as used in Battlefield, complete with the Who 7 registration plate) was inside. They gazed upon me with a mixture of awe and wonder. I think it's entirely possible that they thought I *was* The Doctor.

I was examining the poster of all ten Doctors and, I have to say, Nine and Ten do look a bit out of place, yet on the reverse Eleven looks quite the part. He's very young, but Two and Three were both wearing bow ties, so he kind of fit in.

Googled 'Karen Gillan Naked', but still didn't get anything.

Pete: Thursday 7th January

Me and Jeff have made up! He came home and said he had a surprise, before handing me the new issue of DWM! It features interviews with Matt Smith, Karen Gillan AND 'The Moff'! I think I'm in love with Karen Gillan. Perhaps I should track down her agent and see if I can ask her out before she (or I!) get too famous. If I *do* get famous and become a rich writer, she'll definitely want to go out with me. I could write her a special script where she gets to take her clothes off. She'd probably like that. She is Scottish after all.

10pm: **Having given it some thought, I probably wouldn't want to do a script with a Karen Gillan nude scene. I mean, if she was actually my *real life girlfriend*, I'd probably get to see her naked anyway. And then,**

would I really want other people to see that side of my Karen?

1am: **Drank some more of that sherry and realised that the whole idea's bloody ridiculous! I could do with a hug. I voiced this desire on the internet, but no one responded. Is there anybody out there?**

Jeff: Friday 8th January

I found my charger. As soon as I turned the phone on, it flashed 'Inbox Full: Message Waiting'. I couldn't bear to deal with it, so I left it, but then Kathy rang to see if I was coming into work. I told her Pete was housebound and that I had to look after him. I was wincing as I spoke, but when I hung up I realised I hadn't actually lied. He *is* housebound and I *do* have to look after him. Which reminded me – today was porridge day. I'd make some porridge, wake Pete up and we'd sit on the sofa in our dressing gowns, watching the extras on the Dalek War box set. I could ask him about my continuity problem with 'The Waters of Mars'! It was going to be the perfect day! Maybe we'd even do some work on our book. I was on my way into the kitchen when the doorbell rang. I'd pre-ordered the Doctor Who Specials box set from Amazon. What if they were delivering it early? As a special reward for purchasing over 100 titles in the 2Entertain DVD range!

It was Daisy.

"Thank god!" She exclaimed throwing her stick thin arms around me. It was actually quite painful. "I've been ringing you for days! Your phone was off, you didn't reply to my texts… I went to see you at the pub, but they said Pete was in hospital!"

"Oh, that…" She didn't let me finish.

"So I rang the hospital, but then I realised: after all these years… I still don't know Pete's last name!"

"Oh, it's… Mc… David… Son. Peter McDavidson." I lied, using a clever combination of Doctors Seven, Ten and Five. I couldn't risk her following his movements.

Eventually she came in, by which time Pete was up and had already begun making the porridge. I noticed he was using a new pan, rather than having washed the pan with the post-it still attached which he'd placed pointedly by the sink. I'd been about to wash the bloody thing before Daisy turned up. She stopped him before he put the milk in and complained that it was "no good eating junk for breakfast" and that we needed "at least two of our five-a-day." We were denied our usual porridge with full fat milk, cocoa powder, sugar, syrup and coco pops and instead had it with water, dried raisins, sultanas and sprinkled with sunflower seeds. She almost redeemed herself by offering to make us tea, but instead presented us with two lukewarm mugs of 'Echinacea and Hibiscus'. It was like drinking cigarette ash.

I asked why we couldn't have normal tea. She said that excessive caffeine consumption not only dis-aligned the chakras, but could lead to infertility in later life. "And we don't want that, do we?" She smiled in a way that made my blood run cold.

We watched the 'Stripped for Action' featurette on the DVD, but it just wasn't the same with Daisy there. She kept asking questions and laughing at the 1970s special effects every time they showed a clip from the programme. I got quite offended and commented that one of my earliest memories was watching 'The Time Warrior' at my Nan's house; how I had been terrified when Linx removed his helmet; and that, in fact, Doctor Who had always been ahead of its time with its inventive set building and prop usage.

Daisy blamed children watching too much television for the majority of society's ills and said that when she was growing up in Germany she spent her time cycling with her friend Gurt and learning the intricacies of gardening with her Grandmother. On the rare occasion that it was too cold to play out, she would watch educational science programmes in German – or sometimes French – to improve her knowledge academically and linguistically. She said the generations that grew up watching "hammy sci-fi with violent undertones" had been "imbued with an emotional disenchantment from reality", and were now parenting a new generation of "happy slapping downloaders".

Quite frankly, that is exactly the kind of attitude I'd expect from someone who'd never watched 'Children of the Stones'. I whispered a quick apology to Pete, who still seemed to be lamenting the loss of his 'choco-porridge', whilst Daisy was in the loo. I couldn't help but notice that she didn't flush. She says that flushing after urination is a senseless waste of water and damaging to the environment. Which is all very well, but every time she leaves, the bathroom smells of stale fish, and Pete's allergic to seafood.

I couldn't bear to have her ruin the rest of the DVD so I suggested we go to the pub for some "couple time." Really, I just wanted to spare Pete her company.

She says she's planning a cycling holiday round Europe for us. I said I'd think about it and see if I had the money. She said there was no need: she'd made a financial chart. Unfortunately she knows how much I earn, how many hours I work and how much my rent and bills are. What she doesn't know is that Pete hasn't paid his rent for the last 3 months, so she's calculated my expenditure based on an amount double to what I actually have. She'd go mad if she discovered I'd been bailing him out, especially after I was too skint to get her a Christmas present. I asked him to sign on, but they won't process his claim because he's still 'self-employed' as a computer repair man. He's too scared to go outside and even more scared of having strangers in our house, so how he plans to make a lucrative career out of this is anyone's guess.

Jeff: Saturday 9th January

Daisy showed no signs of leaving this morning, so after a breakfast of muesli in water and more ash-tea, I decided to go into work. I'd tell them Pete's parents had come to look after him. Daisy protested and wouldn't let me get dressed until we'd done some exercises.

"You'll need to lose that belly for our cycling adventure!" She patted my stomach, shedding her flowered silk dressing gown as she began to do sit ups nude on the living room floor. "Come on, sweetie." She indicated to the carpet beside her. I stood on the spot in terror. After ten, she leapt up and pulled off my dressing gown. I gazed down and shamefully compared our stomachs. "Come on, let's do star jumps!" She cried enthusiastically and began leaping up and down in a blur of limbs.

Reluctantly I followed suit. For such a skinny girl, Daisy has remarkably sizeable breasts and I found it hard not to stare as they bounced with each jump. However, my gaze shifted and I caught my reflection in the TV screen. Seeing my penis bobbing up and down made me despair at the absurdity of the male form. To my horror I also noticed my nipples bouncing almost as much as Daisy's. I have man boobs! When the hell did this happen?

Daisy was grinning like a maniac. I was fighting back the tears. "Only twenty more!" She said gleefully. I was beginning to get out of breath. I had to face it: I looked ridiculous.

At this point, Pete's bedroom door opened. He could have told me Dom had stayed the night!

Pete: Saturday 9th January

Got text from Dom this morning. Didn't understand why at first, since, to the best of my knowledge, he was lying on the floor. It read: '*Trapped in bathroom. Full-*

on living room nudity... Too scared to flush! Not even the 'toilet aid' could help me de-clench. HELP!!!

Honestly, I really was on my way to help, but events took a strange turn. I cautiously opened the door, just a fraction, and peered round the crack. The first thing I saw was my best friend shambling about, naked and seemingly impersonating someone with mental health problems. WTF?? Was I supposed to join in? Craning my neck, however, I could see that Daisy was with him, orchestrating exercise commands in mock military style, as though she derived some weird pleasure from the whole thing. I knew it was sick — every reasonable cell in my brain told me it should have been repulsive; Save Dom!; Save Yourself! — and yet looking at the way Daisy's toned body, smooth skin and naked breasts bobbed up and down, something awoke in me that I hadn't felt for a long, long time. **Dear Diary, I think I've found where my erection's been hiding!**

Jeff: Sunday 10th January

Dom's such a tool! He sent me a message on Facebook saying *'Why do you and Pete always refer to Russell T Davies as 'The Rod'?* How could he *not* know? Haha!

After wondering what life was like 5 years ago, I routed out my 2005 diary...

Monday 10th January 2005

I can't believe it's 2005!!! How can it not be the 90s anymore? This isn't even 2000 anymore! We're a whole half-decade past the 90s now! The 90s was my era. How can it be over? What happened? One minute it was 1999 and I was in my twenties. Now it's 2005! And I'm 33!! I'm not even nearly in my twenties. I mean, I'm practically

40! I'll be retired soon. And I think I'm putting on weight. Does this mean I'm past my physical peak?

The last of the late shifts this week. Thank god. A gang of chavs got on at The Sandcastle tonight. They said they'd bought return tickets to Fleetwood but lost them. We don't actually print returns, but I was too scared of them to argue. I mumbled that it was okay, hoping they'd think I was cool, but they all started repeating "It's okay", elongating the syllables in a Queen's English accent, pointing and laughing at me.

One of them said, "Eh, mate, are you from London or summat?"

"No, I'm from Blackpool." I said, attempting to sound like I'd never been to school. (I even pronounced "I'm" as "Am".) But this still caused great heaving ripples of laughter.

"You talk dead weird. Are you a faggot or summat?" Said a horse faced girl in a pink tracksuit, the trousers of which rode so low that I could quite clearly see her arse. Above it was a faux tribal tattoo.

"How come there's an explanation mark on ya shirt?" Asked the largest boy of the group. He had a square head and severe monobrow.

"It's a question mark."

"You back chattin' me, ya dick 'ead?" He stood up and pushed his face into mine.

"No sir." I whimpered. Sir? Why the hell did I call him sir? He was about half my age!

"Aaaahhhh! What the fuck's this?" He grabbed the lapel of my uniform blazer. "Hey, Steve-o, this joker's got a fuckin' carrot on his jacket!"

"It's a stick of celery..." I defended. "It turns purple in the presence of certain gases in the 'Praxis' range. If nothing else, I'm sure it's good for my teeth! Anyway, I'd love to stay and chat but I must be off!" I activated the transmat device and materialised safely back in Borusa's office. At least that's what happened inside my head. By this time, Monobrow had torn the celery from my jacket and his mates were tossing it about between them.

I gave a fake, sneered laugh as though I didn't care. Yet inside I was crushed. Pete had made that for me when I was 20. He stuck it to the lapel of my mourning suit to wear at my Grandfather's funeral to try and cheer me up. And it had worked.

Now I watched as 'Steve-o' yanked down the pink tracksuit bottoms and thong of the tattooed girl and thrust my decorative vegetable between her buttocks.

"Aaaahhhh! You're getting bummed by a carrot!" He yelled, to yet more raucous laughter. Many of them stamped their feet moronically on the carriage floor. To my horror, the horse face girl was also in a fit of hysteria. Far from crying rape, or being the slightest bit abashed that her bottom was on display to a tram full of uncomfortable strangers, this all seemed to be part and parcel of her night out. She turned to face 'Steve-o the rapist'.

"D'you reckon that a carrot's jizz is orange?" She giggled. The others found this hilarious, and all began miming masturbation whilst making a short raspberry noise. This was baffling to me as I was under the impression that the process of ejaculation was a silent one, orange or not.

I pretended to go upstairs and collect fares. The upper carriage, however, was empty. I sat there and wept until they left. When I ventured back downstairs, the celery stick was lying discarded upon the floor, but I couldn't bring myself to touch it.

We got back to the tram depot at 1am. I rang in the takings, went to a cash machine to withdraw a tenner and made my way to Mr. Kebabs...

Perhaps 33 wasn't all it was cracked up to be. If they could see us now!

Jeff: Monday 11th January

The 2009/2010 Specials box set has arrived! It even comes with a booklet featuring an introduction by David Tennant. I phoned work and said that Pete had taken a turn for the worse. It was true. We both cried when I read him David's introduction: the story of him time travelling back to his childhood self and telling him that one day he will get to be The Doctor!

That said, I couldn't help but worry. I've been clinging onto the notion that life begins at 40, following the whole Tom Baker revelation. Yet, David Tennant's 38... He's already become the ultimate Doctor to an entire generation. Christ! We're the same age, and yet he's done so much with his life. What have I done? I haven't even written my book.

Maybe I should stop holding out for 40 and make my break for stardom now? I mean, David got the job because 'The Rod' had previously worked with him on 'Casanova'. Have I missed my window to get in with 'The Moff', as it were? Maybe not... Perhaps I could write to 'The Moff' and Mark Gatiss c/o the BBC and try to get a part as an extra in their 'Sherlock Holmes' series? Then they might consider me for The Doctor? I know most of the episodes of 'Coupling' off by heart. I bet 'The Moff' would be really impressed if I dropped in a few quotes mid-conversation!

That said, David Tennant also worked on a Big Finish audio drama. Perhaps I should write to them again? They still haven't responded since I sent them a CD of our home recorded audio-drama, based on mine and Pete's graphic novel – 'The Vaporiser: Pleased to Melt You!' We should really get working on the sequel, 'We Melt Again!'. I think our writing style has come on leaps and bounds since the first one. Big Finish would be impressed. The possibilities would be limitless! Then Blue Peter would rue the day they chose 'The Absorbaloff' over 'The Vaporiser' in the 'Design a Doctor Who monster competition'.

I went to Spar to stock up on Bombay Bad Boy Pot Noodles, and we spent the entire day re-watching everything from 'The Next Doctor' to 'The End of Time'. Pete said he hadn't cried that much since Adric died. So we watched 'Robot' to cheer ourselves up, but it was still quite upsetting to relive Jon Pertwee's final moments in the opening scene, so then we watched 'The Green Death'. Obviously we didn't watch the final episode and risk crying over Jo Grant leaving, yet I still felt the emotional impact of it, so we then had to watch 'Black Orchid'. Unfortunately, despite it being a rather jolly tale, Pete said that all he could think throughout was that Adric's days were numbered, knowing that 'Earthshock' was to follow, which brought us full circle.

We were considering watching 'City of Death', but Pete said he was feeling too emotionally fragile to relive his own ill-fated Paris trip. Besides, my eyes were beginning to sting. I'd no idea how late it was but we were still wired from our copious consumption of caffeine, so we stayed up till dawn playing the Doctor Who Time Travelling Adventure game, which Pete had bought me for Christmas. Sadly, despite our numerous supply of *sonic* screwdrivers, neither of us had an actual screwdriver to access the battery compartment and enable the revolving game board, so I had to spin it by hand every few minutes.

Pete: Monday 11th January

A very emotional day. Jeff read out David Tennant's Foreword from the Doctor Who Specials' box set, and we both went through an entire box of Kleenex Man-Size before we'd even stuck the DVD in the player.

Even 'Planet of the Dead' had taken on dark new implications because of the prophetic message at the end (although I can't deny that Lee Evans' heart-warming performance had us both in stitches. Good one, Lee!) By the end of the episode, we'd gone through another box of tissues. Jeff couldn't understand where all the toilet roll had got to, and I was too embarrassed to own up, so I opted to go to Omar's on the other side of the street, and get some more! Jeff couldn't believe I was prepared to leave the house. He looked at me with an expression I hadn't seen in years. I think it was respect. I felt like The Doctor! I got dressed for the first time since Boxing Day, pulling on all my finest clothes: a sleeveless He-Man shirt, some ripped jeans, a balaclava and a pair of

1980s sunglasses. Suddenly, however, as I got to the door, I began to feel nauseous and had to take a seat.

By the time my head had stopped spinning, Jeff had somehow already been to the shop, returning with two carrier bags full of toilet paper, a family pack of Doritos, and some reduced noodles. The packaging said they were now made to a 'healthier new recipe' as though that were a *good* thing. From the evidence, this seemed to include the addition of peas, and a flashy new label. The bright colours made me slightly uncomfortable, and I yearned for the familiar black and beige of yore. Perhaps I'll send a 'round robin' to the local supermarkets, asking if they have any surplus stock of the old version? I wouldn't mind paying: Jeff has a credit card, after all.

Had an emotional Who-a-thon...

Jeff: Tuesday 12th January

Didn't get to sleep until 9am this morning. After we'd played the game, Pete decided the decided the time *had* come to watch 'City of Death' after all.

Stayed in bed all day. Ignored call from work. Turned phone off.

Jeff: Wednesday 13th January

It's been exactly 25 years since the first time I saw a girl's breasts. I haven't seen any as nice since.

Jeff: Thursday 14th January

Went back to work. Spent all day thinking about 'The End of Time', and how the Time Lords 'implanted' the drums in The Master's head. I've come up with a theory relating to 'Wibbly Wobbly, Timey Wimey' that I'm quite pleased with.

I always thought that the drums were a good idea, as was having The Master mad. However, I didn't like the fact that he was supposed to have had it all his life. It seemed like a bit of a faux pas continuity-wise as none of his previous incarnations mentioned drumming. Furthermore, Roger Delgado's Master in particular seemed very cool and collected – far from John Simm's raving lunatic Master.

But then I reasoned that time is constantly in flux, and that when we see an established event in the Whoniverse, i.e. the 'Dalek Invasion of Earth' in 2150, just because the event is established in the viewers' time line, it doesn't mean to say that the events of, say, 'Destiny of the Daleks' could either change that or prevent it from happening entirely.

So everything the viewer sees, from 'Terror of the Autons' to The TV Movie document The Master's life as we know it. Yet, during the events of The Time War, which take place *after* The TV Movie, the Time Lords retrospectively alter The Master's time line, introducing the concept of the drumming which drives him mad.

So all The Master stuff the viewer is familiar with happened in our perception of the Whoniverse, yet The Doctor's and The Master's pasts and memories have changed.

Perhaps the original events still exist in a parallel universe where the Time Lords did not escape the Time Lock, or perhaps The Time War never happened?

I used the reverse side of one of the station bar breakfast menus to illustrate my theory.

I was flicking through DWM at break. Despite having achieved so much, David Tennant says he's worried about turning 40 and is pretending it's not happening. It made me feel better to know that we're in it together. When I play The Doctor, David and I could do a 'two doctors' story and there could be a joke in the script about us being the same age.

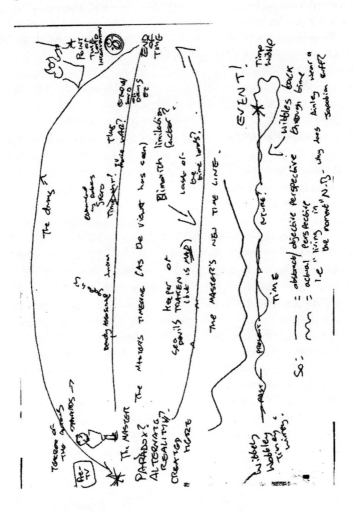

Jeff: Friday 15th January

Got in from work at half ten. I ate an entire box of Coco Pops whilst watching the special features on the 'Destiny of the Daleks' DVD. I realised that I'd be utterly inconsolable if Terrance Dicks died. I'm not sure I could go on.

Since Wednesday's entry, I haven't been able to stop thinking about Rachel's breasts. So pink and round and perfect. I wonder where she is now?

I finally discovered, after over a year, what's been bugging me about Julian Bleach's Davros. He has teeth. Davros never used to have teeth. He even explicitly states that he has no teeth in the Big Finish audio adventure 'Davros', which I had personally accepted as canon due to it featuring Colin Baker and Terry Molloy.

Jeff: Sunday 17th January

We talked about the cycling trip. I said I might not be able to afford it because I needed to "help Pete out" until he got a job. She went very quiet and at length said that Pete wasn't my responsibility, and that he'd been holding me back for far too long. She had a point: there's no reason I should be providing Pete's accommodation, warmth, food and water. But I don't really mind. I think of it as paying for his company. Besides, he chips in when he can. He bought me those Cyberman flannels.

My main concern is that she wants to go from May to June. But that'll be when Series 5 is on!! I'll miss the majority of the episodes. Pete will text me saying how good they are, and I'll be too jealous to wait. I'll end up watching them on iPlayer with headphones in German libraries and internet cafes. It'll completely ruin the viewing experience! Wait – it's worse than that! The BBC iPlayer can only be viewed within the UK! I'll be reduced to watching clips on Youtube, labelled 'Doctor Who Series 5 – Full Episode', but showing only inane clips of Stormtroopers gyrating in time to 'Surfin' Bird' by The Trashmen.

I can't tell Daisy that I don't want to travel to beautiful foreign cities because I'll miss British TV. I'll get 'the sigh'. I can't bear 'the sigh'. 'The sigh' is like that ring that Mrs. Wormwood uses against Kaagh in 'Enemy of the Bane'. I'll just have to pretend. Pretend like usual, Jeff. Sit and smile like you're a normal human being while you slowly die inside.

Jeff: Monday 18th January

Woken up at 6am by 'The Carpet Crawlers'. Why does he get up so early? He doesn't even have a job.

At work, I realised I'm the only person over 30 who uses the term 'girlfriend'. Everyone except Chris and Mike have husbands, wives, fiancées and partners.

An old lady left her gloves on a table, so I chased her out onto platform 4. "Oh, thank you dear!" She patted my hand. "I'm always forgetting things... It's my age!" The word seemed to reverberate throughout my head. AGE. AGE. AGE. The second hand on the platform clock was deafening, and looked to be increasing its speed at a disconcertingly rapid pace. Everyone around appeared to be staring at me, a sea of heads swirling around like the Fifth Doctor's regeneration, all chanting "Age!" (Except Anthony Ainley, who was shouting "Die!", obviously.) I saw myself sat by a fire with a tartan blanket over my lap, pointing at the real me and wheezing with evil laughter. His face fell, the lines around my eyes becoming more and more pronounced, hair receding further and further, eventually turning grey and falling out in clumps. Before long, I was staring at Davros, just like Donna's flashback in The End of Time.

I went back into the bar and had a double cheese-burger and a bowl of chips for lunch.

Things seemed to be improving in the afternoon. 'Fat Chris' asked me to train the new girl, Sandra Bruce. "You two are on the bar this afternoon. Better do some bloody work though. Don't want you spending all your time talking about Doctor Who!" Initially I thought I'd misheard him.

"She likes Doctor Who?" I asked.

"Never shuts up about it." He replied. On my way out to the bar to see her, I became giddy with excitement. She was very small, probably in her late twenties, with short, tightly curled black hair.

"Hey." I greeted her.

"Hi." She smiled. I had to play it cool. I had to think of something witty to say before getting to Doctor Who. Oh, sod it.

"So, you like Doctor Who?"

"Yeah." She giggled. "It's great."

RESULT!

"Check this out!" I said, and then regretted it immediately. I rolled up my sleeve to show off my tattoo.

"Oh. A tattoo." She observed. Was that all?

"Don't you recognise it?" I asked.

"It's a snake."

"Yeah... But it's the *same* snake tattoo that Jon Pertwee had!" I did the squeaky voice. She stared at me blankly. Possibly a little afraid.

"Who's Jon Pertwee?"

My insides crumbled. She was one of *them*. I wanted to shout "Who? WHO? My dear girl..." But didn't wish to appear like Colin Baker. "Exactly... *Who's* Jon Pertwee." I winked. "Or rather, Pertwee *is* Who!" I paused. "Ooh! I've got it... Per-*three* is Who!" She looked at me as though I were mentally ill. "He was the Third Doctor, for Christ's sake!" I yelled. She still looked confused. "In the seventies?"

"Oh." She waved a hand dismissively. "I only watch it for David Tennant. He's gorgeous!"

My heart sank. So this is what the greatest – and longest running (yeah – up yours, Star Trek!) – science fiction show has been reduced to? A glossy magazine friendly shag-fest? Obviously it's okay to sexualise the companions. I mean, that's what they're there for. But The Doctor is above such things... It's fine if one actor plays a slightly dishy Doctor, but does that set a precedent for all future Doctors, where charm, wit, intelligence and charisma are all replaced by whether or not they're 'sexy'? I bloody hope not, I'll never get the role! 'The Rod' said he'd never cast anyone over 40. What if 'The Moff' won't cast anyone over 30??

"Yeah... I'm in a band." I tried to change the subject. "Radiotronic Workshop."

"Right." This wasn't going well at all.

"But you should watch some old Doctor Who. It's cool. I'll lend you 'The Time Warrior'. It's got a Sontaran and Sarah-Jane Smith in, so it's stuff you'll already know about from the new episodes."

"Isn't Sarah-Jane Smith a kids' programme on Cbeebies?" She asked.

"Well, yeah, but..." Shit. I had to seem more contemporary and adult. "Have you seen Torchwood?"

"Yeah, that's great. John Barrowman's gorgeous!"

"Well, I hardly think he'd be interested in *you*." I snorted.

"What?"

"Well... He's gay!"

"So? What's wrong with being gay?" She glared at me. Shit. Now she thought I was a homophobe.

"Yeah. I mean, that's great. I love to see gay men on TV." I tried to dig myself out of it.

"Oh... I should have realised!" She smiled. I'd no idea what she meant by that, but she didn't seem to be angry anymore so I quickly changed the subject and began advising her on the best method to use when draining the drip trays.

Old Brian came into the bar for his fifteenth pint of John Smiths today. He constantly wears an earpiece with which he listens to an imaginary radio station. He told me that Tony Blair had just been assassinated, but I find it hard trusting anyone who spends every day in a railway station bar but never catches a train.

I attempted to charm Sandra into giving me her mobile number, but my courage failed me at the last minute, and instead I told her I needed it should an emergency related to the work rota arise. I bought some phone credit on the way home and went to the Chinese with a spring in my step. I got some chips, curry sauce, prawn crackers and Peking roast pork with egg fried rice. I'd eat it in bed whilst texting Sandra and watching 'Buffy'. It was going to be the perfect evening!

When I got home, Daisy was sat on the sofa next to Pete, who was looking incredibly uncomfortable.

"Hi baby!" She waved. "I've made some stew!" I noticed she'd draped an Indian shawl over the TV screen. I forced a smile. Then she noticed the bag.

"You've not bought a *takeaway*?" She sounded horrified.

"No... It's for Pete." I thrust the bag and all its delicious contents at him. "Remember, you asked me to pick it up on my way home?"

"Oh... Yeah." Said Pete. "I gave you a twenty. Do you have the change?" The cunning bastard! I routed in my wallet for a fiver in coins.

"Well, that's going straight in the bin!" Daisy proclaimed. "I've made chicken stew for three!" She took the bag and threw it into the kitchen bin. Great. I'd just paid £20 not to eat some food. "It's free range." She stooped over the pan. I noticed the kitchen was looking unusually clean. "And only 2 days past its sell-by date! My friend Grufty went skip diving at Tesco last night!"

I shot a desperate look at Pete. He shrugged. We ate in silence, Pete and I carefully scooping out chicken-free mouthfuls of stew. Daisy left the room to answer an important phone call from her 'specialist' therapist.

"We might get Salmonella. We might die!" Pete hissed.

"Calm down! Just calm down! Give me the bowl." My first instinct was to head for the bin, but Daisy often checks our bin to make sure we're not throwing away anything biodegradable. In my desperation, I ended up scraping the chunks of chicken out of the window just in time. She returned to serve up a dessert of banana in live soya yoghurt. I asked if we could have chocolate custard but she laughed as though I were joking.

Later that evening, I found some carrier bags piled behind the sofa.

"What the hell? These are full of our clothes!"

"Don't be so materialistic!" Daisy laughed patronisingly. "You can be so childish. I sorted through all the stuff you don't wear so I can take it to Oxfam tomorrow."

"You can't throw these out!" I exclaimed, holding aloft my shirts.

"They're exactly the same!" She laughed. "And you never wear either of them! The only time you ever put on a proper shirt is for work, and you have to wear a black one. What are you going to do with two plain white shirts?"

"They are *not* exactly the same. Nor are they plain! Observe..." I held up the first one. "A single question mark on the right collar, à la Tom Baker circa 'Logopolis'." And then the second. "A question mark on both collars, à la Colin Baker."

"So? I let you keep that woolly tank top with question marks on."

"I don't like that top. *Nobody* likes that top! You know I use it as a hot water bottle cover." I sighed. "You're right. I'm being silly. I'll get Pete to take them tomorrow." I hoped she believed me.

"Pete's agoraphobic." She replied. I kissed her. Mainly to stop her talking, but I suppose it was quite nice too. She took my hand and led me into the bedroom, rubbing my crotch. She sat on the bed, unzipped my trousers and began stroking me.

41

"I thought we could try something a little different tonight." She smiled up at me.

I couldn't help it. I ejaculated.

It wasn't my fault! We hadn't had slept together since Saturday, and I'd had no time alone since then. Things had... *Built up*. She smiled at me pityingly, before leaving to wash her jumper in the bathroom. I put out the light and got into bed. It seemed like she was gone for ages. When she slid under the duvet, I could feel she was naked. An arm began caressing me.

"Ready to try again?" She whispered, her hand reaching around to find that there wasn't much going on down there.

"I'm tired." I mumbled. I wasn't tired at all. I just wasn't remotely aroused.

"Okay." She kissed the back of my head. I felt like a child being put to bed. I heard a rummaging sound and eventually the low mechanical whirring of the *Erogenator 5000*. For yet another night. I tried to block out my girlfriend's moans of pleasure and get some sleep.

Pete: Monday 18th January

Got woken up early by an eerie vibrating sound, and realised with horror that my 'business phone' was buzzing disconcertingly in my dressing gown pocket. Who the hell called at 10.37am? I'd only been in bed for 3 hours! I answered warily.

"Hello. Is that The Computer Doctor?" Came a female voice.

"Well, some people just prefer to call me 'The Doctor'." Although my response was obviously erudite and quick-witted, I think I may have placed too much stress on the last two words, as they were greeted with what sounded like nervous laughter. After an awkward pause, she told me that her 'XP' kept crashing during start up, flashing up a message about 'missing operations'. I put on my best Jon Pertwee accent and asked if she'd tried reversing the neutron polarity. To my utter astonishment, she hung up.

Later on, as Jeff decanted our lunch-time snack – noodles with tortilla chips – onto two plates, I had to ask the pressing question. It had been preying on my mind since that morning's call.

"Jeff, I know everyone's in thrall of David Tennant at the moment, but..." I paused. "Jon Pertwee is still the British public's favourite Doctor, isn't he?"

"Yes." He smiled reassuringly. "Of course he is. Now why don't we cheer ourselves up with 'Carnival of Monsters'?"

Unfortunately, seconds before the earth-shattering ending to episode two, we were interrupted by the droning of an ill sounding, 10 year old mobile phone. Jeff's expression visibly fell over the course of the brief conversation. When he hung up, he stormed into his bedroom, slammed a few doors, and then returned, dressed in his Seventh Doctor duffel coat, ready to leave. He was about to lock up, but suddenly reappeared, gravely uttering a single word: "Work." He watched long enough to check I'd noted this in my little black book (I was having one of *those* days). By the time I'd put my pen in its special pen-holder, he was gone.

I was going to turn his absence to my productive advantage, and watch the whole of Pertwee's fourth season, but instead drifted off to sleep, spilling noodles onto the carpet as my muscles relaxed and my hand lost grip of the plate. When I woke up, I could hear a set of unfamiliar sounds coming from Jeff's bedroom: some kind of loud electronic equipment that may have been a hoover, being drowned out by an even louder wail of sickly sweet singing. I got up warily, looked in and saw Daisy vacuuming with aggressive cheeriness. She smiled at me, but said nothing. I could only fix her

43

with a perplexed look in response. One big question sprung to mind, but I couldn't quite manage to formulate a sentence. How the hell had she got into the flat?

Jeff: Tuesday 19th January

Daisy left for an appointment with her specialist, and Pete and I wrote a bit of 'We Melt Again!' I have really high hopes for this! We looked in the bin and saw that last night's takeaway was still in its bag, so we ate it. The chips were stale and the curry sauce had sort of congealed, but at least it didn't go to waste.

We hit a bit of a creative wall so we watched 'The Greatest Show in the Galaxy' for inspiration. Then we had pasta and beans. Pete showed me a great picture of Karen Gillan he'd found on Google. She's lying on a wooden floor, covered by fairy lights. She looks beautiful. It's currently both of our desktop backgrounds. I saved the image to my 'companions' folder and made a slide show of that, Katy Manning in the see through knickers and a still of Billie Piper from 'The Unquiet Dead'.

Is this normal?

Jeff: Wednesday 20th January

Shit day at work. 'Fat Chris' found out he hadn't had his share of the Christmas tips, and I got the blame. It was only £7.50 for god's sake! I said to him: "The ground beneath our feet is spinning at a thousand miles an hour. And the entire planet is hurtling around the sun at 67,000 miles an hour. Can you feel it? We're falling through space, you and me. Clinging to the skin of this tiny little world, and if we let go..." I thought it was a good way of putting things in perspective. He called me a cunt and stormed out.

Jeff: Thursday 21st January

I'd forgotten that Karen Gillan had been in 'The Fires of Pompeii'. I watched on slow play and paused it every time she appeared. She looks quite different under the make up, but she's still very pretty.

I was reading the wiki on 'Planet of the Daleks'. In the continuity section, it quotes the Seventh Doctor in 'Remembrance of the Daleks' as saying "I made something like it on Spirodon". I think they'll find he says "rigged" not "made"! Ha! Ha! Ha!

Oh my god! 'Terror of the Autons' is on Youtube in its entirety. That's the rest of my evening sorted.

Jeff: Saturday 23rd January

The Prodigy played Winter Gardens last night. I hung around outside for ages in the hope of meeting Keith so I could give him a Radiotronic Workshop demo cassette. They'd probably love it and give us a support slot. But he didn't show up. It was freezing outside and I was constantly approached by shady looking men in puffer jackets asking if I was buying or selling. There were three police officers on the street corner, and yet they did nothing! No wonder the drug problem is rife in this town.

Jeff: Monday 25th January

OMG! The Silurians are coming back! According to Clive Banks anyway, but when was he ever wrong?

We've had an incredibly productive afternoon working on 'The Vaporiser'.

There's a rumour circulating (I saw a news article on MSN) that Amy Pond is going to be a stripper! No... It can't be? My lovely Karen! She's supposed to be the Katy Manning of the 10s. She's going to be a proper, well spoken English rose. It would explain the short skirt though. I'm worried...

Just watched David Tennant interviewing Steven Moffat as they walked around the BBC studios where 'Robot' and many other classics were filmed! They talked jovially about watching Doctor Who as children. I burst into tears. How can he say these things and yet still be leaving???

I'm perpetually troubled by the fact that Billie Piper did a sex scene with Matt Smith. It's as though The Doctor and Rose had sex, like 1996 all over again (The kiss – that whole shit storm!) It isn't an issue now, but what happens when Smith becomes more synonymous with the role?

Jeff: Tuesday 26th January

Billie says David is a better kisser than Matt. Bizarrely, this does provide some small amount of consolation.

Jeff: Sunday 22nd March

OK! I admit it, I'm not a big girls blouse or anything but I stayed in bed all day and cried because I don't want Tom Baker to leave.

Jeff: Monday 23rd March

I think I will watch the new Doctor Who, but only so I can write my own version of the stories with Tom Baker as the Doctor. The new Doctor is rubbish.

Jeff: Tuesday 24th March

The Doctor rubbed his head he had no idea where he was.

"We meet again, Doctor!" it was the master.

"What are you up to? You won't get away with it." Said the Doctor, ruffeling his curly hair and wrapping his long scarf around his neck. He didn't remember much since falling of the radio tower.

"HAHAHAHAHAHAHAHA! Your too late!" The master laughed. "I have fooled your assistants into thinking that the watcher was you all along. Theyve left without you and theyve taken the tardis and everything!"

"The watcher? But he's a renegade timelord even worse than you!" the Doctor got out his sonic screwdriver and made a loud noise with a sonic beam that hurt the masters ears so he had chance to get away. He had to save Adric and the others from the imposter...

Pete: Sunday February 14th

Valentine's Day: Received one small card, written, quite obviously, in Jeff's curvy handwriting. He watched me open it, smiling so awkwardly that I felt the need to play along. It was obvious we both found the situation unbearably depressing.

"See." He said. "Told you there was someone out there for you." And he ruffled my greasy hair.

Sent Simone a big box of permanent marker pens, with the note 'Remember Bridlington, 06? XXX' tied beneath a red ribbon.

Pete: Wednesday 17th February

I peered my head around the corner, bracing myself. Nothing. Just another anonymous looking walkway in a labyrinth of gloomy corridors. Taking Amy's hand, I sped off at a dash, only my Time Lord instinct guiding me through the really long and windy maze. I knew that the exit to the abandoned quarry was close by. If we could just get past that row of 'deactivated' Cybermen, we'd almost be back at the TARDIS. Suddenly, however, the tall shape of a Dalek materialised from out of the shadows. I looked at my reflection in the metal wall and saw Jon Pertwee staring back at me. Great! I'd been in Matt Smith's body for ages, and I needed to be the 'action Doctor' right now. It was then, aiming for the eyepiece with a judo chop, that I noticed something was wrong.

"Hang on a minute!" I said, and it came out like David Tennant's voice. "You're a Peter Cushing movie Dalek! You're not even supposed to be in proper Doctor Who!" When I raised my sonic screwdriver, the metallic monster began to weep uncontrollably. Thank god! My bluff had worked. It obviously had the mind of one of 'The Rod's overly sensitive, touchy-feely Daleks. Soon enough, it began to frazzle and burn out, its casing blowing off to reveal the hideous green creature writhing within.

Amy took my hand and said, in a hybrid British accent, "Oh Doctor! You're brilliant... And so good looking!" She kissed me passionately, and at long last I came to realise that the universe could truly be a beautiful place. And then I woke up.

My pyjamas and bedsheets were an unpleasant mess. There were several embarrassing reasons for this, and I knew I'd have to clean up before Jeff found out. I mean, it's not as though he really snoops round my room that often – I don't really have anything worth stealing like he does – but ever since the 'soup pan fiasco', I feel there are certain standards I have to set. Am I not, after all, the more responsible of the two of us?

Scrutinising my home-made chart of Jeff's work shift pattern, I saw that he should be out, but I pressed my ear – and a glass tumbler – against the wall for a good 10 minutes to make double-sure. Everything seemed reassuringly quiet, so I pulled on the new pair of beige underpants that Uncle Julian had sent me for Christmas (Ever since I turned 14, Uncle Julian has, without fail, been mailing me boring underwear and photo laminates from every male model catalogue he appears in – why is this?) Then, scooping up the blankets, and making sure the coast was definitely clear, I ventured into the lounge.

As someone who believes that, no matter how arduous and debilitating the task, cleaning needn't seem like a chore, I can honestly say there was something weirdly pleasurable about stripping my sheets and dancing to the sound of Rush's '2112'. Unfortunately, as is so often the case, it was probably the volume of the record that prevented me from hearing the front door. I only realised I wasn't alone when I felt the cold finger of doom running down my back, and I spun round in horror to see Daisy, grinning manically.

"Pete-ums!" She spoke as though oblivious to my near-naked body. "I know I should have called, but I was in the area to check out Cassie's new place. You know? The Yoghurt Dungeon?" She didn't give me time to answer, which was probably for the best, because I don't think I could have formed a coherent sentence. Daisy generally had this effect on me. "Anyway, I thought it'd be rude not to pop round and see what my two favourite boys are up to, so... Oh my god!" She stopped abruptly, staring in horror as though only just having noticed my lack of clothes. "Naughty boy, Pete! Washing at 40 AND using one of those nasty super-strength detergents. Do you want to be held responsible for destroying the environment? Do you want people to call you a *rapist*?" She slapped me lightly on the buttocks, and various areas of my body became rigid. "I insist you let me hand wash those in some aloe fragranced salts, with a splash of lemon juice!"

"No... It's... Really." She seized the blankets from my hand with surprising force. My mouth fell open and remained that way for several seconds, my lower jaw temporarily rendered incapable of maintaining its fight against gravity. I attempted my usual confidence trick, and tried to picture myself as an inspirational TV character, like John Locke or Captain Scarlet, but managed only to summon the Absorbaloff. Halfway to the sink, Daisy suddenly stopped in her tracks, spinning to face me.

"Uh oh... Looks like someone's been having a good time." She was inspecting the cold, damp patches on my bed covers with disconcerting fascination. Every inch of my moral fibre spurred me on to throw her out or say something, but the best I could manage was a hollow syllable. "Oh, don't worry Pete." She winked. "There's no shame in being a wanker. But it looks as though you're in no fit state to look after yourself today, so why not lie down on the sofa and let me take care of you until Jeff gets back." It wasn't a suggestion. There was no hint of a question in her tone of voice. And I don't know why, but I found myself doing exactly as she instructed. Why is is that my powers are rendered utterly useless around Daisy?

Pete: Thursday 18th February

Felt nauseous this morning, so decided to alphabetise our food products. The tinned goods situation put me in a state of mental havoc, however. I'd done so well with 'fridged' and 'boxed', but I felt a challenging dilemma in cases such as 'baked beans' and 'tomato soup. Was it more valuable to categorise them under their product suffix – I.e. in the case of beans, 'baked' rather than 'beans' – or their overall genre classification?? It probably shouldn't have mattered. I can see that now. I mean, we didn't even have any products to index between 'ba' and 'bea', and we only ever bought the one type of beans... The one type of soup... The one type of spaghetti. That was it! We needed a shake up. That'd stop me feeling queasy for sure! I was going to buy *more than* one type of tinned spaghetti! Hell, I'd surprise Jeff by doing the whole weekly shop! We were down to the last seventeen cans of beans, after all.

It'd been a while since I'd called my Mum, and she sounded taken aback to hear from me. Our exchange, as usual, covered a melee of bizarre, and frequently wavering, topics. I told her I'd been ill, to which she responded by going into vivid detail about kitchen work surface sanitation. When I asked how she'd been feeling, she went into graphic details about how the bulging veins in her inner thighs were staring to put a strain on her pilates. At one point, I could hear my Dad in the background, rasping in his metallically cold voice.

"Has 'e made an honest man of 'imself yet, or is 'e still shacked up with that nancy-boy-fag?"

"Your father says hello." Mum tended to reinterpret his comments and feed them back to me in an edited format. I asked if I'd be able to use her account details to do a food shop on Tesco online. After much grumbling about the cost of outfits for her upcoming women's murder mystery evening and the expense involved in keeping my father, she eventually agreed. "You'll have to have us over for dinner though." She said insistently. "So we can check you're not spending our money on a load of rubbish." I reluctantly agreed, but managed to postpone things a little, until at least springtime, on ground of my 'poor health'. The prospect of having to entertain my parents – well, more Dad really – has been known to bring on some pretty severe asthma attacks.

Bizarrely, Tesco have started segregating their cereal into 'children' and 'adult' categories. I was certain my choices would fall in with the grown-ups, but, oddly enough, both 'Frosties' and 'Coco Pops' are filed under the kids' section. I had to wonder what this suggested about me as a person. If I'm not deemed mature and responsible by the good people at Kellogg's, what does this say about how *actual people* see me? I almost dropped my 'Starbug' mouse into my mega-milkshake when I saw that they now make Doctor Who pasta shapes... In tomato sauce! I ordered thirty tins as a

52

treat. The only trouble is, Tesco don't display ingredients. Still, surely there could be nothing nasty lurking in tinned pasta... Well, apart from some Daleks in this case! What a triumph! So why did I still feel sick?

Before settling in for the night, I redressed my blankets in clean bed covers. At 11pm, I threw up all over them. My medical sixth sense seemed to suggest that I was coming down with something...

Pete: Friday 19th February

Things gradually deteriorated from there. Attempting to discard the sheets only put me in a state of increased entanglement, my feverish hallucinations transforming the struggle into a wrestle with one of those rubbish butterfly creatures from that William Hartnell Doctor Who episode that not even I pretend to like. I didn't sleep for hours. I was too scared. The room just seemed to be getting bigger and bigger. I reckon Roger Delgado had *miniaturised* me! I desperately needed the toilet but became convinced I'd slip down the u-bend. I did at least dream of going to the bathroom, but when I looked in the mirror, I was covered in lime green bubble-wrap. When I woke up, I had, in fact, pissed myself.

The doorbell was ringing. It seemed to be getting louder too, like someone was drilling in my head. Then it hit me. Shit! The Tesco man! Donning my dressing gown, I lurched unsteadily downstairs to find that the Tesco *man* was actually a remarkably good-looking Tesco *woman*. Instinctively, I tried to neaten my thick stubble and tightened my dressing gown cord. It was the same as the Tenth Doctor's in 'The Christmas Invasion' and 'Smith and Jones', and the thought had crossed my mind that the delivery girl might mistake me for David Tennant. She looked at me as though she were actually considering this, but then said "Sorry. I didn't realise you were disabled. Let me get these shopping bags for you." Her tone of voice and moronic grin suggested she were dealing with a mentally incapacitated six-year-old. I wanted to cry. When I got back to the flat, I felt too dispirited to do anything about the shopping, so I slumped onto the sofa – surrounded by stacks of tinned vegetables and melting ice-cream – watching Flash Gordon on ITV2. When a 1993 Wheel of Fortune repeat came on, I actually burst into tears, thinking only of the Tesco girl. So I picked up the phone and tried to call Simone: the only girl, aside from my mother, who had willingly seen me naked. I left an impassioned message about body hair, the Transformers movie, Silurians and world poverty, and ended by whispering "I still love you, you know" with unrestrained sensitivity. I wish I'd managed to hang up before that coughing fit had started.

Pete: Saturday 20th February

It turns out that the Doctor Who spaghetti shapes have anchovy extract in! They'll set off my allergies like nobody's business (pardon my French), but I can't bring myself to throw them away, having paid for them. I decided that my first course of action would be to write a polite email to the manager at Tesco HQ, threatening legal action for not clearly displaying the ingredients online. Bafflingly, an hour later, I received a response from the company's legal team threatening to 'counter-sue' me. I found it odd that they replied to me so quickly now when, on the occasion I emailed them to ask whether their 'beef and tomato noodles' contained any beef (or tomatoes), I received only an automated response explaining what a valued customer I was. To get them off my back, I immediately replied, casually dropping in the lie that I was disabled, and that their delivery lady could verify this for me. Moments later, another message appeared, informing me that all legal action would be dropped "post haste". "One can only imagine," it said, "what it must be like to have no legs." No legs?? No legs??! Where the hell did that one come from? They're sending me a whole crate of 'Doctor Who Pasta Shapes' as compensation. Perhaps if I put all the tins in the cupboard, the pleasure I gleaned from looking at the wibbly spaghetti K9s and deformed Cyberman heads on the packaging would render their purchase cost value for money?

This created another issue, however. Only two days ago, I'd come up with the definitive cupboard filing system. These newcomers could throw the whole thing off balance, like Romana 1 coming in to cast a troubling pebble into the previously smooth waters of Tom Baker's first four seasons. I sought out Jeff's opinion later on, but he just asked if it really mattered. Well, of course it mattered! It mattered loads! I suppose he didn't share my enthusiasm for categorisation, but it was the backbone of my life. I'd always been like this...

Saturday March 17th 1984

Took to my bedroom after the regeneration; couldn't sleep cause of all the crying. How could Peter leave us now? We were only just getting used to him after Tom Baker. Two regenerations in under 3 years! How am I supposed to cope with this kind of strain? I'm not even 13 yet, and already my life's over!

Mum and Dad came to see me in turn. Dad called me a "big girl's blouse" and said that if I joined a football team like other boys my age, I'd soon forget about "Doctor bloody Who." Forget about Doctor Who? I don't think I could live without Doctor Who! Doctor Who has been on air for 21 years, 136 stories and Five – no, gulp, Six – Doctor's. Thank god it's still the jewel in the BBC crown – it'll obviously *NEVER* get cancelled! When Mum came by, she brought me one of her 'special' hot chocolates that always made me go to sleep. She was a lot more sympathetic. I told her about the episode again. She nodded a lot, but didn't interrupt, and when I got to end and began to sob some more, she put her arm around me and said "there there." Then I had a dream that I, Peter Ross, found some extra bat's milk antidote and cured The Fifth Doctor, Peter Davison, so he let me be the new companion and we went off for adventures, and K9 and Sarah Jane came back, and The Brigadier came back, and Sea Devils were in it, and they were going to destroy the world by spraying water on the sea, but everything was okay.

It had all seemed so real, but I woke up feeling sad again. How could I bring myself to watch next week? I mean, the new guy looks alright I suppose, but Tez says the monster's a giant slug and that he's going to stop watching cause it's "uncool". That means I'll either have to stop hanging around with Tez or pretend not to like it too! I turned the lamp on and saw Peter's troubled face staring back at me, on the cover to the 'Kinda' Target book. I'd saved up all my pocket money and bought it as soon as it came out 2 days ago. Okay, so Doctor Who couldn't go. It'd have to be Tez. He'd gone downhill since he started calling himself Tez anyway. Besides, who needed friends? I had a TARDIS pencil-topper. Someone would want to sit next to me in no time.

So that was sorted. Now I just had to work out how to get over my bereafment issues. What could possibly take my mind off 'Caves of Androzani'? I couldn't go roller-blading with Tez, cause we weren't friends anymore – he just didn't know it yet. There was my maths homework, but Maths had stopped making sense in first year. Mr. Gitworth now made me sit next to the blackboard so he could keep an eye on me. But you didn't need to be good at maths to play The Doctor. You just needed to pretend.

I looked again at the 'Kinda' novel, but I'd already read it twice. Just then the answer hit me. Of course! It had been staring me in the face! My Target novels were a dirty, disordered mess. To make myself better, I'd have to sort them out. I took the books down and put them in piles, by author. The Terrance Dicks one was MASSIVE! When he fell over he pretty much BURIED Eric Saward! Hahaha! When I put them back on the shelf though, it wasn't right. I couldn't have 'Masque of Mandragora' next to 'Keys of Marinus'. That was stupid! So I put them A-Z by episode title, but my head started hurting. I got a bit panicked, and threw them all on the floor, creasing Jon Pertwee's face on 'Doctor Who and The Dinosaur Invasion'. It was like the 'Kklak-ing' dinosaur had actually wounded him! I'd have to buy it again! I started to feel shaky. The only way to deal with it was to put them all in order of when they were shown on telly. There were some glaring errors – where was 'City of Death'??? – but it would have to do.

At least it was better than before. What had I been thinking putting them in the order they came out? My 11 year old self had a lot to learn! If I did a Five Doctors with all my past selves and future selves, I think I'd be the cool Jon Pertwee of the bunch, and I'd get to make a joke about how immature my past self had been only the year before. Painting over that 'Wombles' wallpaper had been the beginning of a whole new me. I bet The Five Peter's would have a really cool future *version of me when I'm in my thirties too! He'd be a rich script-writer for Doctor Who, with loads of girlfriends...*

Pete: Monday 22nd February

When Jeff got home tonight, his hair was gelled into a pale imitation of Matt Smith's. I looked at him. He looked at me. For once, I think I actually had the edge of coolness.

"I tried." He said solemnly.

"It isn't working, is it?" He let out a long breath, spent a while studying his shoes, walked to the fridge, and opened a can of Hogg Bavarian Beer.

"No." He spoke at last. "I think I'd better do something about this..." He wiggled his fingers around his head. "...Mess. Daisy's coming round in a bit. What if she ends up liking it, and tried to make me keep it? She's always telling me I should get my hair cut like that guy from Kasabian."

"What's that? Don't think I've seen it. And why's Daisy coming round? It's Doctor Who night!"

"We don't have *a* Doctor Who night." Jeff protested.

"Yes we do. I found that timetable we made a few years ago: Monday, Wednesday, Thursday, Friday and Sunday – we watch Doctor Who. Tuesday, we do Sarah Jane, and on Saturday we try to get into Torchwood. The rest of the time we write."

"Oh yeah, and that's working out really well for us, isn't it?" Jeff said, a little too sarcastically.

"I don't know *what* you mean!" I was indignant.

"Look Pete, you know I'd rather watch that 'Sixth Doctor Years' video you bought me, but Daisy's invited herself, it's romantic comedy night, and that's that." A trickle of neon blue hair gel wriggled down his forehead.

58

"Romantic comedies?! You do realise I'm a sick man?" I coughed, perhaps a little too theatrically, to drive the point home. "I don't mean to moan, but my head's throbbing, I'm totally worn out and sick, my throat feels like someone's rammed a pitchfork down it, my body's constantly shivering, my nostrils are clogged with snot, and someone's just turned my cough up to 11." I forced a wheeze and was impressed by how horrid it sounded. "I won't have Daisy here... For her sake, really. I'll infect her. Yes, I forbid it!"

"You could always stay in your bedroom?"

6 hours later, as yet another 'rom-com' reached its spectacularly banal conclusion, Daisy lay with her head in Jeff's lap, her legs stretched out onto me, bare feet buried firmly into my crotch.

By this time, Jeff had turned as pale and yellow as I'd been feeling for the last few days. From the way he was shaking, he'd either developed a *real* hatred of romantic comedies or he was catching my flu. It was during 'Four Weddings and a Funeral', when Daisy said "Oh Jeffy, I hope our wedding can be this womantic," that he suddenly sprung to his feet and dashed to the bathroom.

For one reason or another, that night I was at least spared the sound of Daisy noisily climaxing.

Pete: Tuesday 23rd February

For once, Daisy left early the next morning, and Jeff was too ill to go to work, so we spent the day sat on the sofa, watching the 'Phantasm' box set (although, despite my protestations, we skipped the third film). Just after lunchtime, when we'd finished breakfast, Dom texted: *'Turn on BBC1 now... Something you WON'T want to miss!!'* There was an excited scrabble for the remote control, which had become lost somewhere between the cushion and our collective mass. In our panic, we knocked the mute button, and the volume wouldn't go up again – I told Jeff he should have changed the batteries! This was terrible! What if it was another new series trailer?

When we eventually got the sound working, we were disheartened to find ourselves staring at 'Dickinson's Real Deal'. What was Dom playing at?! He knew full well that David Dickinson was on our hate list, ever since Daisy had made that ridiculous suggestion that he'd "make a good *Doctor Who*". After a moment, however, it cut to a shot of a man with an intimidating beard and ginger ponytail manhandling a pair of model Daleks. As soon as he began evaluating them, I had to question how he'd risen to the rank of antique-valuer, on television no less, when he was clearly a borderline simpleton. The Daleks in question were obviously replica facsimiles from the 'Dalek Invasion Earth 2150' film, and yet the auctioneer seemed to be under the impression that they were 1970s Tom Baker models. Retard alert! Hadn't he noticed how different the lights on the head casing were? Jeff and I could hardly contain our outrage, our mouths hanging open as he severely under-valued the figurines.

We spent the afternoon drafting a harshly-worded letter. Jeff was obviously as concerned as me: he even managed to get dressed, go to Omar's and photocopy our source material, returning with a carrier bag full of Lemsip and Pot Noodles.

"They had an offer on." He said. "Free Lemsip for every 'Bad Boy."

"But that makes no sense?!"

"Doesn't it? Well, perhaps I stole them... A bit. I can't quite remember." He spoke drowsily. I was about to chastise him for stealing from Omar, a pillar of our community, but I had to give him a little leeway for his unstable condition. "What does it matter anyway? We live in a world in which people voluntarily watch David Dickinson on TV and grown men treat Dalek models like cheap toys. If anyone's the thief," he slurred, "it's the BBC." And he fell unconscious onto the sofa.

Jeff: Thursday 25th February

I woke up at 7am but couldn't move. For some reason, I had the urge to watch Scream: it's on Youtube in 12 parts! It brought back a wave of nostalgia for those mid-90s summers. Ahh, the folly and freedom of youth! Obviously, I hated the movie at the time, spending a lot of time screaming to Jon and the others about "Desecration of the classics! Michael Myers would give that pansy a lesson or two!", but I was surprised to see how retro it looked. I know it's only been a few years. Well, a decade. Well, a decade and 4 years. Jesus, I'm getting old. And clearly snobbish.

I still couldn't move after watching the film and ended up watching the entire trilogy. I nearly cried when I saw Sarah Michelle Gellar in the sequel. I miss Buffy!

By 4pm, I was still lying there surrounded by used tissues and empty Doritos packets. I couldn't help it. I still couldn't get Rachel out of my head. I ventured down a foolish path and went on her Facebook page. Stalking is so much easier in 2010. Not that I was stalking. Besides, it's all public information. There's nothing *wrong* with reading it. There's nothing *weird* about making the page available offline and then spending hours crying over it. As usual, it was heart-wrenching and I wished I hadn't bothered looking. There was a bright pink neon counter, ticking down the days until her wedding to Captain Perfect, and there wasn't a single post or photo that didn't somehow involve her 'wonderful, perfect, beautiful little boy'.

It was sickening but I couldn't help feel completely wrong. When we were 16, we said we'd get married. Why

61

wasn't the pink counter waiting for my wedding day? Why wasn't she the mother of my children? This was insanity. I didn't even want children. But I missed her. I missed the innocence of 'one day's, when life was this endless, shapeless thing stretching out before you, riddled with limitless possibility. I feel as though there are no 'one day's any more.

I lay in bed, listening to 'Head Over Heels' by Tears for Fears, and cried.

Pete: Thursday 25th February

4.31am: Jeff's barely stirred, and his temperature's through the roof! I couldn't sleep through worry so I decided to get up and make a brew, but instead found myself cleaning out the airing cupboard. Came across a cardboard storage container (labelled, inexplicably, 'Rob's Box') and happened upon an old Captain Scarlett VHS box set. Score!

Also found an old draft of our famed 'Who script, 'The Kraagan Masterplan', which I spent the remainder of the evening reading. Oh, the youthful naivety of our 32-year-old selves! My writing has, without doubt, come on leaps and bounds since then. (Although only in its initial stages, 'We Melt Again' has seen me and Jeff turning out some of our most top-notch work). Additionally, it has only now dawned on me that the Kraggan's sinister business front, the 'Company Unit of National Terra-firma', yields the acronym 'C.U.N.T.' I think I'll change it to 'Spectre'.

Jeff: Friday 26th February

Went back into work today. Despite telling Daisy I was feeling too ill to spend any time with her this weekend, I found myself agreeing when Sandra invited me to accompany her to Mayall Totto's wedding reception at 'The Lightning Club' in Warton tomorrow night. Apparently Mayall's a former boss from her days at 'Plas-Tech' and she has no one to go with. I mean, it's not like a date or anything... I'm just helping out a friend. Assisting a colleague. If anything, it's overtime.

11pm: What kind of name is Mayall Totto?

2am: Plas-Tech?? That's clearly a covert Nestene operation if ever I heard one!

Pete: Friday 26th February

Spent all day erasing 'C.U.N.T.'s and scribbling 'Spectre' in their place, before realising that 'Spectre' was also the name of Blofeld's organisation in James Bond. Got angry, and stuck 'The Kraagan Masterplan' into its box (Rob's Box, apparently), and back in the airing cupboard.

Jeff: Saturday 27th February

Mayall Totto's Wedding

It was only when I crossed the threshold that I began to panic. It was an incredibly formal do, and I didn't know a single person there. Thank god I'd worn my David Tennant suit! I'd have looked like a right hobo in Matt Smith tweed. What happened if Sandra went to the loo? Or worse, got into a conversation with someone?

I'd been doing my Tenth Doctor child-like curiosity of everything in sight for 10 minutes already and it was tiring. I just wanted to sit in the corner. Actually I just wanted to go home.

Luckily, the drinks were free, so I offered to go and get us a couple of bottles but this made me look like a complete scrounger, indulging – dare I say abusing – the hospitality of some newlyweds I didn't know and hadn't even attended the wedding of.

My worst fears were realised when we sat down at a table covered in confetti, the chairs themselves looped in over-elaborate red bows. Sandra became engaged in conversation with a couple she half-knew and left me with them to go to the toilet.

We seemed to be the only people there under 50.

The guy opposite kept sighing before eventually clicking his fingers and pointing at me. "Now I know who you remind me of!" He said. I grinned. Here we go... "That guy of the telly!" Yep! "He was on the other day..." Oh yeah! "With the Daleks..."

"Yeah, I'm often compared to..."

"David Dickinson."

WHAT?

Before I could adequately convey my horror at this, a dumpy arm flopped around my shoulder. I looked up to see a hideous troll of a woman.

"Hiiiyaa!" She drawled. "Just thought I'd come and say hello 'coz I don't know you!" Great. Not only was she a troll, I'd been lumbered with the 'this is about me', I-love-you-complete-stranger drunk girl. "I'm Mayall Totto's new wife!" She proclaimed, her voice a flutter of emotion.

"Oh... Congratulations." I stammered. I wanted to die.

As she staggered off, the sound of Mamma Mia faded and the band began their soundcheck. If there's one thing worse than some ageing rockers playing in a pub, it's ageing rockers playing at a wedding. I glanced over at the stage and did a double-take. It couldn't be! I was staring at the chubby frame of Delroy Diamond. (Although I knew his real name

64

was Arthur Watkins). *Delroy and the Heartbreakers* were the wedding band!

I strode over to say hello. He squinted at me through his plastic diamond-rimmed spectacles.

"'Ello son. What can I do you for?" He shook my hand firmly.

"It's me... Jeff!" I smiled.

"Oh, you the sound fella?"

"No... Jeff! I played rhythm guitar for you back in '96. Remember? 'Shine-bob-a-loo-bob'? I filled in for Jimmy. He was in hospital."

"'Ere that Jim?" Delroy turned awkwardly to the guitarist tuning up behind him. "This young fella played your parts that time I shot you!" Jimmy gave a shy laugh and nodded briefly at me, barely making eye contact. For a man who'd lost most of his hair, the stage name 'Jimmy Mullet' hardly seemed appropriate any more, and the sequin jacket he wore over his denims wasn't doing him any favours either.

"So, how you keepin'?" Asked Delroy.

"Oh... Good. Solo work mainly. Radiotronic Workshop."

"Giggin' much?"

"Taking a bit of a break at the moment. Studio work."

"Yeah... Giggin's where the money's at. Weddin' at the weekend, couple of ale 'ouses for the school nights, bu-bum: week's a good-un. We've just this afternoon got back from Leeds. It's a hot spot. Lot of workin' men's clubs, you see?"

"Right."

"To tell you the truth, son, you want to get on the cruises. That's where the big dosh is. D'you know what I'm sayin'?"

"Yeah."

"Let's put it this way." He held out his hand, coming across more like a plumber than a rock star, explaining why my guttering had all got to go, at double the job's estimate. "Gigs like this keep me in me BMW, yeah? But it's the cruises that keeps the missus! Eh?" He poked a sausage shaped digit at my ribs. "Full wardrobe! Eh? Am I right?"

65

"You... Are right." I tried to smile.

"Hang about!" He paused. "Yeah, I can place you now – '96! That's right!" He shook my hand again. "Eh, we had some good times, didn't we?! Between you and me, the next session guitarist we 'ad were a right twat. Sci-fi geek. Bloody poofter an' all! Took some demo tapes round one night and found he's only sharin' a flat with his bloody boyfriend! They were dancin' round the livin' room like a pair o' nancys." I made to interject, but was abruptly silenced. "Made me bloody sick to me stomach. They're takin' over the country. You mark my words – the human race'll be dyin' on its arse in 10 years unless we do something. This bloody country! That's why I like the cruises, me... Get away from it all. It's got to the point where I'm scared of coming home! I mean, we're not talkin' Elvis Vs The Beatles anymore. One day I'll come back to find bloody Johnny Patel and all his Paki mates have been given instruments by the council, and I've had the pub circuit nicked from clean under me feet."

Luckily, I glanced back to the table and saw that Sandra had returned. "Anyway, I'd best get back to the missus." I excused myself. Why had I called her my 'missus'? Was I harbouring subconscious desires for Sandra? No, of course not. I was just trying to sound like Delroy so he wouldn't hate me for leaving. I chanced a look back to see he was pointing at Sandra, giving me the thumbs up and nodding his head. I was out of earshot, but from the way his lips were moving, it appeared he was making something like a "guuuuerrr!" sound. He then began groping an imaginary pair of breasts in the air before him. I quickly turned away, but couldn't shake the horrific feeling that he was now thrusting, and the image was burning into my back.

After the first half of their set, which seemed to alternate between Elvis covers and chart songs (including a hilariously atrocious version of 'Bad Romance' by Lady Gaga), the free buffet (a hog roast) was wheeled out. Sandra said it was awful and that she only ate meat she couldn't

66

identify with, so I offered to take us to a nearby curry place. Although I convinced myself this was purely a culinary necessity, I couldn't ignore the smallest sensation of butterflies at the thought of us being alone together. A bottle of wine... A candlelit table...

I'd read a great review of this place online, although when we arrived it felt more like we were in an American diner off some deserted highway. Upon entering, the phrase 'food hall' seemed more appropriate than 'restaurant'. It wasn't until we sat down and I noticed a poster on the wall that I realised what the racket from the far side of the room was.

"Tonight – Live Entertainment: Bryan Thornhill *is* ROBBIE WILLIAMS!"

Still, it was better than Delroy and the Heartbreakers.

Jeff: Sunday 28th February

Managed to drag myself out of bed at 3pm to go to Booze Busters, where I got some Corona and Wotzits. Then we watched most of 'Lost' season 5. It'd been a while since we'd seen the show and, all in all, we were a bit confused. The landing wall needs redecorating anyway, so we drew a 'continuity line' from the front door to the living room. I'm sure Daisy will lecture me about this. I'll blame it on Dom.

Jeff: Monday 1st March

I texted Rachel, asking if she wanted to go for a coffee and catch up. I couldn't stop checking my phone. I ended up concealing it in my locker to remove the temptation. I was beginning to annoy myself.

3am: I got a reply! '*Ha! Coffee? What's that? Mummies don't have time for coffee. Would be lovely to catch up*'.

I've been reflecting on this some some time. It seems to be something of a mixed message. It would be lovely to catch up? Does this mean she'd like to, but can't? Or have we now made some kind of arrangement? Jesus, you don't have this kind of vague bullshit from men. Maybe I'll just ask Pete to go for a coffee instead.

5am: Just remembered that Pete hasn't been outside for about 2 years, so the chances of that coffee are pretty slim too. Why don't I know anyone who isn't a complete freak?

Pete: Friday 12th March – 2pm

"Why do the villains never learn that the aliens they side with always turn against them? They always end up crawling back to The Doctor for help. Ridiculous!" Jeff was clearly exasperated, but try as I might, I just couldn't focus. After watching Jo Grant flirting with Captain Yates in 'Day of the Daleks', I suddenly had an overwhelming desire to look at *that* infamous Katy Manning photoshoot. I mean, it's a design classic, and it's okay to appreciate the female form from an objective viewpoint. It had nothing to do with wanking! Unfortunately, when I locked my bedroom door and fired up the laptop, it only got as far as the Karen Gillan wallpaper before conking out. Come back to me Karen! I pressed the 'on' button repeatedly, but nothing happened. If only my knowledge of computer repair spanned just a little way beyond any machines manufactured in 1998.

Shit! I was going to fasten my trousers and ask to borrow Jeff's.

Shit! Pete wants to borrow my laptop. Ordinarily, I keep all my 'sensitive materials' in a folder labelled 'cars', in a folder called 'pics', in a folder for 'windows default pictures' – but that's no good for long term usage. He could easily stumble upon my extensive collection of companion... *erotica*. I mean, I'm the cool one. I have a girlfriend. I have a sex life. I'm not supposed to be locking myself away, lusting over stills from 'Secret Diary of a Call Girl'.

I was going to have to delete them.

I thought about saving it all to a memory stick, but that was far too dangerous. I could lose it – and then Daisy might find it! I'd just have to download them all again once I'd got my laptop back. I could deal with losing the pictures of Lalla Ward from 'Vampire Circus', and all those Leela close ups, but there were almost tears in my eyes as I deleted my prized collection of Billie's sunbathing pictures from The Daily Sport. I managed, however, until I got to the *crème de la crème*: the Katy Manning 'Girl Illustrated' shoot.

I mean, I had *that* Dalek picture as a poster. Pete bought it for me, for god's sake. I shouldn't be ashamed of having it on my hard drive – we have it framed over the fireplace. There was the rest of the shoot, however. On that bed with the absurdly retro flowered duvet and those see-through knickers. A personal favourite. Ahh, Katy! I was 10 years old when I first saw those pictures. It was like the world had been turned upside down. I'd never seen a *girl* naked. Then, all of a sudden – Jo Grant! It was the *birth* of my libido...

I had no idea which website I'd found these on. What if I was unable to retrieve them? Calm down, Jeff, this is 2010: downloading pictures of naked celebrities is just like buying a carton of milk these days. I highlighted them all, but my resolve failed me before I could hit 'delete'. In my desperation, I logged onto Yahoo and set up a new account, under the name 'Matt Thascales' (you_will_obey_me1963@gmail.com) and then set up another fake account for 'Frazer Manning' on gmail (warrior_from_the_deep42@gmail.com) and emailed the entire folder from 'Matt' to 'Frazer'. The sordid materials were safe and secret in cyberspace, allowing me to delete the folder from my laptop. I grinned. I was like MacGyver. Or Michael Schofield from Prison Break. My smugness was short lived, however, as I realised: no Jeff, you're just a wanker.

Pete: Friday 12th March – 3.45pm

Jeff was ages with the laptop! I was almost losing enthusiasm for the whole idea when – after a lengthy series of unidentifiable noises, a little profanity and, finally, a triumphant "Geronimo!" - he eventually appeared from his bedroom, an oddly accomplished grin on his face.

"Thanks." I said, as he handed it to me. "You know I wouldn't normally ask, but the Working Tax Credit guys are chomping at the bit to see those work spreadsheets!"

"Well." He made an odd gesture which could easily have been misinterpreted. "It's hardly as though you're going to be using it for internet porn!" We both laughed boisterously, too loud and for too long, slapping the front of our legs, even though no one actually does that. This brought a surge of blood back to my nether regions and I remembered the purpose of my mission.

I was surprised to see that Jeff didn't also have the Karen Gillan background. In fact, it was a picture of William Hartnell in that silly hat. What was sexy about that? Surely Jeff wasn't trying to pass himself off as an ordinary human being??! Things worsened. I presumed he'd already have the Katy Manning photos saved to his hard drive, but I looked in all the obvious places

and they were nowhere to be found! The 'Default Pictures>Cars' file actually had pictures of cars in it! Even the folder labelled 'Inferno' was empty! Obviously, Daisy had cracked his user area password – 'thegreenjeff' – and given it the nudity hoover treatment.

And there was me thinking she was a feminist too. What a hypocrite!

In the end, it came down to me and a bit of creative Googling. In the space of a few minutes, not only did I find the Katy Manning shoot, but numerous other companions too. Lalla Ward, Louise Jameson, Billie Piper – they were all there! Of course, there was the small problem that I'd have to delete all trace of them from Jeff's hard drive once my 'research' was done, but it was nothing a mature, focused IT professional like myself couldn't handle. Now, if only I could prize that squashed toilet roll out from behind the radiator.

Pete: Friday 12th March – 6pm

I deleted my internet history, cleared the toolbar and was halfway to the door when I realised. Bollocks! Had I altered his search settings?? I just couldn't remember. Maybe what my Mum used to say about memory loss was true. To make sure all the incriminating evidence was gone, I powered back up, clicked in the address for Google, and changed his internet 'Safesearch' settings from 'Moderate' to 'Strict'.

By the time I returned the laptop, I was nervous but Jeff was more interested in grilling me about my own. He seemed to think I'd know the technical details of what was up with the thing, and this wrong-footed me somewhat.

"I mean, isn't it your job to fix these things?"

71

"You're right." I laughed nervously. **"I'll be sure to give it the full Peter Davison treatment tomorrow."** I was glad he didn't ask me to explain this comment, as, even now, I have no idea quite what I meant by it.

Jeff: Friday 12th March: 9pm

Got the laptop back. Whatever Pete was doing, he's wiped the history so it now no longer remembers my login details for the new email address. Shit... I was sure the password was 'Peladon' or something?

After a while, I gave up and had to reacquire the pictures. I think Google must be broken. I tried 'Girl Illustrated', 'Katy Manning Dalek', you name it. All I got were pictures of Kylie in her (far, far inferior) Dalek photo, which people had commented on as being reminiscent of the real thing, not to mention endless Lego imitations of the image I was actually looking for, yet nothing remotely titillating! Is this the latest blow from the 'Bildaberg group' that Dom's always going on about? First public smoking, now good old fashioned perving from the comfort of your own bedroom!

Jeff: Monday 15th March

I remembered one of the passwords ('doctorwho')! I can't really be forgiven for forgetting that one. It was for the Matt Thascales account: unfortunately, the one I had sent my Katy Manning pictures *from* and not *to*.

Given that the account was only 2 days old, and belonged to someone who didn't exist, I was slightly surprised to see that I had an email waiting for me.

From: warrior_from_the_deep442@gmail.com
To: you_will_obey_me1963@yahoo.co.uk

Subject: Hi

Hi Matt! Not sure I know you, but thanx for those pics. Dey were HAWWWT!

So, you wanna swap pics? ASL? Douglas.

Oh no! I'd typed 442 instead of 42! And what the hell did ASL mean? What if it was an acronym for 'Anal Sex League'? There was a file attached, which I opened with some trepidation, only to discover a grainy camera photo of the bottom half of a man in incredibly tight white jeans, the crotch of which looked disturbingly damp.

I deleted my email, deactivated my account and vowed *never* to use the internet again.

Jeff: Friday 26th March

We opened the Jagermeister from under the sink, that I've been hiding from Daisy, to celebrate having watched Matt Smith on 'Jonathan Ross'. I'm still dubious about the new sonic screwdriver, but there was a collective cheer when we saw the picture of William Hartnell from 'Vampires of Venice'.

I consulted our 'continuity log' and confirmed that Hartnell is now officially head of the 'flashback table'.

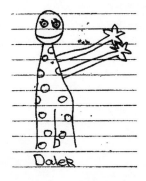

Dalek

73

Jeff: Friday 28th October

Revenge of the Cybermen has been released as a videogramme! I went straight to Woolworths after school to look at it, it looks dead brilliant! Even though the Cyberman on the cover is one of the new ones. Dad won't buy it because it's £39.99 but wed also need a home projector for it and I've never seen one of them because they cost nearly a thousand pounds.

Maybe I can persuade them to play it at school and say it will help us learn about the solar system and stuff because I think it's set on Jupiter. I don't remember much about it apart from I saw it when I was little and I was dead scared of the cybermats! I had enough pocket money to buy the Target novelisation by Terrance Dicks so that will have to do for now.

Jeff: Sunday 30th October

I need to start taking drama classes more seriously if I'm going to play the Doctor one day. But it's hard because I think Mr Haytread is a right pervert. He makes us wear black lyrca and then he watches the girls rolling around on the dance mats to the eurythmics.

When I'm the Doctor I'll make sure I have a decent costume, not like something from a Pantomime.

Jeff: Monday 31st October

I was outside school and it was raining. I met a girl who smelled like Christmas. She has long dark hair and is beautiful. Her name is Rachel.

Pete: Thursday 1st April

I was having another of my really good Karen Gillan dreams, when I was disturbed by what sounded like the mournful ruminations of an angry cow. It took several seconds of panic-stricken flailing before I realised it was my mobile. God! The vibrate setting on this thing was really getting vicious in its old age! It was a text from Dom, reading 'Spoiler Alert! Tom Baker confirmed to make appearance in 11th Hour!!!' and then, in caps lock: 'THIS IS AN APRIL FOOL!' I couldn't help thinking he was somehow missing the point.

The door abruptly swung open, and in crashed a bare-chested Jeff, simultaneously dribbling toothpaste, making monster noises AND warbling the 'Who' theme. The man was a genius! I immediately sprang into action, grabbing one of the sonic screwdrivers from my bedside table, and shouting 'he's hyperpodulating!' Then we both fell about laughing.

These japes got better every year!

Jeff: Thursday 1st April

I steeled myself, staring into the mirror. "I'm The Doctor. I'm a Time Lord. I'm 903 years old..." Okay... It was time. Although it wasn't really working. I'm a bit fatter than David Tennant. "Hey Pete!" I greeted him far too cheerily.

"What's wrong?" He looked terrified.

"Nothing. Well... You know I said my parents were going away for Easter? Well... My cousin's not at college at the moment and he can't really stay at home by himself..."

"What do you mean 'not at college'?" Said Pete, aghast.

"It's Easter. Half term."

"No, I mean, why's he still at college? He's 27!"

"You know why." I sighed.

"Because he's retarded?"

"Kevin is not retarded! He has mild autism." Pete frowned. "Alright, it's pretty severe, but he's not retarded. You can't say that anymore."

"But if I *could* say it... Then he'd be a retard?"

"Shut up. He's coming to stay."

"What?!" Pete looked like he was going to cry.

"Just for the weekend!"

"This weekend? *My helicopter?* This weekend??"

"Yes, this weekend..."

"But it's Doc-"

"Yes, yes, I know! But what could I do? I'm not retard-err- Autistic. I'm the grown up, sensible one, my Mum asked me a favour and I can't say no because we're watching kids' TV in our pants all weekend. I couldn't say that. I'd get the sigh."

"I thought it was Daisy that did the sigh?"

"It's just women in general. He'll be here tomorrow, but don't worry. I'll sort something out."

Jeff: Friday 2nd April

My parents dropped Kevin off on their way up to Scotland. As usual, my Mum stayed in the car and my Dad lingered reluctantly on the doorstep, clad in his immaculately pressed security guard uniform, despite the fact he was going on holiday. And retired.

"Are you sure you don't want to come in for a quick brew?"

"No, we're scheduled for arrival at Fort William at 1200 hours. I've allowed for two 7 minute long toilet breaks, but you know how *women* are." His moustache seemed to sway from side to side as he spoke. "You be good now, young sir." He mock-punched Kevin on the shoulder. There was something quite depressing about that. He used to treat him like that when he was 4 years old. That kind of exchange is normal between a father and a small boy, but when they're 59 and 27 years old, it's quite unsettling.

"Okay, Uncle Dad." Kevin mumbled. (When he was adopted by Ronald, at the age of 4, Kevin couldn't get used to the concept of his uncle now being his Dad, and has since referred to him as 'Uncle Dad'.)

Anyway, it was probably for the best they didn't come in. The 'Lost' continuity guide was still scrawled all over the wall. (We eventually scribbled the words 'FUCK IT' across in red marker pen.)

"You okay?" I asked Kevin, in a resigned sort of way. The question was a formality. I knew whatever I received in reply would be unintelligible or irrelevant.

"Yeh." He shrugged. "Is Pete about?" He spoke with a completely false sense of casualness. He couldn't keep eye contact as he asked the question. He's been terrified of Pete ever since they first met 24 years ago. Pete had long hair, and for some reason this distressed Kevin. Every time Pete came round he used to hide in the airing cupboard.

"Yes." I wanted to say. "Pete's here. He's just next door. And he's got a knife." Just for the fun of it.

"No." I said. (He was asleep.)

"Oh. Where am I sleeping?" Kevin speaks very quickly, so this all came out as one word. He's also not too clever when it comes to the letters L and S.

"On the sofa."

"What if Pete wants to sit on it while I'm asleep? He might hurt me." He visibly paled.

"He won't. Do you want a brew?"

"Yeh. But not with that weird milk. It's not the weird milk is it?"

"What are you on about? We only use one kind of milk. The normal kind."

"No, you have the weird milk in a carton. I like it out of the bottle."

"It's UHT. Everyone drinks UHT."

77

"It tastes funny. I like it from the bottle."

"Well, we don't have any."

"Right. Can I have some orange juice instead?"

"We don't have any. It's water, tea or Carlsberg."

"BEER?" He looked at me like I was forcing him to take heroin.

"It's all we have."

"I bet you've got big cupboards full of beer. People will think you're like a crazy person." He paused, staring in horror at the wall as though he'd just realised he only had a few hours left to live. "Ooooh, nooo... Pete's not gonna get drunk is he?"

"Not unless it's a special occasion."

"Oh no! He's gonna be drunk. Can you tell him to go away?" His voice began to tremble.

"What do you mean 'go away'? He lives here."

"Yeah, but it's your house too. *Please*, can't you just tell him to go away until Monday?"

"No! I couldn't do that... He's not well." I lied, but I thought playing the sympathy card might help him see Pete in a different light.

"Oooooh noooo!" He clamped the sleeve of his jacket over his nose, backing into the corner of the living room. "It's not the Millennium Bug is it?" His voice was shaking.

"No. That's a bloody computer virus! And it doesn't exist!"

"Don't swear!" He shrieked, pointing at me accusingly.

"He's not ill. He's just, you know, under the weather."

"Bet it's the Millennium Bug..." He mumbled

"Do you want a drink or not?"

"Can I have shandy?"

"Yes." I lied. We'd got some pretty weak Sainsburys' own beers in. I could put a teaspoon of sugar in and say it was shandy. Of course, that would make it flat... Ah! Of course, I could dilute it with the Organic Cucumber Presse Daisy left in the fridge. (I asked if she was going to drink it, and she said it was a flower in a barren garden. I think it was some kind of metaphor comparing cucumber juice to Carlsberg Export.)

We walked through to the kitchen, or rather I did. Kevin hovered in the doorway. Luckily, this gave me time to pour some 2% beer into a glass and dispose of the can. I popped the kettle on but then decided: sod it, who cares if it's 10:30am? He'll think I'm drinking shandy. Besides, it's Good Friday. I'm allowed a treat. I know I'm working later, but I work in a railway station bar... So it's like market research.

Kevin started looking at the model Daleks on the windowsill.

"Which garlics are these?"

"Daleks."

"Yeh, which ones are they?"

"I got them from that convention. Remember, the one we went to in Manchester when you were 10?" I remembered. He'd run out screaming.

"Yeh, but which garlics are they? Are they Davros' garlics or the renegade garlics?"

"It's just a model Dalek."

"Yeah, but it's gold. The gold garlics are from the 70s, aren't they?"

"It's just that colour because you're supposed to paint them."

"Yeh, but the gold garlics were from the 70s."

I wanted to go into detail that there had been a gold Dalek in the 70s, in 'Day of the Daleks', and of course the black and gold movie Dalek in 'Planet of the Daleks'... But there was never more than one. And the ones that *were* gold weren't gold all over. That would look ridiculous. But I couldn't do it. I'd sound like some kind of sci-fi geek!.

"Yeah. They're from the 70s."

"With the old man?"

"Jon Pertwee wasn't an old man!"

"Right... Yeah... You know the, err, Undertaker? And John Cenna? Well, Cenna won at Backlash..." Oh god, not WWF. He always ends up on WWF. He's been obsessed with The Undertaker for about 20 years and I still don't know what the hell he's on about. The amount of sentences which begin with "You know the, err, Undertaker?" And I just zone out.

In his bedroom at home, one half of the wall space is dedicated to the Royals (specifically the Queen Mother and Princess Di for some reason), and the other is a mural of WWF posters. Oiled, muscular men in leotards grimacing. No wonder he's never had a girlfriend.

By this time, the conversation – or, rather, his monologue – had turned to the time he tried to get a goat in the back of his 'Uncle Dad's car, and the hilarity that ensued when they were pulled over by the police and the officer found a goat in the back, munching its way through an old A-Z.

Every time he starts ranting on about WWF, it always ends up with the goat story. And I never heard about this story in the first place. I mean, his 'Uncle Dad' is my Dad, and he never said anything about a goat. It's always relayed so fast that it's hard to distinguish most of the individual words, so I just let him get on with it.

I made to go through to the living room and Kevin froze in the doorway. "Oooooh, nooooo!" He wailed. "There aren't any cydermen are there?"

"Not unless Pete's been upgraded!" I quipped. He didn't get it.

"Pete's a cyderman?" He regarded me with a look of genuine confusion on his face.

"No. There are no *cyber*men." I informed him. I'd made a routine check before he came round to remove anything featuring – or relating to – cybermen, from the living room. I'd shown him 'Attack of the Cybermen' when he was a kid, and he'd been so scared of the scene where the Cybermen crush that guy's hands that he'd had to have counselling for about 4 years after. (That was the reason he ran from the convention in '93, although bizarrely he was more frightened of Sophie Aldred than the guys in Cybermen costumes. He was running along a corridor screaming

"Don't let the scary lady get me!" Thinking he was having fun, she ran after him shouting "BOOM!") And in the 80s, the Cybermen were made of tinfoil, so for a few years he was too scared to go into the kitchen. He got over that eventually, but to this day he's still frightened of cling film.

"What about DVDs? You've got cyderman DVDs!"

"Yeah... In the DVD rack. You can't see the covers?"

"Are the cydermen on the sides?"

"No! It's just grey with a picture of The Doctor. You're not scared of The Doctor are you?"

"You won't make me look at it, will you?"

"Why would I want to do that?"

"Dunno. Oooooh nooooo! You're not gonna make me watch The Earthshocks are you?"

"No. And it's called 'Earthshock'."

"I need a wee."

"You know where the bathroom is." He trundled off and I quickly ran to get another beer. It was only as I opened the fridge that I remembered: I hadn't removed the Cyberman flannels from the bathroom...

Pete: Friday 2nd April

"Look after him??" I protested. "But I was all set to watch 'Battlefield' tonight. Can't you take him to work with you?"

"Oh shame!" Jeff smiled to himself, obviously impressed by the apt timing of his quote; now I was going to have to put another quid in the 'Bambera jar'. "I can't take him to work with me. You know what he gets like around strangers. What if he tries to climb into the chiller again? Kathy'll go mental!"

"But it just won't work. We both know how he feels about me! Besides, what if I'd been planning to go out?"

81

Jeff tilted his head. "Let's face it Pete. Kamilian's had more outings than you in the last few years!"

"Well, tonight could've been the night!" I was more than a little hurt. How *could* he compare me to that stupid, poncey robot – the blight upon the otherwise tolerable 'King's Demons'? "Anyway, how would Kevin react if I was planning to have Dom round? He's still *got* long hair."

"Dom's not coming round." He spoke sternly.

"He might be..." Grinning, I reached for my mobile, which was buried beneath somewhere in the vicinity of my FHM pile.

"Dom's NOT coming round!" I could tell I'd wound him up. "Now, I'd better go. I'm going to be late for work."

When I went through to the lounge, Kevin was nowhere to be seen. I searched frantically, and began to curse under my breath. "Fucking hell! This is bloody ridiculous!" A gasp of shock sounded from near one of the lounge chairs. Kevin had given himself away.

"Don't swear!" He was hiding behind the sofa, surrounded by a makeshift fort of cushions. "You won't go to heaven." I removed one of the cushions from his head. "Don't hurt me!" He whimpered.

"Kevin." I tried to sound calm and reasonable. "I'm not going to hurt you."

"But I did a bad thing..." He inclined his head down to where a damp stain was spreading on his already soggy trousers. "I'm dead sorry." His lips trembled. "I didn't mean to. I was scared. I heard you say Don was coming round."

"It's DOM!" My teeth were gritted.

"Ahhhh!" He screamed pathetically.

"Come on." I tried to hide my exasperation and sound sympathetic. Thank god the carpet wasn't white: we couldn't afford to hire one of those electric cleaners. The combination of Kevin's mortal terror for everything unfamiliar (which was pretty much *everything*, full stop), and his weak bladder, meant that he was a volatile house-guest. Last time he stayed, we ended up having to replace a whole set of bed covers after our towel, which had a picture of Shrek on it, gave him nightmares. I grabbed his arm to hoist him up, but he began to wail pitiably.

"Geroff! Geroff me! I'll call a policeman. I'll tell him you've been drinking pot!" He shot up, ran into the kitchen and went to hide beneath the table. I came through just in time to see him knock it off-balance, and, from then, everything seemed to go in slow-motion. A beer bottle swayed precariously on the brink, but mercifully came to rest. A Marmite jar slid to one side, stopping just in time. A teapot tipped and lost its lid. Miraculously, however, it didn't smash.

For a brief moment, it seemed as though everything was going to be okay, but then the unthinkable happened. The K9 biscuit barrel, that Jeff had bought for my 21st birthday, fell to the ground and shattered into tiny pieces. The noise sent Kevin into some kind of fit, and I had to call Jeff back. When he eventually got home, I'm not ashamed to admit that I was slumped dejectedly on the floor, staring at a fragment of K9's ear and weeping.

Jeff: Saturday 3rd April (am)

I flexed my fingers, hesitating before I picked up the phone. It seemed like a slightly immoral thing to do, but I'm sure William Hartnell would have handled the situation in a similar way. I grabbed the receiver and called Dad's sister, 'Mad Margaret'. She'd had a long career as a health and safety inspector until she fell out of a bulldozer and into a slate quarry. She's not been the same since. She can't leave the house without a clipboard and insists on inspecting everything from flowerpots to belt buckles.

"Hellllllooooooooo?" She answered. She speaks like an pantomime witch.

"Hi, Margaret? It's Jeff."

"Jeff? But I don't know a Jeff."

"It's Jeffrey. Jeffrey Greene."

"Ohhhhh! Jeffrey Slater! Our Ron's son!" She's never really been able to accept the fact that Ronald isn't my biological father and that we have different surnames.

"Yeah... Listen, I need a favour. Kevin-"

"Kevin?"

"Yeah. Kevin. Your nephew? He's staying at mine for the weekend, but there's been a bit of an emergency and I was wondering if he could stay at yours for a bit?"

"What kind of emergency?"

"Well, this guy at work... Wilfred... Got stuck in a, sort of, glass cabinet. So the health and safety officer... David... Had to get him out. Now we need a new health and safety officer, so I'm having to check up on the new guy – make sure he's up to the job."

"Well, that sounds very complicated."

"It is. The new guy, Smith... Matthews... Smith Matthews is coming to the flat for a formal interview, and, well, Kevin needs full supervision what with his... Disposition."

"What's wrong with him?"

"You know. He's mildly autistic."

"Oh! I always thought you were the retarded one."

Pete: Saturday 3rd April

The anticipation was too much. I couldn't sleep, so I was up by 11 – *the eleventh hour*. I skulked cautiously around the house, checking for signs that the deed had been done: sleeping bag empty; big puddle on the bathroom floor; discarded pairs of tracksuit bottoms slung over sofa, cooker door AND record player; spilt UHT; trail of Rice Krispies leading towards the exit; and everything *blissfully* quiet. I breathed a sigh of relief. Kevin had left the building, and the rest of the day was mine to enjoy!

A part of me was pleased to be out of bed so early – I could put on that exercise video Uncle Julian had sent me, make a start trying to repair the laptop, clean the house, write a novel. Another part of me, however, knew that it'd be like childhood Christmas Eve all over again – that I would rattle round the house, feeling tense, wringing my hands, going slightly mad, running baths and then letting the water go cold without taking them, bidding on ebay for German car parts and football memorabilia.

As it was, I ended up on the sofa (inevitable, really) using duct tape to bind together the TV, DVD, video and Freeview remotes (somewhat less so). This actually proved decidedly fiddly, and I was still going at it when Jeff walked through the front door. He looked at me, before his eyes turned excitedly to the remote controls as he dropped a pair of shopping bags, and raised his arms aloft.

"The Megatron returns!" He shut the door. "Pete, you're an absolute genius!" He locked the door. "I mean, there was me abandoning the whole idea..." He bolted the door. "...After Daisy got that hi-fi remote stuck to her arse..." He put the chain on the door. "...And went all..." He pulled a face and waved his hands frantically, before shoving a wedge beneath the front door. "And here you are, br- wait! Have you unplugged the phone?"

"No. Wh-"

"You twat!" He ran to the extension cord, yanking it out in a jittery, panicked movement.

"Jeff, is there a reason you're being so security conscious?"

85

"Just want to make sure no one disturbs us during Doctor Who." He stopped to catch his breath, before adding guiltily. "Plus, I just stole shitloads of stuff again. Now come on!" He snapped his fingers.

"Erm, Okay... But you are quite sure you're not going to get caught sooner or later?" His eyes widened considerably.

"Yes... Maybe... It hardly matters! Did Tom Baker play by the rules in 'Genesis of the Daleks'? I think not!"

"Oh, come on! You can hardly compare a life-changing moral decision like that to you nicking-" I rustled through the shopping bag. "...Slim-a-Soup, motor oil..."

"I'm an outlaw..."

"Value brand tampons?"

"A vigilante..."

"You're a kleptomaniac!"

"For God's sake, Pete, as if *I'm* the one with the problems!" He slammed a can of extra-chunky dog food down onto the kitchen table.

"And just what's that supposed to mean?" He fell silent, biting his lip, and when he blinked, it seemed like whole minutes passed in the time it took him to shut and open his eyelids.

"Never mind." He said at last, smiling genially. "How about I make us one of those special hot chocolates while you do the important work?" He waved a stolen pad of paper, and accusingly red Biro. "We've got six-and-a-half hours, ten doctors to get through: do your worst!"

It proved to be an impossible task. By the time Jeff'd made a hot chocolate, the page was still completely blank. By the time he'd had a bath, I'd managed to write the name of each doctor down, but had got no further. By the time he'd cleaned out the kitchen,

86

tidied the lounge and barricaded the door, my head was in my hands and there were so many crossings out that I had to start afresh. And by the time Daisy came round and nearly *ruined* everything, the list looked a complete mess.

Jeff refused to shift the furniture and let her in, shouting through the peep hole that he was "very ill".

"Aww, but Jeffy," Daisy squealed, "don't you want me to come in and wook after you?"

"Daisy, there's nothing I'd like more than for you to come and 'wook after' me, but I've got..." He fumbled at thin air, as though it would provide him with a suitable end to his sentence. "...Smith's Disease." He said at last, a little too triumphantly. At least Daisy wasn't able to see him punching the air. "And it's tewibly contagious."

"OMG!" She screamed, banging hard against the door. "Phoenix from 'Lentil Fetish' had Smith's Disease, and he nearly lost a hand! You have to let me in so I can bath the affected area in lavender essence!"

The exchange continued like this for some time. We thought we were in trouble when she threatened to mount a doorstep vigil, and her medley of Bryan Adams' love songs proved to be a particularly bleak moment. The Radiotronic Workshop could show her a thing or two! When she finished, I shouted that Jeff had taken to his bed some time ago. I'm a terrible liar, and felt sure she'd know that he was stood right next to me, eating a waffle, but it seemed to work. After 15 minutes pawing at the door, she eventually left. Somehow we'd lost most of the afternoon.

The rest of it rapidly vanished in the time it took to boil the kettle, prepare the experimental schnitzel-sausage-noodle sandwiches, artfully arrange the Twiglets, sufficiently defrost the ice-cream, arrange the Twiglets again, decant the crisps, set up the video recorder, and rearrange the Twiglets to perfection.

Before we knew it, the moment was upon us... The Eleventh Doctor had arrived...

<u>William Hartnell</u> = An Unearthly Child,
The Daleks, ~~The Web Machines~~, Dalek Invasion
of Earth, ~~Web Planet?~~ LoL! Time Meddler,
Tenth Planet ~~MARVEL!!~~ ~~Massacre?~~ ...
The Chase? nahh...

Patrick Troughton - Tomb of the Cybermen
? Fury (scary scene), Invasion ~~and~~ War Games
Dominators? Seeds of Doom ~~The other~~

<u>Pertwee</u> - Spearhead, Terror of Autons, Green Death
Frontier? - "SPIDERS", Daemons, Sea Devils
too long ~~Robot~~ Android Invasion?

<u>THE 4th DOCTOR</u> - Genesis, Terror of Zygons
City of Death, ~~can't face~~ Image of Fendahl!
Seeds of Doom. The Key to Time? Talons of W.C.

<u>Peter Davison</u> - Earth Shock, Androzani,
Ressurection o.t. D's - Arc of Infinity? undead, Black
Orchid. The Five Doctors. KINDA TIME CRASH?

<u>Colin Baker</u> - The Two Doctors (ish)

<u>Sylvester McCoy</u> - Remembrance. Greatest Show
all of Season 25? too long - loose Canon light
Rad + Comm Enemy Within. Easy! Reck

Christopher Eccleston - The Empty ~~Too finale?~~
Father's Day, Parting child Unquiet
of the ways Dead

David Tennant - All of Series 2 - ~~not the~~ ~~Daleks~~
fucking ABSORBALOFF! Human Nature, Blink,
Utopia, ~~Lazarus~~, Evolution of Daleks,
Turn Left, Poison Sky, Doc's ~~Daughter~~
Unicorn? Journey's End, Stolen Earth
The End of Time. ~~Madame~~

Jeff: Saturday 3rd April (pm)

We just sat there in silence. The odd glance was exchanged, but neither of us gave any sign of emotion. There were many "Well, it was..." And "It's kind of..." But no real sentences. We mutely watched 'Confidential', but didn't even get another beer. Even though it was still early, we both got up. Without a word spoken, we both knew the other was going to bed.

"What d'you think? Beginning of the end?" Pete asked tentatively as he hovered in his bedroom doorway.

"Well..." I began, but luckily he'd retired before I had to think of anything to add to that.

2am: Pete and I burst out of our bedrooms simultaneously, almost colliding. We regarded each other, and after a brief pause threw our arms into the air.

"WAAAAEEEEYYYYYY!!!" We exclaimed in unison, before hugging, bouncing up and down on the spot. "WAAAAEEEEEYYYYYY!!!!!" We fell to the floor, our throats sore, sobbing with joyous laughter.

"Matt Smith... *IS* The Doctor!"

"Let's watch it again!"

"I'll put the kettle on. You get the oven chips in!"

Jeff: Sunday 4th April

We watched the 'I am The Doctor...' speech fifteen times on Youtube.

Too excited to eat.

Unfortunately, I was racked with guilt by 1pm, and drove round to Mad Margaret's to reclaim Kevin. To make matters worse, Daisy was at the flat when I got back, Pete shooting me terrified glances. We'd planned to watch the repeat at 8, followed by 'Confidential', and it was looking like they were going to talk all the way through.

"There aren't any cydermen in it are there?" Asked Kevin.

"No. Well, yes, but only for a second. I'll tell you to look away."

"Oh no! I don't want to see it. Can I get in the cupboard?"

"No! If you don't want to see it, go to my room."

"Come on, Kevin! You want to see Doctor Who fighting the monsters, don't you?" Daisy asked in a sickly voice, as though she were addressing a child.

"S'pose." He murmured.

By this time it had already started. I could see Pete was gripping the arm of the sofa in tortured, mute frustration.

"Where's The Doctor?" Kevin seemed troubled.

"The Doctor's right there, silly!" Said Daisy.

"That's not Doctor Who." He shook his head fiercely.

"Jesus Christ! Where the hell were you on New Year's Day? He's regenerated! It's Matt bloody Smith now!"

"Don't swear!"

"Stop being mean, Jeffy!" Daisy poked me.

"You know the, err, Undertaker?" Kevin began.

The rest of the evening continued in much the same way, and is far too painful to relate. Later on, as we lay in bed, Daisy snuggled up to me.

"What do you love about me, Jeff?" She said sleepily.

I had no idea.

"You're... Kind?" I proceeded to rack my brains for romantic lines from films. This seemed to satisfy her. But it was then that I realised: I don't love Daisy. I don't even like her that much. Why the hell are we still together?

Jeff: Monday 5th April

My Dad picked Kevin up before I left this morning. Thank god.

I was thinking about new 'Who episode titles that sound like they fit in with the classic series, and composed this list at work:

The Empty Child / The Christmas Invasion / Tooth and Claw / Rise of the Cybermen / The Age of Steel / The Impossible Planet / Army of Ghosts / Evolution of the Daleks / The Lazarus Experiment / The Family of Blood / Last of the Time Lords / Time Crash / Voyage of the Damned / The Fires of Pompeii / Planet of the Ood / The Sontaran Stratagem / Forest of the Dead / The Waters of Mars / The End of Time / The Eleventh Hour / The Beast Below / Victory of the Daleks.

Ah, if only it had been 'Vampires *of* Venice' and not 'Vampires *in* Venice', it would most definitely have qualified for the list!

I nipped out at lunch and went to the sci-fi shop, Omega's Tomb. The owner, Mad Frankie was in. He's a great guy, but he spends the majority of his time exploring the astral plain. He also bears an uncanny resemblance to Rick Wakeman from Yes. I don't know if it's his hypnotic mode of speech, or perhaps he really is a wizard, but he has an uncanny knack of being able to make me buy things. Even if they're rubbish or I already own them. Only last week I bought an old VHS copy of 'Daleks' Invasion Earth: 2150 AD'. He charged me a fiver for it because it was 'rare'. Rare? I've got it at home on DVD, as part of the Dalek collection. And it's terrible!

I managed to escape having only bought a K9 annual from 1983. When I arrived back at the pub, Kathy was stood in the staff room, her arms folded confrontationally across her chest. She was clutching a piece of paper.

Shit! My heart sank to my converse.

"What the fuck is this, Jeff?"

"It's just a list..."

"What does it even mean? *Empty Child, Christmas Invasion, Tooth and Claw...*"

"Alright – it's just a list!"

"We're not paying you to stand around making lists! Don't you remember the Seven Steps to Success? If there's nobody that needs serving, it's: 1. Check the barrels. 2. Does the the counter need cleaning? 3. Do the snacks need replenishing? 4. Do any tables need cleaning? 5. Do any customers look in need of assistance? 6. Is the entrance litter free? 7. Do the toilets need cleaning? And if none of the other steps apply, go and help out in the kitchen. How can you expect us to run a successful establishment if we don't follow the Seven Steps?"

"Look, I was just..."

"Do you have your keyfob?" She snapped.

"Yes." I pulled the little plastic 'square of doom' from my pocket, where it swung suspended from a pink plastic twisty thing, hooked to a belt hole on my regulation trousers.

"Now, tell me Jeff: where on the keyfob does it say 'Make pointless lists about Sci-Fi?"

"Well, obviously it doesn't..."

"Right! Good! We've made progress." She waved her hands in a messianic fashion. "This is your last warning, Jeff. Any more of your bullshit and you're out. Do I make myself clear?"

"Yes."

"Right. It's 2:30. Time to check the toilets."

Went home and ate three pot noodles whilst watching 'Eleventh Hour' on iPlayer before the evening shift. There are some small pleasures in life! I also composed another list of episode titles that were pure 'Rod', and not remotely Doctor Whoish.

Rose / Dalek / The Long Game / Boom Town (for Tom's sake!) / The Doctor Dances / Fear Her (too pretentious) / The Runaway Bride (too dreadful to comment!) / Smith and Jones / Daleks in Manhattan (sounds like a gay musical) / 42 / Blink (why the hell wasn't it 'Don't Blink'? That would have been perfect) / The Sound of Drums / Partners in Crime / The Doctor's Daughter / Turn Left / Journey's End.

Back at work, I went through to the storeroom to retrieve a box of WKD and found Kathy waiting for me again. "Here." She said frostily, and slipped a piece of paper into my hand. Shit... Was this it? My dismissal? I was on my last chance! I hadn't used that up yet!

What if she'd seen the error of her ways and composed a list of *her* favourite Doctor Who episode titles? I was wrong. I was also slightly astonished when I unfolded the note.

Stacy – 07787952107 x

Surely this wasn't real? Surely this only happened in films? Or America... Or at least to attractive people? But somebody cared... Somebody fancied me. I'm bloody Casanova!

I got home at 3:30am to find we were out of Bacon Crispies, but I was in such a good mood that I drove to the 24 hour Tesco, playing 'Ebeneezer Goode' at full volume. Ahh, '92! With the window down and the night wind whipping my face, I felt truly alive for the first time in years.

Jeff: Tuesday 6th April

I rapped cheerily on Pete's door at 2pm. "Breakfast!" I called.

"What are you..." He stumbled sleepily out of his room. "Oh my god!" His eyes lit up with joy as he surveyed the culinary masterpiece I had prepared. "You're a genius! This is better than your pasta and beans triumph!" He complimented, tucking into his fish fingers and custard.

Jeff: Wednesday 7th April

I've been looking at Stacy's number repeatedly ever since Monday, but still haven't had the nerve to ring. If I never ring, then nothing can ever go wrong, and this will forever be a good thing. Albeit a small one. And of course there's the Daisy issue. I mean, there's nothing wrong with phoning someone. It's not like it's cheating. Although I'd be lying if I said I hadn't conjured a mental image of Stacy, and mentally undressed her several times...

Jeff: Thursday 8th April

Horror of all horrors! An email from Dad:

Dear Jeffrey,

This is a bit of a sensitive subject concerning your mother. You know how women are. Your mother in particular has always been a bit of a feminist, what with her pottery classes in the 80s and that race for life sponsorship she gave. She is reaching a stage in her life where I think she feels the need for grandchildren. What with Kevin's condition, this clearly isn't on the cards from his division.

It is, therefore, that the duty falls to you. If you could reply to me with your feelings on the matter that would be greatly appreciated, and then together we could perhaps devise some kind of strategy. The idea of spawning offspring may initially seem daunting, but I think you will eventually find it satisfactory and fulfilling, and will be surprised what an emotional bond exists between you and your child.

Regards,
Ronald Slater (Your Father)

95

I bashed out a quick reply, typing stuff about "money", "work", and the "not too distant future". It seemed to do the trick, but it was a close one. However, it did put a dampener on my recent cheeriness. I lay awake, wondering why I feel like a failure.

1. I don't have an expensive car.
2. I don't own a house.
3. I don't have kids
4. I'm not married.
5. I work as a poorly paid barman.
6. I don't go on regular holidays to Greece, Tenerife or Portugal.

But the more I thought about these things, the more I realised I didn't want any of them. The Fiat is reliable. Who cares if the seats hurt and the passenger door doesn't open? Owning a house worked out very badly last time, and doing it again would just tie me down... What if I needed to up sticks and move to Cardiff to join the Doctor Who team? There'd be a mountain of paperwork. As for children, I can't stand the noisy little buggers. I do sometimes wonder about the magic of sitting down with a son, watching Doctor Who together and reading him Target novelisations at bedtime, but the dream is pierced by the fact that he'd probably be infuriating and unappreciative. He'd probably be more interested in modern kids shows like 'Power Rangers'.

I started to wonder about what I really wanted out of life, and all I could think of – the ideal scenario – was just drinking beer with Pete and watching Doctor Who, maybe with a curry. And we do that all the time. Obviously, I'd like more money, but I don't really want to have to work for it... So having a minimum effort job and a relatively small income seem to balance each other out. As I feared, Daisy didn't fit into the equation anywhere.

The more I thought about it, the more I realised my ideal scenario was basically my life the way it was right now, but without Daisy and without work. And seeing as I'm resigned to having no money anyway, I might as well just sign on the dole... That would give me more time to lounge around the house. Maybe I'd write my book, or finally get round to watching Firefly. But, of course, then I'd have no job and even less money... And my feelings of failure would be tripled. Because that's where it all falls through. It's all very well and good saying my life is perfect give or take a few minor details, but then why do I feel so awful all the time?

Let's face it – I'm just going to have to get married and have kids. Maybe it's one of those things – I won't realise I want it until I actually have it. A bit like Matt Smith! Nobody wanted him to be The Doctor. "Bring back David Tennant!" We said. "He's too young!" "It's the beginning of the end!" But we love Matt Smith! (Matt Smith *IS* The Doctor!) We just needed him to be part of our lives (or at least part of our regular TV schedule) to fully appreciate this.

Jeff: Friday 9th April

If I am going to get married and have children, it can't be with Daisy. There's only so much misery I can willingly resign myself to. Jesus, I'm going to have to break up with her. I haven't broken up with anyone for years. I'm supposed to be mature now, but all I want to do is get Pete to ring her up and do it for me.

I can't think about this! I'm banning all depressing thoughts for the time being. For a start, they're depressing, and more importantly I don't have the mental capacity to make sensible decisions. I'm too excited. 'The Beast Below' is on tomorrow!!!

97

Jeff: Monday 12th April

9am: I woke up this morning and lay in bed troubling over the plot holes in 'The Beast Below'. I looked up at the shelf and the first thing to catch my eye was the Davros box set – the comforting silver Doctor Who logo glimmering the way it does on the DVD box sets. Daisy says it's immoral that I own the same collection on DVD and video, but I'm not convinced. Anyway, the point is that once I'd noticed the logo – it was like Bad Wolf – it was everywhere. DVDs on the shelf, the Dalek poster on the wall, the Target/New Adventures books on the bookshelf. The TARDIS USB port, the LED Dalek phone spinner, the pen caddy that was filled with sonic screwdriver pens! (96 movie replica, Tenth Doctor's, Tenth Doctor's with UV nib, Laser Screwdriver pen, and the sonic pen from 'Partners in Crime'.)

I love Doctor Who. I've always loved Doctor Who... But right now this was scaring me. It was like I'd somehow let this TV programme take over my life! Take away the merchandise and the DVDs, the takeaway evenings in front of the TV (or should I say, behind the sofa!) with Pete, and literally what is left of me?

I tried to remember the last time I didn't watch Doctor Who. Of course: last Monday. Although I did spend the whole day making Who related lists... And, now I think about it, I did actually watch 'The Eleventh Hour' between work shifts. When had this happened? When had I stopped being a proper human being? I'm sure it wasn't always like this! I routed through my old diaries to find out when my life had gone wrong...

Saturday 3rd April 2004

Went to the beer garden at The Farmers Arms with Pete, and told him I think I'm finally over Emma (The Terrible Zodin, more like!). It was a really great day. I felt like myself again.

Ever since I met Daisy, it's like Emma doesn't even register on the emotional scale anymore! I'm meeting her tomorrow. We're going for lunch.

Sunday 4ᵗʰ April

Went to a veggie place called The Dolphin's Beak (or something) in Lancaster, and inadvertently ended up joining in some kind of anti-war demonstration afterwards! It was like the old days. Daisy's such a free spirit. It's amazing how much we have in common. We were both at a lot of the same raves and festivals when we were younger. It's a miracle we never came across each other before! The fact that we've been gravitating around each other for so long... It's like fate or something!

Monday 5ᵗʰ April

Daisy's surname is Padbury! *It's meant to be.*

I got a call from work today. It'll be tram season soon. Do I really want to spend another summer collecting fares? Daisy was saying she's been planning a cycling trip round Europe. I know the money I've been saving was for the deposit on the house – but this could be a once in a lifetime chance! Why should I be tied down? Why should I be part of the system? I should be living! Thank god for Daisy! If she hadn't woken me up, I could have ended up stuck in a dead end job, sharing this grotty flat with Pete indefinitely!

I tried to think about something – *anything* that wasn't Doctor Who related – but all I could think of was Colin Baker's face beaming at me.

Something had to be done.

7pm: "What?" Pete stared at me incredulously. "You're giving up Doctor Who?"

"I'm not giving up! I'm abstaining. Just for a while. It's like that time you gave up watching any episodes with the Daleks in for lent."

"It's nothing like that! This is... It's just..." He made an explosion noise.

"I think you're taking it too seriously. I just feel like I spend too much of my life watching TV. I want to prove to myself that I can do other things too."

He clearly wasn't won over.

"So what about audio dramas?"

"No, I'm just generally trying to steer clear of that whole area."

"Target books?"

"No Doctor Who!"

"What about Sarah Jane?"

"That still counts as Doctor Who."

"WHAT?" Another explosion. "You can't compare Sarah Jane to Doctor Who!"

"Why not? It has K9, Sontarans, The Brigadier... Oh yeah, and The Doctor!"

"What about Torchwood? We could finally watch 'Children of Earth'?"

"No! Can't we... Play chess or something?"

"We only have Dalek chess. I presume you're above that now?"

"Monopoly?"

"We have the 'Star Wars' edition."

"Jesus Christ! This is my point exactly: we don't have or do anything that normal, adult people are supposed to!" There was an uncomfortable silence. "Look, I'm going to the Chinese. At least that's normal. You want the usual?"

"What about the Peter Cushing movies? They don't count."

I brought home a couple of king prawn satays and some barbecue ribs and we ate in silence, watching 'Family Guy'. But there was no escaping. In the episode, dope was legalised and a comment was made about the ratings for Doctor Who going up.

By 11pm, I was broken, and we watched 'The Caves of Androzani' in tears. I'd had my phone off for ages. Afterwards, I bit the bullet and looked at it. The usual onslaught of messages from Daisy ensued. I may have lost resolve in giving up Doctor Who, but I could still be a grown up in other areas of my life. I was going to take charge. I was going to be a man! I sent her a message saying '*We need to talk*'. No kiss, no smiley face: just cold-hearted indifference. Shit. I'd done it now. Thrown a stone into the pond of my life and everything was definitely not okay. The ripples were coming. The Pandorica was opening.

Jeff: Tuesday 13th April

Daisy came round tonight. I told her I thought we should break up. She cried for half an hour, and then we had sex. She's currently asleep in my bed. What does this mean?

Pete: Tuesday 13th April

Finally got round to reading that Mark Gatiss book, 'The Vesuvius Club', that Jeff got me for Christmas. I don't get it. The Doctor hasn't been in it at all yet! I suppose it could be a Doctor-lite story like 'Blink' or that shit one with Peter Kay, but what if The Doctor doesn't come into it until right at the end? Should I persist that long?

I have also spotted something about Gatiss that he has hitherto concealed from the public. I reckon he could be gay! I'd better not let this slip to my Mum. She once described 'The Idiot's Lantern' as "alright" because of its "inaccurate but amusing 50s references".

Shit – that reminds me! I still haven't had her and Dad round for dinner! I mentally ran through my list of excuses: feeling ill, tooth hurting, was thinking, snow

might jam mechanism on Dad's voice-box again, like the time he sounded like the start of 'Invaders Must Die' for the whole bank holiday weekend. No: I was going to have to deal with this. Somehow, however, my resolve to pick up the phone fled and, the next thing I knew, I was on the sofa, watching 'Green Death' featurettes and eating a comically shaped baked potato.

Jeff: Wednesday 13ᵗʰ April

"You didn't really mean what you said last night, did you Jeffy?" Asked Daisy. She looked too tragically cute... So forlorn.

"No." I lied. "Of course not." I told her I was very confused and stressed out at work. I said I needed some space to "sort my head out". Thank god – we might get to watch 'Victory of the Daleks' in peace!

Jeff: Thursday 14ᵗʰ April

I had an email from my Dad. The subject read: 'Birthday'.

Dear Son,

I am writing with regard to your birthday, scheduled for 18/05/10. In spite of the recent recessionary times, finances have been kind to us this year. Coupled with the recent development that my wife, Mrs. Slater (your mother), had a small bit of luck betting on the horse 'Big Bill' in a recent competition, we feel more comfortable this year in terms of 'loosening our belts'.

Therefore, I propose that we are prepared to invest a sum between the amount of £50 and £70 toward a gift in celebration of your birth.

Please outline the kind of gift you would prefer. The deadline for this decision is 1200 hours on 25/04/10, to allow for product availability, or postage if required.

Warm Regards.
Your (Non Biological) Father,
Ronald Slater.

I had a think about the stuff I *really* wanted...

The Forgotten Army / Apollo 23 / Night of the Humans / K9 Tales box set / Myths and Legends box set / Matt Smith's sonic screwdriver / A tweed jacket / Braces / A bow tie / Buffy the Vampire Slayer Season 8, Volume 1 – The Long Way Home / Buffy the Vampire Slayer Season 8, Volume 2 – No Future for You / Buffy the Vampire Slayer Season 8, Volume 3 – Wolves at the Gate / Buffy the Vampire Slayer Season 8, Volume 4 – Time of Your Life.

There was more. Loads more. But I could never tell anyone any of it. (Except Pete, obviously). I found it much harder to try and compile a list of the things I'm *supposed* to want...

Socks / A cafetiere / Aftershave / Leather iPod case / Avatar DVD / The Girl with the Dragon Tattoo.

That would have to do. I didn't really like 'Avatar' that much, but there are posters for it everywhere and Amazon keep recommending it, so hopefully it'll seem normal. Maybe I could send it back and exchange it for 'The Creature from the Pit'! I don't even know what 'The Girl with the Dragon Tattoo' is, but it's in a lot of best seller lists.

Jeff: Friday 16th April

I had an argument at work with Sandra, who insists that Doctor Who is now "rubbish".

"Matt Smith looks like a little boy!" She growled. "And he's just like 'whatevvvvvvvaaaa, I'm gonna kill a Star Whale' and, like, just saying, like 'the Time Lords are all dead, it was a bad day...' but David Tennant would have been in tears all the way through the episode!" The more frenziedly she spoke, the lower and gruffer her voice became.

"You weren't there at the beginning!" I snapped. "You don't know how good it was!" (Neither was I technically, but she needn't know that. I bet she has no idea who William Hartnell is.) "The Doctor isn't supposed to cry all the time. He's supposed to be... The Doctor! And Matt Smith *IS* The Doctor!"

"Nahhhhhh." She elongated the word, and by this point had begun to sound like a Yeti. "Only River Song can save the series now." She clapped her hands to her chest, her voice suddenly back to normal. "Ahhh, she's *such a princess*!"

I was too afraid to respond to this.

At home, I downloaded the Daleks "For Victory!" poster from the Doctor Who website and waited until I was sure Pete was asleep. I printed loads and stuck them all round the living room, accompanied by the Union Flag streamers I'd had kicking round in a draw since Euro '96. (Now that was a good year. One of my favourites. August was a bit dull though!)

By the time I was done, I felt a massive sense of accomplishment. The living room was looking very World-War-II-ish! I couldn't wait to see Pete's face in the morning!

Jeff: Saturday 17th April

Russell T Davies has most definitely left the building! Somebody give Mark Gatiss a cigar! Finally, an episode with the Daleks that didn't feature the words 'But how did you survive the Time War?' Let's face it – by the time of 'The Stolen Earth', nobody cared.

Jeff: Sunday 18th April

Was woken by a frenzied hammering at my door. It was Pete.

"Did you get it? Did you get the message?" I pulled myself up groggily, and checked my phone. It was flashing '1 Message Received'. It was also 7am. I opened the text – it had been sent by Dom at 3am: *'Drwho exhibition on in Lanabsues today only! I peabo BBC's now donated ALL the props&costumes from tennant era... Plus a special guest appearance from u know who @ 10am!*

I opened my bedroom door, amazed to find Pete up and dressed. But not just dressed as in wearing underpants. I mean dressed. He was wearing his Tom Baker scarf.

"What the hell?"

"We have to go! If we go now, we can get there in time!" He trilled ecstatically.

"What do you mean? We're not going to get to Scotland in 3 hours."

"Scotland?"

"What? No – Lancaster! He was using predictive text! There's a bus in an hour. It'll get us there for half nine, then we've got time to look around and properly enjoy it before we become too star struck to take it all in!!!"

"Star struck?"

"By Tom Baker of course!! The special guest appearance!"

"Tom Baker?! Tom Baker's going to be in Lancaster?"

"Well, who else would it be? Tennant'll either be dancing with spastics or in Hollywood, Troughton's dead, Pertwee's dead, Matt Smith's in America doing that promotion tour and no one likes any of the other Doctors. It has to be *Tom*! Process of elimination!"

"But a guest appearance..."

"Special guest appearance!"

"Whatever. That could mean anyone. Not necessarily one of the Doctors. It could be Eric Saward for all we know."

"Duh! The phrasing of the text! You know... *Who*. It was a cryptic clue! He doesn't want to tell us it's Tom because he knows we'd be too excited to catch the bus. I might even do something irresponsible, like let you drive me there."

"There's nothing irresponsible about my driving."

"Anything over 20 miles an hour is voluntary suicide."

"You're... Hang on? Voluntary suicide? There's no such thing as voluntary suicide! What would the alternative be? *Involuntary* suicide? That's just death!" I stopped. Pete was clearly pained. "Sorry, I'm just being grumpy 'cause it's 7am. You've got a point. It could be Tom."

"Come on Jeff. This could be our big chance! He could confirm everything we've been hoping. I mean, he – The Doctor – would literally tell us that "life begins at 40". He could get you in with 'The Moff'! You would be the Twelfth Doctor! We could give him 'The Kraagan Masterplan'... And 'The Vaporiser'! I bet he knows loads of agents and publishers! He might even be up for reading an audio book of ours! This is it! The big chance! The golden ticket!"

"Hang on... You're going outside?"

Pete inhaled deeply, and fixed me with a proud smile. "Yeah. I am."

We got to the bus stop only to discover that Pete had looked at the wrong timetable. It was Sunday and the first bus didn't leave until after 1pm. We found much the same result at the train station. I couldn't work out if Pete was wearing his full Tom Baker costume (minus the curly wig) because of the convention, or just to help him deal with being in public. I hoped it was the latter. I mean, he looked great, but I wasn't sure if Tom would be a bit freaked out by it. Then he surprised me for the second time that day...

"We're going to have to drive." I couldn't believe what I was hearing, and I wasn't going to argue. We ran back and chucked everything onto the back seat.

"Copy of 'Who on Earth is Tom Baker'?"

"Check."

"'The Boy Who Kicked Pigs'?"

"Check."

"Vinyl copy of 'The Pescatons', narrated by Tom Baker?"

"Check."

"'Kraagan Masterplan'?"

"Check."

"'Vaporiser'?"

"Check."

"Book of ideas for seasons 32 – 40 of Doctor Who?"

"Check."

"Sick bucket? And spare pants?"

"Check."

Okay... This was it. Pete opened the car door and froze. "Jeff... Approximately what speed will you be travelling at?"

"29 miles an hour, Pete. 29 miles an hour." I winked.

We got into Lancaster at half nine. Pete spent the entire trip in tears, with the scarf wrapped around his eyes. He was sick eight times, and we had to stop four times for bucket emptying / trouser changing. But on the whole it went quite well.

We arrived at The Judge's Lodgings, where the exhibition was to be held, and I was slightly confused. The sign just said 'Museum of Childhood'... No TARDIS... No inflatable Daleks... I couldn't even hear the theme tune emanating from anywhere. After paying entry, and following a maze of portraits and mocked up Victorian classrooms, we were on the verge of giving up. Maybe it was the wrong day? Maybe we'd got the wrong venue? Maybe it was in Scotland after all... We asked a member of staff on the top floor, and she said there *was* a Doctor Who exhibition on, directing us towards the end of the corridor. Then we saw it. The door of the room was painted to look like the TARDIS! We ran through, giddy with excitement, to find... not much at all.

The small room was empty, save for a few glass cabinets, mainly full of stuff we already had. An entire wall dedicated to the Target novelisations? I may as well have stayed in my bedroom! And as for all the retro toys, it was all stuff I'd had in the 70s, most of which was either in the drinks cabinet or at my parents' house or on our mantle piece.

"Wh... Where are all the costumes?" Asked Pete, looking forlorn. In a far corner of the room was a mannequin, with a sheet of paper pinned to it: 'Awaiting Costume: Doctor Who'. "Wh... Where's Tom?" He mumbled pathetically, tightening his grip on a pile of papers that which basically amounted to our life's work. I checked my phone. It was 10:10.

"DERRR DERRRRRR!" The special guest burst through the TARDIS door. It was Dom. "Oh hey. Look, they've got the Matt Smith sonic screwdriver!"

Jeff: Monday 19th April

"Well, nobody liked that Dalek episode, did they?" Said Mad Frankie, as I perused the shelves in Omega's Tomb. I noticed they had 'Attack of the Cybermen' for five quid.

"What? I thought it was incredible! The best one yet!"

"No. No one liked it. Nothing happened." He stared at me intently. If he were a stranger, it may have been intimidating, but this was just his way. I knew that he was really staring into the vastness of the cosmos. "I've got some friends – proper Doctor Who fans who've been watching it for years – and they all agree that it was the worst episode of

Doctor Who ever made." He swayed a little as he spoke, and I noticed he hadn't blinked once.

"The worst episode ever?? I'm sorry... Were they asleep for the entirety of the 80s? Have they forgotten the sham that was 'Trial of a Time Lord'? And what about fucking... 'Dragonfire'?"

"I suppose. Better than that Children in Need thing."

"No, I quite like that one."

I went back to work and spent the rest of the day kicking myself for not buying 'Attack of the Cybermen'. I know I already own it on video, in the special edition collector's tin with 'Tenth Planet', but it was only a fiver. And having things, especially Doctor Who things, just feels good. After half four, I could no longer bear it. I feigned a telephone call and ran out on the pretence of having some emergency, only to find it had been sold! I felt crushed, denied. I'd had my heart set on owning it, and the opportunity had been stolen! There was only one thing for it. I was going to have to buy it from HMV, even if it was £15. But they didn't have it, and neither did CEX. What the hell was going on? I was going to have to get it from Amazon.

Jeff: Tuesday 20th April

It turned out they had 'Attack of the Cybermen' for less than a fiver on Amazon, so I won! They also had most of Colin Baker's episodes going quite cheap. They were all there – 'Twin Dilemma', 'Vengeance of Varos', 'The Mark of the Rani'... I mean, none of those stories were actually any good, but they only came to £17 with super saver delivery!

The till roll ran out at work. Despite having worked there for four years, I've still never got the hang of it. This was it. Time to be a man. Time to be a proper, resourceful, useful person. The kind of guy people like to have around. Matt

Smith saved the world in 20 minutes. There was nothing to stop me replacing a bit of paper in a machine.

"Okay..." I breathed. "No TARDIS. No sonic screwdriver. 20 minutes to change the till roll. I *can* do it!"

10 minutes later, I was bent extremely close to the till, not to get a good look, but to hide my tears of shame and despair. I'd threaded a new roll in, but now the bit that held it no longer turned when you pressed the till button, and the more I forced it, the more it tore, until the whole thing was just a mess of shreds. I had to get 'Fat Chris' (who still isn't really speaking to me) to do it for me, and went to the toilet to carry on crying.

Jeff: Saturday 24th April

The injustice of having to work a late shift, which meant rushing from the house before the end of 'Confidential' was one thing. Getting stuck with Sandra was just rubbing salt into the wound.

She was doing the Yeti voice again, reminding me of the 'bottle of orange juice' sketch from 'League of Gentlemen'. "Ahh, the angels are so scary. It's like 'noooo, look out Amy, you've got an angel in your eye'. I mean, The Doctor was RUBBISH as usual. He looks about 9, and he's all like 'whatevvvvaaaaa, I'm not going to save any of you. It's fine. I'll just lock Amy in a big metal room to die. I mean, David Tennant wouldn't have left her like that, and David Tennant would have been crying his eyes out when Bob died, ButRiverwasAMAZING!! She was like 'Yeeeeeaaaahhhh, I know how to fly the TARDIS'."

"Are you quite finished?"

"I think River Song should be the next Doctor Who. It's about time there was a woman Doctor Who. Amy would be a good Doctor Who too. Well, anyone would be better than Matt Smith! If there was a woman Doctor Who, maybe she would be called Mrs. Who... They should do an episode where you find out what Doctor Who's real name is."

"Are you out of your fucking mind?" I screamed, causing Old Brian to jump and spill some of his John Smiths. "If The Doctor had a name, what the fuck would they call the programme? The whole point of it... The whole fucking premise is that we don't really know who he is. D'you think that if it had been called 'The Adventures of Dr. Derek fucking Walton' in 1963 that it'd still be on today? Of course it fucking wouldn't! And as for the whole 'River Song should be The Doctor'... What does that even mean? How can one character *become* another? If anything, you mean Alex Kingston should be the next Doctor, which is utterly fucking preposterous because-" She burst into tears and fled from the bar. It was only then I realised that I'd overstepped the mark. Kathy stood in the doorway, her arms folded menacingly.

"Jeff. In here. Now!"

Jeff: Sunday 25th April

Pete was not going to take it well.

"You got sacked? But... But... How are we going to pay for food?" He shrieked.

"Never mind that. What about the rent?"

"What? Rent?"

"Yes, you know, the rent on the flat. That thing you never contribute to."

"But I thought this was *our* flat?"

"Yes, it's our flat. It's our flat which we rent!"

"But..."

"It's fine. I've got enough to keep us going for a couple of months at a push. I'll just find another job as soon as I can. I'll see if they'll have me back on the trams."

"But didn't you..."

"...That was a long time ago. I'm sure they've forgotten about that by now. Besides, it's probably a good thing. This means I *definitely* can't go on that cycling holiday! Ha! Didn't put that on your graph, did you?" I punched at the air.

"Graph?"

"Oh, never mind. Besides, all that commuting was doing my head in."

"But won't you miss everyone? Fat Chris, Mad Frankie, Old Brian..."

"No. They were all... Sort of... You know... Arseholes."

"What about that gorgeous girl that likes Doctor Who?"

"Yeah, I may have... She's even worse. And she looks like a fish in jeans."

"But she likes Doctor Who!"

"No! No, she's one of *them*."

"Oh no!"

"Yeah."

"A post 05-er? Shit. Well, there's bound to be *someone* you'll miss. What about Cancer Dave?"

"Oh yeah. I will miss him. He doesn't actually have cancer, you know."

"What?!"

"Sorry, I've been meaning to tell you for ages. I got it wrong. It's actually Oliver who has cancer."

"You mean... Cancer Dave doesn't have cancer? But we've been calling him Cancer Dave for years!"

"I know... I know..."

"I even sent him that 'get well soon' card! When he didn't reply, I thought he'd died! But he probably just thought I was mental."

"Come on, everything's going to be fine. Let's watch the 'Time of Angels' repeat."

I was looking at the new sonic screwdriver toy on Amazon and ended up reading a customer review. I found it very useful until I walked in on myself and realised the absurdity of it all. I was a soon-to-be 39 year old man looking at toys, and reading an absurdly detailed description of said toy by another – presumably equally pathetic – grown man.

"Pete! You've got to hear this!" I walked into the living room holding my laptop. "Can you believe someone went to all this detail about the new sonic screwdriver?! It's a kids' toy for Christ's sake! '*Matt Smith Turns the Sonic Up to ELEVEN: I read a lot of negative reviews for this product, and it nearly put me off purchasing it. Being fully ordained into the Church of Whovianism, however, I just couldn't resist. I ordered it on 24 hour delivery: needless to say, when the postman showed up this morning, I felt sick with excitement and haven't been able to stop playing with it for hours! Ignore the naysayers. All in all, it's a pretty impressive piece of kit! After carefully unboxing it, I was astonished to see just how big it is compared to its forerunners. Other people may have criticised this, but – I must say – it's much better on the size and shape front: a perfect fit, one might say, whether gripped in the palm of your hand or whipped out, defeating monsters! Plus, it's so big that there's very little chance of misplacing it, so collectors will be pleased to hear there'll be no more losing it down the back of the sofa – unlike those pesky David Tennant models! One downside to this is that it's difficult to fit it snugly in your trousers, which might cause some difficulty to show fanatics who like to take their screwdriver everywhere with them. Perhaps the 'Character Options' toy company can incorporate some dimensionally transcendental pockets into their future Who range?*

In terms of functionality, I regret to say it's not all plain sailing, so strap on your seat belts! There ARE teething troubles. The fact that you need to install the batteries before you can lock and load has been a persistent problem with the sonic screwdriver range, and I'm afraid to report that this model falls at the same hurdle. If anything, the fact that there are FOUR tiny screws buried deep into the plastic recess means that this latest upgrade is the trickiest of the lot when it comes to

113

battery installation. I spent a good half hour studying the manual, and saw that it instructed me to 'twist the emitter one-tenth anticlockwise, then pull away from the handle'. Easier said than done! It was such stiff business that although I gripped it firmly, I was too nervous about breaking the end to use much force. I went limp-wristed trying to manoeuvre the delicate-looking components, and after several attempts, brute force was all that would prevail. Another problem is the lack of indication which way the batteries go in, and I'm afraid to say I fell victim to this transparency fault, having to repeat the whole process again. We haven't all been to the Gallifreyan academy, after all! This version also takes more batteries than the previous ones, but that's forgiveable considering the size, not to mention some hidden little surprises...

After a cup of strong Horlicks, I took a little time out to get to know my new sonic screwdriver. One thing I noticed upon reappraisal was that the distorted exterior of this iteration highlights the sub-par manufacturing quality which has persistently dogged its predecessors. The extended 'claw' feature at the tip of the shaft feels flimsy and fragile, whilst the hollow space inside gives the whole device a more obviously synthetic feel. Perhaps gone forever are the days when my Mum would ask if it was the real prop from the show!

But fear not! The new screwdriver is fully equipped with bright green light and spring-loaded head to soothe those ultraviolet blues. The extendible 'claw' feature is really quite something! You can almost feel it throbbing with power, and the way the 'claw' opens up lends a further grandiosity to proceedings. I tried it out on the gas man when he came to read our meter and he admitted that he "wouldn't want to run into me in a dark alley!" Next to the extension catch, a switch activates the light and comforting 'whirr' familiar to Whovians across the world. I couldn't help but let out a contented 'Ahhhh!' But zounds, I say! It doesn't work when the shaft is extended. What are the manufacturers playing at??! Thankfully, when extended there is a second button revealed beneath the elongated protrusion. It is so small, however, that those with stubby fingers may struggle to enjoy the full range of diverse features on offer. As if this didn't complicate issues enough, there is a third button, hidden behind a secret hinge. I had to question what the point of this bright red switch might be, but I suppose it adds an extra dimension (in time!) for young users.

One of the most exciting aspects of the new model is the addition of extra sounds: there are four in total, each one completely individual! The operation button appears to be equipped with a slight time delay, allowing the discerning user to trigger through a number of modes. A single press creates the standard 'whirring' noise, three presses stimulate the end to repeatedly flash (accompanied by a sound a little like a burglar alarm – I would appreciate it if someone would point out when this is ever used in the series). The fourth press gives the device the appearance of being broken... Or maybe I just purchased a faulty one? I'll have to check with one of my friends. The sounds were so exciting that they almost rid the memory of my traumatic battery experience, and should hopefully be enough to satiate the desires of even the most stringent Whovian.

All in all, I'm pretty satisfied with my new screwdriver... Although I don't think I'll be putting any shelves up with it! For those who are experiencing similar difficulties as I, however, I've set up a support forum and will be welcoming your emails with any queries, both functional and technical. It does take some getting used to, but experiment with the different features and I think you'll find you've invested in a trustworthy model. And invest you certainly should!' Can you believe this guy? He must have no life whatsoever! He wrote an A4 page essay about a toy that essentially lights up and makes noises!"

Pete remained still, looking hurt. "I wrote that." He said. "I bought it as an early birthday present for you."

Jeff: Tuesday 27ᵗʰ April

I had to go into work to get my P45. I waited until evening so I knew that Kathy would have finished her shift. 'Fat Chris' handed it to me in silence, whilst Sandra made a point of not making eye contact. The only person who seemed pleased to see me was old Brian, who explained to me in his grizzled tones that he doesn't "just drink beer here. I drink it

115

at home as well. I drink whiskey too." I had to be honest. I wasn't going to miss the place.

As I was leaving, someone called my name. At first I was confused. She must have been calling to someone else, as I had no idea who she was.

"I'm Shtacy! I gave you my number. You never called." She made a sad face. I couldn't believe it. I'd long since convinced myself that it had been some kind of joke, but she was real. She wasn't amazingly attractive – a little chubby perhaps – but she wasn't hideous! And she liked me! She had long, light brown hair and wore jeans with a white tank top that struggled to contain her, almost intimidatingly, large breasts. Her face was rounded, but with a long nose and very pretty eyes. She spoke with some kind of accent, but I couldn't quite place it. Polish? Russian? That was it: she spoke like a Bond villain!

"Yeah, sorry! Been really busy... D'you want to go for a drink?" I didn't realise it was a bad idea until the words had left my mouth, but I couldn't put them back in so off we went.

One drink turned into several, and then the pub turned into a club. I don't remember much other than being pushed up against a wall as she kissed me. The next thing I knew, it was the morning after and we were in her bed.

Jeff: Wednesday 28th April

I awoke with a jolt and my first instinct was to wretch. Sunlight filtered into the room in that sickly yellow way it only seems to do when you have a hangover. My mouth was dry and my head was pounding. I had no idea how much I'd had to drink last night, but I knew the real reason for my nausea was the taste in my mouth. I felt like someone had poured an ashtray down my throat. Stacy had been chain smoking for most of the evening. It hadn't seemed to register at the time. I hadn't noticed the foul taste each time

116

she'd kissed me. Why had that never bothered me when *I* smoked? Now I recalled with horror her bitter, nicotine flavour saliva mixing with mine with every violent kiss. I suppose she may have used the word 'passionate', but there was definitely an aggression to her technique, and the tongue piercing didn't help matters.

She lay next to me, fully clothed beneath the covers, whereas I was inexplicably naked from the waist down. Bit by bit, the events of last night came back to me...

Oh God! I had to get out of there. I also had to think of a lie as to where I'd been. The ash taste was obscuring all thought. I nudged Stacy. She was dead to the world. Was I really just going to leave? Yes. As quietly as I could, I retrieved my missing items of clothing and crept from the room. I took one last look at her, trying to remember if she had seemed at least vaguely attractive the previous night. It was a blur. I was racked with guilt. Should I at least leave a phone number? Well, I didn't really want her to ever call me, so no. What about an email address? Or was that just adding insult to injury? Surely an email address means 'never call me ever'. And there was always the risk that she might actually email me. Of course! There was a solution. I grabbed a broken pencil and scrawled the 'warrior_from_the_deep42@gmail.com' address on a bit of paper, placed it on the bedside table and crept from the house.

It was a hot, sunny day with a cloudless sky, and I felt dreadful. I'd been wearing the same clothes since yesterday, I was sweaty, half asleep, hungover, dehydrated and hungry. And I had twelve missed calls from Daisy. I got a sausage roll and a coffee on my way to find the car, but I knew I wouldn't feel human until I'd had a shower. Even then, I wouldn't feel *good*.

Pete: Thursday 29th April

Shortly after Jeff left this morning, I was driven out of bed by a loud knocking, so I pulled on my dressing gown to go and take a look who was calling. I couldn't see anyone through the peep-hole, so I edged the door open slowly to see that there was, indeed, nobody there. On the floor, however, was a small package, with 'FAO The Computer Doctor' scribbled on the front and a note – in big, curvy black marker pen writing – reading 'problem booting up. Please could you take a look over this for me, and email me on sexybexy@gmail.com?' This was most worrying. I knew I shouldn't have advertised my address in the Yellow Pages! What was I going to do? I mean, I could try to fix the computer, but then that would almost certainly end up with me having to admit that I couldn't actually *fix computers*! That I was, in fact, totally unqualified for my job.

I took several deep breaths. Stay calm. Just... stay calm, Pete! If I strained my ears, I could just about hear footsteps in the downstairs hallway. For all I knew, 'sexybexy@gmail.com' could still be down there. Perhaps I could talk my way out of things. I dashed down the staircase, and ran straight into a grizzly looking pensioner. He seemed, if anything, even more bemused than me, and, oddly enough, wore the same dressing gown.

"Whoa! I'm..."

"You're..."

"...it's..."

"...quite..."

"But..."

"...sorry about the..."

"...noggin..."

"computer..."

"...pocket watch." Just as we had talked over one another, we stopped simultaneously, and proceeded to scratch our mutual heads. It was like looking into a particularly unflattering mirror. The odd thought occurred to me that the man could be me from the future. He did look a little like an older version of me, albeit thinner around the face, fatter around the waist, and with, what can only be described as, a crazed mass of mad hair. But it didn't make sense. The likelihood that I'd discover time travel in 40 years and still be looking so unhealthily misshapen didn't correlate somehow. Surely I would have gone back and altered my own timeline to turn myself into a more adequate human being? It'd be a like a Moff storyline. I also noticed that the door to the downstairs flat – which, in all my time of living here, had remained locked – was ajar.

"Erm, you wouldn't be sexybexy@gmail.com, would you?" Even as the words left my mouth, it seemed pretty doubtful that he'd reply in the affirmative.

"No, I most certainly am not," his voice wavered precariously, "my name is Mr. Harrison." Although he spoke sharply, he sounded like he looked: old, peculiar, musty. What if this really *was* me aged 78?? He reached into his dressing gown pocket and pulled out half a custard cream biscuit. Leaning into me, he whispered "I've been asleep for three-and-a-half years, you know!" Before laughing, and gliding back to his flat.

As he left, he reached into the folds of his dressing gown and extended a shaking hand. In it was a heap of crumpled letters – so that's where my postal vote got to! On the front of the envelope, 'Vote Saxon!' was scrawled in spidery handwriting. The mind-aching possibility that this guy actually *was* a future-me made me made me feel a little grey inside. I imagined my hair instantaneously going white and frizzy, falling out in clumps all at once. I imagined the prospect of Cod

Liver Oil pills suddenly becoming appealing. I imagined watching daytime television as a recreational pursuit, and then remembered that I did that already. Hell, Mum had even bought me the complete *Murder, She Wrote* box set last Christmas.

I was suddenly struck by a terrifying thought. I was getting old, and Karen Gillan was NEVER going to be my wife.

Jeff: Friday 30th April

Possibly out of a desire to make my life better, but probably out of guilt, I phoned Daisy. She seemed pitifully delighted to hear from me and insisted we go for lunch at the Soy Bean Abattoir in Liverpool. Apparently the name is ironic, but why we had to go to Liverpool, to eat Mexican bean wraps with fruit cakes and beetroot smoothies, is beyond me, when there's a perfectly good little cafe in Blackpool.

She said she was glad I'd "come to my senses" and that we should do something "womantic" for my birthday. She also seemed pleased that I'd left the pub, but I *had* lied, saying I'd quit to pursue better things.

Maybe it was because I felt bad, or maybe it was because she doesn't taste of ash or have a tongue piercing (Or the *other* piercing which Stacy had referred to as the "jewel" in her "Lady Box"), but I felt much more affectionate towards her than I had in a long time. Especially the way she sometimes stopped midway through a sentence and blushed, lowering her head and looking up at me with cheeky eyes. It was one of the first things I'd liked about her. She reminded me of a classic companion. It was a look I could imagine Jo, or Zoe, giving. That said, she was still boring the shit out of me.

120

Pete: Friday 30th April

After sitting awake doing a lot of thinking about me and the future, I was all set for a philosophical discussion with Jeff. I sent him a text, saying we needed to talk as soon as he got back from Liverpool; cleared the kitchen table; put a can of lager and notepad at each side; and filled the kettle just over maximum level (my brush with mortality issues had obviously brought out a rebellious streak).

I was planning to tackle the issue head on as soon as he got home, but he rushed back early, saying that my 'uncharacteristically serious' text had got him worried, and caught me unaware: I was midway through the online shopping, and my brain just wasn't ready.

"Jeff," I said, still fixing my gaze upon the screen, "I've been doing some thinking, and... Oh my god!" He sprung to my side, a look of concern about him. "They've got a Three-for-a-pound deal on rice pudding!" Unfortunately, things quickly derailed from there. Jeff threw in THE 'unlimited rice pudding' quote, and then the whole evening would have just felt wrong had we not watched 'Remembrance of the Daleks' in its entirety. Something to do with that Chaos Theory bit in 'Spaced', I think. Anyway, basically, if we hadn't watched it, we would have been fucked.

I did consider trying to talk future again when we'd done, but my words just weren't coming out in the right order. Perhaps it was the overwhelming weight and responsibility of the serious issue at hand. Perhaps it was the lager six-pack. Who knows?

We fell asleep watching *Remembrance of the Daleks* for a second time, with the commentary playing.

Jeff: Saturday 1st May

Probably because I'm a pathetic creature of habit, I went to Preston just to talk to Mad Frankie. That's what used to happen on Saturdays before I got sacked. But I was put off by his tirade of abuse concerning Matt Smith. Honestly, why can't people just appreciate Doctor Who? And if they don't like it, then why bother watching it?! I sped home for 1pm. Only 5 hours until 'Flesh and Stone' and I had to decorate the house with Weeping Angel masks.

Jeff: Sunday 2nd May

My problems with 'Time of Angels'/'Flesh and Stone':

1. Why do the angels no longer send people back in time? Why is this not explained?
2. The Tenth Doctor stated, in 'Blink', that when the Weeping Angels are observed by any living thing "they literally turn to stone" - surely insinuating that when not being observed they are, in fact, flesh and blood. So why, in this episode, do the statues appear to come to life?
3. When did the angels become malevolent? In 'Blink' they are simply feeding off temporal energy. The Doctor says they are "creatures of the abstract" and "the only psychopaths in the universe to kill you kindly". And yet now, with no explanation whatsoever, they are suddenly the most evil creatures in the universe? Which, by the way, is what The Doctor said about the Daleks in 'Victory'! So, come on 'Moff' – which is it? There can only be one "most evil"!
4. What is good about River Song? Is there something I'm missing there?

5. If the image of an Angel becomes an Angel, then how come the people who saw the Angels in 'Blink' (I.e. the entire cast) didn't end up suffering the same fate as Amy?

6. The Angels were talking through Bob how exactly? And wasn't that done in 'Silence in the Library'?

7. Why were the Clerics there in the first place? What was their mission? They didn't know there was an army of Angels, so why go to one abandoned, dead planet to stop one single Angel. Surely that would be the best place for it?

8. If the TARDIS makes its noise because the breaks are still on, then why does the Master's TARDIS make the same noise? Does he leave the breaks on too? Not likely that two of the cleverest minds in the galaxy would make that mistake. Although, it would make sense considering the fact that the TARDIS simply appears and disappears without a sound in 'Colony in Space' when being controlled remotely by the Time Lords. However, this is flawed by the fact that the dematerialisation noise is heard not only when the Time Lords return the Third Doctor's dematerialisation circuit in 'The Three Doctors', but also when the Time Lord appears to The Doctor at the beginning of 'Terror of the Autons'. It just doesn't make sense!

9. When The Doctor leaves Amy, but then returns, he is quite clearly wearing his jacket, which was taken by the Angels in the previous scene. Is this deliberate? Has he time travelled back, or forward, to this moment from a different point in time, or is it simply a costume continuity error – like the wardrobe farce that is 'The Empire Strikes Back'?

Pete: Sunday 2nd May (am)

All my opinions and excitement about 'Flesh and Stone' were swept aside by a confusing wave of emotions over the ending. Why does she want to shag Matt Smith and not me??? Okay- he may be younger, richer, better looking, more socially mobile and charismatic than me, but at least I've got a less angular head. Surely that must count for something?

Despair overtook me. It wasn't long before I found myself in bed, eating handfuls of dry sugar puffs from the box. When the packet was empty, the ensuing sugar rush sent me a bit mental, until I crashed out.

Pete: Sunday 2nd May (pm)

I'm not quite sure what happened last night. I will not apologise for my behaviour, nor will I be held accountable for it. All I know is that the bed covers were full of sticky cereal bits; my pants were hanging out of the window, flapping inelegantly in the breeze; and my wall of Karen newspaper cuttings was smeared in hard toothpaste.

Pete: Monday 3rd May

Put advert on online dating site: 'not-unattractive male with normally shaped head seeks Amy Pond lookalike'. I didn't have many up-to-date photos, so I had to settle for one of me and Jeff at *Whogasm '06*. I'm sure the fact that he's in full Davros costume, and I'm wearing a Cyberman helmet will only help to endear women towards me.

Pete: Thursday 6th May

Dating site page views, so far: 0 (zero).

Pete: Friday 7th May

Partly out of wanting to seem like a normal grown-up, partly out of wanting something culturally relevant to talk to girls about on all the dates I'm soon *sure* to be going on, and partly out of boredom, I watched the election coverage with Jeff.

"So, Tony Blair's not the Prime Minister anymore?" I scratched my head.

"Erm, no." Jeff looked oddly perplexed. "And he hasn't been for about three years. When was the last time you watched the news?"

"Not including that American woman in *The End of Time*?"

"Well, no. That *definitely* doesn't count." I must have looked a bit too crestfallen, because he gave me a friendly dig on the shoulder and added cheerily, "Well, I mean to say it doesn't count in *our* world, obviously, but in a parallel universe... fuck yeah!"

We watched a bit more of the TV report. A nervous looking, balding man, with a pointy chin and not-insubstantial nose came on screen and announced to us that "the British public have spoken. We're just not sure exactly what it is they've said." There was something oddly comforting about someone with such an important sounding name and posh accent admitting that no one had a clue what the hell was going on anymore. Maybe we're not doomed.

Jeff: Saturday 8th May

Wow! 'Vampires of Venice' was a triumph! And it is *of* and not *in*! However, I couldn't help but notice that Toby Whitehouse seems to have recycled the 'School Reunion' script and done a 'find and replace' with the words 'Krillitane' and 'Vampire'. Not convinced?

A box of plot for 'Doctor Who and the Interchangeable Script'...

A young man is jealous because his girlfriend has been whisked away by a mysterious stranger known as The Doctor, and they are having adventures in time and space without him. Nevertheless, the three team up to investigate sinister goings on in a school, the spooky leaders of which seem to be using the children for some evil purpose.

Adopting false aliases, our heroes get themselves into the school with the help of psychic paper, only to discover that the teachers are really aliens, and only appear to be human, but have the power to change their form. They are caught and, narrowly escaping, regroup to come up with a plan of attack. Shortly after, The Doctor confronts the leader of the aliens, telling them to leave in peace. The leader knows of the Time Lords and is surprised at The Doctor's involvement and actions. The villain offers an alliance with The Doctor, who refuses before leaving politely whilst promising to destroy the aliens. Inexplicably, they let him go nonetheless.

Sure enough, The Doctor comes up with a scheme to stop them. But by this stage, the aliens' plan has entered its final phase.

The boyfriend, meanwhile, is feeling left out and unspectacular, but then proves himself in an unexpected moment of bravery.

There is a big explosion, lots of sonic-ing, and everything is fine. The Doctor then allows the boyfriend of his companion to come with them for further adventures in time and space.

Pete: Sunday 9th May

Had sultry dream about Vampire Girls, woke up feeling excited, bounded out of bed to check my inbox. This was it. Today was the day I'd get a response from the dating site. I could feel it. I flicked to the hit counter at the bottom. Page views: 0 (zero).

Jeff: Monday 10th May

My Colin Baker DVDs arrived today. Pete asked why I had wasted money I didn't have on episodes I notoriously disliked and already owned on video.

"I mean, just tell me you're not going to go crazy and buy 'Trial of a Time Lord' or anything..."

Jeff: Wednesday 12th May

The 'Trial of a Time Lord' box set arrived today! Pete demanded to know why, and I broke down and confessed that I'd become convinced that owning Colin Baker's entire tenure on DVD would make me feel as though I'd accomplished something with my life.

"Has it worked?"

"No!" I wailed. "It somehow feels incomplete with 'Dimensions in Time'!"

"But that was shit!"

"Nevertheless, it's canon." He made a cup of tea to calm me down.

Pete: Tuesday 11th May

Watched Nottingham Forest V Blackpool game with Jeff and Daisy. I'd pleaded with Jeff to stop her coming round, but he'd argued that if she came round during football, he would earn boyfriend points for legitimately spending time with her without actually having to talk. I had to agree that this was a "valid point".

Unfortunately, my comment that "Nottingham must have a positively tropical climate, because all the players are black" didn't go down too well. For some reason, the moment I followed it up with my winning "Good job it's not dark!" joke, Daisy went on the defensive, telling me I was xenophobic.

"Maybe, but at least I'm not a racist." I argued. "I just appreciate racially motivated humour." She slapped me on the leg, said that she refused to share the sofa with a bigot and would be leaving imminently. Me and Jeff exchanged hopeful glances, but, by the time of Blackpool's triumph at end of the game, she was still there, going on incessantly about feeling ill while me and Jeff jumped up and down with joy.

Why she's still here is beyond me. All I do know is that my knee still stings, and I can still hear Jeff having reluctant sex in the next room.

Pete: Wednesday 12th May

I can't believe it!!!!! My ad's got a response!!!!!!!! From someone actually called Amy Pond!!!!!!!!!!

Hey there, cutie! Couldn't believe it when I stumbled across your profile. I may not look exactly like your ideal partner, but we do share more than a passing

128

resemblance and – get this – the same name. Also, I LOVE guys with symmetrical heads. How weird is that? Your photo made me feel fuzzy inside – I love that silly hat you're wearing. It's really zany! I'm gonna put a pic up soon as I get my webcam working, but check this: I live in Layton. I'm not usually this forward, but hows about we meet up sometime?

I finished reading and instantly reached for my inhaler, taking several slow puffs. Okay, Pete: let's not get too carried away. For all I know, she could be a seven-foot-tall dykey-ex-convict-type, or a wheelchair-bound Ogron lookalike with Shane MacGowan teeth. But then again, what if it was the REAL Amy Pond???

I only wish I could have replied, but my dongle got in the way. At that moment, it lit up at the end and started to go haywire, so I had to yank it off. After that, it was spent for the rest of night. The more I tried plugging it in and out, the less signs of life it showed. I must have drained it. If only I hadn't got so over-excited!

Pete: Thursday 13th May

I've been thinking about this all day. There was no question of not responding to the message. It was just a matter of how to sell myself. Would I focus entirely on looks? Would I try to show myself as playful and humorous, or witty and erudite? The thought struck me that I probably couldn't pull off any of the above convincingly: hardly anyone – apart from maybe Simone, when she wanted to borrow some cash, or Jeff, if he was trying to be reassuring – had ever described me as attractive, fun or particularly sharp. Come to think of it, plenty of people had said the opposite.

129

Things didn't seem to stack up too well in my favour. Let's face it, I was fucked.

I decided what I needed, more than anything, was some friendly support. But Jeff was at work. In my despair, I texted Dom, asking what my best features were. Two minutes later, my phone flashed up the '1 New Message' logo. Dom's reply read: *'Well, you're certainly no William Shatner, but then again, you're hardly a Rod Stewart either'*. I think he was trying to be diplomatic, but I had no idea what he was talking about. Was whatever he was suggesting a good thing or a bad thing? Was it somewhere in between, or none of the above? Maybe he was being sarcastic? I just didn't know.

Whilst I chewed over this, I sat at the table, eating the discount rice pudding cold, from the tin, all the while aware that Amy Pond was slipping away from me.

Pete: Friday 14th May

I've done it! At last!! I managed to respond to the message in a way that was honest, but didn't make me seem like a failure, a massive twat or a subhuman cave-dwelling mutant from *The Mutants* or *Mutant!*!! And to think I thought I wouldn't be able to do it without sounding pathetic, awkward or desperate.

```
Oh my god! I can't believe someone
actually replied to this! And there was me
about to delete it! HAHAHA! What an idiot
I am! ;-) Anyway, SOOOO glad to hear from
you! :-) I'm not really very good at this
sort of thing, so maybe you can tell me a
bit about yourself. Did you watch the
match the other night? What do you look
like? What's your favourite Doctor Who
```

episode ;-)? Who did you vote for in the election? What do you think about the situation in Iraq? Do you enjoy eating food sometimes? Do most of your social situations take place indoors/outdoors (delete as appropriate)? What do you look for in a man? Hope all these questions aren't too scary, haha. It's a bit like James Bond, isn't it? And I'm the villain! :-) I've been expecting you, Mr... POND! We have ways of making you talk. HAHAHA. But seriously, I REALLY hope I haven't scared you.

I thought the smilies were a bit of a risk. I'd never normally use them, but I didn't want to appear too uptight.

4am: Can't sleep, can't breath. I think the winks might have been too forward.

Pete: Saturday 15th May

We were sat in an unusual silence, me reading the *Web of Fear* Target novelisation, Jeff tinkering with his new sonic screwdriver, when both our phones lit up at once.

"That's weird." Jeff looked up at me, arching an eyebrow.

"Yeah, a bit *Twilight Zone*." As it happened, it was the same message from Dom, but as I read it and sighed, forcing my mobile back into the tight pocket slit of my jeans, Jeff spat out a mouthful of tea and sprung to his feet.

"Colin Baker... A signing... I had no idea... I can't believe it... " He rambled, grabbing his keys, swinging a coat over his arm. "I can ask him if he pitched our edited *Nightmare Fair* script to Big Finish yet. It's..."

131

"Obviously another joke." I cut in, waving my book dismissively. "Nothing more to it." Jeff's whole frame visibly sank. It was as though he'd lost several feet in height.

"Well..." He sounded wounded. "I happen to think it might be for real."

"I thought we agreed we weren't going to trust Dom after..." I mimed some air quotes. "'The Lancaster incident'?" If this was a film a grave shadow would probably have fallen across both our faces, but it wasn't, and it didn't. "I thought you said, and I quote, that he was a bounder, a scoundrel and a cad?"

"Yeah, well, I had to win you back on side so you'd get in the car. Anyway, I'm going, and if he's not there, then there's plenty of other ways to entertain yourself in central Blackpool, like..." He picked up a local tourism leaflet and scanned the adverts on the front: The Circus of Death, The Tower of Death, The Odd-Cod Chippie, The *Wheel* of Death and Nadine's Massage Parlour. "Well, I'll find something. And you should come too- you'll stagnate in here." He picked up a sock, which was draped over the rim of a mug, as if to exemplify this.

"Jeff, you're a moth to a candle flame." I mentally awarded myself another ten points for dropping in a Jethro Tull quote. "It's like a few weeks ago, when I warned you about not looking in the Radio Times, on pain of seeing Alex Kingston's breasts. You just couldn't resist having a look, and, I quote, you were scarred for life."

"So, am I to take it you're not coming then... And will you please stop quoting me?!"

"No, because I'm 99.99% sure that he won't be there. It'll just be Dom, trying to get our attention by wearing a silly cravat, or bearing his arse or something."

"Yeah, well don't say I didn't try." He made to leave.

"I won't, but just you wait: I'll be having the last laugh."

Jeff: Saturday 15th May

What a day! I routed out my old Colin Baker coat and ran into town, brandishing my brand now sonic screwdriver! Luckily, it was Gay Pride weekend, so no one batted an eyelid. Daisy followed reluctantly at my heels on the promise that we'd go for some tofu curry afterwards.

I sped into Planet Who half an hour early, but he was already there – The Sixth Doctor! I mean, he was grey haired and wearing crocs, but who cared! All of a sudden, my dislike of 80s era Doctor Who disappeared and I felt the tears welling in my eyes. I remembered what it was like to be 13 years old and watching 'Revelation of the Daleks' for the first time. I wasn't aware of the shit production and terrible acting. It was all just so magical. I was back in that mindset, in the presence of The Doctor!

After marvelling at the toys and making a mental wish list – if only I was with Pete and not Daisy! – I joined the queue upstairs, which snaked its way around a collection of tables where some overweight kids ate McDonalds takeaway and played some kind of fantasy card game. How pathetic! My attention was soon distracted, however, by a display of 'Buffy' action figures.

As we neared Colin, I was giddy with excitement. It was then that I noticed one of the role-playing children was slightly bigger than the others, wearing some kind of ridiculous hat and an eye patch.

"Kevin?" I called, aghast. "What are *you* doing here?"

"I come here every week." He explained. "These are the guys." He had referred to 'the guys' before, but I'd always presumed he meant that troupe of 'specially abled' students he was herded around college with. I had no idea that my 27

133

year old cousin spent his Saturdays hanging out with acne riddled teenage geeks. It was all a bit frightening.

Pete: Saturday 15th May – 3pm

Unable to stop myself crying, I crushed an Eiffel Tower pen with one hand and hurled my phone at the wall with the other. Jeff had just sent a photo of him, Colin Baker, and a kid dressed up as the sixth doctor, all with their arms round each other. A cut-out Sontaran lurked to one side of the screen, and the message caption read 'The Doctor with his new companions: let battle commence!"

Pete: Sunday 16th May – am

1am: **I was just short of throwing myself out of the window when I eventually got my temp-computer fired up and was able to check my messages. Amy has given me her mobile number! I was too scared to call, but we've been texting all evening. I've bitten the bullet, and invited her over for a drink tomorrow. I know you hear all these stories about lonely middle-aged men luring unsuspecting girls to their flats then taking advantage of them, but I've assessed the situation and I'm definitely safe. The evidence stacks up overwhelmingly in my favour: I'll be on my own turf, I'm a man and I'm *far* too old to be a victim of paedophilic lust. In fact, it occurs to me with some excitement that statistically *I'm* more likely to be the child abuser of the two of us! And I'm DEFINITELY not, so it'll all be fine.**

Got text just before bed: '*Can't wait to meet you tomorrow, handsome. Goodnight XXX*'. I replied '*You too. Goodnight, Pond XXXXX*', and went to bed

feeling happy, warm, contented, but, most of all, excited to get out of bed the next day for the first time in ages. Everything really WAS going to be okay!

6.33am: I felt as though my stomach was trying to leap out from underneath the covers, I couldn't keep my legs still and my eyes were so wide open that I couldn't seem to blink (which would be PERFECT if there was a Weeping Angel in the vicinity, but not so good considering I was trying to sleep). It was an unfamiliar feeling – probably excitement – but sleep proved impossible, so I got up to make a brew. I could hardly believe my eyes when I opened the door. Jeff had blue-tacked a signed picture of Colin Baker to the frame: '*To my good friend Pete. My dear boy, where were you?? All the best, Colin*'. He'd put 'Colin'!! It looked like we knew each other!!! Wait until I showed Dom. If only it was 1986 again. I'd have been the envy of Science Club! Creepy Johnson wouldn't have known what had hit him. I'm not ashamed to say that I found myself welling up, and wanted to thank Jeff there and then. But I knew he'd be asleep, so I crept into his room and left a generously full cup of tea on his bedside table.

Half an hour later, I heard his alarm go off as 'Fireflies' started playing, followed by what sounded suspiciously like a cup falling on the floor. That, in turn, was followed by a prolonged period of swearing. Oops! I hope he didn't think it was some kind of deliberate trap. My guilt, strangely, was accompanied by an immense feeling of super-villainy. Perhaps I *could* play the next Master after all. Okay, I wasn't as young and slim as that time I sent in an audition tape to be in 'The TV Movie', but people had said to me, on more than one occasion, and I quote, 'even *you* would have made a better Master than Eric Roberts'.

Pete: Sunday 16th May (pm)

Today was a day of firsts... or at least 'first-for-a-long-time's. I got up before 10am, and decided to experiment with press-ups rather than masturbation. I got through thirteen of them, before collapsing in a sweating, breathless heap. But that didn't matter: today was the start of a new regime. This sort of stuff would be second nature to me soon, and I'd be fit enough to go bicycling around the Cotswalds with Amy at the drop of a hat in no time. From now on, I'd be a new Pete Ross. I made beans on toast, cutting down my usual six slices of white bread to just five, before jumping into the shower. I shaved; I used deodorant; I brushed AND flossed my teeth, dislodging several bits of questionable looking food; I even combed my hair! Of course, it refused to do as it was told, going perfectly flat up until my ears, so that it looked horrible and greasy, then springing out in a mass of unruly, mad scientist curls. It looked a bit stupid, but then if Colin Baker hadn't looked a bit stupid, he probably wouldn't have got the part of The Doctor!

Choosing my clothes for the day was a tough one. I was toying with the idea of raiding Jeff's wardrobe and dressing up as one of the Doctors, but I thought that would look a bit geeky, so I settled for my 'Masters of the Universe' T-Shirt, with a white blazer over the top, and a pair of brown chords. After all, I'd been saving this outfit for a special occasion.

I made sure the place was all clean too. Once again, before going to work, Jeff had left the bathroom towels in a heap on the floor, soaking up the puddles of overspill bathwater. For some reason, there also seemed to be a big smear of jam on the edge of the fridge, some of which ended up on my jacket when I tried to wipe it off. I was sure Amy wouldn't notice.

136

After all, she said I looked 'cute' from my online picture, so obviously either her eyesight wasn't up to much, or she was an 'inner beauty' sort of girl.

When the house was spotless, and I couldn't find anything else to occupy me, I paced up and down, checking my calculator watch frequently. Eventually, there was a sharp knock at the door, and I rushed to open it, almost tripping on the way. There was a momentary pause when I got there, a swell of sickness and excitement rising in my stomach, until I turned the handle and saw the figure on the other side: a man, with bright red hair and freckles, holding a bunch of pink flowers in one hand, and a bottle of rosé wine in the other.

"Hi!" He spoke in an overly-confident, almost desperate sounding, American accent. "I'm Andy Pond!"

My heart sank. I knew instantly that I must have made a typing error, and I felt utterly stupid: a grown man still behaving like a teenager. For days, all my hopes had been pinned on this meeting. I'd built whole stories around it: intricate plot-lines that would spring from this moment. I'd dreamed about them. I saw myself regenerating into a real person, walking round the streets arm in arm with the pregnant Karen from 'Amy's Choice', people smiling at me, and feeling like I wasn't such a loser. And, just like everything in my life, it had come to nothing. I wanted to slam the door, to be done with all this nonsense right now, but Andy still stood there, the smile on his face somehow pleading and desperate. And that was my biggest first for today- when I invited him in, not wanting to crush his hopes in the same way mine had just been, and played along... at being gay.

Pete: Monday 17ᵗʰ May

I'm giving up on online dating. I'm going to become a model railway enthusiast instead, and attend conventions full of men in bow-ties. Bow ties are cool.

I took a look on three websites – 'Choo-Choo Loco', 'Head of Steam' and 'No Train, No Gain' – and realised I didn't have enough money to collect model railway paraphernalia just yet. So I turned my attention to other things and saw 'sexybexy's laptop glaring at me accusingly. My thoughts returned to the dire situation at hand and realised I'd come full circle. So I put on the Tom Baker-era episode 'Full Circle' and realised that the E-Space trilogy wasn't as good as I remembered it being.

All in all, the day ended with a vague feeling of not having achieved anything, so I dealt with that situation by getting pissed.

Pete: Tuesday 18ᵗʰ May

"Whoa! You're up early..." Jeff mumbled groggily when I crept into his room, trying to shield his eyes from the light. I didn't want to admit that I hadn't actually been to sleep yet. *BBC iPlayer*, birthday preparations and Andy Pond anxiety had kept me up all night.

"I wanted to do something special for your breakfast." I kept one hand behind my back. "I've made your favourite!"

"What? Chicken Dansak?" He shot bolt upright. "Full English? Sunday roast?? Those weird pizzas?!"

"No, erm..." I swung my arm round to reveal five slices of white bread (the expensive kind that you need an engineering degree for just to fit it in the toaster), stacked on top of one another, a single candle perched atop the crust. "...Toast. Happy birthday!" Suddenly it seemed like an anticlimax. Jeff slunk back down into the covers, and the already-feeble-looking candle extinguished itself.

"Ah. Put it on the side, will you?" I angled it in such a way that he'd notice the Marmite-shaped '39' on the top slice. He smiled when he saw it. "Haha. Keep it quiet, will you?! I said I was 31 on that audition tape I sent to 'The Moff', remember?"

"I *do* remember. Your costume's still hung up on the back of my door."

"Hmmm..." He made a face. "I wish I'd been sober when I'd done that. I still think it might have been the pirate wig, Elizabethan ruff and green tights that put him off calling me back. Anyway, you haven't made a big fuss about this whole," he waved a dismissive hand, "*birthday thing*, have you?"

"Er, no." I grinned, pushing the door to and fro with my foot. Jeff got out of bed, put on a dressing gown and tried to walk into the lounge. Standing in the doorway, however, was a life-sized Matt Smith cut out, wearing a Christmas-cracker party hat with the number '39' scribbled on in pink marker pen. I'd bought the matching Karen Gillan one for myself, but she stood by the sofa, holding a banner which read 'Happy 39th Birthday'. A balloon hovered near the ceiling, featuring the same message, but with '*Geronimo!* 40, here we come!' underneath. I'd covered various items of furniture in shredded tin foil, and the floor in bits of polystyrene, to create that authentic Patrick Troughton era alien planet look. I think I can feel a future career in interior design beckoning. Andy Pond probably knows Laurence Llewelyn-Bowen. I'm pretty sure he's gay too.

"Wow... You've turned our living room into Pinewood Studios." Jeff's voice wavered somewhere between jubilation and bewilderment. Maybe I'd gone a bit far with the Bacofoil. Lack of sleep does that to you. "And it's like you weren't even worried about the mess."

"I took some pills." I smiled proudly.

There was a moment of silence, as he took it all in, before letting out a big Matt Smith "Haha!" He began to jump up and down with his arms around my neck, which went on until his dressing gown nearly fell open. Taking that into account, I probably picked the *most* inopportune moment to say...

"Jeff, have you ever done something really stupid, like..." I hesitated. "*Accidentally* ended up being gay?" He looked down at his almost open robe, and knotted his eyebrows. "No, not you, you... twat!" (Had to throw in a bit of blokey banter.) "I mean more like... Well... Have you ever lied to someone to spare their feelings?" He looked worried. "...Then put off telling them the truth because you were scared of hurting them?" He seemed to be counting something on his fingers, the corners of his mouth turning downwards. "And you tell yourself you're *not* doing anything wrong, but everyday you don't tell the truth, you somehow dig yourself in a bit deeper, until you're in a big..." I stirred at the air like it was soup. "...Quagmire of deception?!"

For a long time everything was quiet, until, at last, he said a forceful "No". But he said it in such a way that it actually sounded more like 'Yes', and I knew he was feeling guilty about Daisy. Sensing we were drifting into potentially dangerous territory, I decided to move things on quickly... back to my own humiliations.

"Well, you know I had that date 'thing' yesterday?"

"Oh yeah- Amy Pond?! You were pretty quiet about that when I got in!"

"I was in bed!" The words came out sounding more snappy and defensive than I'd meant them to.

"Exactly. What the hell were *you* doing in bed before midnight? Don't you usually spend Sunday nights checking for DVD subtitle inconsistencies until 2am? Nah... You were just trying not to make me jealous, weren't you?" He boxed at the air. "So spill the beans. All the gory details..." I rung my hands frantically. I had to get it out, otherwise I was *literally* going to explode, but Jeff wouldn't stop talking. "Go on, you old devil! Did she have the hair? Was she wearing a mini-skirt? Oooorrrr," his eyes lit up, "was she not even *wearing* a skirt?"

"*She* was a bloke." I muttered.

"Wh-hoa! And there was me thinking I'd be the one getting all the birthday pres-" His eyes suddenly widened, as though, somehow, my last sentence had only just arrived safely at his brain. "Hang on. She was a tranny?"

"More than that..." I replied solemnly.

"A big fat tranny?!!"

"Jeff! This is no time for Tim Bisley quotes. This is an emergency..."

"Sorry. It was an accident. Honest: you know much I've struggled to watch anything with Simon Pegg in since..."

"THE LONG GAME." We said it mournfully, as one, and conversation was inevitably derailed, hurtling several miles off-topic towards a long list of post-*Shaun of the Dead* Pegg disappointments. I swear a shiver passed through the room when we reached *How to Lose Friends and Alienate People*, and suddenly lying to Andy Pond didn't seem quite so bad. "It turns out, I never wrote '*Amy* Pond' on my advert. I wrote..." Inadvertently, I seemed to be stifling my mouth with a cushion. "...Andy." The lump abruptly returned to my throat. "But by the time he got here, I was already in too deep. He looked so helpless and pathetic. He was like a walking, breathing version of that feeling I get when I look in the mirror most mornings..."

"...'The scary door'..." Jeff nodded sagely.

"...So I invited him in, and..."

"Gayed it up?! Couldn't you have just made him a brew and explained your way out of it?"

"He had pink wine, Jeff. *Pink* wine! There was no getting out. As soon as he spotted the *pink* flowers on the table, and Daisy's *pink* sweater slung over the chair, I knew I was done for! And all those pictures of me and you with our arms round each other didn't help either. He instantly assumed that you were my ex, and that I was having a hard time letting go."

"And I presume you put him straight?" He chortled to himself. "No pun intended."

"Sort of... I... Erm... Well, basically, I told him you were in a coma."

"You killed me?!" He sprung up.

"Not *killed* you. Just... put you to sleep."

"That's what they say to dogs when they give them the lethal injection!" He sank back melodramatically. "God... I can't believe you *killed* me. And the day before my birthday too. I had so much to live for... Probably." He seemed to be counting down on his fingers again, a worried look creeping over his face. This wasn't going well.

"Look, it's not as though I want you in a coma. That's the last thing I want... Unless there's some MASSIVE leap forward in cryogenics, and we freeze ourselves for thirty years until they've invented time travelling microwaves and... Computers that make toast. Anyway, I thought it was a pretty clever excuse. Every time he made a move, I just went on about not being over you properly, how I needed some space, and he backed right off."

"You managed to get rid of him without any trouble then?"

"Well, pretty much... He *was* crying, and he *did* kept putting his arms around me, telling me I was a 'beautiful, brave man'."

"Hmmm, so you think you'll hear from him again?"

"Erm, I reckon I should be okay. He probably thought I had too much baggage."

"You do. You've got more baggage than Cassandra. And I wouldn't go getting too optimistic just yet." He pressed the red button on my mobile phone, and handed it to me: 17 missed calls.

"It could be... No, wait. Dom doesn't do calls since 'The Event' – only texts."

"This is going to be a tricky one..." Jeff put on his best Matt Smith accent, and, appropriately enough, the Doctor Who theme started. It was my ringtone. Instinctively, I reached for my comforting sonic screwdriver. But it was no good- the batteries had gone.

Suddenly, the failures of the few weeks came back to haunt me all at once: the screwdriver was dead, K9 was gone, I'd failed to meet two Doctor's and I'd become gay by proxy. Surely, I reasoned, things couldn't sink any lower from here? As if on cue, the 'happy birthday' balloon broke from its ribbon, drifted towards the lightbulb and unceremoniously burst.

Jeff: Tuesday 18th May

I haven't had my hair cut for a while now. I've been keeping up the pretence that it's laziness, but it's not. It's my birthday. And I'm allowed to treat myself. My hair was finally long enough. It was time!

I marched into the barbers. "Give me the 'Matt Smith' look!" I grinned.

"Who?"

"Oh, sorry..." I rummaged in my bag for the clipping from the Radio Times.

"Oh, you want to look like Doctor Who. Fancy dress party, is it?"

"Yeah?" I lied. The tweed jacket and bow tie were already waiting, spread out on my bed. I was going to look fantastic!

Jeff: Wednesday 19th May

"You look like a paedophile!" Daisy exclaimed in horror. "Or some kind of pervy Catholic school teacher. I thought you were growing it?" She sulked. "Now that you're free from the tyranny of the establishment..." I presumed she meant the pub. "And who wears bow ties?"

"Bow ties are cool." I protested.

"They are not cool. They are a symbol of the higher classes and their oppression of the poor. Anyway, I need you to give me a lift to the bank. I start my shift at 3."

Pete: Friday 19th March

Celebrated Embankment Day by watching Tom Baker's sixth season in its entirety.

What the hell was going on with Davros' voice in 'Destiny of the Daleks'??? I mean: "Ya see??!!! WTF, FFS!

Jeff: Saturday 22nd May

Daisy was right. I am free from the "tyranny of the establishment", which meant we were able to spend the entire day watching 'The Silurians', 'The Sea Devils' and 'Warriors of the Deep' in preparation for 'The Hungry

144

Earth'. Pete's face was priceless when he came out of the bathroom and I surprised him by leaping out wearing my Silurian mask.

But by the time we were ready for the big moment, I unveiled my masterpiece. I'd bought thirty Sainsbury's Basics noodles and filled out big pan with them. I added a frightening amount of curry powder and some dried peas, filled it up with boiling water and created what must have been the largest pot noodle in the world by pouring it all into a small plastic bin. It was *clean* – I'm not some kind of slob!!

It was the only snack worthy of accompanying what was surely the best episode of Doctor Who since 'The Curse of Fenric'! For the first time since 'Rose', I genuinely felt like I was watching an episode of Doctor Who! No worries, no reservations... Just sheer joy!

Jeff: Sunday 23rd May

We have now watched 'The Hungry Earth' eight times. I was on my way to Sainsbury's to stock up on more giant pot noodle ingredients when I noticed I had a text. Shit! I couldn't deal with Daisy now. Only it wasn't her: '*How about that coffee? Rachel x*'.

Jeff: Friday 16ᵗʰ March

I have to admit it – the caves of androzani was quite good. I'll probably watch the last part tonight. When I was in the school library I thought I should give Peter Davidson another chance so I got the Target book of castrovulva out to have a read, even though he looks like an idiot with a stupid grin on the cover.

"He's changing, The Doctor's regenerating" were the first words. It made me think of Tom Baker and I got tears in my eyes, which was dead bad because Rachels brother had just come into the library. When he's around I know that I have to act cool because he might tell her what I've been doing. I didn't want him saying I was a geek because I was reading a rubbish book from the sci-fi section. I tried to hide it under a newspaper but it was too late and he was sat at the table opposite so I tried to look at it like I was laughing at how rubbish it was so I was kind of sneering. I hope he doesn't think I have some kind of muscle disease. Why couldn't I have picked up a good book like the book of star wars by Alan Dean Foster?

Johnny Psychosis came in after a bit and everyone knows hes dead cool so hopefully Chris will tell Rachel that I'm friends with him. He had put studs all over his blazer and it looked brill. I'd like to do that with mine but I don't know how.

Jeff: Monday 19ᵗʰ March

I've joined Johnny's punk band, we're called Sod Collin and we're going to play at the school concert. Mrs Trout says we cant be called Sod Collin because it's offensive, so we said we'll change it to The Collins, but when we play we'll have a flag with the real name on hahaha! She also thinks that we're doing a song called "Crazy Love" but really it's called "Lie Back and Stink of England"! We wrote the lyrics in Geography, it's dead Political. I hope Rachel comes to the concert because Melody Maker is always saying that girls fancy men in bands. Johnny says he will get his mum to put studs on my blazer.

Jeff: Wednesday 21ˢᵗ March

Got called into the headmasters office because of my blazer. Rachel was there too! She was in trouble for having her eyes painted like Suzy Sue. He said we were a disgrace to the school, but that just means we're cool. It was like he was the Brigadier and I was the third Doctor!

Me and Rachel walked home together. I showed her the words to "Lie Back and Stink of England" and she thought it was great. She said if the world heard the song it could bring down the government. I'm not really sure what she meant by that – don't we need a government? Who would sort out the drains and pay dole money and stuff? I suppose The Doctor and Leela got rid of the government in The Sun Makers and that all worked out OK.

We could be the Tom Baker and Leela of punk! I think Rachel would look dead sexy in a cave girl outfit.

Jeff: Thursday 22ⁿᵈ March

I can't get the image of Rachel in Leela's costume out of my head. Who needs Razzle?

Pete: Sunday 30th May

It took us at least 45 minutes to stop crying about Rory after 'Cold Blood'. I'm not quite sure how, but we'd already been through two full boxes of man-sized tissues this weekend. Jeff had to go to newsagents. He said the fresh air would probably do him good, but when he returned sometime later, he looked more emotional than when he'd left. Apparently, he'd broken down in the shop, inadvertently collided with a shelf and 'accidentally' punched a hole through box of coco-pops. Omar had to take him into the back and make him a cup of milky coffee.

Whilst I had the flat to myself, I tried watching the endings of 'Earthshock', 'Doomsday' and 'The End of Time' in order to accurately update my empathy response chart, but the emotional commitment was just too much. Instead, I flicked through the channels hoping to find something to cheer me up. It'd been a while since I'd stepped out of my DVD comfort zone, and I wasn't prepared for the horror of prime-time entertainment. Over the course of 17 channels, I saw teenage girls dressed in revealing snow white outfits, dancing provocatively with effeminate dwarves; people in tanks trying to stick five-pound notes to their slime-covered bodies; a Yorkshire Terrier pulling a cackling man in a skiing armchair round a brightly lit studio to rapturous applause; and Graham Norton attempting to goad David Dickinson and Alan Sugar into eating Maltesers off one another's bodies.

I longed for the days when Patrick Troughton saying "My giddy aunt!" was the most provocative thing on Saturday night TV. Was I born in the wrong decade entirely?

Jeff: Tuesday 1ˢᵗ June

I sat fidgeting in Caffe Nero. I was half an hour early, and
my plan to sit coolly sipping a latte was thwarted. I'd been
so nervous I knocked back the whole thing in 5 minutes.
My tongue still hurt. I couldn't just sit there with an empty
cup... They might *arrest* me or something. I had to go and
buy another drink. But what if she walked in? It would look
so undignified, for her to see me fiddling with change and
balancing sachets of sugar. Also, I'd have to drape my coat
obviously across my chair and a part of the table to make it
clear that it was taken in my absence. If she saw that, she'd
think I was a naturally untidy, reckless sort of person.
(Which I *am*, but I was hoping she might have forgotten.)
Also, if she caught me just leaving the till, it would be rude
of me not to have bought her a drink, so I'd have to queue
again and that would spoil the whole greeting thing... So
should I buy two coffees? But then if she didn't get here
soon, it'd go cold. You can't give cold coffee to someone
you love. It'd be like telling them to fuck off. But, I suppose
if it started to cool and she wasn't there, I could drink it and
then feel less bad about occupying space in a cafe without
actually drinking anything. That could work. But no! Wait! If
anyone saw me sat there alone with *two* coffees it would be
bad enough, but if they saw me drink the *second* one they'd
know I was some kind of lonely freak. But I'm not – I'm on
a date. No, it's not a date. Not a date.

I checked my phone but then abruptly switched it off.
There was another conundrum. I had to check it regularly to
make sure she didn't text to say she was late or not coming,
but I couldn't leave it on in case Daisy called. I'd have to lie,
and I'm no good at lying to Daisy. Like that time I told her I
couldn't go travelling because a potential job had opened up
at Lazarus Industries in Cardiff. (The trip clashed with series
3.) Anyway, it's not like I had anything to hide from Daisy. I
was just meeting a friend for an afternoon coffee. Where
was the harm there? But when you've been in love with this

149

'friend' since the age of 12, it still somehow feels a bit wrong.

Shit – I had to concentrate on looking good. What would The Doctor be doing right now? He'd have probably noticed that the coffee machine was behaving in a way that could only mean severe alterations to the displacement hyper-time vortex. The manager would be calling him a madman and insisting he leave; The Doctor (Tom Baker in this one) would fix him with a stern glare and say "Listen to me. You're all in grave peril. It's of the uppermost importance that you get these people out of here right now." But I couldn't do that. The coffee machine looked to be working just fine.

I thought about it. I hadn't seen Rachel for 11 years. In fact, I think it was here that I last saw her. Before the kids, before the engagement to Captain Bastard. *He* was the king of France. Yeah? Big deal. *I* was the Lord of Time! I snorted inwardly.

I smelt her before I saw her: the same imitation Vivienne Westwood perfume she used to wear at school. She looked the same too. My heart exploded and I was 13 years old again. We talked about the usual rubbish. Work, TV, our families... But the way she looked at me, it was like nothing had changed. Like, despite the fact we were grown ups having coffee, it was just a façade, and underneath we were still two kids sharing an illicit cigarette behind the science block. I don't know, maybe I was imagining it. I didn't really hear most of the words, but being there was just magical. Rain was cascading down the windows and a radio hummed faintly in the background. The rain made me think of 'Blink'. *"I have until the rain stops."*

"Oh, I love this song!" She said, all of a sudden.

"Me too." I nodded and smiled. I'd never heard it before in my life.

"Well, I'd better get back. I need to pick James up." She laid her cup to rest on the table and with those words and

150

that gesture the bubble was broken and it was 2010. "It's been really good to get out of the house. It can all get a bit... You know? I mean, thanks. It's been really lovely to see you. We'll have to meet again soon." We hugged, she walked out into the summer rain and it stopped. I could still smell her.

I sat back, reeling from it all and then did something a bit ridiculous. I threw my coat on, jumped over the table and ran up to the man behind the counter. "Listen to me!" I did my best Tom Baker voice. "It's of the uppermost importance that you tell me what that last song was right now!"

"What?" He looked a little afraid. "Err... Muse, I think." I had to buy it! I tore down the street to WH Smiths and asked the girl behind the counter where the singles chart was. She looked at me like I was insane. How can they not be selling singles anymore? How are songs going to get into the charts?

Jeff: Wednesday 2nd June

The song was called 'Undisclosed Desires'. I had it in my head all night, but awoke to a revelation. I could buy it online as one of those newfangled MP3s!

I went onto Amazon to see it would only cost 79p for one song – what a bargain! However, when I proceeded to the checkout, it said I couldn't download an MP3 without installing an Amazon MP3 installer.

After waiting 20 minutes for the infernal thing to download, I was asked to visit the MP3 store. What about the one I'd already bought? When I clicked, it opened the MP3 store in a different window, using Internet Explorer. I didn't even think I had Internet Explorer. I use Firefox!

Which meant I had to go about signing in all over again. Once more I found the song I wanted. I clicked 'add to basket' only to be confronted by the 'this page cannot be displayed' message. Refresh. Try again. Add to basket. 'This page cannot be displayed'. At this point, I may have screamed the word "fuck" very loudly. I'd been at this for over half an hour. How was this any better than buying a CD from a shop?

I gave up, opened a new window in Firefox, found the track and added it to my basket, only to be told that I couldn't download an MP3 without installing an Amazon MP3 installer. "I already have a fucking installer!" I yelled at the screen.

After a few minutes shaking my fist, I eventually discovered some small print, telling me to click if I already had an installer. I clicked. I paid. An Amazon icon appeared on my desktop. What happened now? Did the song just start playing? Another icon appeared, informing me I had to launch the installer, then the first icon disappeared and I was informed the MP3 was 'being downloaded'.

Five minutes later, Media Player launched of its own accord. I clicked play, and the screen went white. 'Windows Media Player is not responding.' I shut it down and sent an error report to Microsoft that I somehow felt they wouldn't be too eager to reply to. I sat waiting. I clicked the Amazon MP3 icon, but all that did was start installing the installer again. Where had my song gone? I scoured my files: My Music, My Downloads; I even looked in the Recycle Bin, but to no avail. I'd now been sat at my computer for an hour and 11 minutes and had singularly failed to achieve anything. I burst into tears and flung the laptop at the wall. The screen shattered and keys flew across the carpet.

Before I really knew what I was doing, I found myself kneeling in Pete's doorway, wailing "I need a computer doctor! I NEED A COMPUTER DOCTOR!"

Jeff: Thursday 3rd June

It's been over 2 weeks since I signed on. Where's my money? For a start, I need to get a new laptop...

I called the claims processing department, and, after being on hold seemingly forever, I was informed that my claim had been "shut down".

"What? Why?"

"I'm afraid, Mr. Greene, that you were claiming the wrong band of income support." Band? "Our records show that you're caring for a child. You'll need to re-apply for 'single parent living allowance'."

"I'm sorry... What? I don't have a child!"

"Yes you do, Mr. Greene."

"No! No! Really, I don't... I don't even have a wife..."

"You don't need to be married to have children, Mr. Greene."

"That's not what I mean... I'm footloose. You know? Fancy free!"

"Footloose and fancy free, Mr. Greene? May I remind you that you are only eligible for income support if you are actively seeking employment. It's not our responsibility to fund a lifestyle of decadence." A lifestyle of decadence on forty quid a week?

"But you said I can't have income support anyway!"

"Nevertheless, you made a claim. We take fraudulent claims very seriously, Mr. Greene. You could face a fine, or even a custodial sentence."

"Look... I'm not committing fraud, and I don't want to go to prison! I just want the benefits that your leaflet said I was entitled to!"

"I've already told you, Mr. Greene. You are not entitled to income support whilst caring for a child."

"But I'm not!"

"According to our records, under living arrangements, you stated you were living as a single parent at your recent meeting."

"No! I didn't say that at all! I said my flatmate had the mind of a child! It was a joke!"

"The benefits office is no place for tomfoolery, Mr. Greene. May I remind you that you signed the form to certify that all the information given was correct."

"I thought it was!"

"Very well, but we won't turn a blind eye the next time you decide to abuse our system."

"So, does this mean I can have my money?"

"No. I told you, Mr. Greene, your claim has been closed. You will need to open a new claim."

"But how long will it take to get my money?"

"The claim will take 14 working days to process. You can fill out the online re-application form..."

"I don't have a computer at the moment. Could you post it to me?"

"No."

"Why not?"

"Print is dead, Mr. Greene. If you insist on filling out a form, you must obtain one from your local office."

"So I can go to Blackpool and-"

"No, Mr Greene!" I wasn't entirely sure, but it was almost as if I could hear him banging a fist on his desk. "Our Blackpool outpost is merely a sorting office. You must visit a designated processing department. You're nearest department is Preston. Good day, Mr. Greene!"

I drove to Preston Job Centre and filled out a form with information they already had, and then noticed it came with an envelope labelled 'Processing Department, Preston'. What was the point in that? I was already there. I could just give it to them. I made my way over to the information desk.

"Ahh, no. I'm afraid we can't accept this. It has to come through the post." A suited man frowned.

"But... Why? I mean, it's here. Now. What's the difference?"

"Yeeaahhh. It's just that all standard issue claims have to be received internally. I mean, I'm just here to give information. I don't actually know who to give this to." He pulled a face and shrugged.

"So, you're saying I have to go across the road and post this... So you can get it tomorrow?"

"No, no, no. As I say, it has to be received *internally*. Hand that in at your claims office and they'll forward it to us."

"What? In Blackpool? But I've just come from there!"

I was beginning to despair when an idea struck me. I picked up a leaflet from a stand: 'Invalid Carer Allowance'.

Pete: Thursday 3rd June

A Mr. Harrison, of South Shore, Blackpool, was on a radio show about disability today. He said he'd had agoraphobia and, at one point in his 30s, couldn't leave the house for *years*! The voice sounded oddly familiar, so I ran downstairs as soon as the interview had finished and knocked at the ground floor flat. It was as I suspected. No one replied, and I couldn't hear anything coming from within. So if this *was* the same Mr. Harrison I'd met a few weeks ago, it proved it – he couldn't be me from the future, because I DEFINITELY didn't have agoraphobia!!

Pete: Friday 4th June

Jeff thinks I have agoraphobia. It all started when I tried to fix 'sexybexy's laptop. I don't know quite what happened, but it wasn't fifteen minutes before the whole thing was in bits on the floor, each component artfully laid out. I found myself asking 'How did I do this? Did I black out or something? If I can dismantle computers, maybe I *can* repair them!' My new burst of confidence was short-lived. When I tried to work out what the actual fault was and attempted to put it back together, I soon realised that any old sod can take things to bits when they're bored. Conversely, it turns out that wiring circuits to the motherboard, rewriting core programming, hooking up a monitor display, removing software viruses, and getting the 'S' key to actually mean 'S' (rather than 'F') does seem to require some level of skill.

When Jeff walked in, things were looking bleak.

"I think I've thrown a spanner in the works!" I whimpered.

"I can see that." He looked at the memory card slot, into which I'd jammed a spanner. "How long have you been at this?" I couldn't rightly say. I'd lost all perspective of time, but I pointed him in the direction of an absurdly large heap of teabags, spilling off the edge of the table. "Shit." He shook his head mournfully.

"I thought I was on a roll. I got *all* that marmalade out of the USB socket."

"Did you manage to get rid of the lisp?" He cocked an eyebrow.

"Well, I... H-how did you..?"

"The 'S' key doesn't work, right?" I didn't reply. Had Jeff been psychic all along?! Listening into my thoughts? It was too terrifying to contemplate! Whilst on the outside, I appeared personable, normal and well-adjusted, my inner monologue revealed an, otherwise absolutely *invisible*, mundane and petty streak. "When you press 'S', you get 'F', so if you were to go onto a forum and type... 'I'm stumped by recent developments in the sci-fi genre', you'd actually be saying 'I'm ftumped by recent developmentf in the fci-

156

si genre'... which doesn't really make sense, unless you're a total moron!"

"Jeff?" I shuffled back cautiously, my voice wavering. "Do you have special powers?"

He was laughing. "Well, that's *got to be* it, hasn't it? Unless, hmmmmm, let me think..." He stroked his chin. "The only other way I could possibly know is if... I used to own this compu- but, no. That defies sense!"

"Yeah, I'm not totally stupid!" (I wasn't even convincing myself). "Just cause you used to own a laptop *exactly* like this, you can't fool *me*!" Even as I went for the old self-confident head tap, I could feel myself faltering. "I happen to know for *sure* this isn't the same one?" Why did that come out as a question? "This one belongs to..."

"Sexybexy."

"That's absolutely... Wait! No... Because!" I jabbed my finger into the air, and clapped a hand to my forehead. If only I'd been David Tennant, my moment of mental revelation would have been accompanied by a liberal amount of hair ruffling, and some snappy editing. But I wasn't. I was just some guy, you know? Some guy who felt as though his brain was trying to leap in two different directions. I reached for the nearest beanie to prevent it doing so. Thank god I'd spent last night alphabetically categorising my collection of mediocre hats. Didn't want another Morbius on our hands!

"It was me, Pete. I'm Sexybexy."

"Noooo..." My self-confidence shifted down an octave. "You're Jeff. Look, I can prove it." I snatched a notepad, on which he'd doodled the words 'Jeffmeister' repeatedly: was this some kind of nervous habit, or was he planning his own TV show? "So, if anything, it'd be SeffyJeffy, and that doesn't even work. It sounds like a brand of lavatory cleaner. So..." I tried to think of a suitably witty and urbane put-down. "Fuck off!" He just sat there, examining his nails. "Alright... So, why did you do it? Was it some kind of joke?"

"Of course not. I was trying to be nice to you."

"*Nice* to me!? Couldn't you have bought me chocolate or flowers or something *normal*?"

I counted as he tried to start at least eight different sentences before any actual words came out. He chewed his lip, ruffled his hair, dug fingernails into his arm. I was about to get up and put the kettle on, when he said "Pete, this isn't the first time I've said this, and it won't be the last: I love you. BUT – and this is a big but..." (He'd already insulted my arse: things could only get worse.) "You're a *hopeless* computer repair man, you've got some serious stuff to work through, and I can't be your Dad forever." A formless, numb, 'O'-shaped sound escaped my lips, as he finished. "But I *could* be your carer..."

"Are you trying to suggest..." I croaked. "...That I've gone a bit mad or something?"

"I don't mean to be, well, mean... But look at you, Pete: you can barely leave the house these days, you're surrounded by toys and bits of circuit board. It's 6pm and you're half naked in a bobble-hat!"

"It's not a bobble-hat." I protested. "It's a beanie. And I'm not mad... And some of these toys are *yours*!"

"Mine aren't toys. They're authentic collectors' memorabilia." He sounded unusually tetchy. Surely he wasn't growing up. If he did, I was screwed! "The difference is that *I* don't line them all up and have pretend battles, setting fire to tiny cardboard castles with little matchboxes. And I didn't say you were mad. But I do think you've got agoraphobia. There's nothing wrong with it. It's not all that bad really. The computer thing was to prove a point: I don't think you stand much chance of working if you can't leave the house, and I'm not gonna be able to pay for this place on my own anymore, so I think you need to try and

158

sign up for Disability allowance. The government have money for people like you."

"People like *me*??!" I leapt to my feet, strode into the kitchen furiously and slammed the door. My initial plan was to go on hunger strike. Unfortunately, however, the fridge was empty, and the emergency cake I'd left beneath the sink had gone damp, so I'd have had no staying power. I spent the evening building a 3D Death Star jigsaw, ignoring Jeff, and trying to unremember what he'd said. I'd prove I wasn't mad for sure! I laughed long into the night.

Pete: Saturday 5th June

"Hahahahahaha!" I cackled, not remotely maniacally. Breath probably didn't expect such a jeffless greeting the moment he emerged from his bedroom, so I grabbed him by the dressing gown sleeves in case he tried to escape to the bathroom.

"I couldn't sleep after last night." I shouted. He looked guilty. "Andiwasdoingsomethinking." It all came out as one word; a formless mass of syllables; a creature from the pit.

"Are you alright? You eyes look kind of bloodshot."

"I'm fine... Just... Fine. Been drinking a lot of coffee, but I'm definitely... Just... Fine. Just... Look, I don't know quite how to say this." I took a deep breath. "I've been doing *a lot* of thinking about some pretty serious stuff, and I'm not gonna pretend I'm not worried." I took six more deep breaths. I was going to have to spell this one out slowly. "One day... Stephen Moffat..." Jeff nodded. "Is going to leave... Doctor Who." I waited for the shock to resonate, but he seemed more concerned with trying to shrug his arms free. It was as I thought. I knew I wasn't just being paranoid. He was going to lock himself in the

159

bathroom and initiate a siege. If that happened, I wouldn't get to tell him my plan, and, to make matters worse, I'd have to piss into the 'Meals for Mums' Tupperware. I shifted my weight to block the door. "If you think about it logically..." I realised I was ranting a bit and tried to appear calm by winking, which, in retrospect, probably didn't help. "...Mark Gatiss isn't going to end up running the show. So – and I mean this seriously – and I'm not trying to sound egotistical – and you'll need to stick with me on this – but the *only* people I can imagine taking over as head writers are... Me and you."

"Bu-"

I cut across him before he had time to say anything. It's a well known fact that people *always* come round to your way of thinking if you talk continuously for a long period of time. "Thinkaboutit: how many men in their 30s can there be that know as much about the Whoniverse as us?? Who've seen every surviving episode, and own the Target novelisations of all the missing ones? Who've religiously purchased 'Doctor Who Magazine' every month since 1979? Even during the dark 1990s when there was *literally* NOTHING to write about? Who actually listen to 'The Pescatons' despite its dubious canonicity? Who have a cupboard full of Dalek mugs, and disappointingly inedible spaghetti shapes? *AND*, we've got all these..." I rifled through a Kwik Save carrier bag, labelled 'Script Ideas: 88 – Present', with obvious enthusiasm. Some of them were written on the backs of cereal packets, such was the furore of our late night creativity. "You can't argue with titles like... Countdown to F.E.A.R., Mutopia, The Kraagan Masterplan, Timeray!, Doctor Who and The Scary Door, All Aboard the Horror Express, The Nightmare Machine... They're all potential classics, Jeff! And I've been working on what could be our *pièce de résistance*: let me introduce you to... The

160

Armageddon Factor! Twelve episodes full of horror, adventure, and masterful plot twists. I tell you, there's no way the BBC are gonna turn this baby down. So, what do you think?" I picked up a toy spear. "Isn't it time we called Broadcasting House?"

"Well, I don't know quite how to tell you this, but... Most of those ideas are... Terrible... And there's already been an episode called 'The Armageddon Factor'... And it was shit! And..."

I grabbed his shoulder with one hand, and pressed a finger to my lips with the other. "Is that crack in the wall making noises again?" I felt my eye go into an involuntary spasm.

"Pete, have you taken your pills?"

Pete: Monday 7th June

We hadn't spoken about it for days, but sooner or later I knew the agoraphobia monster was going to rear its ugly head, and it would be much scarier than the one in 'Vincent and the Doctor'. I couldn't help empathising with Van Gogh, but much as I tried to argue my case to 'Comedy Dan' on 'Forum from the Deep', I knew I was no genius. Vincent's bedroom was full of brilliant paintings. Mine was a mess of mouldy mug-o-soup, creased magazines, 'vintage' cider bottles and 'Kwik and E-Z Noodle' wrappers. You wouldn't even have to see the price to know that it was cheap. All the packaging was orange and white, and the labels were spelled out in text-speak, as though to sound cool and modern. I picked up a half-crushed bottle and read the imitation-handwriting slogan: 'Tastes like shit, but getz u pissed'. It was so old and faded I couldn't tell whether the drawing of a downcast-looking homeless chap cradling a possibly deceased dog was part of the design or something Dom had scribbled on.

How had I let myself get like this? When had it all started? It wasn't as though I'd intentionally stopped getting dressed and leaving the house. I just hadn't fancied it for a while... surely? Deep down, I suppose I knew the answer. Under my bed was a stack of old diaries. All I had to do was find the one with the David Tennant stickers all over it... Except that they all did. If I'd found one of them in the street, and didn't know they were mine, I probably would have guessed them to belong to an eight-year-old. I rifled through until I found the one from...

Tuesday 13th February 2007

"Yes! Yes! Yes!" I sprung up from my bed at the sound of a vigorous banging coming from the living room. I was still a bit dazed – it was, after all, not quite lunchtime – so the thought that Jeff might be sweating and naked barely crossed my mind.

"Back of the net! Spawn has left the mothership!" Jeff said, somewhat confusingly.

"What's with all the commotion?" I asked cautiously.

"Come and have a drink with your uncle Roger!" I didn't know what the hell he was talking about. A whole range of terrifying thoughts ran through my head. Was he on drugs? Was I going to have to restrain him, steward a rave or prevent an orgy? He indicated a spot on the sofa, shuffling up and flinging a bundle of yellowed tissues to the floor. I was careful to put a cushion over the chair before sitting down. "You may need to sit down." He wore a serious expression now.

"I, erm... I'm already sitting down." There was definitely something weird about him – he was pointing at the screen with a trembling hand.

"I've just... Made the winning bid..." He was breathless with excitement, and I suddenly saw why.

*"...On a Tenth Doctor... FLOOR LENGTH COAT!" I
was speechless. This was massive. Perhaps he'd let me
wear it. I almost wished I wasn't going to France so I
could see it arrive. That said, if it came right away,
maybe Jeff'd be okay about me taking it, and people
would think that I – Pete Ross – was The Doctor. I –
Pete Ross – WAS The Doctor...*

"So you're going for it then?"

*"Yep. Gonna stop at The Crescent for a bit of Dutch
courage first, but then I'm going to march right in
there..."*

*Jeff raised a hand. "I wouldn't 'march' if I were you.
I don't think they're allowed to sell to mad people, and
you already look a bit... you know... since you permed
your hair."*

*"You know why I did that!" I snapped testily. "If I'm
gonna go to Paris, then I'm gonna give it the full Tom
Baker treatment. I've got the scarf, I've got the pretty
girl. I needed the Fourth Doctor's curls to complete the
look."*

*"Yeah? Well you look more like Leo Sayer. Ooh, by
the way, will you be around later? Daisy's coming
round and we're gonna watch 'Spearhead'. I showed
her a clip on the website, and she said the Autons
bursting through the shop window was 'grisly'. Isn't
she great?" He didn't give me time to answer, which
was good because I didn't have time to tell him that
Daisy had condescendingly referred to it as 'Spearmint
from Space'. "So, you know what you're going to say in
the shop then?"*

*"I think so. I mean, it's not really that different to
buying cling-film or balloons, is it?" I tried – and failed
– to shrug nonchalantly.*

*"Just remember: everyone does it, everyone uses
them. Be forthright. Be strong. Brave heart, Pete!"*

I strode confidently to the counter, looked the cashier square in the eye, held out a fifty pence piece and – in my most authoritative, blokey voice – said "I'd like to purchase a condom please". Except that the sound which came out wasn't authoritative or blokey at all. More... pathetic and already in default defensive mode, as though I were battling away a fresh wave of high school 'Spotty Pete' insults all over again. Here I was, 35 years old, and I was back in the schoolyard. Except that my tormentor had a name badge, a degree and the sort of rehearsed smile you only got on a training course.

At length, I realised that the man behind the counter had been talking and gesticulating wildly for some time. Shit! I hadn't taken in a single word. I tried to smile apologetically, but came out looking like one of those mad people who talk to bus drivers. When I repeated my request to shut him up, it came out sounding rude.

"And what kind would you like, sir?" I couldn't tell if it was out of spite, or a sincere desire to be kind and helpful, but he spoke in the same patronising voice that Daisy used to talk to Bucky (the intolerable midget) when he wasn't wearing his 'Miracle Grow Extend-O-Stilts'.

"Well, er, I don't know. It's not like I've measured anything down there for a while, if that's what you mean? Just the usual, I guess..." Saying that made me think of country pubs, handled glasses and listening to 'Heavy Horses' on the jukebox, so I added "And a pint of bitter please!" But it didn't seem to illicit a laugh. What was wrong with him? Dom would've been in stitches.

"What do you usually get?"

"I usually just come in here for deodorant, anti-odour foot spray and sensitive skin face cream." He

164

narrowed his eyes. *What else did he want from me?* "I've got a sensitive face."

"No, I mean, sir..." He elongated the 'ir'. "What about the condoms?"

"But I don't think you're supposed to put them on your face." My scalp was getting sore from all the head scratching.

"Oh, for god's sake!" I was getting the slightest impression I'd irritated him, though I couldn't for the life of me work out why. "Which one of us here is a qualified *chemist?*" I shot him a puzzled look, unsure of how to respond. *Was he having some kind of personal crisis, or merely being rhetorical?*

"It's you, isn't it... Surely?" He folded his arms, and my unique understanding of people told me it was time to move things on. I ended up asking for one of everything and took out my credit card.

He returned to the counter with a very full carrier bag, and said "Stick it in whenever you like", folding his arms expectantly.

Oh my god! Was he making a move? It had certainly sounded forward. *He didn't actually think I wanted to..? No!* "I'm sorry." I stuttered. "You're not my type."

"I'm talking about the credit card, you wanker!" He slammed his fist onto the table.

I knew that going round to Simone's with the entire 'Big Mates' Contraception' range in a carrier bag would look a little unsubtle, so I concealed it in her bush before attempting to gain entry. Her housemates, Joanne and Kitty, answered the door, giggling as soon as they set eyes on me. They always did that, like I was the butt of some kind of in-joke.

"Is Simone about?"

"Upstairs." Joanne OR Kitty inclined her head – I've never been able to tell them apart: they both dress in that ironic studenty way, have curly hair and often finish each other's sentences. "She's with Rik."

"Goth Rik?" I could barely contain my outrage. "What's she doing with that loser?"

"She's, er..." They smirked as one. "...Helping reboot his hard-drive."

"Oh. She's been stealing all my business since I paid for her to go on that computer course. Rik should've come round my gaff. I would've given his hard-drive a good reconfiguring too." This provoked a whole new wave of giggling, as though I'd said something hilarious. "Well, can I come in?"

They led me through to the living room, where the usual array of half-drunk alcopops littered the table, cigarette ash floating in the dregs of pink, sugary liquid. There was a vigorous and persistent banging coming from the ceiling above.

"Is that Simone?" I asked awkwardly. "Or do you need to get a man in to take a look at your pipes?" More giggling.

"Must be." One of them replied. "Charlene's over at Greg's." Charlene? Greg? Who were these people??!

"She must be giving his system a really good going over." Smirked the other girl. I had to get away from these two harpies. Think, Pete, think! What would James Bond do?

"Mind if I pay a visit to the little boys room? I'm bursting for the loo!"

"Yes, but... Oh... My... God! Kitty, will you take a look at Simone's washing up?!" She clapped a hand to her lips in exaggerated shock. Kitty responded in kind, her mouth dropping open, like the scary bit in 'Fury from the Deep'.

"Oh, Jo'sers! She treats us like slaves!" She whimpered. "And it's not even our responsibility!" Theatrically, they both folded their arms and faced me as one. I knew that they were trying to manipulate me, *but that wasn't enough to stop the waves of crippling guilt. This was probably what being married was like... Well, to a woman, at least. Now there were two of them, and the Helvetica Scenario was upon me. I was going to have to do someone else's washing up. They'd probably have me cleaning the toilet with a toothbrush and ironing their knickers next, while they peered over my shoulder, eyeing every crease critically and screaming if I got something wrong. I was their eunuch, their manservant... And I was powerless to stop them.*

It was a good forty-five minutes before I emerged from the kitchen, having finished a mass of washing up, covered in soap suds and pasta sauce. I recognised very little of the mess as Simone's, and many of the plates were mysteriously marked with Js and Ks. The living room was free of its former annoyances: Joanne and Kitty seemed to have vanished elsewhere, and the rhythmic banging from upstairs had ceased. Sure enough, however, Goth Rik was slumped on the sofa, stroking his goatee beard and leaning heavily upon a cane. A trilby hat was pulled over his dirty-blond hair, and his whole posture exuded the air of practised despondence. Even his roll-up hung wearily from his lips. I think he thought it made him look cool. It made him look like a cunt.

"Rik." I acknowledged him with a nod.

"Steve." He nodded back dejectedly.

"It's, er, Pete... actually." He didn't respond. Only an icy silence followed, punctuated occasionally by the sound of muffled swearing from above. "So, erm, what're you doing here?"

"I was passing..." He took a deep breath. Every syllable was laboured, like the energy was constantly being sapped away from him. I'm sure he imagined

that this sounded distant and enigmatic. "...On my way back from Skeletor's house."

"Skeletor?!"

"His real name's Tony." He croaked, and no further conversation was forthcoming. As soon as I left the room, I felt the tension lift from the atmosphere. Before I went, I shouted upstairs to Simone, eager to catch a glimpse of her so that it didn't feel like a completely wasted trip. After much clattering, and an exchange of words so strong they probably should have come with a 'parental advisory' warning, she called back "What do you want?"

"Just wanted to check we're still okay for tomorrow? 8.30? Squire's Gate?"

"Yeah, yeah. I'm packing now. Christ!" She sounded unnecessarily pissed off for someone who was about to be taken on an all-expenses-paid romantic break.

"Do you want me to take one of your bags while I'm here? Save you carrying it?"

"Nah, there's stuff in here I don't want you to see..." She wavered hesitantly. "...Yet. Girl's stuff." I could barely contain my excitement. Tomorrow night was the night! I could feel it! Although when she said, somewhat bluntly, "Now go, will you?" my spirits were dampened.

I shouted "Farewell, my Rose!" but didn't get a response, although I swore I could just about make out the sound of an eerie giggling drifting ghostlike down the stairs.

As I was on my way out, I lingered over a picture by the front door. It showed Rik, Simone and the girls halfway down a roller-coaster drop. Everyone had their hands in the air, mouth's wide open, apart from Rik, who looked as bored as always, still smoking a cigarette and still leaning on a cane. Simone, pressed next to him, looked happier than I'd ever seen her. I had to wonder where I was. I searched desperately on the pinboard for even the smallest photo, but I didn't feature at all. I tried to convince myself that it hadn't been updated recently, but couldn't ignore the niggling fact that last week's date was printed in the bottom right corner of the most recent one – a shot of Simone, drunkenly leaning into the camera, a fake bridal veil on her head, and 'Just Married' scrawled across her cleavage in marker pen.

I stopped for a few drinks with Big Dougie on the way home, who wanted to read me his latest poetic ode to the male genitalia, so Jeff was already in bed by the time I got back to the flat. But he'd left a CD on my bed, with the note: 'Something for you to listen to on the train back' (I bet it's full of romantic songs!) 'And just remember, whatever happens, I love you.' The big poof! He must have been pissed.

The following pages were all scribbled over in black. The trip itself was written up in another diary. I had a feeling I knew where it was, but I couldn't bring myself to deal with it just then. Instead, I went through to the kitchen with the intention of making an Irish coffee. But I ended up filling my cup with whiskey to the top, and lay on the sofa, shovelling teaspoons of coffee granules directly into my mouth. Then I got a bit overexcited, wrote an incredibly moving short story about talking potato and forwarded it to all my email contacts.

Jeff: Saturday 12th June

It started just like any ordinary day. I'd been lying on the sofa, eating Frosties and idly comprising a list of what

169

Christmas present each Doctor would be likely to get you. I think it's remarkably astute...

William Hartnell – An expired book token.
Patrick Troughton – A recorder.
Jon Pertwee – A molecular hydrolic polarity reverser.
Tom Baker – A bag of Jelly Babies.
Peter Davison – An illustrated children's bible.
Colin Baker – A cake made of play dough and an ABBA CD
Sylvester McCoy – Would have forgotten, but wowed you at the last minute with a remarkable performance on spoons.
Paul McGann – One Jelly Baby. However, he would magically and theatrically produce it from behind your ear.
Christopher Eccleston – A lump of coal and a clout round the ear.
David Tennant – A winning lottery ticket (smug bastard).
Matt Smith – A bow tie (bow ties are cool) and a bowl of custard.

Finishing my list, I realised it was past midday, so it was no officially socially acceptable to get pissed. I went to Bargain Booze and got a four-pack of Tuborg lager and some Quavers, which I then consumed whilst watching 'Stones of Blood'. It was only as I was folding away the cardboard and stuffing it in the bin (Thank god Daisy wasn't there – we were using her cardboard recycling bin as a footrest) that I noticed the enthusiastic font on the inside proclaiming 'Congratulations! You have won 2 tickets to the Glastonbury festival!'

Pete: Sunday 13th June

I'm not ashamed to say that we cried fat tears of sheer happiness watching Matt Smith play football in 'The Lodger', and laughed like schoolboys during The Doctor's hilariously ill-timed 'Annihilate' speech.

As soon as 'Confidential' finished, I fired off an email to Omar, advertising for a lodger. It's not as though either of us actually wants one. It's not as though we'd even have room if someone showed up. But you never know: we might end up with Matt Smith! He'd *willingly* watch Doctor Who with us; we could do amusing 80s montages; and we wouldn't even have to tie him up in the shower, like that bloke in Preston claimed to have done with Christopher Eccleston.

I couldn't wait to see the look on Jeff's face when he found out!

Jeff: Monday 14th June

I can't go to Glastonbury! I'm too old for all that now. I know my 18 year old self would be appalled, but I've grown quite fond of showering regularly, watching daytime TV and wearing shirts. When you're younger, you think you'll never change, and that if you do it will be some kind of massive compromise, but the thing you never anticipate is that you actually begin to genuinely enjoy some of the things you once shunned. Like slippers, pyjamas and 'Trisha'. I suppose this is why The Doctors never get on in multi-Doctor stories. I bet the First Doctor never imagined he'd end up saying "Sor' of, yeah" or dancing to Soft Cell, just like the Sixth Doctor probably wouldn't have thought he'd one day wear all black. And I bet the Eleventh Doctor is really embarrassed by the fact he used to wear that cat badge...

And that dreadful question mark tank top! I think I'll watch 'The Happiness Patrol'...

Jeff: Tuesday 15th June

Daisy was on the phone, lecturing me about how we never do anything nice together, I never have time for her and I never leave the flat. I couldn't help it. The words just tumbled out of my mouth...

"How can you say that? I'm so hurt! Here I've been, planning an amazing surprise for you and everything..."

"A surprise? Really? What?"

"Daisy, I'm taking you to Glastonbury! So we can get back to our roots! Commune with the... Meridians... And all that."

"Glastonbury? Jesus, Jeff! Why don't you just take me out for a romantic lunch at Burger King? This isn't 1994 anymore. The whole thing's just a big, corporate firework display of capitalism and convention! I mean, who's playing? U2?"

"Yes, actually. And, erm, Snoop Dog?" She was silent.

"Besides, I can't get the time off work."

Thank god. This is probably fate intervening. I can't be away on the 26th. It's the season finale! I had to hang up because there was someone at the door. I was a little unsettled to see a seven foot transvestite in a catsuit wearing UV make up who said he/she had "Come to move in."

Pete: Wednesday 16th June

Jeff stormed angrily upstairs, looking aggravated, and pulled the TV cable from the wall.

"Oi! I was watching 'Richard and Judy', you bastard!" I spoke between mouthfuls of mashed potato.

"What the hell do you think you're playing at?" He demanded. "Advertising for a lodger? Did you think Matt Smith – Matt *Fucking* Smith – was going to show up or something?"

"No..." I mumbled guiltily.

"I've had to turn away a nun with a prosthetic hand, someone dressed as a giant cockroach and a guy with a bag full of hacksaws!" He replaced the plug.

"Ooh, hacksaw man's still doing the rounds, is he?"

"That's beside the point, Pete. You've got to..." But he was distracted by the TV. "Ooh, wrestling!"

Jeff: Friday 18th June

I received a letter from the council about my housing benefit claim. Apparently there was a 'problem' and I had to contact them straight away.

"Ahh, yes." Said the claims advisor, a rotund balding man, as I sat in his office at the town hall that afternoon. "We've been asked to investigate your claim, as we have reason to believe you may be having a relationship with your house mate."

"WHAT?!"

"As you know, different rates apply for live-in couples, married or not, Mr. Greene."

"But, I... I mean, well, he's... For a start, he's a man!"

"Don't think we don't know what goes on, Mr Greene! Our records show that you've lived together for the best part of a decade. Why is this?"

"Well, we just... Do. He"s my friend." The adviser gave a mirthless laugh.

"You recently ended employment as a barman, but I see your partner, Mr. Ross, was unemployed during this time." He peered at me over the silver rims of his spectacles with keen eyes.

"Yeah..."

"I see. So tell me a little about your living arrangements. Rooms?"

"A kitchen-"

"Shared?"

"Yes." He made a note of this. "A living room-"

"Shared?"

"Yes... A bathroom-"

"Just the one?"

"Yes."

"Shared?"

"Yes..." He raised an eyebrow.

"Most irregular. Do continue. Bedrooms?"

"Two."

"Shared?" How can *two* people share *two* bedrooms?

"Yes, we share them... One each!"

"According to the plans of the building, one is a double and the other is a mere box room!" His voice raised an octave in triumph.

"Yeah, but we keep most of the toys- I mean, the stuff – in the living room. And obviously when Daisy stays over, I need the extra room, so-"

"Ah! So you have a tenant. You should have declared this, Mr. Greene. Falsifying a claim can result in a fine or custodial sentence!"

"She's not a tenant. She's my girlfriend!" He considered me dubiously.

"Do you and your flatmate shop individually?"

"Yes. Well... No."

"And does Mr. Ross ever prepare your meals, Mr Greene?"

"Yes, but-"

"And the cleaning, the household chores. Who deals with those?"

"Well, Pete. I mean, I'd like to, but the man's a clean freak!"

"Do you ever socialise together?"

"Well, yes..."

174

"Do you go out?"

"No. He's agoraphobic."

"I see. Cosy evenings in, eh? I think we have all the information we need, Mr. Greene. We'll be in touch."

Pete: Friday 18th June

I found it buried at the bottom of a box, which was otherwise full of vintage comics: *the book of doom.* Considering all the heartbreak I'd come to associate it with, it looked inappropriately cheery, with its embossed Eiffel Tower silhouette and picture of a poncy-looking French couple riding a bicycle on the front. A cruel irony or just one more thing to hate the French for? Inside, all but a few pages had been torn out. Although I knew exactly what was written on the remaining ones – the diary of my last trip outside – I couldn't face reading it at that moment. Going back there would be like admitting defeat.

I was relieved when there was a knock at the door. I answered it to Andy Pond, and instantly began crying, except this time I wasn't putting it on. When he came in, we barely said a word: we just sat next to one another, drinking cup after cup of tea, both of us in tears. I had to wonder what *his* excuse was.

Before he left, he said "I hope you don't mind, but I've told my therapist all about you. He thinks this is really good for me. Same time next week?"

Pete: Wednesday 14th February 2007

My heart skipped a beat every time I heard somebody walking over the bridge, and I couldn't help but check my watch at least every thirty seconds: the minute hand never seemed to move. It had settled comfortably

175

somewhere in the region of Rose Tyler's pink hoodie, nestled into her breast; who could blame it? It was 8.42am, and Simone was a good 10 minutes late. Scrap that. A good 10 minutes was probably a bad choice of phrase. There had been nothing good about them. As if the morning hadn't been stressful enough having to get up at 4am; packing, packing and repacking – just to make triply sure; constantly scanning the tickets, scrutinising the dates and travel times, convinced they could shift at any moment so that we'd miss our Euro-tunnel connection; unpacking to organise the contents of my holdall more efficiently; changing footwear at least seven times. I'd rung my hands so many times they'd come up in a rash, and now, here I was... alone.

Short of calling the whole thing off, I tried one last desperate attempt to call her, but just as the phone picked up a dialling tone, I heard footsteps edging slowly down the stairs. I hung up and spun round, full of hope and relief, only to be confronted by twin horrors: an angry looking chav lolloping towards me, and the train pulling into the station. This was it. Make or break time! Obviously, there was no question of me getting on the train. Simone must have been in some kind of trouble and it was up to me to rescue her, whisk her away to Paris and give her the night of her life. I'd be her David Tennant, her knight in shining armour, her prince charming, her – the train pulled in and I saw my reflection in the window – her... twat in a trilby hat.

"Oi, mate!" The chav snorted. "This the Kirkham train?" I nodded, and tried to make my exit, but he carried on talking at me. "Ah, thank god. Me bird's gonna be well pissed. I said I were only goin' out for an hour, or... A couple'r hour, or summit." He made a noise like a tumble drier and heaved a glob of mucus onto the platform. "Thing is, I was out with Steve-O, an' Gary and Brian last night, and let me tell yer about

176

Brian, right? Brian... is a twat. And he, like, ended up getting' into this fight wi' this bouncer. It weren't 'is fault like. 'E 'ad it in for him from the start. Know what I'm saying?" I didn't know what he was saying. I hadn't the slightest idea. "Anyway, 'e only went an' landed himself in the Vic..." Hang on! What had happened? Somehow, I was on the train and it was moving. How had I not noticed getting on? Climbing up the steps? Taking a seat? I looked at my ticket and saw that it had already been stamped, but I had no memory of a conductor coming round. Had this moron's conversation really been so scintillating that I'd channelled everything else out??!

"I'm terribly sorry, erm, mate..." I started to say, but he cut in again.

"Hey." He looked me up and down, a threatening glint in his eye. Thank god I'd packed the punishment spray. "I like yer t-shirt."

"Really?" I looked down. But I was wearing my 'Keep Watching the Skies' shirt. No one liked this shirt! Not even I liked it!

"Are you like..." He rubbed at his nose and made an unpleasant face. "One o' them sci-fi geeks or summit?" Once again, I didn't have to say anything, because he saw my scarf. "Eh, lookarthat! Ah, let me tek a picture to show me mates. You could play the next doctor who!" Oh no... He'd done it. He'd made the ultimate mistake. It didn't matter that it would almost certainly end up with me getting kicked to death. I was going to have to correct him. But, just then, there was a timely intervention. "Ah, don' worry about it, mate. This is my stop." What?! We were in Kirkham already? Bloody hell. I was almost halfway to Paris, and I'd yet to do anything about the Simone situation. My overly-friendly antagonist left and I was relieved when no one else took his seat. I could make a phone call. One *phone call to save the world. Except that I didn't have a signal. Bollocks!*

I'd tried to relax on the London train, but my heart filled with disappointment each time I looked at my phone screen – which was frequently – and saw it blank – which was all the time. Not even a message from Jeff. He must have been on his 6am shift at work... the lazy sod!

I went and sat in 'Subway' when I got to Euston, not knowing what to do. After fifteen minutes, a waiter in a silly hat came over and told me that people usually tended to buy food in order to reserve a spot in the cafe, so I chose a sandwich at random and cried inwardly when I realised I'd picked the most expensive thing on the kids' menu. Then the phone started blinking, and, for a moment, I thought everything was going to be okay, but it was just a message from Dom. It read 'I AM Destruktor-on!' He must have been having another ego attack. What a tool! No sooner had I put it down, however, than it started ringing. I snatched it up immediately, nearly flinging it into my Monster Truck Cola in the panic.

"Simone..." One huge sigh of relief. "Where are you? I was beginning to think you weren't coming?"

"Oh my god! I can't believe you'd think that! You're so nasty to me sometimes. Anyway, that thirty quid you left me for a taxi went missing..." I heard her take a long drag on a cigarette, and suddenly got the feeling I knew exactly what had happened to the money... But I couldn't bring myself to voice the suspicion. Jeff said it was like she had this weird hold over me, but that was just rubbish. "Anyway, I definitely am coming to Paris, but I'll just need you to transfer me a little bit more money." It wasn't a question. It was an instruction.

178

From here on in, what I actually thought and what came out of my mouth were polar opposites.

"Of course." *No way, you penny pinching bitch.* "How much would you like?" *Bleed me dry, why don't you?*

"Erm, not too much. Perhaps just like sixty? Seventy pounds? Just enough to get me to London. I mean, it's not like it's as far as... Sheffield, is it?" She laughed in an oddly humourless way, and I reciprocated in kind.

"Well, that is quite a lot of money..." *And I'd already booked our tickets, you stupid cow, so now I'm going to have to pay twice.* "But, this is your big week, so I guess I can get over to the nearest bank, and I'll wait for you here?"

"Oh, I wouldn't want you standing around. You get going, and I'll meet you there. Just, you know, send me the money, will you?"

"You're going to meet me? In Paris?" *So, it's come to this. You obviously can't bear the thought of spending any time with me. We're fucked.* "But you've never even left Lancashire?"

"Well, I've been reading this really good magazine recently, and it said that expanding your mental horizons is a lot like expanding your physical horizons."

"Oh, erm, that's profound." *But the only physical horizon you've been expanding has been your waistline.*

"Yeah, well I'm a very deep and spiritual person, Pete, and it's about time you... Oh, I've got to go. 'Loose Women's just starting."

"Right... But you are coming, aren't you?" *Please don't make me check into the hotel alone. Only a complete looser would book a double room for one on Valentine's Day.*

"Oh yeah, for sure. Just you concentrate on wiring me that money."

"Okay. And I'll meet you outside Gare Du Nord at 9?" No reply. "I love you." A mirthless laugh, and the sound of a phone hanging up. Even though I had a really bad feeling about the whole thing, I found a Post Office outside King's Cross and sent her one hundred pounds, to be on the safe side.

It was shortly before 11pm that night, stood outside the station, when I came to regret that decision. I'd been there for well over an hour-and-a-half, freezing my balls off; everyone that passed seemed to be pointing at me; and I'd just fended off yet another wave of Romanian beggars in Nike trainers when I decided to give up and go back alone to my hotel room. The arrivals board had been blank since about 10pm. I knew, deep down, that I'd been deluding myself, and about a LOT more than just the train timetables. The only thing that could possibly save the situation was an expensive French pint, but when I reached my hand into my back-pocket, I found it empty. I'd been mugged!

Pete: Thursday 15th February 2007

Even though the sheets were brown and cigarette burned, I didn't want to get up. The world outside sounded noisy and chaotic, and I wasn't sure I could cope with it all. But the Moroccan hotel manager kept banging on the door, and shouting at me to "clear out", so I was forced to drag myself up and, without showering, left the room in the clothes I was already wearing – the clothes I'd been wearing since yesterday.

"Many wonderful things to see in beautiful city of Paris, my friend." The hotel manager pitched his voice somewhere between politely affable and threateningly hostile, his hand on my back, all but steering me towards the exit. The city didn't look all that beautiful

from the porch. Cars screeched through the streets at frightening speeds, their horns wailing angrily; pedestrians walked shoulder to shoulder, pushing past one another; litter covered the already filthy ground; and pushy street-sellers spoke at a million-miles-an-hour, jostling for attention, peddling their cheaply made crap upon unsuspecting tourists. Well, I certainly wasn't falling for that!

"Electro-pens. Just five Euro!" A surly looking guy in a dirty vest grabbed me by the wrist and reeled me in. What the fuck were electro pens? I wanted to ask. "Top-of-range high-quality gifts, to give to your family? Your girlfriend, no?" He'd hit my weak spot, rendered me powerless. He'd located my kryptonite. Somewhat against my will, I found myself buying one of his 'electro pens' (a tacky, light-up thing with a glowing Eiffel Tower perched on top) and the sort of journal that no right-minded writer would be seen dead with... Except that I didn't have anything else to do, other than keep a diary of the things I wasn't doing, and the fun I wasn't having, so it wasn't all bad news.

I found the nearest bar, bought an eighteen Euro half of lager and began writing. Maybe this would be a turning point in my life: the legendary holiday where the legendary Pete Ross begun his legendary Doctor Who script. Inspired, I set my stupid-looking pen to work, but fifteen minutes later, all I'd done was draw an anthropomorphic clove of garlic, dancing with angry baguette in a striped jumper.

I was relieved when a squat man in a tailcoat pulled up a bar stool next to mine and began talking to me in a language I didn't understand, presumably French. If only I remembered anything from lessons at high school. No, wait. I did remember something: reciting 'My Daily Routine' over and over again – constantly, pointlessly, incessantly – for FIVE years!! I understood now. All that 'talk to strangers abroad' and 'cycle round

*youth hostels with Pierre and Stefanie' stuff was
bollocks! The whole course was geared towards
learning 1 minute of mindless drivel by rote, and
reciting it to grade C standard. And the worst thing of
all was that it obviously worked, because, whilst I
couldn't say anything useful, I could remember the
whole fucking routine! So why didn't I just keep my
mouth shut, finish my drink and leave apologetically?
WHY did I think it would help my situation to recite it
all? None of it was even true anymore. I told him I was
15 years old; that I lived with my parents, in a house
with eleven bedrooms, and that I had a gerbil. That
had been a lie even back then. Dad always said pets
were for girls and told me I wouldn't end up a
company director if I was too busy poncing around
with a sodding rodent. The French man put his hand
on my shoulder, and shook his head, a darkly defiant
look about him. What did this mean? By the time I got
to telling him about travelling to school on a yellow
bus, he was shrugging wildly, a hint of frustration to
his muttering. I continued, moving on to my uniform
and the contents of my pencil case – had this stuff
always been so mundane? – but he kept repeating a
single word over and over again.*

*"Porquoi? Porquoi?" What could it possibly have
meant? He looked agitated and I was about to back
away when he saw my drawing and seemed to take
offence. I was on my feet when he gave me a shove,
and it was only when I stumbled backwards that I
noticed he wasn't on a bar stool at all. He was in a
wheelchair! Oh, god no. How could I fight back if he
was disabled? I could just see the headlines: 'Brutish
Brit Thug Vents Vicious Race Hate on Innocent
Foreigner'. If I could just get my bag back, I could leg
it. I lunged for my belongings, but he seemed to think
I was making an assault, threw a leg out and kicked
me.*

"Please... Just leave me alone!" I whimpered, holding out the remainder of my drink to him as a peace offering. He pushed my arm away, and the contents of the glass spilled down my shirt. It was clear that I stood no chance of getting my bag back. I was just going to abandon my dignity and leave. I dashed towards the door, trying to block out the torrent of abuse and cruel laughter, and didn't stop until I was down a deserted alleyway. I'd lost my mobile phone, my lunch and yet more cash. They'd all been in the bag. On the plus side, I'd managed to salvage the notebook and pen, which I hadn't actually wanted in the first place. On the minus side, however, I was hopelessly lost.

It was late when I found my way back to the hotel. I checked every pocket of my suitcase, but it was no use. All my cash was gone. I was down to the remaining balance of my credit card, but I'd already used most of that to bail Simone out and pay off the double room where I slept alone. I felt panicked, like the dirty walls were closing in all about me. I needed some air. I hadn't managed to get the window open last night. It had been painted with emulsion so thickly that it was jammed completely shut. I wasn't going to bother trying again now. I didn't have the energy.

I left the room in a daze, not even bothering to lock up. Everything of value to me was gone anyway. What did it matter if my ultraviolet security pen and Speedstroke swimming trunks got taken? Outside, tense looking waiters stalked the pavements, trying to beckon even the poorest looking passers by into their overpriced, unpleasant looking restaurants. One woman leapt out, waving a menu intrusively into my face and I slipped over the kerbside, onto the road, where a camp looking police man shot past on a bicycle, blowing his crime whistle. What the hell was going on? I hadn't signed up for this! I ended up running down into a metro station for safety. Seeing that it wasn't staffed, I jumped over the ticket barrier and onto the first train. Tonight I'd been planning to take Simone to see the tower. I had no great desire to go on my own, but descending into the claustrophobic tunnels at fearsome speeds brought a knot to my stomach, and, seeing that Trocadero was the next stop, I ended up there anyway.

Emerging back into the icy winter air, I was a little baffled that the tower was nowhere to be seen. As soon as I rounded the corner, however, I reeled back. It was HUGE! I'd watched 'City of Death' countless times, but it looked a lot bigger than on the telly. Perhaps it was because we only had a thirty-six inch screen. Fairy lights twinkled along the side, drifting down like snowflakes, and long beams cast an eerie, sonic-screwdriver-blue glow onto the steel frame. Leading up to it, a long paved area descended down some steps, to fountains, statues and a park, where the frost on bare tree branches glittered under the moonlight. Cold and lonely as I felt, there was no denying that it was beautiful. But everywhere I looked, happy couples seemed to be strolling hand in hand, wrought with emotions and feelings I couldn't even begin to imagine, throwing their heads back and laughing at jokes I couldn't hear – jokes that were probably at my expense. I wrapped my coat tighter about my chest, my lip trembling. At first I thought it was just the cold, but then I began to sob, and it wasn't just like the sobbing me and Jeff had descended into when The Doctor said goodbye to Rose at the end of 'Doomsday'. It came from deep within. I couldn't remember ever feeling as sad as I did now. I looked at the tower, and then at myself, wondering who would miss me if I jumped. There didn't even seem much point in trying to reason with myself. I was going to do it.

When I saw the lines and admission prices, however, I realised I couldn't actually afford to commit suicide. So I went for a Thai Green Curry instead, which was marginally cheaper and, even though everyone seemed to be looking over their shoulder and snickering at me, decidedly less uncomfortable. I mean, I could've got myself killed!

Pete: Friday 16th February 2007

I miss Britain! I miss Marmite, and Doctor Who, and tea that tastes of tea, and Monty Python, and, most of all, I miss Jeff! There was another lone Englishman at the communal breakfast this morning, and I breathed a sigh of relief when he came to sit with me. Finally-intelligent conversation! He told me his name was Anthony Carmichael, and that he'd been a rap music pioneer, but it hadn't really worked out for him, so he'd gone on to work in sales.

"I was a rap music pioneer," he said, "but it didn't really work out for me, so I went on to work in sales." On reflection, it seems he said little else. Every time he repeated the sentence, the words came out in a slightly different order, and it always seemed to end with a little chuckle, but I couldn't work out which bit was the joke. Nevertheless, I laughed along with him heartily, in the hope that the other diners would mistake us for good friends. I'd had this horrible feeling everyone had been staring at me ever since I got here, like they knew I'd been stood up: like they could actually see the depth of my shame and embarrassment. I kept hoping me and Anthony'd have the opportunity to start reminiscing about good old Blighty together, but I never got chance to communicate my homesickness.

When I went back to my hotel room to pack my stuff up, I realised it had been broken into. They'd taken just two things: my ultraviolet security pen, and my Speedstroke swimming trunks. I was far too puzzled to even give it a second thought. One of the biggest advantages of being serially robbed is that it makes your bags considerably lighter. Plus, if I hadn't lost all my money, I only would have spent it on useful, interesting and entertaining things... And then I would have had to carry them around. I had to check out of the hotel at 10am, but my return train wasn't until 6, so I had to cart all my stuff around with me for the day. Thankfully, the entire contents of my belongings now entailed a moth-eaten scarf, a packet of Digestive biscuits and a lifetime supply of unused condoms that would probably never see the light of day. I think I knew who was winning...

Unfortunately, my good mood didn't last. It wasn't long before I found myself stood in the middle of a dual-carriageway, too scared, or at least too numb, to move. Every time I thought I'd got my head round the left-hand drive thing, the polarity of the neutron flow seemed to reverse, and a fresh onslaught of cars would hit warp speed in my direction, as soon as my toe touched the tarmac. It was an inauspicious start to a nefarious day, in which – for a brief period – I descended into the ranks of Jack-the-Ripper-esque villainy. Loneliness can do strange things to a man, and I wasn't proud of that day's crime spree, but I hold Simone entirely responsible. It all started when a woman with a pram pulled up next to me at the crossing. On top of her pushchair was a yellow cassette Walkman. I didn't mean to steal it. It's just that I hadn't seen one since 1993, and I wanted to take a look. The next thing I knew, I'd jumped a bus and was sat at the back, loudly humming Paul McCartney's 'Live and Let Die', kicking seats for percussion. I was thrown off somewhere round the Arc de Triumph, stumbled directly into the nearest supermarket and stole two bottles of red wine by concealing them under my jumper and pretending they were just ordinary breasts: the kind you'd see on any ordinary woman. Classic.

I don't know why, but the more I drank, the more lonely I felt, the more angry I became and the more I wanted to drown Simone in a vat of warm peanut butter (she hated the stuff – it was what had brought us together in the first place, and now the cruel irony would be all mine!) I spied a record and DVD shop in the distance, and knew that it was the only place that could give me any solace, so I dashed towards it, all the blood rushing to my head, in the same way it had done when Colin Baker had unexpectedly regenerated, causing me to have a miniature fit. Out of nowhere, a Polish woman sprang at me, immediately trying to extort money out of me by waving around a photograph of a black child dressed in Pirate gear.

"The poor child." She said, in a disjointed accent. "He embarrassed, because he have to dress in Pirate gear. Gimme some cash, and I buy him real clothes... I make him a man, like his mother. No?" She followed me, reeling off this sort of crap for some time, but I was preoccupied. I'd just remembered pinching a handful of complimentary sweets from the hotel reception as revenge against the pushy Moroccan owner, and the sugar rush had hit. I escaped from the Polish woman and into the record shop, going into such a frenzy that I blacked out.

When I came round, I was slumped by the river, a CD named 'The Best of the Spice Girls – sung in French!' tucked just inside my coat, and a life-sized cardboard cut-out of the singer from Tears For Fears standing over me, his mad hair stood accusingly on end. Where'd he come from? I didn't like Tears For Fears or the Spice Girls! I felt terrible, but any negative thoughts

187

were swept away by the elated feeling of knowing I'd soon be going home, to tea and toast, and to the end this horrifying ordeal. That was, until I checked my watch.

"Oh god, no." It was twenty-past-six. My train home was due to leave at any moment, and I was nowhere near the station. The floodgates opened and I broke down there and then. If I couldn't get home, back to our lovely flat, back to daytime television, back to junk food, back to Blackpool and back to Jeff then I really did have nothing left worth living for. Simone was gone, all my most treasured possessions were gone, and I was stranded in fucking France!

I stood up and walked to the water's edge, staring down into the dirty, slimy depths, teetering precariously on the brink. The water was so black, you couldn't even see the reflection of the city. The pollution alone could swallow me whole. I took off my jacket and unbuttoned my shirt, the cold hitting me instantly, making me feel sick. Then I picked up my chemist carrier bag from the bottom corners and let its contents tip into the Seine. Before long, condoms of every different shape and size were bobbing up and down along the water. What with this being France, people would probably be diving in to retrieve them before long, but the only way they'd ever be any use to me was if I decided to make an army of 'Green Death' maggots. Out of the corner of my eye, I spotted a police man running towards me, shouting at the top of his voice, but I knew he wouldn't make it in time. I put one foot out. Was I really going to do it? Could I? Really? I shifted my weight, but then a thought prevented me from going all the way, and, before I knew it, the policeman had seized me, pulling me back onto the hard stone floor.

"Sir. What were you doing?" How did he know to speak to me in English? Perhaps it was my

188

overwhelming air of erudite sophistication, or perhaps it was the fact that I was overweight, carrying an ungainly amount of luggage and wearing a silly hat and Tom Baker scarf over a stretched Blackpool FC shirt. Either way, I didn't care. God – or Patrick Stewart – had intervened, and I wasn't going to die today. This policeman had saved my life, and that meant somebody did give a fuck about me... Even if it was just his job to give a fuck when people were about top themselves. But then he said "Ze River Seine iz a public heritage spot. How could you litter it with your zex aids and fat English body?"

"I was planning to commit suicide by drowning myself," I said frankly, "but then I remembered that I didn't have any swimming trunks." The policeman shook his head and put me in handcuffs.

I was racked with terror as he drove me to the station. I'd seen what they did to criminals on 'The Bill'. But then I remembered that this was France, and that the police force solved crime at a leisurely pace, stopping for a morale boosting sing-song if need be. When we arrived, the sergeant was playing cards with one of the criminals in a cell. They were laughing heartily, drinking from a tankard of wine between each move, and the room was filled with acrid smoke.

"What did he do?" I asked.

"Stole a cake from the patisserie... a LARGE cake." He said threateningly. I was thrown into a cell with a man who'd 'nearly made things difficult' for another busker by playing his accordion too loudly, and a man who'd got a bit tipsy and ridden his bicycle down the central aisle of a church. We spent the evening singing woozily, even though none of us seemed to speak the same language, until someone came for me.

"Where are we going?" I asked warily.

"To the airport." They were the last possible words I wanted to hear. I'd been terrified of flying since the age of 7. I couldn't fly. I was aeroplaneaphobic. I felt sick and panicky, like I wanted to jump out of my own skin. Something in me tried to do just that, but it only made my head hurt more, like a pressure building up so badly I thought I might explode, or scream. But, in actual fact, I found I couldn't say anything. "We searched your bags, and saw that you'd missed your train. Think of this as us being merciful, if you like, after all the trouble you've caused for us."

"I didn't mean to... honest! My girlfriend left me, and I went a bit mad, and I may have stolen some stuff, and I may have beaten up a cripple... But I didn't mean to. Really I didn't. Please don't make me get on the plane. Please." I wept.

"If you refuse to cooperate, we will have to sedate you."

"Plllleeeeaaasssseeeee!" I was in tears. The policeman took out a syringe, which appeared to be full of red wine, and plunged it into my arm. I started to feel tipsy instantly.

"I'm afraid you leave me no choice. You are being deported, and if you ever return to our country, I must inform you that we've taken serious measures to prevent your embassy bailing you out again. I hope you realise the severity of your crimes." My head was swimming, until he said. "Is that clear, Mr. Carmichael?"

"You can't make me get... WHAT?" I stopped dead. "But my name's not..." And then I blacked out.

Pete: Saturday 17th February 2007

I didn't know what time it was when I found myself in the passenger lounge at Manchester Airport. I felt so weary and nauseous. What had been in that lethal French concoction? I lurched to my feet and had to steady myself on the headrest to stop a sudden fall. A group of teenagers with big hair and fluorescent, cartoon-strip hoodies, who sat opposite, seemed to find this hilarious. They were drinking a similar looking concoction to the stuff Simone always had lying around. I could see from the bottle label that it was called 'Nuclear Waste', the graffiti style caption underneath reading 'survive the fall-out from this holocaust, dude!' When had the world become so horrible? Why weren't people nice to each other anymore? Why had everyone stopped treating each other with courtesy and respect? And WHY THE FUCK was everyone pointing at me??!

Obviously, I couldn't afford the train fare back from Manchester, so I spent the entire journey hiding in the onboard lavatory. Despite the overflowing, tissue-clogged sink and faint musty odour, I found the privacy of an enclosed, windowless space strangely comforting and was reluctant to leave. Of course, when I did, I had to walk the rest of the way, through the windy streets; past the pub advertising 'one-weekend-only classy and professional Las Vegas weddings'; left at the 'Sunny Horizons Dating Service' (with a misplaced apostrophe); and straight on past the karaoke bar, where a colossal woman wailed her way through 'Stand By Your Man'.

When I got home, it took a good degree of fumbling to get the key to turn. Just as I was about to walk in, a thuggish looking kid on a tiny bike drew to a halt outside our gate, pointed at me and let out a single hollow laugh. It was all I could do not to hurl a rock at the little bastard. Up in the flat, I drew all the curtains, and, as soon as I knew no one was looking, burst into floods of unstoppable tears. Simone had broken me.

191

Jeff: Saturday 19th June

I had a text from Daisy: *'I'll be getting a lift down with Lumpy and Mudd, but there's only one seat in the van. You'll have to get the coach down. Hope that's ok! Love you x'*. I had no idea what she was talking about. Lumpy and Mudd?

I replied *'Who? And where are we going?'*

'Glastonbury of course! You know Lumpy and Mudd. We had a three way polyamorous relationship in the 90s.'

I couldn't deal with this. I turned my phone off. The Pandorica was opening!

Jeff: Monday 21st June

I woke up and realised I was late for work. I scrambled around frantically for a pair of socks but then, to make matters worse, I couldn't find my uniform anywhere.

It was only after 20 minutes of chaos, fist waving and tears that I remembered I didn't have a job anymore. How can I be expected to remember such trivial details? My mind was shit to pieces. The universe has *exploded*. Rory is an Auton. Amy is dead! The Doctor's imprisoned for all eternity... And, to make matters worse, River seems to have decided she looks good in furs. I was just about to get back into bed when there was a knock at the door. Maybe Tommy Asbo had finally come round to drop those videos off?

I opened the door, dismayed, to find that it was just some fat, ginger bloke. "Look, I don't want to join a cult, alright..."

"What?" He looked upset. "No, I'm just here to see Pete..." And that was when I realised. He was speaking in an American accent. This was the infamous Andy Pond.

"Oh, okay. He's still in bed." For some reason, Andy looked crestfallen.

192

"Shall I tell him you called?"

"Well... Perhaps I could come in for a cup of tea?" I hadn't replied before he invited himself over the threshold. "You know, you look really familiar..." He eyed me suspiciously.

"Really? I don't think we've met."

"Hang on! It's you! You're Jeff! But I thought you-" It was at this point that Pete emerged from his bedroom, his face a mask of terror. He looked at me, pleadingly. This was going to be awful...

"Jeff? No." I said. "I'm Colin... Collins."

Andy looked me up and down, and then at the many pictures of Pete and I on the mantelpiece. "I see." He said, tight lipped. "I think I know what's going on here..." He lifted his head upwards in a camp attempt at dignity, trying to prevent the tears welling.

"Look, I can explain..." Pete darted towards him.

"Oh, it's not your fault honeykins!" Andy threw his arms around Pete, who was looking pretty scared. "I know what you were feeling, but no matter how much Colin looks like Jeff, it's not going to bring him back. You have to move on!" He clasped Pete's hands and held them to his heart. "Find what's right for you." He took a deep breath and turned to me. "I think you should get dressed and leave now, Mr. Collins. Pete and I have things we need to work through."

Leave? But I had nowhere to go! And it was raining. But Pete looked desperate and helpless, so I decided to pay a spontaneous visit to Daisy at work to show how much I cared. I made toward my bedroom door to get some clothes.

"Ah ah!" Andy wagged a finger at me. "Pete doesn't like people going in that room. It's perfectly preserved the way Jeff left it." He pointed towards Pete's door. "Take your things, and geeeedddd outta here!" He wiggled his hips as he said this and, for a second, I thought he could have been a female soul singer.

Of course, Andy thought I was just some gay swinger Pete had picked up in The Pink Handbag who had obviously spent the night... Well, it didn't bear thinking about. The point was, I had to go into Pete's room and pretend to get my clothes, which meant I had to borrow some of his.

I felt slightly self-conscious going into HSBC wearing a pair of Troll walking trousers, a 'Who Gives a Toss' t-shirt, and duffel coat two sizes too small, from which my arms protruded somewhere below the elbow. I had no doubt that this would provoke some kind of lecture from Daisy. Yet, as I approached her kiosk, she simply said "Oh, hi! Thank god you've stopped wearing that bow tie!"

Jeff: Tuesday 22nd June

I've been having a recurring dream that I'm at the alter on my wedding day. The bride is next to me, but her dress is made of such blinding light that I can't make out her face. I glance around. Everyone is smiling at me, but I'm utterly miserable. My heart feels like it's made of lead. I feel the way I always imagined I would if I were in court, being served a jail sentence. I'm drenched in sweat, and so tired that my arms are sagging forward. The priest is beaming at me expectantly, as though I'm supposed to say something, but I'm gripped with fear and can't speak.

But then it happens – a hot white burning sensation stabbing at my breast. There's something in my blazer pocket. I fish it out to see the TARDIS key glowing beautifully. It's ready! The enthusiastic strings of the Eleventh Doctor's theme kick in from nowhere, as I spin on my heel without looking back, and vault for the door, cries of chaos and pandemonium behind me.

I ignore them all and sprint out of the churchyard, across the village green to where a blue box sits waiting in an orchard.

And then I wake up. What the hell's that all about?

Pete has been begging me not to go to Glastonbury, but what can I do? I promised Daisy. Well, worse – I told her I'd bought her a ticket...

Jeff: Wednesday 23rd June

The coach left Preston at 7am. I realised, to my dismay, that the new DWM was out today, and I'd be denied the chance to read it. Surely missing Doctor Who itself was punishment enough?

I managed to get on first, grabbing a great seat by the window, until a man asked me if we could swap so he could sit next to his wife. I couldn't exactly say no. I ended up sat by the toilet, where the floor was mysteriously sticky, next to a mad looking, gangling man who was staring into the middle distance.

We called into a service station, where I was appalled to find thirty-two different types of porn, gaming magazines, horse magazines, gun magazines, golf, pro-swimming, cake decorating... But no Doctor Who! What kind of world do we live in?

By 3PM, the traffic was at a standstill, somewhere round Mendip. A weird fault had developed that meant, whilst the air conditioning was broken, the heating was stuck on. It was becoming unbearable. I checked my bag for snacks, but the chocolate bars had melted and the juice had gone warm! For the first time in 8 hours, the staring man spoke.

195

"Are you from Preston?" Each syllable was extensively elongated, and sounded as though it were being dragged across gravel.

"Err, no – Blackpool. But I used to work in Preston."

"They won't let me in the library."

"...Okay..."

"Something about my card not being right. I can't make it rain indoors. That's *ridiculous*."

"Well, no, of course not..."

"And all that stuff that happened with the..." The last word was mumbled, but I had this horrible feeling he'd said 'children'. "I just don't think I should be treated this way."

Him? What about me? "No, of course not!" I nodded.

"I blame *him*." He waved a finger menacingly. "Where do you work in Preston?" The finger dropped and he was suddenly mellow.

"I don't work there anymore."

"What happened?"

"I got sacked."

"Oooohhhhhh." He closed his eyes and began massaging his forehead. I wasn't entirely sure, but I think he may have been crying. "The bastards!" He moaned. "They're bastards. They stab you in the back. Don't they? Don't they stab you in the back?"

"Yeah..."

"They stabbed me in the back. They're bastards. But, you and me... We're the same."

At that moment, I got a text from Daisy: '*Hey. We've just put our tents up. We're in the dragon field. What a beautiful day! X*'. I seethed inwardly.

The driver offered to let people off the coach to walk alongside the static traffic, and about half of them did, but, being alone, I didn't fancy it. After half an hour or so, I'd seen a dozen people climb back on board with frosty beers, pints of scrumpy and ice creams. I couldn't take it anymore,

196

so when the scary staring man got up, I decided to follow him.

All we encountered were some bushes and a roundabout. It was when we drew level with the roundabout that, somehow, the traffic eased completely. It happened in slow motion, like something from a disaster movie. Our coach overtook us and disappeared into the distance, leaving a mocking wave of swirling dust. I felt a scrawny arm slide around my shoulders.

"You and me, *we're the same*."

Jeff: Thursday 24th June

I arrived at the festival on foot, luckily having kept my ticket in my pocket, at midnight. I'd been exhausted and wanted to sleep right where I came in, but I had to trudge over to 'Gate A' where my 'missing' luggage had been left. Missing? Ha! It had left me in the middle of a fucking field. By the time I'd reacquired my belongings, it was nearly 2am. I had no intention of trying to find the 'Dragon Field' or 'Trash City', where my girlfriend, Spanner and Lamppost – or whatever their names were – were partying the night away, so I pitched my tent on the first field I found. This morning, I discovered it to be next to 'Dance Field', which explained why I didn't get any sleep.

I didn't remember any of this. What had happened to all the travellers? The huge fence and all the security... It was like being in prison.

I texted Daisy to find out where she was: '*The Chakra Horizon Holistic Sauna in the Tipi Field*'. At length, I found it, and was somewhat taken aback to see that they were all naked, sat around a campfire.

"Hey mate... It's not fucking Marks and Spencer's." Laughed a hairy man, reclining on the grass with his legs horrifically apart.

"Jeff, this is Mudd." The hairy man nodded. "And that's Lumpy." She pointed to a tall guy, stood by a paddling pool and wearing a miniskirt, a turban of dreadlocks piled on top of his straggly head. I could tell this was going to be even more fun than my afternoon with 'Jones', the scary staring man who, when I asked if he'd left his ticket on board, had looked confused and said he was under the impression our coach was the 'Fleur de Horizons' tour bus, and assumed I'd been appointed his carer for the day.

Jeff: Friday 25ᵗʰ June

After being dragged to yoga at 9am, forced to endure a 'spiritual massage' workshop and then some experimental jazz on the 'Lost Dolphin' stage, I flatly refused another sauna and was left to my own devices.

I made my way down to the main festival site – the normal bit they show on TV – away from the dragons, laughter classes and men in dresses. More importantly, it was the bit where they sold alcohol. The billboard outside the beer tent was advertising Sunday's football match. It was worth a try...

"You have a TV in here?" I shouted over the crowd.

"Yeah, for the football."

"I don't suppose... Is there any chance... You could show Doctor Who tomorrow night?"

"Fuck off! You can just stay at home and watch TV, you moron! What's the point in going to a festival and asking to watch TV?" He was right. He was making a very valid point. I could have just stayed at home.

Jeff: Saturday 26ᵗʰ June

After a morning of chanting, chanting, some lentil mush and more chanting at the Hare Krishna tent (they give you free food if you endure the chanting, and Daisy has been refusing to spend any money on site after hearing that Prince Charles was here yesterday – I have no idea why), I put my foot down and insisted on going to see some normal bands. I went to the main stage and saw The Lightning Seeds. I'm not ashamed to say I cried with nostalgia and patriotism when they played 'Three Lions'. As the crowd dispersed I realised, to my horror, that 1996 was 14 years ago.

I wandered around aimlessly for a bit, bought an overpriced burger, a way overpriced pint and went to sit on a bench. This was it: the most important day in history. Amy's wedding day! The base code of the universe! The date of the explosion! And I was in a field in Somerset, banned from television. I felt like The Doctor in 'Flesh and Stone', knowing that 'something' was exploding out there right now, somewhere in time. 'The Big Bang' was happening right now. It was out there in the ether. The TV signals containing its encrypted data were all around me, but I couldn't see them!

I tried to console myself with the fact that Orbital are playing tomorrow night – that it would somehow make everything okay – but deep down I knew that it would pale by comparison to their 1994 set. We were all old men now. I felt like some kind of ghost, haunting a lifestyle that no longer belonged to me.

I was interrupted in my sulking when a man clutching a bongo came and sat next to me, telling me that the pyramids were built by lizards from space.

Pete: Sunday 27th June

After 'The Pandorica Opens' had finished, and after I'd stopped hyperventilating, I made a list of all the unanswered questions The Moff had left us. Would he wrap it all up cleverly in an entertaining twisty-turny

plot, or would he do a 'Rod' and lazily leave it to the world of fan-fiction to properly explain why Donna's head didn't explode when she remembered The Doctor, *par example*?

1. Why does the Doctor appear with his jacket on in 'The Time of Angels' after the angels have taken it from him?
2. Why does 'Little Amy' hear the TARDIS when she's sat on her suitcase in 'The Eleventh Hour'?
3. Who is saying 'silence will fall'?
4. What is 'the silence'?
5. Why doesn't Amy remember the Daleks?
6. What's the significance of the duck pond, without any ducks?
7. Why mention the Cyberking?
8. Is there any further significance to the date 26.06.10, other than Amy's wedding?
9. Why are there 'too many empty rooms' in Amy's house?
10. What happened to Amy's parents?
11. Why was 'Little Amy' left alone in house?
12. Who is piloting the TARDIS, and why is it being weird?

After 'The Big Bang', I was a bit too baffled to form a proper opinion, but I couldn't believe he'd answered nine-out-of-twelve, while the other three are obviously a deliberate future story arc. Clever stuff, Moff! I watched the episode again, and actually managed to enjoy it once I'd get my head round all the intricate twists. In fact, it was brilliant!!! I wanted to text Jeff, or call him to talk about it, but I knew he wouldn't have been able to watch it at Glastonburgh.

I just hope all the 'orient express in space stuff' is a joke and that the rumours about the Yeti coming back are true! At last I'll have another excuse to dig out my favourite Halloween costume!

I posted my list online, but it only got one response, from 'Marc of Infinity', accusing me of being 'anally retentive'. Does this mean I now have bowel problems as well as agoraphobia?

Jeff: Sunday 27th June

I was sat next to a stone circle, having a cup of tea and trying to ignore Mudd's speech. He was stood on top of one of the stones, shouting "The total victory of the working class lies in the destruction of capitalist society! The wealth of society is produced by the workers, and yet most of this is converted into profits for the shareholders and business people who own the fucking production lines! So make wage demands! We need a bigger share of what is rightfully our own! What I'm saying is SOLIDARITY! Yeah? Constant oppression of the enemy!"

Daisy was beaming and clapping enthusiastically whilst Lumpy stared vacantly into the distance. It was at this point that I noticed two policemen slowly making their way toward the circle. I'm not really sure what happened. It was all so fast. But, the next thing I knew, Mudd flew from atop the stone and took off across the field, the police hot at his heels. The second officer radioed for backup and, just as Mudd seemed to be making good his escape, he tripped over his feet, landing painfully on his head. The first policeman dived at him, but missed. Mudd attempted to wriggle away, and the officer crawled after him. It was like watching a primary school scrap. However, when Mudd got to his feet, he was swiftly rugby tackled into the soil by the second officer, who quickly handcuffed him. He wasn't moving. He looked like he might be dead. They dragged him to his feet and began escorting him out of the field.

Daisy immediately got up and sprinted after them, whining "Excuuusssee me... Two officers to one person? That's *against the law*!"

I sat there, quietly amused, and continued to drink my tea as Lumpy stared at me. "Duuuuhh... Errrrmmmm... D'you wanna come to my house?" He asked.

"Where do you live?"

"Telford. We could, just, like, go... Or something?"

"I think I'll go and get a pint."

I went back to the beer tent that was showing the football. Luckily, the angry anti-Doctor Who man wasn't there. Only the World Cup could redeem this whole situation now. Only a sterling victory for England could make my world a good place.

By Germany's third goal, a man with a square head sidled up to me. He reeked of Lynx and fish. "It's a fuckin' apology for a team!" He snorted, as though gargling phlegm. "What's the excuse, eh? What's the excuse?"

"Exactly... What's the excuse?"

"Is that ref fuckin' blind? Lampard's shot was fuckin'... *200 feet* over the line." He paused, sniffing the air feverishly. "I smell pussy!" He declared. "Pure virgin pussy!" And then ran off. I had to get out of this place.

As I was fighting my way through the crowd, I had a text from Daisy: '*They've arrested Mudd on some jumped up charges of selling coke and having sex with a minor. Can you believe it? I've got to go and post his bail, so I guess I'll see you back home. Thanks for a great weekend x*'. That was it! I was free! I could go... I was struck with a wave of inspiration. If I left now, I might be able find a hotel with a TV and watch the Doctor Who repeat! It was perfect. As I scurried back to my tent, however, I was pulled into a procession of congaing people.

"Hey, mate. Are you on your own?" Asked a guy in heart shaped glasses.

"Yeah, my friend got arrested..."

"No way! Have some cider." A bottle of Olde English was thrust into my hand. The next thing I knew, I was suddenly best friends with about twelve complete strangers, raving my tits off at 'Club Henge'. I'd bought a t-shirt with cartoons of Matt Smith, Tom Baker and K-9 standing by the TARDIS, and I didn't feel old. I was just a guy having fun at a festival. This was no different to 1994! In many ways, it was the same... Maybe even better! I'd just been having a shit time because I'd been *expecting* to have a shit time. Maybe all that new-age positive thinking stuff I used to believe was true! Maybe the power of positive thought *could* change the world for good. Well, either that or the fact that I was rid of Daisy, Stewpot and Caravan. Whatever, I felt happy.

My phone was vibrating. Shit. What did she want? But it wasn't from Daisy. It was from Rachel. *Do you ever think about the past?*

I went along to Orbital with some of my new best friends, who told me they were called Woody, Buzz and Mr. Potato Head. I suspected these names weren't on their birth-certificates. Buzz became less lucid as the night went on, grabbing my arm at regular intervals and screaming "I have seen the great cobbley" right into my ear. By the time they played 'Satan', he seemed to be communing with the great beyond. I didn't think I'd ever seen anyone go without blinking for so long. I wondered if he knew Mad Frankie. When I asked, he told me he WAS Mad Frankie. I thought it wise not to push the matter any further. Instead, my attention was diverted by a little girl who looked remarkably like little Amy. (Or maybe it was just the MEGAPILL! I bought from the legal highs stall.) She tugged at my sleeve, complaining that she couldn't see. Swept up in the euphoria of the moment, I allowed her older sister to lift her onto my shoulders and we danced to 'Halcyon'. I couldn't believe it. It was the 90s! I'd actually gone back in time! And I hadn't even needed The Doctor. Maybe I *was* The Doctor...

It was all over too quickly. They only played the 8 minute version of 'The Box' – not the half hour one from the EP – and everyone seemed to be heading off. Reality was beckoning. But I wasn't ready to leave yet!

"I don't want to go..." I found myself muttering. But then, through the dry ice, a lone figure appeared on stage. He *definitely* wasn't in the band. He had hair, for a start. Maybe it was all over. Maybe he was a roadie come to pack everything away. But then...

"Helllooooo Glastonbury!"

Hang on. I knew that voice... No! It couldn't be...

"Let me hear you cheer!"

Matt Smith! MATT *FUCKING* SMITH!!!

Pete: Monday 28th June

Orbital... Playing the Doctor Who theme? With Matt Smith... *The* **Doctor?! Wearing the head-lamp glasses?! I think one of my two hearts just skipped a beat! I was like a child who'd eaten too much sugar on Christmas Eve, watching the footage over and over again, running around the house playing with all the different settings on my sonic screwdriver, hiding in my TARDIS wardrobe, racing my remote control Davros against K9. Then my Mum called and I had to be a proper grown-up. Shit! It had happened. They'd finally invited themselves for dinner...**

Jeff: Monday 28th June

I stepped into the hallway and was confronted by an unusual sight. Pete was there, some post clutched in his hand, and a wiry girl with tangled blond hair and feverish eyes held him in a headlock, as he struggled pathetically to free himself. In her other hand, she held a crumpled piece of paper. Of course. It was Psycho Sharon from the other flat. We rarely see her, but often hear screaming and furniture being dragged about.

Shit! What would The Doctor do? He'd probably raise his hands and inch toward her, saying "Listen to me, listen to me! Whatever's wrong, I promise you I can help, but first you've got to let her go!" (Because, obviously, it would be Amy and not Pete.) The evil blond woman would writhe and say "Hahaha! Never! You're too late DOK-TOR!" He'd consider this for a moment and then say "Amy, you trust me, don't you?" She'd nod and, in a flash, he'd whip out the sonic screwdriver and the lights would go out. When the emergency generator kicked in and illuminated the corridor, we'd see that the shards from the shattered lightbulb had blinded their assailant, who would stagger down the stairs, wailing "Blllauurrrgghhh!"

But that wouldn't work. I didn't have a sonic screwdriver. Well, I did but it was just a plastic toy. I had to distract her. I needed to say something that was friendly, yet disarming and a little confusing to throw her off guard. I needed to be witty, charming, mysterious, trustworthy yet stern, urbane and fun all at the same time.

"What the fuck?" I spluttered.

"Did you hear that?" She shouted at me. "Is there a van outside?" She relinquished Pete, who stumbled breathlessly against the wall. "There are wires in the walls!" She punched the door frame. "Fucking wires in the walls, man!" And she sprinted away.

Jeff: Tuesday 29th June

We were sat wearing our fezzes, watching 'The Big Bang' yet again, when we were interrupted by a knock at the door.

There was a smart-looking, small man on the doorstep, who smiled at me but then looked uncertainly at the fez.

205

"Hello there. I was wondering if you had the telephone number for your landlord?" He asked.

"What, Lovely Kenny? Trust me, you don't want to speak to him..."

"I have an arrest warrant for Sharon White, across the hall, and I need to get into her flat."

"So, are you a police officer?"

"No, no." He laughed jovially. "I'm a warrant officer."

"But you've come to arrest her?"

"No, I just need to serve her with this warrant." He brandished a piece of paper. "We have contacted her twice previously via post, but she hasn't responded, so I'm here to serve her with the warrant."

"So... You wrote to tell her she was under arrest... And wondered why she didn't get back to you?"

"Well, yes."

The peculiar events of the previous afternoon were beginning to make a little more sense. "I'll give you his number, but he's not going to be happy!" I warned him.

"You know..." I said to Pete, as I strolled back into the living room. "I something wonder whether we're the only normal people on the planet."

"Tell me about it!" He laughed, adjusting his fez and handing me a fish finger. "The custard's just cooled a little. I'd say it's at optimum dipping time."

Jeff: Saturday 5ᵗʰ January

I missed the first episode of the new Doctor Who to go on a date with Rachel, so I must really love her! Pete reckons it's going to be the best episode since Tomb of the Cybermen. I've never seen it but the cover of the Target novelisation looks OK so I agreed with him. We went to see The Terminator and it was brilliant! The effects were dead realistic, not like tin foil cybermen and green bubble wrap! We were kissing for ages when we waited at the bus stop. I had my hand on the top of her leg the whole time and I felt dead nervous and a bit sick but not in a bad way. I think it's what people mean when they say they have butterflys.

Jeff: Sunday 13ᵗʰ January

This has been the best weekend ever! I went to the Blackpool game with dad yesterday and we won 3-0! Then I saw the second episode of Attack of the Cybermen and it was amazing! Colin Baker is so much better than Peter Davison, I think he could possibly be the best doctor yet. I hope they put it out on video soon so I can see the start.

Then today Rachel came round to my house. She brought some of her records round. We kissed a lot and listened to Songs from the Big Chair and Hyæna really loud, then she let me lift up her top!!!!!!!!!!!!!!!

Jeff: Saturday 19ᵗʰ January

Me and Rachel went to the cinema again. We saw a really funny film called The Breakfast Club, but I felt sad at the end. I'm not sure why. I had tears in my eyes a bit, so had to try really hard not to cry in case Rachel thought I was a poof. There was a girl in the film called Allison who reminded me of Rachel, but not as pretty. I was annoyed when the lights came on because it had been nice just sitting there in the dark with our arms around each other.

The only bad thing about going to the cinema was that I missed Doctor Who. But it didn't look very good anyway, the radio times said the villain was a little worm called Sid or something. I don't really mind, I suppose I'm too old for Doctor Who now. It is a children's program after all. The Breakfast Club was good because it had loads of issues in it like steryotipes and stuff. I'm in a relationship so I have grown up responsibilities now, if I don't start acting my age I'll become a geek like Pete Ross!

Jeff: Monday 11ᵗʰ February

PATRICK TROUGHTON IS COMMING BACK!!!!!!!!!!

Jeff: Thursday 1st July

"Wow." Said Pete, slightly breathless.

"Yeah." I nodded, much like when Amy showed The Doctor her wedding dress.

"I mean... Just... Wow." He fumbled at the air in an attempt to find the right words.

"Yep!"

"Well, I suppose it had to happen some time..."

"You know, now it's gone..." I began tentatively. "It's like... I don't..."

"...Miss it. Yeah, I know. I actually, you know, kind of *prefer* it this way."

He was right. Replacing the life-sized cardboard cut out of David Tennant in the bathroom with the new Matt Smith one was the best thing I'd done all year.

Jeff: Friday 2nd July

I had a message from Rachel on Facebook saying she'd like to meet up again! I was in such a good mood I found myself just pacing up and down, listening to the new Doctor Who theme, too euphoric to actually do anything. Which was a shame, because before I checked my messages, I'd been getting some sterling work done on our new 'Vaporiser' novel...

Drew Ardon stalked the futuristic corridors of the metallic bunker. Penelope Foxxworth was captive somewhere within the compound, and if he didn't get her to safety by 1500 hours, his ass would be on the line, and he knew all too well that the Senator slapped asses with a scythe.

Just as he rounded a corner at the end of the corridor, there came a sound from far down the corridor to his left.

"So you have returned!" A sinister voice crackled. Drew didn't need to look around to see who it was. When he did, there was no mistaking

it. The crash helmet, the custom green Nikes, the spandex body warmer. The Vaporiser! "We melt again, Mr. Ardon! Hahahahaha!"

Jeff: Saturday 3rd July

It's pissing me off that Open Office insists 'Vaporiser' is a spelling error, telling me to spell it with a 'Z'. I'm not American!

Jeff: Sunday 4th July

Upon further reflection, perhaps I should spell it with a 'Z', to make it a bit cooler, more modern and transatlantic. Sex it up a bit.

Jeff: Monday 5th July

No. That whole 'Americanisation' thing is a terrible idea. We don't want another 'Doctor Who – The TV Movie' on our hands!

Jeff: Tuesday 6th July

I awoke to find a slightly bizarre text in my inbox: '*Brilliant. I'd love to be friends. Maybe we can go for a drink sometime? I'll even wear the costume! Your pal, Adric.*'

Pete promised me he wasn't the culprit, but I wasn't convinced.

"Jeff... Why has Daisy put up a 'Women's Nutritional Chart' above the sink? We're both men. And I've never heard of a..." He squinted at the word. "*Celeriac.* Jesus! It looks like an Ood."

"D'you reckon the Ood count as *proper* Doctor Who monsters?" I asked, trying to ignore the chart.

"What?"

"Well, I mean, I was thinking about K9, and how iconic he is. But he kind of missed all the good stories, didn't he?"

"I don't... Really... What are you... Hang on! What about 'City of Death'?"

"You can't count 'City of Death' just because Tom Baker says 'Hello K9'!"

"He is still *in it* though."

"That's not the point. The fact is, K9 is synonymous with Doctor Who." I held aloft my Doctor Who mug and pointed at the picture of K9 to prove my point. "And yet, he came in fairly late in the game. Don't you think it's weird that by the time we first heard about The Master, the show was already a decade old?!"

"8 years." Pete abruptly cut me off.

"Whatever. But... You know? Doctor Who is: Time Lord, TARDIS, companion, sonic screwdriver, Daleks, Cybermen, Sontarans, K9 and Autons. But some of those came pretty late on."

"Ooh! Wait! I'll draw a chart!" He squealed excitedly.

"Well, that's not really what I-" But he'd already got out his marker pens, and was hastily scribbling.

"And the winner is..." He announced proudly, spinning it around for me to see. "The Daleks!"

63 – Daleks / 66 – Cybermen / 67 – Yeti / 67 – Ice Warriors / 68 – Sonic Screwdriver / 70 – Autons / 70 – Homo Reptilia / 71 – The Master / 74 – Sontarans / 75 – Davros / 77 – K9

"Actually, I think you've proved my point!" I boggled. "That's it. 1977 must be the cut off point! I mean, that stuff's all *proper* Doctor Who! Can you imagine how excited people would be if the Ice Warriors came back?"

"What about the Zygons?"

"They were only in one story. Does that count?"

"Of course it bloody counts. I'm putting it in! *Zygons... 75...*"

"But seriously... Did they invent anything new in the 80s? Anything that people would actually get excited about if it returned?"

"I don't think... I mean, there was *literally* nothing."

"Just Cybermen standing around saying 'Excellent'! And I can't really imagine the Glam-Droid from 'Visitation' making a welcome comeback..."

"What about Sil?"

"Oh, come on. You can't compare Sil to the Autons!"

"At least he got to be in it twice. It's like, they invented all these aliens like the 'Terileptils' and the Vervoids, but they didn't have the audacity to bring them back because even the writers knew they were rubbish."

"'Terror of the Vervoids' is a-" I leapt to its defence, but Pete held up a hand to silence me.

"Whatever you're about to say, forget it. You can't seriously compare 'Vervoids' to 'Genesis of the Daleks'!" He was right. "The 80s was just a big rehash fest! I mean, they even reused The Black Guardian!"

"Yeah! And that weird, big-headed Omega in 'Arse of Insanity'."

"We said we'd never talk about that!" He yelled, his eyes widening. "Omega dies at the end of 'The Three Doctors' and that's that!"

"Sorry... So... What was I saying? Oh yeah, the Ood! Are they a proper Doctor Who monster now? What are the new modern standards?"

"I don't think we'll know for at least a decade, but I can't realistically see anyone getting excited by another Slitheen story."

"You're right. Celeriac *is* a weird vegetable. And I have no idea where that chart came from."

Jeff: Friday 9th July

It occurs to me... Uma Thurman was in two films in 1997 – 'The Avengers' and 'Batman and Robin' – which were, on separate occasions, both voted the worst film of all time. Whereas, to my mind, 'The Avengers' is one of the greatest films ever made. That's all I really have to say on the matter.

Jeff: Saturday 10th July

I had a route under my bed and found the *box of doom*. At the bottom were all my high school love letters from Rachel, all perfectly preserved in a plastic wallet. I listened to 'Undisclosed Desires' as I leafed through them. Valentine's cards, Christmas present tags, photos, drawings... I came across my favourite, torn from the geometric page of a maths notebook and speckled with black dots where the ink had run as I'd stood reading it in the rainy schoolyard. In the top right hand corner I'd drawn stick figures of the two of us, holding hands outside the TARDIS.

...It's hard to tell you how much I love you because there just aren't enough words to describe it. I don't even mind about having to go to school, because it means I get to see you. I love you so much. I've never felt like this before. I want us to spend the rest of our lives together...

I went on Facebook again and looked at the countdown to her wedding day. I suppose this happens in every relationship eventually. One of you gets a fairytale, and the other gets an old box stained by raindrops that fell a thousand years ago, somehow still wet.

I was dragged out of 1984 by the buzzing of my phone. Bloody hell – my Mum? What did she want?

"Hello?"

213

"Jeff? It's your Mum."

"I know." Try as I might, I still couldn't get her to understand the concept of caller ID.

"It's your father. He's gone a bit... Mad."

Jeff: Monday 12th July

"Where the hell have you been?" Shrieked Pete, as I stumbled home at 1am.

"You know how you always said my Dad was mental for spending all day pacing up and down Hound's Hill shopping centre in his security guard uniform?" I sighed, sinking into the sofa.

"Even though he retired ages ago?"

"Yeah. And I always said that he was just very proud, and that he was just making sure they were getting on okay without him?"

"Yeah?"

"Well... I think you were right. I think he probably is a bit... Mad."

"What happened?" Pete raised an eyebrow.

"Well, he was pacing around as usual, but then he caught someone shoplifting."

"Well, at least he's still being useful-"

"Except they weren't actually shoplifting. It was just an old woman trying to fit a bag of cakes into her trolley."

"Oh."

"Yeah."

"So, what happened?"

"Well, the police arrived, but he insisted she was a criminal. So when they refused to arrest her, he accused them of being imposters."

"Imposters?"

"Yeah. Well, specifically Russian spies, disguised as police officers on some sort of mission to overthrow the monarchy."

214

"He's always had it in for the KGB, hasn't he?"

"So he took the old woman hostage with his air rifle, and barricaded himself in that chicken shop. I had to go and reason with him until he let her go."

"You were a hostage negotiator?! That's amazing. You're like Sylvester Stallone or something... You'll definitely get a job at the BBC now!"

"It was my Dad. I don't think it counts."

"So you were negotiating until 1 in the morning?"

"No, we had to go with them down to the station."

"He's in prison?"

"Out on bail. They've suggested counselling."

Jeff: Wednesday 14th July

Daisy and I went to Comet. I'd forestalled getting a new laptop for too long. Before I was even fully across the threshold, I'd been pounced upon by a salesman. I told him I wanted a decent laptop.

"What you need is the Advent Roma 3001!" He trilled. "Would you like to be introduced?" I thought this was a highly unusual thing to say. Was this computer sentient?

"Introduced? It's not... Self-aware or anything, is it?" I asked, as he led me to a glass cabinet.

"Almost! It's terribly interactive. It's time to step into the 10s!"

"Well..." I was uncertain, slightly afraid of his almost inhuman demeanour. "...I suppose I'll be up to date at last."

He unlocked the window and pointed to the laptop on its little stand. "Intel, Celeron Dual-Core T3100, Genuine Windows Home Premium 4096 MO, Hard Drive: 250 Gigabyte, DVD-RW Rewriter, sexy black shell, 15.6 Widescreen and Immediate response!"

"It's not *that* impressive." Daisy snorted.

"What?" The salesman looked hurt. "It has seven computer languages and five protocols!"

215

"Protocols?" I asked.

"Yes. That's how it talks to other computers." He gave me a well rehearsed wink. "The FBI and the CIA use Advent computers, sir. They're favoured universally and used for all sorts. You could design ships. Run power stations. Oil! Gas! Who knows where the energy industry would be without Advent computers."

I ended up leaving with a Compaq for a hundred-and-twenty quid.

"You have a nice day now, sir!" The salesman yelled, before sidling up to me and whispering in my ear. "Oh, and by the way sir, I strongly suggest you marry the girl." He winked in Daisy's direction. I left feeling a little unsettled and with the strangest sense of deja vu.

"I've had a really productive day!" Proclaimed Pete, as I stepped through the door.

"Right." I found this hard to believe, as it was 4pm and he was sat in his underpants, drinking a Mars Bar milkshake and watching the Spice Girls movie.

Jeff: Thursday 15th July

I am now officially and inescapably in the red. I've exceeded my overdraft and I maxed out my credit card buying the new laptop. And still no sign of any benefits! I bit the bullet and rang them, only to be informed that my claim was in "processing hell" and that if I was desperate for cash, I should apply for a "crisis loan". He transferred me to another department.

"Hello? I'd like to apply for a crisis loan."

"Can I take your number please?"

"National Insurance number?"

"No. The number you were assigned in the telephone queue."

"Oh... Err... 6."

"Okay, Number 6. May I have your National Insurance number?"

"WH 24 11 63 O."

"I see. Unfortunately, Number 6-"

"Stop calling me that. It's weird! My name's-"

"I'm afraid we take a very strong stance against individual personality in our clients. It creates room for bias, Number 6. As I was saying, it appears that you already have a claim open with the DWP. I cannot authorise a crisis loan to someone already receiving benefits."

"But... I'm not getting any benefits! My claim's in processing hell!"

"In that case, Number 6, I suggest you take it up with your local Job Centre."

"But they told me to call you!"

"That will be all, Number 6. Be seeing you."

Jeff: Friday 16th July

"What the hell is this?" Asked Pete, as I placed his tea in front of him.

"It's bangers and mash." I said.

"These aren't bangers! They're carrots!"

"I couldn't afford any sausages!" I snapped. "It was either this or carrot and potato stew."

"Stew? But only old people eat stew. It's just stuff with bits in!"

"Exactly. So shut up and enjoy it."

"When are we going to get some real food? My parents are coming over soon!"

I couldn't help it. I sniggered.

"What?"

"You know. It's just..."

"What?!"

"I thought his life support system was so efficient he didn't need to eat. I thought he lacked teeth. And taste buds."

"That is *not* funny!"

A silence fell. "It is a *bit* funny..."

Jeff: Monday 19th July

I tweaked my bow tie (a red one today!) and surveyed myself in the mirror.

"Come on, look at me! No plan, no back up, no weapons worth a damn. Oh, and something else: I don't have anything to lose! So, if you're sitting up there in your silly little spaceships with all your silly little guns, and you've got any plans on taking the Pandorica tonight, just remember who's standing in your way!"

I was ready for my appointment at the bank.

"So, Mr. Greene. I understand you wish to *extend* the overdraft facility on your account?" Said the chubby man with the moustache. He looked like a Dickensian villain.

"That's right, yes." Shit... Was the bow tie a bad idea?

"And the reason for this?"

"Oh, just a temporary cash flow problem. I'm between jobs right now... Looking into going into... You know how it is... Can't make money without spending money. Haha!"

He asked for my NI number, mobile telephone number, email address, and the name of my favourite uncle. I squinted at his name badge: '*Mr. William Eckerslike*'. After a few minutes of frenzied tapping at his keyboard, he eventually spun the computer monitor around and I was a bit confused – if not downright horrified – to find that I was staring at my Facebook page. "According to your latest status update, Mr. Greene, you are – and I quote – 'Skint! Skint! Fucking Skint!' Would you care to elaborate?"

"Well, you know how it is..."

"I'm not sure I do. This evidence hardly convinces me that you are a reliable investment, and hardly capable of repaying a larger overdraft – especially in this time of recession. If I may take a moment to review your situation, you are an unmarried, non-home-owning, unemployed debtor, with no savings or premiums, who currently owes £400 on his credit card, and is £250 over his £2000 overdraft limit. You have an outstanding library fine of £24, and..." He peered at the screen. "...You owe someone called 'Dom' a tenner. Given the circumstances, I am *reducing* your overdraft. We'll introduce a repayment scheme as of today."

Jeff: Tuesday 20th July

I received a letter from the DWP, telling me that my claim for benefits had been rejected.

Dear Mr. Greene,

Unfortunately, your claim has been rejected by the computer.

I refer you to the payslip for £800 from Blackpool Transport Ltd, dated 1st July. This exceeds the amount you are permitted to earn whilst claiming benefits. May we remind you that we take fraudulent claims very seriously. In future, you could face a fine or even a custodial sentence.

Regards,

Mr. Ratcliffe

I examined the attached payslip, and saw that it was dated 1st July 2005. Still, it wasn't all bad. Now I wasn't technically receiving benefits, I could re-submit my crisis loan application before correcting their error! I reached for the phone.

"Hello?" Came a dull greeting.

219

"Hello. I'm ringing about a crisis loan."

"What is your number?"

"Err... 6." I said, somewhat uncertainly.

"Ahh, Number 6. I'm afraid you are not eligible for a crisis loan as you do not currently have an open claim for benefits."

"But I thought I couldn't get a loan if I *was* on benefits?"

"Yeah. It's just that if you don't have a claim registered on the system, the computer won't recognise your existence."

"Well, what can I do? I need to pay the rent!"

"Well, according you your Facebook page, you live in very close proximity to your parents. I suggest you ask them to put you up."

"I'm 38!"

"39, actually, Mr. Greene."

Pete: Wednesday 21st July

I normally find my life busy, hectic and fulfilling but today turned out to be a bit of a non-starter, so I decided to deal with all the tedious jobs I'd been putting off for ages. I reasoned the place was probably due for a clean up before my parents came anyway. The soul of my slipper got stuck to the sticky lino this morning and ripped clean off when I lifted my foot. Even though I'd bought them from 'Shoesaverz' 8 years ago, that probably wasn't supposed to happen.

I cleaned the kitchen; stacked the pans in order of size and brand; combed the sofa; changed my sheets; dealt with that green area on the carpet, where me and Jeff had drunk too much Horlicks and decided to try our hands at alchemy; scrubbed between the bathroom tiles with a toothbrush; and re-applied any posters that were peeling. Then I checked my watch. Shit: it was only 11:31am. Why is it that when you clean out of obligation, it seems like an unending task of unbearable tedium, but when you do it willingly, you breeze through it? I'd have to turn my attention to matters of personal grooming to kill some more time, but even when I'd showered, plucked my eyebrows, shaved, rubbed my entire upper torso in roll-on deodorant and done my clenching exercises, it was still only lunchtime.

I was going to have to do it. I was going to have to go through all my unread emails. I started with junk mail. I couldn't believe the number of messages telling me I needed cheap Canadian medicine to help my libido, rid me of alleged erectile dysfunction and – mysteriously – add an extra couple of inches to increase the size of my penis. It defied logic. Where was that extra length supposed to come from? Did the pills come with their own plastic surgeon or was it all done by some kind of rudimentary torsion machine?

It was all getting a bit depressing. I was about to give up when I saw a message reading 'Comedy Dan has suggested you rejoin the Facebook community. Why not catch up with all those old friends who are missing you?' I was reasonably sure I didn't have any friends that actually liked me enough to seriously miss me, apart from maybe Jeff, and I'd just seen him a few hours ago, so if he was itching to get in touch again so soon, I'd be a bit worried. Nevertheless, setting up a Facebook profile would kill a little time.

I'd originally deleted my account, after I got a crazed phone call from Dom telling me that the whole thing was a secret brain experiment set up by the giant lizards, but now that I thought about it, that didn't seem particularly plausible. I *was* mildly freaked out, however, when I followed the link and found that it remembered all my details. Photographs that didn't really look like me anymore; an insincere biog that made me sound like a confident, fun and outgoing socialite (all bollocks, of course); and, disconcertingly, my credit card number. It was as though I'd never really been gone at all! Even all my old school 'friends' were there. Why? It didn't make any sense that the sort of people who used to beat the crap out of me now wanted to be best friends. Craig Brickstock, who once held me by the ankles and poured milk into my nostrils – before stealing my shoes – had become a Community Support Officer with six kids. In year 8, Jenny Goldstein humiliated me by tearing up the 'Caves of Androzani' Target Novelisation, in which I'd written her a love note, in front of our whole food studies class. Now she looked like Blackpool's answer to Delia Smith and had repeatedly 'poked' me (not literally, it turns out) for failing to 'fertilise her Little Green Patch'. What did it all mean?! Was it some kind of sexual innuendo, or a new development in hyperspace flirting to which I was completely ignorant? There was something else niggling at me too – all these people seemed to be doing quite well for themselves. They all looked 'normal'. Push the thought out, Pete. Just ignore the bad thoughts and they'll go away.

It wasn't all bad, after all. Terry Williams, who I hadn't seen since primary school, had sent me a 'friend request'. I quickly perused his photos to make sure he wasn't doing *too* much better than me before accepting. Overweight – check; balding – check; wife/girlfriend – negative; embarrassing mid-life crisis car with flame transfers on the bonnet – check, but I'd let him off the hook for that one. Not only was I going to add him, I was going to send him a message and invite him over for a drink. Perhaps a healthy dose of reminiscence and pointless nostalgia would help me work out where it had all gone so drastically wrong. I wrote out a couple of friendly, concise emails and then picked the one that made me sound the least weird. I was proud of myself. I hadn't agonised over it for too long, and I'd even included a little joke.

Sure enough, it was only a couple of minutes before a new message came through. I opened it eagerly, my head swimming excitedly with warm recollections of the past. Except that it was from that girl Daisy had tried to set me up with, Tracey: '*Sure. I'd love to come over for a drink! Wait until you see my new Chinese dragon dress. It's REALLY tight!! XXXXX*'.

Shit. Shit. Shit! I pressed the 'back' button a few times and glanced in horror at my 'friend requests' page. Tracey had been the next one down from Terry. But all of a sudden, I was struck with a genius plan, and reached for my mobile to give Andy Pond a call.

Jeff: Wednesday 21st July

It was with a heavy heart that I logged onto Job-Finder.net. Its homepage was garish and yellow, depicting a smiling Asian woman with a disfigured lip, sitting in a wheelchair. She had short, spiked hair, an eyebrow piercing and was brandishing a selection of power tools. I clicked on the 'situations vacant' tab to see a picture of some pest control officers in a sewer, all with their arms raised and inane grins on their faces. A caption below read '*Proud to be a TEAM!*'

I couldn't take it anymore and crawled into bed, where I spent the remainder of the day eating Coco Pops from the box, and reading 'White Darkness'.

Jeff: Thursday 22nd July

I decided to be assertive and go to the Job Centre. I'd tell them that the payslip was 5 years old and try to find a job that wasn't subterranean. After breakfast, of course.

I watched 'The Avengers', just to occupy me, whilst I ate my toast. But then Pete got up and suggested we eat spicy beans, so I watched a bit of 'The Infinite Quest' whilst he prepared them.

By midday I was ready to leave, but decided to check my emails first. After watching a really well put together Youtube video, featuring every single jelly baby reference in Doctor Who, back to back, I was straight out!

Just as I was leaving, Pete handed me a 'Value Noodle-Pot' and said there was something I just had to see that would blow my mind.

By 3pm, having watched the silent, black and white footage of the film crew from Fury from the Deep, I was at last at the Job Centre!

The man behind the desk apologised for the mix up, but said it would be at least 14 days before I received any money, and suggested that I apply for a crisis loan in the meantime. He handed me an application form. I reigned in the impulse to scream, stuffed the form into my tweed jacket and made my way to the War Machine type things that were supposed to help find you a job.

I typed my details in using the touch screen. I explained that I had a degree in English Literature, almost 20 years of work experience and a cycling proficiency certificate. I specified that I was looking for something in the media. Who knows – it might get me a job at the BBC!

It took a few minutes to digest the information, before returning its findings: '*The following position is suitable for you: stripper*'.

Pete: Friday 23rd July

For the seventh time in a row, an electronic voice had just interrupted a polyphonic ringtone version of Vivaldi's 'Four Seasons' to apologise for keeping me on hold. This always got to me. Unless they'd installed

224

this particular robot with some sort of empathy chip, how could it possibly make a sincere apology? I'd been putting it off for weeks, but had finally decided to take the plunge and phone about sickness benefits. There was something about the whole process that made me kind of uneasy. Admitting it to a legitimate government agency seemed like making my 'condition' official, and I wasn't sure I was ready to admit it to myself yet... They'd told me to think of the call as an 'informal chat', but then warned me that it would include some pretty rigorous questioning (interrogation?) and would last about 45 minutes. I'd been waiting nearly that long already. Time wasted whilst I could have been getting on with my life. 'Deal or No Deal' was due to start any second, and Mum mentioned that Noel Edmunds has stopped colouring his beard. I couldn't miss that!

Just as I was drifting off, a polite – if clinical – female voice announced its presence.

"You're not a computer too, are you?" I quipped. My humorous remark didn't go down well. Her tone instantly became frostier, like a school teacher sternly reprimanding a misbehaving child.

"May I remind you that this call is being recorded."

"Bu-"

"And furthermore, antagonising a Benefit Officer for Sickness Services will only result in a delay in your claim."

"But it was only a joke." I protested.

"A joke? Didn't think there'd be much time for fun and games in your condition, Mr. Roth." She reprimanded me. "Perhaps you're not as depressed as you say you are?"

"I'm not depressed. I'm agoraphobic!" I already felt like hanging up. "And it's Ross, not Roth."

"Surely you're not accusing the government of keeping inaccurate records?" Her tone became even more stern. It was as though she tensed with every word.

"No, I'm just saying that my name's Ross."

"Could you spell that for me, please?" I did, and listened to her spelling out the letters, scribbling with a pencil. "So that's... R-O-T-H." I ground my teeth, but couldn't be bothered correcting her again. "Okay, so let me just get your details up on the computer. Ah, yes... And... I see... So you filled out a postal application, and..." She stopped dead. "Oh dear." That didn't sound good.

"What is it?" I asked nervously.

"Well, it says here that you don't have a doctor's note to authenticate your claim?"

"Yes, I do!" I didn't mean to sound so hostile, but Doctor Kowalski had been very reluctant to make a house call. He showed up in a foul mood, possibly drunk and conducted a very forceful examination which I now realise might have been a bit 'hands on'. Surely confirming a patient's psychological condition shouldn't involve anyone dropping their trousers?! "I spent bloody ages trying to fax a copy of that thing over." Already, I was on the verge of tears. No one had used the fax machine for years since it had 'gone rogue' and eaten a poisonous plant.

"I apologise." She sounded even less sincere than the robot. "I'm afraid there must have been some sort of processing error." I was gripping the phone so hard that my knuckles had turned white when I heard these words. "It seems that there *is* a medical report on your file, but it's not yours."

"Then who the hell's it for?!"

"It's for a Mr. Pete Ross. I can see how they'd have made such a silly error. What with you two having such similar names."

"We don't have *similar* names. We have the *same* name. *I'm* Pete Ross."

"No. I'm afraid it says quite clearly on our form here that your claim is registered under the name 'Pete Roth'."

"Look, I don't want to argue about this, but that's only because it's not open to discussion. I think I know my own name." She paused for a moment. I could hear the sound of long fingers drumming against a desk.

"Well, the way I see it, there are two options here. Either you *don't* know your own name as well as you think you do, or you've just submitted a fraudulent claim under a false identity, which is a criminal offence. Which is it to be, Mr. Roth?"

"Look..." I tried to sound authoritative, but my lip was trembling. In the space of one short phone conversation, or 'informal chat', this woman had got me down on my knees begging to be acknowledged as the sort of certifiable idiot who doesn't even know his own name, in order to avoid a prison sentence. "Isn't there any way I can sort this out?"

"The only thing I might be able to do is book you an appointment at your local job centre."

"But I can't leave the house."

"Can't leave the house, Mr. Roth? That's not the sort of attitude we take too kindly to. How are you supposed to get yourself a job if you can't be bothered to-"

"No, I mean, I have agoraphobia. We've been through this. It's what this whole thing's about."

I heard her take a long breath, click a series of keys on her computer and sigh heavily. At length, she said "Have you heard of a website called Face-Book?"

"Yeah, of course I have. Everyone's on it." Why was this relevant? "I only restarted my profile a few days ago."

"That's not the point. I draw your attention to a photograph from the folder 'birthdays', which shows you, dressed as a medieval knight, *outdoors*. Does this

227

foray into the outside world – presumably to consume some kind of hallucinogenic drug – sound like the behaviour of a so-called agoraphobic?"

"No, but that was taken four years ago. And I wasn't dressed as a knight. I was dressed as a *Cy-ber-man*." I knew that rejoining Facebook was a recipe for disaster.

"Be that as it may, Mr. Roth, I'm afraid things don't look good. I've keyed in all your variables into our computer, and it hasn't been able to output a single directive. Obviously we can't act without instruction from BOSS."

"Can't you just... Hang on – sorry..?" I hesitated. "What did you just say?"

"It looks as though we're going to have to terminate your claim."

"No, I mean... BOSS. What's all that about?" I'd been about to hang up, but now I was curious.

"Oh, BOSS is our new computer. It stands for Benefit Officer for Sickness Services. We let him do all our thinking round here."

"Riiiggghht..." I really should have hung up. Any minute now, a giant maggot was going to crawl from behind the sofa. "And might you be able to tell me what your name is?"

"Stevens. Letitia Stevens."

That was it. It had all got too weird. I hung up. There was no doubt about it. They were giant insect larvae. They were in league with Facebook. They were the league of evil. Maybe Dom had been right about the lizard people.

Jeff: Friday 23rd July

Stayed in bed all day with phone off.

228

Pete: Saturday 24th July

It was an ordinary Saturday night – Jeff was cooking up something in the kitchen, the Quantum Leap repeats were on in the background, and I was sat on the floor eating a cornflake toastie – when the sofa started making a weird noise. I craned my head down to the groove between two cushions, recoiling in horror when I heard it.

"Je-efff?" I called. "Have you still got your new phone set to 'caller announce'?"

"I don't know." He appeared in a spattered apron, 'Smoke Me a Kipper' written across its front. "I can't work out how to turn the bloody thing off. What does it say?"

I swallowed hard. "Hello sweetie."

"Oh no... She hasn't? Surely?"

"What is it?"

"Daisy said she'd done something *hilarious* with my phone, to surprise me when she called. She must have changed her contact name."

"And she thinks *that's* funny? Doesn't she realise that any issue relating to Alex Kingston is no laughing matter? You're going to have to change it." I chucked him the phone.

"I don't know how. You do it! You're The Computer Doctor." He chucked it back.

"*This* isn't a computer!" I threw it back again.

"I know!" He wailed. "If it was, it'd have a mute button and I could shut the fucker up!" He swung his arm back and hurled the offending phone towards the wall. I couldn't let him smash up another one. Daisy would have lectured me about 'provoking him with my negative chi' again. I lunged to catch it, but knocked the answer button in doing so. Shit! A wave of panic flooded through me. Jeff left the room, and I was forced to do the only sensible thing a man in my

229

**position could. I pressed the receiver to my mouth, put
on my best comedy Welsh accent and pretended it was
a wrong number.**

Jeff: Sunday 25th July

Pete won't let me eat anything yet, even though his parents
won't be here for another hour. I persuaded him to let me
have a slice of toast, but things didn't look good when I
opened the 5kg tub of butter. (At the same time as buying
all the Doctor Who pasta, Pete also bought twenty catering
sized tubs of butter. He'd watched the news for the first
time since 1996 and was starting to panic about nuclear
war.) It was coated with a layer of green fur. We'd only
opened it yesterday! I resisted the urge to gag and began
scraping off the worst with a dessert spoon.

"What the hell are you doing?" Pete yelled, as he caught
me about to throw the offending matter in the bin. "You
know what my parents are like with their cleanliness
inspections! You can't just put mould in the bin. It'll grow!"

"Well, what d'you want me to do? Eat it?" I snapped.

"We'll have to flush it down the toilet. It's the only
solution." He proclaimed.

Following a lot of scooping and four flushes, the greenish-
yellow mass was still bobbing around defiantly in the toilet
bowl.

"They'll be here soon!" Pete wrung his hands frantically.
"They can't see this!"

"We could scoop it back out with a fishing net or
something?" I ventured hesitantly, cringing at the thought.

"No... Then we'll be back to square one. It's too solid to
flush. We're going to have to melt it."

"*Melt it?* How?"

"We'll pour boiling water on it. It's the most logical solution. It's what Peter Davison would do!" I wasn't convinced, but Pete was already tearing towards the kitchen.

10 minutes later, it still hadn't melted, but did seem to have expanded somewhat. Pete was becoming frenzied. "Just one more! That'll do it!"

"Pete, I'm not sure if there's any more room in the bowl..." He flew back to the kitchen and promptly returned with another kettle full of boiling water. Despite my efforts to apprehend him, he poured the lot in and the toilet overflowed.

"Shit! Flush! Flush!" He yanked the handle.

"That's the worst thing you could've done!" I cried. The flush caused another surge of water to cascade out of the toilet bowl, not only saturating the bathroom floor but ejecting the offending article which began to float towards the doorway. Then the doorbell rang.

Pete: Sunday 25ᵗʰ July

The day was upon us. Doomsday. The end of time. My parents were coming round for Sunday lunch. This meant trouble. There's no way I'd be able to relax. I'd have to spend the whole time attempting to impress my Mum, whilst simultaneously trying not to disappoint my Dad, and keeping Jeff's Dalek impressions to a minimum. So then my brain would be in three different places at once – four if you counted the one inside my head. I'd be bound to wrong foot it somewhere. And to make matters worse, Mum said she had important news. If she didn't tell me what it was _right away_, I'd spend so much time trying to guess what horrible thing it might be (and how it would affect me) that I'd suddenly realise I hadn't been listening. Dad's voice-box could be difficult to understand at the best of times.

I hadn't really slept properly. I woke up shortly before 5, clutching a Clockwork Robot head. This made for a puzzling start to the day. Not only had I no memory of getting up in the night to get it, I didn't remember buying it, being given it, or ever owning it before, so god only knows where it had appeared from. Had I sleepwalked to 'Thunderbooks', broken in and nicked it? No, because that would involve going outside and I wasn't convinced that even my *subconscious* could handle that sort of strain at the moment. But it didn't seem like the kind of thing I would forget about owning either. The thought did occur that it was the actual real head of a Clockwork Robot, but I quickly dismissed that and got up to do some obsessive tidying. The naked Katy Manning shot on the mantelpiece was replaced with the boring geranium vase photo I always put up when Mum came round. The sofa stains were easily concealed with one of Daisy's brightly-coloured Indian throws. I even dug out my most up-market clothes: a green and red stripy blazer with those trendy big lapels like John Travolta had, a pair of brown flared suit trousers, and a swirly orange shirt – button up, no less! Even Peter Davison had never looked this good.

Lunchtime came, however, and things didn't get off to the best start. Whilst Jeff tried to soak up the tide of butter, the sofa started talking again. It was that new phone, and this time I knew I hadn't misheard it.

"Jeff?" He ran from the bathroom, frantically wringing a greasy dishcloth.

"This better be important! We've got a race against the clock on here. And one of our pans was practically *on fire* when I went back to check on the food a minute ago." He whispered it, looking cautiously over his shoulder, as though the very mention of fire might send dinner up in flames again. "Why did you insist on cooking with alcohol anyway?"

"You know my Dad won't eat anything unless it tastes of whiskey. Anyway, why's your phone saying 'Davros'?"

"It,erm, isn't... For sure." He looked guiltily down at his slippers. "It's Dave – Dave Ross. Your Dad must be calling to let us know he's nearly up the stairs. That's good, isn't it?"

"No, it's NOT good, but I don't want to get into that right now. I've got to be calm – not stressed. That's not easy though, when your fucking phone's *quite clearly* saying 'Davros'!" I punched the wall. "Which is completely discrimina... Well, disable-ist, or... Something. The point is, it's not funny. That's what it is. Isn't! Ah, forget it. But I tell you what: if we get through this lunch alive, I'm divorcing you as a friend!"

"I *knew* it!" An electronic sounding voice rasped accusingly from the doorway. I spun round to see Dad, leaning heavily on its frame. Oh god – he'd heard me talking about divorce. It was going to fuel yet another round of cruel jokes about me and Jeff being gay lovers. Except he started going on about something else entirely. "I *knew* you wouldn't have installed that stair-lift. You just want to watch your old man suffer. That's it, isn't it? Can't think of any other reason you'd live on the top floor. Well, ha! Cause I win. 10 quid!" He stretched out his hand, but remained where he was. How he'd got this far when he was only supposed to be able to walk a few steps unaided was a mystery. The answer soon presented itself. My Mum hobbled into the room, out of breath from carrying his heavy looking, state-of-the-art wheelchair. Dad fixed her with a disparaging glower. "42 seconds from car door to here, woman." He tutted. "I could have been dead by now!"

"Calm down, dear." She shot him her 'be on your best behaviour or else' look, as Jeff sauntered into the

233

room, wisps of smoke rising from his singed sleeves as he served up drinks. "Thanks, love. And don't you listen to him, Peter." She sunk gratefully into the sofa, mercifully stifling Jeff's mobile. "He's got his wires crossed again. It was *Stanley* who bet you he'd put a stair-lift in." The way she spoke, it was like she was talking to a child, or someone with an extremely limited intellect.

"Yeah, well 'es a lyin' bastard an' all! Didn't even pay up!"

"He had a stroke!"

"What? Is that *Sex-Offender* Stanley you're talking about?" Jeff took a seat.

"Yes!" Mum's eyes lit up. "He used to be something of a 'player' back in the day!"

"I don't think that's quite how they put it in the paper."

Nobody was paying any attention to my Dad, so he pressed the 'emergency help' button on his wheelchair, and, when everyone turned round, started to complain about the lack of central heating. Mum told him off, pointing out that it was the middle of summer, and then launched into a long description of someone-I'd-never-met's holiday plans. Dad began talking about how the gas company were trying to bleed him dry, and how they would rue the day they crossed him. Jeff kept trying to usher people to the table. And I hadn't said a single word in the 15 minutes since they'd arrived. It was exactly like my house when I'd been growing up: everyone talking, but no one listening to each other. I may as well have not even been there for all the input I had. I could have put my cardboard Matt Smith cut-out at the dinner table and saved the bother of having to hear Dad recount what seemed like every one of my childhood sporting failures. He even dug out his old 'results book' from when we used to have head-to-head general knowledge quizzes at mealtimes, to show how I was "inferior stock". He laughed at this remark like it was some sort of joke, but no one else joined in. Instead, Mum kept looking at me apologetically. After pudding, everyone was relieved when Dad was escorted to the bathroom for his regular post-dinner toilet session.

"I was tempted to press the big red self-destruct button." Jeff muttered when we had a moment to ourselves. The last part was in his best Dalek voice. Even Nicolas Briggs would have been impressed.

"You'd never believe he used to write romantic poetry before we were married." Mum spoke mournfully.

"Whatever did happen to Dad's poems?" Hearing my own voice at last sounded strange.

"He thought the Communists were going to come and steal his identity, so he burnt them all." I could hear him laughing maniacally from the bathroom. Mum lowered her voice. "Look, that's not why I came here today. I wanted to talk to you about something without your Dad interrupting. I'm afraid I've got some bad news..."

"Oh no..." A sense of foreboding flooded through me. "Tedric's not fallen apart in the wash, has he?"

"No, It's about your Uncle Julian." Mum continued, placing a sympathetic hand on my leg. "I'm afraid he recently... passed away."

I couldn't help but find myself saying "Oh". I didn't really know what to think. When I'd thought of Tedric's furry arms disappearing and being chewed up by the lint trap, I'd felt close to weeping. Did it make me a bad person that I was relieved when I found out it was just my Mum's step-brother? I mean, don't get me wrong. Julian was a nice guy, if a bit peculiar, but no one in my family really saw much of him. It didn't seem like especially big news. Of course, I couldn't be totally nonplussed, but I couldn't break down in hysterics either. As far as I was aware, there was just no etiquette for the adequate amount of fuss to make in this sort of situation. But maybe that was just because all my reactions and emotional responses came from TV and books: they *never* made a fuss when minor characters, who'd only ever been mentioned a few times, died.

"The only consolation is that he died doing what he loved, and he probably went in the way he wanted."

"Oh right. So... He was sleeping then?"

"No, erm, sadly not. He had a violent heart-attack whilst on a photo shoot for a new brand of extra tight-fitting swimming trunks." Jeff immediately covered his mouth. I hoped it was through shock, and not because he was trying to stifle a laugh.

All I could think to say was "That's... Unusual." Why do we always make such inane comments when someone dies? Are we really that emotionally immature that we can't deal with it head on? If only Tedric had been here. He'd have made it all better. Mum's grip on my leg tightened as we heard the toilet ominously flush.

"Look, I can't go into detail now, because your Dad isn't going to be very happy about this, but I've been looking over your Uncle Julian's will, and... Well, it seems he must have taken quite a shine to you that time you met, because... And you might want to brace yourself... He's left all his money... to you."

At that moment, Dad emerged from the bathroom and rolled towards us. Evidently he'd heard about the inheritance, because the veins in his neck were protruding more severely than I'd ever seen. "What did you just say?!" You could tell how angry he was from the amount of feedback resonating off his voice-box. "This insubordination will not be tolerated!" He seemed to become more angry with each syllable, spittle flying from his wrinkled lips. "That money should have been mine. My campaign money to become president of the golf club!" He was working into a frenzy, stuttering and repeatedly striking the side of his chair with his burnt hand. "I should have been a *god*!" Mum looked terrified. Jeff was in stitches. I felt too numb to feel much of anything.

The Doctor Who cliffhanger music should have gone there, but it didn't. Mum poured my Dad a large drink to calm him down, but he just sat seething in the corner as she got ready to leave. She told me she'd call about Julian's estate. As they were about to go, Dad rolled up to me, a dark glint in his remaining eye, and whispered just out of Mum's earshot. "I've left a little unpleasant surprise for you in the bathroom. Think of it as a parting gift." And cackling, he left. Only then did I notice the huge clump of butter clinging to his wheelchair spokes. Oh god- it was going to go in his booklet of things to humiliate me with at our next 'dinner party'. I'd never hear the last of it.

I went through to the toilet, ready to deal with something horrific, but it was just a note taped to the cistern: 'I haven't forgotten that stair lift, you bastard. I WANT my tenner!'

Jeff: Monday 26th July

Daisy came round and asked me to go to Hamburg with her next weekend. I said I couldn't afford it and she started nagging me about getting a job. My mind raced desperately for a way to placate her.

"Yeah, but... It just doesn't seem right, you know? I mean, there's little kids starving to death in Greece-"

"Greece?"

"I mean Ethiopia!" I should have remembered that one. It was on South Park. "And here we all are..." Think, Jeff, think. Something clever. "It's like half the world's starving to

237

death, and the other half's too fat to do anything about it!"
Ha! Nice one, Eccleston!

"What's that got to do with getting a job?"

"Well, there wouldn't be all those problems in the third world if we didn't keep buying stuff. Probably. So, it's like, how can I be a part of a system that's destroying the world?" This was easy. If only the Job Centre people were this easy to convince, then I could just stay at home watching 'Shakedown' everyday.

"Aww, Jeffy!" Her voice went all gooey and she gave me a cuddle. "It's so sweet that you care! But all we need is love! A revolution won't bring down the system. We just need to start loving everything, even the stuff we don't agree with. The system is *afraid* of love. It governs by *fear*. So the best way to fight it is to love it! Embrace it. Finding the joy within the soul of capitalism is the only way you can help all the poor and needy in the world!"

"Right. Yeah." Shit. She's going to force me to become a stripper.

Pete: Monday 26th July

After seeing the way my Dad behaved last night, it got me thinking about myself. Obviously, we lead very different lives, but I had to wonder if the demon gene might kick in at any time. Was I in danger of turning into him? I came to the conclusion that if there was any chance whatsoever of this happening, then I'd have to rebel against my DNA. From this day forward, I'd take the high ground. I'd be a mature, sensible adult: considerate, intelligent and emotionally developed. This was the day when everything changed.

Pete: Tuesday 27th July

Pacmaaaaaaaaaaaaaaaaaaaaaaaaaaaaaaan!

Jeff: Tuesday 27th July

What's the point in anything? Life is shit, and then you die. I got round to drinking that Morrisons own brand whiskey and filled out my crisis loan application form. I explained I needed £5000 to fund the construction of a death ray.

Jeff: Wednesday 28th July

OMG! The new DWM has the most adorable picture of the gang from Amy's wedding day on the cover. Rory, you lucky bugger!

Pete: Friday 30th July

I logged on to Facebook and saw that my Mum had added me as a friend. When I accepted, and looked at her page, I realised that she'd had a profile for ages. Surely this was the ultimate generational reversal? I was supposed to be The Computer Doctor, but not only was she more technologically advanced than I was, she had a better social life too. Her photo albums were numerous: attending 1950s style soirées with her friends, sequence dancing classes, a Women's Institute flapper's evening. My Dad wasn't on any of them. So that was how she coped with him... They were never in the same house together.

And then I got a message from her. It'd only been a few minutes since I'd pressed 'accept'. So she could type quicker than me too!

Hello Peter, I thought I'd catch you on here
to talk about your inheritance somewhere your
Dad can't listen in. He's doubled his
medication since the weekend, and keeps
droning on about how you tried to murder him
with margarine (?) Anyway, I see from the
'status updates' page that you're apparently
in love with a man named Andy? What's going
on, dear? Surely you've not decided to sample
the rough and tumble world of homosexuality?
It's not as though I have a problem with...
That sort of thing... But your Dad would go
spare. You know how he gets. When England got
knocked out of the football cup, I only
managed to confiscate his gun after he'd shot
three pigeons.
  By the way, you'll be pleased to hear that
Eloise Cartwright's hip replacement went
swimmingly. She'll be tangoing again in no
time! Keep in touch. Mum XXX

I was immediately struck by two thoughts. 1.) Who
the fuck is Eloise Cartwright? 2.) Why has Andy
broadcasted to the world that we're in a relationship?
This called for direct action. It was time to put phase 2
of the plan into action. I picked up the phone and
dialled for Comedy Dan.

Pete: Saturday 31st July

"Comedy Dan?!" Jeff was aghast, as I spooled through
the adverts on our 'Pic N Mix' video.

"Alright! Keep it down, will you? 'Horror of Fang
Rock's about to start, and we always end up talking
through this one."

"That's because it's *sub-par*." His mouth was full,
but even that barely stifled his comment. He must still
have been in shock about my brilliant plan.

240

"Shhh... Do you *want* Terrance Dicks to hear? Let's just keep quiet and watch the episode, shall we?" Despite my stern tone, I gloated inwardly about the brilliance of my brilliant plan. It was brilliant.

"Alright then." He was quiet just long enough to see the TARDIS materialise on the rocks. "Who else is coming to the meal from hell then?"

"Well, obviously Andy Pond has to be there... Then there's Big Dougie. Oh, and Tracey of course. Now, come on – we said we wouldn't talk."

"Yeah, you're right. I suppose I owe Fang Rock another chance." He was silent for all of 8 seconds. "So remind me again why exactly you want to invite this bunch of losers over... on your birthday? Don't you want to give yourself a fighting chance of getting your 39th year off to a good start? Why don't you just go all out and invite your Dad? Oh, and Eloise Cartwright whilst you're at it?"

"Who *is* this Eloise Cartwright?"

"No idea." He shrugged. "I just made her up."

"No you didn't! My Mum was going on about her yesterday, so either you've developed ESP, or you've been spying on me online." I fixed him with my best accusatory squint, but he barely flinched.

"Yeah, well like you said, maybe we should just keep quiet and watch the episode." A-ha! The words of a guilty man! The Doctor had just met Reuben. They were exchanging some witty dialogue. Although, watching now it didn't seem as witty as I remembered. In fact, it was pretty tedious. This had scared the crap out of me when I was 8! Come on, Pete, must keep quiet. Got to set the precedent.

"Thing is, Jeff..." He jumped. "I'm going to need your help. On my birthday, I mean."

"Uh-uh. I'm not sticking round to share dinner with The Munsters, birthday or not."

241

"Go on... I'll buy you a milk chocolate Magnum?" He seemed to consider it for a moment.

"Well, alright... You've twisted my arm, but just this once. So what's the plan?"

"I'm going to take care of Tracey Grimeford and Andy Pond... Once and for all."

"Take care of them? Shouldn't you hire a contract killer for that kind of thing..." I could see he was trying to think of a suitably witty name to call me. "...Dr. Evil?" 5-out-of-10.

"I'm not going to kill them. I just need to lose them."

"I don't think that's going to be easy. It's not like misplacing a quid down the back of the sofa."

"Ahh, but you haven't heard my brilliant plan in full yet! I've done some pretty thorough research on Tracey's profile, and it's *full* of pictures of her spilling out of PVC dresses, trying to cop off with big biker blokes covered in bad tattoos. And who do we know that fits that description?" I waited. "Exactly! Oh... You didn't answer. Why didn't you answer?"

"Big Dougie." He said wearily. "But isn't he a bit suspect? You know? Writing all those poems about cocks?"

"He's just asserting his masculinity."

"Yeah... But... *Poetry*?"

"He's in touch with his emotions, no matter how violent or warped they may be. And come on: he wears leather jackets and chains; that tattoo he's got's full of grammatical errors; plus he's been a builder, a police man *and* in the army. What could be more manly than that? Tracey'll love him. We won't even need to *try* and force them together. But Andy and Dan might be more difficult, and that's where you come in. Now, I've made this choreographed seating plan..."

"Can I just stop you there? I know Andy Pond's deluded enough to think you're actually interested in going out with him, but don't you think he'll be a bit turned off by Dan's... Problem?"

"Ah, no! That's the beauty of it. If I know my Andy..." I stopped. Had I just said *my* Andy? Jeff didn't seem to have picked up on it. Backtrack. Backtrack. "If I know Andy, he loves a sob story. He's bound to find Dan's stutter charming. I just need you to sit with them, and sort of gently, non-intrusively – and in a completely not obvious way – drop hints about what a wonderful couple they'd make."

"But what if they make me talk about gay things? They might take a shine to *me*. I've been there, Pete. That time Daisy made me go to The Pink Handbag, cause she said I was prudish and homophobic? I don't want to go there again."

"It's fine. I'll be there... Although we can't sit together, obviously." His face fell.

"So you're putting me in unfamiliar territory? Making me handle a potentially dangerous situation? And we're going to be separated? It'll be like Year 10 science class all over again. Boy-girl-boy-girl seating, surging hormones and Bunsen burners didn't go together then. This sure as hell isn't going to now. And you do realise I'm not exactly flush with cash at the moment? I presume I'm paying for this meal?"

"Well, it *is* my birthday. And we talked about this. I'll pay you back when I get my inheritance."

"You've no idea how much that inheritance is worth yet though. I know Julian got a lot of work doing those dodgy underwear shoots, but what if he blew all his cash? You might only get a couple of hundred quid."

"Great! I could pay you back, buy a proper computer, stock up on Series 5 toys, and get a pair of new shoes with the change... Right?" Jeff's face tensed in a way that showed up all the encroaching wrinkles of his future, but he didn't reply. 'Horror of Fang Rock' part 1 was drawing to a close. The ship was heading for

243

the rocks. "Hang on..." A revelation suddenly dawned upon me. "I've never picked up on it before, but I *think* that boat might just be a toy! And that used to look so convincing when I was little..."

"Nooooo! Next you'll be telling me that submarine in 'The Sea Devils' is just 4 inches long." He rolled his eyes. "Look, I don't know about this whole dinner party thing."

"How about I make it *two* milk chocolate Magnums?" The title sequence music started.

"I've got a bad feeling about this..."

Jeff: Sunday 1st August

It's August! We're getting old and we're going to die!

Jeff: Monday 2nd August

Shit! It's Pete's birthday in less than two weeks. When did that one sneak up on me? I need to get some presents, but there's still no sign of any benefits! I rushed into town to at least buy him a Matt Smith themed birthday card, but to my horror the Doctor Who rack had been replaced by Twilight cards. Oh God! It's all over! It's 1985 again. Any day now they'll be releasing "Doctor In Distress 2010"!

I'd allowed myself £20 for the rest of the week, but I spent £15 on a copy of Doctor Who Adventures, a sticker book and a Matt Smith action figure from Thunderbooks. How could I resist? It could be my last chance to buy Doctor Who merchandise for fifteen years!

Jeff: Tuesday 3rd of August.

I realise that I may have over-reacted slightly yesterday. I made some instant noodles and sat down to watch the 'Who Peter – Partners in Time' featurette on 'The Horns of Nimon' DVD when there was a knock at the door. Maybe Tommy Asbo had finally brought those DVDs round! It was the police.

"Jeffrey Greene?"

"Yes?" I stammered.

"I'm arresting you on suspicion of terrorism."

Jeff: Wednesday 4th August

5 am: Just got back from the police station. I was kept in a cell for three hours, waiting to be interrogated, without any idea of what it was I had allegedly done.

Eventually, when I was taken into the interview room, my blood froze as I saw, laid out on the desk, my plans for the "Death Ray 2000", which I had sent to the Job Centre, encased in a clear plastic evidence wallet like you see on TV. I begged them to understand that it was just a joke, but was firmly told that terrorism was no laughing matter.

"I understand your claims for benefits have been repeatedly rejected." Growled the inspector. "That you have been denied several loan applications and..." He peered at the file before him. "...You owe someone called 'Dom' a tenner. But this is no excuse to start threatening deadly violence. We saw in you the potential for a crazed gunman." I didn't know what to say, other than reiterating that it was just a joke. A stupid mistake. It was then that he produced an iPhone and loaded my Facebook page. "May I refer you to your status update on Sunday the 20th of June: 'I can't wait until The Big Bang! Just counting down the days now!' Think very carefully before you answer, Mr. Greene, and

245

remember it is an offence to withhold information. Are you planning a terrorist attack?"

"It's an episode of Doctor Who!" I was in tears by this point.

"A later status update..." He carried on regardless. "Simply reads 'BOOOOOM!!!!' Do you have an obsession with destructive weapons, Mr Greene?"

"I was quoting Sophie Aldred! In 'Battlefield'!"

The conversation carried on in much the same way. I began to think that prison was inevitable until the doors burst open and Constable Fox, the chubby guy with the massive side burns who'd arrested my Dad, marched in. He insisted that I was a hero who had saved the life of an innocent shopper and that the terrorism charges were "A load of Claptrap". I was released immediately with a caution.

4pm: Far too traumatised to look for work. I spent the day lying on the Sofa and watching 'Attack of the Clones'. Whilst I was waiting for my Spar microwavable cheeseburger to cook I wrote this:

Dear Mr Yoda,

We are writing with regard to your claim for incapacity benefit. Unfortunately, this claim has been cancelled and and we must insist you repay the £857.45 you received in benefits.

In your interview, you claimed that you could not walk without the assistance of a stick. I refer you to a light saber duel with Count Dooku dated space-year 5000. During this fight, you quite clearly displayed agility contrary a to person eligible for disability living allowance. You also requested home help in the form of our nurse, Miss Horny Lovebottom, on the basis that you could not reach many of the appliances in your home and needed assistance in the shower. It has come to our attention that you are a fully trained Jedi Knight – a fact which you omitted on the benefits application form under 'qualifications' – and, therefore, are able to move objects without touching them.

In light of this, we request that you also pay £1000 to cover the costs of Miss Lovebottom's services over the past months.

Please call us immediately to organise a repayment scheme. Remember – we're here to help!

Haha! I'm a comedy genius! I'm going to have to post that online.

Jeff: Thursday 5th August

I switched on my laptop this morning, eager to know what the world had made of my hilarious post, only to be confronted with a tirade of abuse! It had 54 comments. I skimmed down the list.

Hannaluvzchezzi91:
I just watched all of Yoda's scenes from Phantom, Clones, Sith, Empire and Jedi to make sure, but I'm fairly certain he doesn't mention being on benefits in any of them. He certainly has a job in the prequel trilogy, as he is head of the Jedi council. I'm guessing they provide food/accommodation but it's not the Jedi way to be materialistic, so he shouldn't need anything else. And when he's living on Dagobah, I don't think there is a government. I think he just eats stuff from the swamp and makes his own furniture. Hope this helps.

Columbo:
Yoda e un carattere da guerre spaziali!

Teh_Geetarist:

YODA FTW!!!!!

manufc4evs:
Leave yoda alone u fukin gay

raith_sienar:

Christ! As if I wasn't busy enough updating all the n00bs on the 'Lost' forum about the basic principals of the infinite universe theory, I log on here and find another moron asking questions which are easily explained when you take the time to think about it!

First of all, there is no such thing as "space-year 5000." 'Attack of the Clones' takes place 22 BBY. Secondly, it is true that Yoda needs his staff to walk with, as he is 900. Because Yoda is a grand Jedi master, he has learned to become one with the living force, and in sequences in which he appears more agile, that is the Midi-chlorians in his body transcending his physical existence. I refer you to his line in 'The Empire Strikes Back': "Luminous beings are we. Not this crude matter (muscle)". May I suggest you read the excellent novella 'Jedi: The Dark War', as this delves into this in more detail and I am way too busy. Please get your facts right before wasting peoples' time in future.

I couldn't deal with it anymore. What a bunch of geeks! Had they no sense of humour? It seemed like "Raith Sienar" was living his life in accordance with the world of fan fiction. Some people need to get out more! I deleted my IMDB profile, turned off the laptop and vowed never to use the internet yet again. Then I got back in bed to finish re-reading 'The Dimension Riders'.

Saturday 7th August

I went for another coffee with Rachel, a little less nervous than last time. Although the perfume still got me.

"James loves Doctor Who!" She said. "He wants a sonic screwdriver for his birthday."

"I've got a-" I began, rather enthusiastically, but then remembered I was supposed to be playing it cool. "...An idea where you could get one of those. Amazon." I nodded.

"Uh-huh." She mumbled. I had the feeling that my information hadn't really helped that much. "He's always asking mad questions. Maybe you'll know this one: why does the TARDIS look like a phone box?"

"Well, it's a chameleon circuit. It can change its form to blend in perfectly with its surroundings!"

"So... That's why Doctor Who looks human?" She looked puzzled.

"What? No..."

"So what does he really look like? Is he a green blob or something?"

"Green blob? No, that's the Daleks!" I shrieked.

"I thought the Daleks were robots?" She asked. I buried my head in my hands.

"The Daleks are *not* robots! They're the mutated remains of the Kaled race in a Mark 3 travel machine of bonded polycarbide armour!" I felt the conversation was slipping away from us.

"So... how many days now? Until the wedding?"

She fixed her eyes on mine. "D'you want a proper drink?"

Pete: Saturday 7ᵗʰ August

Where was Jeff?! He said he was only going for coffee. Coffee! How long could that take to drink? And what was he doing drinking coffee anyway? He was a pint man. Everyone knew that! I sincerely hoped he wasn't trying to pass himself off as a regular, functioning person again? Cause it takes a lot more than just switching your lager for latte to achieve that. It was that Rachel! I'd have to give him a stern talking to when he got in... But I couldn't do that on an empty stomach. I looked in the fridge: one carton of milk which had separated into a cooking oil-like substance; some margarine that had gone black; a tub of 'Athlete's Foot Remedy' (?); Daisy's organic yeast gloop; and an open tin of dry Spam with an even dryer teabag perched on top. Maybe if we had any bread in the freezer, I could use the athlete's foot cream as spread? But we didn't. The freezer was equally devoid of edible content. Which only left the... But no! Surely I couldn't eat the Doctor Who spaghetti shapes. Jeff might come home to find me having a spasm of some kind. I scrutinized the ingredients, however, and saw that they only contained 0.07% anchovy extract. Why did they even bother? Surely that wouldn't kill me...

Unfortunately, the tin was without a ring-pull and I'd never been able to master can openers. But this was the future, so maybe it was one of those tins where the lid gradually peeled itself off the hotter it got. They existed, didn't they? Dom had mentioned it. Yeah, course they did. So I stuck the whole thing in the microwave and turned the dial. 3 minutes. Great! Time to go to the bathroom.

When I returned, 2 minutes later, the microwave looked like it was about to take off into space-time. The inside was rippling with blue sparks – little lightning forks of radioactive electricity – at its epicentre, the Doctor Who spaghetti shapes. I didn't know what to do. Was this a unique feature to compliment the nature of the product? It did seem like an awful lot of trouble for the good people at The Mill to go to, just for a cheap snack-food, complete with smoke and... FLAMES! Shit! I ran to press the eject button, but just then there was a small explosion, and all the power went out.

Thank god for my numerous supply of sonic screwdrivers, which double as great torches! I inspected the damage. The base of the microwave oven had melted. I'd have to hide it from Jeff. If he asked, I'd just say we'd never owned one, and that he'd imagined it. I put the whole thing in a box, and hid it under my bed. It'd be *fine* down there. It couldn't be *that* radioactive...

The power had just overloaded. I threw a trip switch and it was fine. But we didn't seem to have any hot water. What if I had to call a plumber? I'd be required to stand around and banter with them, pretend to be a real man: etiquette demanded it. I'd have to worry about it another time. Jeff had just shambled through the front door, clearly pissed. He moved towards me as though he couldn't bend his knees, steadying himself on the furniture, and then my shoulder.

"Have you met the French?!" His expression was gleeful.

I shot him a stern glare. "What time do you call this?" He seemed to be having some difficulty lifting his hand from my shoulder to check his watch, then remembered that we had a clock in the living room. In fact, we had eleven clocks in the living room: one for each Doctor.

"Ah yes, got a bit waylaid. But it's all going to be fine, 'cause me and Rachel are definitely getting back together."

"WHAT?!"

"Yeah, I know. Great, isn't it?" He threw both arms into the air and started singing "champions!" – football style – until he could no longer stay upright, and collided with the sofa in a roughly sit-down position. I perched on the arm, to one side, listening to Jeff twitter on about how fantastic he was, what a fantastic night he'd had, and how fantastic everything was going to be from here on in. All I could think was 'what about me?'.

"Obviously there'll be certain complications." My ears pricked up.

"Oh yeah. Like the fact that Rachel's getting married?"

"A-ha! But she's not! There's no way she'll go through with it. She wants to start a new life with me, for sure."

"Right... And she did definitely say that, didn't she?"

"Didn't need to." Oh dear.

"Well, what exactly happened then?"

"Ah, you wouldn't believe it! We went for that coffee, and as soon as she walked into the room, she couldn't take her eyes off me. I couldn't blame her, of course. It couldn't have helped that the Jeffmeister here was socking it to her in the charm department." So that was why his tie was loose. He seemed to be under the impression that undoing enough buttons to show a little chest hair in public was 'charming'. "Anyway, I was all like – you gonna go through with this sham wedding then, or do you reckon we should give things another crack?" He emphasized the word 'crack' as though it held huge comedic value. This was accompanied by an obscene mime. "And she was like – Oh Jeff, I want to get pissed with you and relive the glory days of your parents bedroom! To hell with the consequences!"

"She *actually* said that?"

"You bet your ass! So we went to the pub, and she was all over me. Her hand must have touched mine, like, four times or something. And you won't believe this, but when we were about to go, she leaned over, and it was obvious she was going to kiss me." I raised my eyebrows, somewhat sceptical. "She didn't. Made some excuse about reaching over to get her handbag, which was *obviously* a lie."

"Oh right. So her handbag wasn't actually behind you then?"

"Well, no... It was. But that just proves it, doesn't it?"

"Does it?"

"Of course! She deliberately left it in a position where she'd end up in an 'accidental' clinch with me."

"So, let me get this straight. She said she wanted more than coffee..." Jeff slicked back his hair. "So you went for a proper drink; you talked about old times, 'cause that's what old friends who haven't seen each other for a while do; she touched your hand a few times, and was careless enough to leave her handbag out of sight, behind your back. And, because of this, you think she wants to get back with you? Have I missed something?"

"Yes. No." Visible confusion set in. He had the look of a dog chasing his own tail. "Not just because of that. Because she said so."

"But did she actually say words like, or to the effect of, 'Jeff, I want to give things another go'?"

"She didn't need to. It was clearly implied."

"Okay. But what did she actually say?" He didn't answer me. I could see him going through his mental filing cabinet, racking his brains. Then his whole head tilted slowly downwards. I'd burst his optimism bubble... And I only felt a *bit* guilty. After a moment, he staggered up and, with some effort, made his way silently to the kitchen. Shortly afterwards, he called back "Didn't we used to have a microwave?"

Pete: Sunday 8th August

I didn't even bother getting into bed. I knew I wouldn't be able to sleep. My mind was too full of worries, each of them swirling round to form one big incomprehensible mess, but all individually jostling for attention. Okay, so Jeff probably wasn't going to leave me for Rachel... But what if he was? Would I have to enter some kind of unholy alliance with Daisy – like Yates pretending to be part of Global Chemicals – in order to woo him back? We hardly made the most compelling team. But then if he *wasn't* getting back together with Rachel, which seemed more likely, I'd have to deal with him moping around, being all hungover and heartbroken in the morning. Then there was the sinister green glow coming from under my bed. I couldn't take it outside myself, but I couldn't tell Jeff to do something about it either. What if the radiation started to have a detrimental effect on my body, and I got out of bed one morning to find that I'd left a foot – or my arse – behind?

I came to the conclusion that I'd probably have to deal with all this stuff, or I'd never sleep again, and the only issue I had any sort of handle on was our lack of hot water. The internet wasn't working, and the router was in Jeff's room. I didn't want to wake him, so I rifled through the Yellow Pages in search of a plumber. I always find Yellow Pages listings a bit difficult to follow. Search for takeaways and it sends you to all manner of sub-categories, located at confusing extremes of the alphabet, making it difficult to compare adverts. Look for taxi services and you'll invariably end up at 'Escorts – discreet and flexible'. *Flexible?* At some point in my search, I always seem to end up on the same page: it features a cartoon pig, dressed in builders' dungarees, carrying a cement hod on his shoulder, and winking. I think it's supposed to look cute, but it always fills me with nightmarish images, a bit like that picture of the dogs playing poker: squealing swine clamouring over the outside of the house, swinging from scaffolding and pressing their pink bodies against the window. However, when I came across it tonight, I knew I must be close. I found the page for plumbers, then realised it was 3am and there'd be no use whatsoever in trying to phone one. But just as I was about to close the book, an advert caught my eye: 'Maxi Gold 26-Hours-a-Day Plumbing Service. We gonna sort you out!' 26 hours a day? That was even *more* than 24! And the poor command of English in their advert probably meant they were cheap! Almost certainly Polish or something! Brilliant!

If we couldn't speak the same language, I wouldn't have to do man-talk. I picked up the phone and gave them a call.

6am: Was sat reading when there was a knock at the door. I peered through the peep-hole, then edged it open cautiously. These guys didn't look like plumbers. The tall one at the front sported an immaculately clean overcoat, with side-parted hair and a suit that would better fit a game-show host. He wore sunglasses and an enthusiastic grin. The guy behind him was dressed up like he was going to a wedding, complete with silk waistcoat and pink carnation. He carried a briefcase in one hand and a 1980s ghetto blaster in the other. When he saw me, he dropped the case, lifted the stereo above his head and pressed 'play' on the tape deck. It began to play the 'Knight Rider' theme tune.

"Bombastus Fantastico at your service!" The one in the sunglasses boomed confidently, no trace of an East European accent. He stretched out his hand and I saw that he wore black gloves like The Master. "And may I introduce my esteemed assistant, Pierson Forbes!" Portable cassette player still above his head, the assistant nodded. "Mr. Forbes here isn't much of a talker, but he's the best sidekick a man could ask for! Makes up a selection of mix-tapes for while I'm doing my duties; passes me my tools; that kind of thing." Out of all the people I'd ever met, this guy definitely had the loudest voice. And the stereo was now playing 'The A-Team'. What if Jeff got woken up?

"Sorry? Mix-tapes? *Disappearing policemen?*" Was this really happening, or had a I nodded off? "And did you say sidekick?" I inched back into the lounge. They followed me in. "You *have* come about the hot water, haven't you?"

"Ah, Peter, Peter – my good friend. You underrate us!" I didn't remember giving my first name over the phone. "Water isn't the only thing that's hot about me and Mr. Forbes. Did I mention he makes the best cup of tea in all of England?" He clapped his hands, and his 'sidekick' obediently scuttled to the kitchen, appearing only seconds later with a tray of hot tea, in cups and saucers I didn't know we owned, with a side helping of Digestive biscuits that we *definitely* hadn't had in the cupboards earlier in the night. Bombastus checked his watch – I noticed it went up to 13 – and asked to be shown to the boiler. Only when he was inspecting the pressure gage and scratching his head did he look anything remotely like a real plumber. He spun round, a serious expression on his face. So here it came – the tradesman's spiel: 'Who did this last time?' 'It's gonna cost ya.' That old shtick.

I braced myself, and was utterly taken aback when he placed his huge hand on my shoulder and said "I couldn't possibly charge you for this. It will take but a minute to fix, and the job satisfaction I glean from allowing your hungover friend in there to have a hot bath when he wakes up in the morning will be more than enough payment for me." The 'Lord of the Rings' soundtrack started up. How did he know about Jeff??? Pierson abruptly opened his briefcase, its compartments filled with all manner of strange-looking tools, and Bombastus steered me towards the sofa, telling me not to look around as he worked. "It's probably best if you don't know. We might blow your minds."

"Minds? I only have one." But he was gone. There was a blinding flash of light, a cry of "I LOVE plumbing!" and the next thing I knew, they were finishing their tea, packing up their tools and making ready to leave. I wanted to ask them not to go. If they could show up in the middle of the night and sort out this problem so efficiently, why couldn't they sort out my others?

As if he'd read my mind, Bombastus knelt down to me, taking a bite from the last biscuit. "Don't worry about your friend in there. He's not going anywhere. The best thing you can do is have a Full English Breakfast ready for when he gets up. Mr. Forbes has just left the ingredients in your fridge – no charge. They cost us nothing. Let's just say that the people at Marks and Spencers owe Bombastus Fantastico here a few favours. By the way, I'd get that microwave sorted soon if I were you." And with that, he made to go. I felt as though he should have a swishing cape behind him. But just as soon as he'd vanished beyond the door, his head reappeared. "Oh, and delete your internet history."

Jeff: Monday 9th August

A letter about our housing benefit:

Dear Mr Greene,

It has come to our attention that you are not receiving any form of income support. We have determined that the only logical explanation for this is that you are in full time employment, and therefore have cancelled your housing benefit. Please see the attached form to organise a repayment scheme for the £234.94 you have received **ILLEGALY** *so far. Please remember that benefit fraud* **IS ILLEGAL** *and in future you could face a* **FINE** *or even a* **CUSTODIAL SENTENCE.***

Don't be a moron!

Mr. H. O. Nimond.
Master of Finances.

Stapled to the letter was a drawing of a yokel floating in a tank of water, whilst a cowboy sheriff stood beside it, scratching his head. In bubble letters below it read *"Don't be a moron! We're here to help!"*

Jeff: Tuesday 10th August

I've become addicted to daytime TV. I can even predict which advert will come on at any given time. I clicked my fingers and yelled "Disaster Lawyers 4 U", only to find a fat, walrus-like man marching toward the screen.

"Ave you bin injured?" He barked. *"Worried about that Hadron Collider? Are you a victim of the threat of terrorism? Feeling a vague sense of unease? If so, pick up the phone now! Phil McQueen was feeling slightly unusual because there were too many immigrants on his street. With our help,. He sued the local 'Costcutters' for FIFTEEN THOUSAND POUNDS!"*

I reflected upon this... I had a vague sense of unease about that letter from the council. Perhaps I could *sue* the council..?

Jeff: Wednesday 11th August

I opened the post and screeched with joy. By the power of Rassilon! I've been paid! £300 of backdated income support! I could buy Pete the new Cyberman Box Set for his birthday. I was disturbed by a knock at the door. Maybe Tommy Asbo had come to bring those videos round? I was surprised, however, to see our landlord, Lovely Kenny. But I thought he was still supposed to be in prison?

"Whovian?" He asked. I remained still, slightly baffled.

"I'm sorry?"

"Whovian?" He repeated, sounding irritated.

"Well... More of an enthusiast, really. It's not like I know who the script editor for 'Timelash' was!" Eric Saward. "I mean, it's not as though I bought 'Doctor In Distress' or anything!" I faked a laugh. I bought three, I wanted to get it to number one. Lovely Kenny didn't look impressed.

"What the fuck are you talkin' about? I've come to fix your Hoover. Your mate Tinky Winky sent me an email sayin' it were broke." He barged his way in, opened the cupboard next to the bathroom and dragged out the vacuum cleaner. On the bag, in a font that might have looked futuristic in the 80s, I noticed the brand name: *Hoovian Turbo Vacuum Cleaner 2000*. He plugged it in and flicked the 'on' switch. It rumbled pathetically and then cut out all together. Lovely Kenny scratched his greasy, balding head for a second before giving me his professional diagnosis.

"It's broke."

"Well... Yeah. Can you fix it."

"Me? I'm a busy man. It were workin' when I last checked, so it must've been you what broke it. It's coming out of your deposit, you'll have to sort yourself out with a new one. 'Ang on – what's that?" He saw the letter I was holding and snatched it from my hand.

"Benefits? I'm not havin' bloody dole scum under my roof! Your tenancy agreement pacifically states no Benefits!"

"No it doesn't-"

"It does. I've revised it since you last looked. No dole scum."

"But ... Why?"

"Too much bloody paper work! I 'ave enough trouble with Mr. Lock at number 63. His 'ands fell off, you see, and I fill out all 'is housing benefit forms. What's your excuse? Get yourselves proper jobs. You've got a week, or you're out on your arse!"

Jeff: Thursday 12th August

I had a bowl of Ricicles, and then resolved to get a job.
Good old Captain Rik was winking at me from the box like
he was encouraging me. Like he knew I could do it.

I fired up the electro box. No harm in checking the
Doctor Who site for news first. Who knows – they may
have announced details about guest appearances from all
eight surviving Doctors in the Christmas special!

After I'd filled out a BBC questionnaire asking me to rate
the Doctor Who website (I gave it 10/10 for it's recent
inclusion of classic series clips – not like the elitist Rod era),
it was bugging me that I couldn't remember what the
computer was called in The Tomorrow People. A bit of
Googling not only unearthed that it was TIM, but that the
whole series was on Youtube! And the 90s remake! I'll get a
job tomorrow.

Pete: Friday 13th August

**For once, I was actually looking forward to the
postman's arrival. I rarely received mail, and, when I
did, it was usually bad news. But this being my
birthday, I was eagerly anticipating a few cards and
letters. I got four, although only one of them was really
relevant. Of the other three, one was addressed to 'Mr.
P Roth', and so went straight in the bin; one bore the
name 'Peter Harrison', presumably intended for our
weird neighbour, who it seemed – disconcertingly –
was also named Peter; and one – postmarked from
Switzerland, dated nearly a month ago – was a cheque
from Uncle Julian, complete with a letter suggesting I
use the money to visit him in Zurich. Well, there was
no way that was going to happen now. I immediately
recognised my mother's neat handwriting on the
remaining envelope. Enclosed was a £25 'Edinburgh**

Woollen Mill' voucher. One to add to the stockpile from my last nine birthdays, I suppose. Prior to that, I always used to get HMV vouchers. I didn't have the heart to confess that I'd never even been to Edinburgh; whereas an HMV gift voucher would come in much more useful, allowing me to buy essential materials, like Steve Hackett's new album or that Jon Pertwee box set. (We have all the DVDs individually, of course, but were cruelly robbed of our chance to own the special packaging.)

None of that mattered really though. Any other presents would only have fallen under the mighty shadow of Jeff's: a Matt Smith action figure!!! I applauded. I cheered. I wept. I assured him it was *way* better than the one Dom had got me, which was obviously just Action Man with a crudely made Hessian jacket, and red woolly bow tie. Epic fail! Despite this, Jeff remained worried that he hadn't bought me enough stuff. He'd even gone scrounging round at Daisy's for a last 50 pence. Apparently, she'd lectured him on the evils of capitalism; suggested he buy me something useful, like stationary or organic bean mix; and then made him sit through an excruciatingly detailed description of her new iPhone. He'd bought a Matt Smith action figure, AND endured an hour of Daisy's sanctimonious crap... Just for me! Yet he still felt guilty. I could measure this level of guilt on the amount of rubbish he'd bought – or, rather, stolen – from the pound shop, as birthday extras: '20 Powertron Extreme-o Batteries'; a giant plastic frog; a gaudy picture of a lumberjack holding a singing fish; some multi-coloured women's tights; a bumper-pack of 'family' colouring pencils; a CD by 'Madness Tribute Band'; and a beer mug in the shape of a golf-bag, complete with plastic golfer handle and the slogan 'tee off to a bright future!'.

When Big Dougie showed up, he said that he had the lumberjack picture on his wall too, before proceeding to stick the Madness CD on and asking why I had a pair of 'Ken' dolls. I switched to masculinity mode and joked that it was just good having a few more blokes round the house to watch the footie with, punching his arm.

Dougie said "I know what you mean. You're on my level, lad." Then, squeezing my shoulder, added cryptically "After all, there's nowt wrong with it, is there?" Nowt wrong with what? I laughed, doing my best to sound deep and booming, and was spared any further awkwardness by Tracey's arrival. I was slightly taken aback as she stepped from the shadows. It had only been a few months since I'd last seen her. She'd been slightly chubby then, but now it looked as though she'd eaten an elephant! Of course – the rip-cord effect! Thank god Dougie was wearing a Meat Loaf shirt. He obviously liked big women. I just hoped he wasn't put off by her awful, two-tone hair: straw-coloured roots running almost to the edge of her scalp, where it suddenly shifted to her usual jet-black dye. It had the disquieting effect of making her appear bald on top, with a bad comb-over. She *looked* a bit like Meat Loaf actually. Why did I keep thinking of Meat Loaf? Of course – God was obviously tossing me a conversational olive branch, and I'd been ignoring all the signs.

"Dougie here used to be in a Meat Loaf tribute band..." I ventured.

"Yeah..." He snorted. "Malt Loaf. Thing is, the big man 'imself got the name 'cause 'e was a fookin' vegetarian. So we got us a veggie name cause we all loves our steaks. Although..." He laughed. "That ain't the only meat I like to sink me teeth into." A tattooed arm jabbed into my ribs. "Eh? Eh?" He winked. "*You* know what I mean, don't you?" No. What *did* he mean??

"You were in a band?" Tracey steered him towards the table, where an array of buffet food was laid out. "I LOVE men in bands." Thank god – they were talking. This would be easy. Deep breath. Deep breath. Okay. So why was I feeling so stressed? Something was bothering me. Something I needed to go and talk to Jeff about. But what was it? Maybe if I could just sit down for a moment... But it wasn't to be.

"Happy B-B-Birthday, P-Pete!" Fuck. Comedy Dan was here. I wasn't ready for him yet. He was supposed to arrive last, so I could cleverly engineer a conversation between him and Andy. At least he'd bought me a present. Although it wasn't wrapped... Or particularly good: 'The Series 1 Villain Figurine set: All your favourites, including The Moxx of Balhoon, The Editor, and The Ann-Droid!' It still had the price tag on: a clearance sticker with 'Reduced – 99p' written on the front.

"Thanks." I tried to sound as sincere as possible. "I'll just go and stick them on my bed." And I made my way over to Jeff's room, entering without even knocking.

"Do you mind?" He looked aggravated. "I was trying to work on my novel." I looked at his laptop and saw that he'd managed to write three lines.

"Wow. The novel?" I feigned interest. When he didn't elaborate any further, I moved onto the more important matters at stake. "Jeff... What do you make of Dougie?"

"Dougie... Erm, which one?"

"We only know one. *Big* Dougie."

"Oh right... It's just that you always called him Big Dougie, so I sort of presumed there must be a small Dougie out there somewhere too?"

263

"That's preposterous! But... I don't know quite how to word it... Do you think there's something a bit... Peculiar... Queer... Do you think there's something queer about him?"

"Well, he's a bit odd yeah. But I wouldn't worry about him not liking Tracey. I'm sure she's exactly his type. And it's not as though he's gay or anything. He was in *the army*, remember?"

"Oh yeah." I breathed a sigh of relief, instantly reassured. "I should have thought of that. Now, are you coming out? We're all here, pretty much. We need to get this nightmare buffet rockin 'n' rollin'."

He cringed, accompanying me back to the living room. "Just promise you won't *ever* say that again." I nodded solemnly. "Eh up, looks like we've got more company..." Andy Pond was leaning against the door frame, his arms folded impatiently. As soon as he saw me, he ran over, flung his arms tightly around my waist, and, without explanation, burst into tears again. Why? Why? Why was he always doing this?

"What's *he* doing here again?" He eyed Jeff scornfully. Oh yeah- I'd totally forgotten about that. But I couldn't have him forcing Jeff out onto the streets again. I needed him tonight. It was time to tell the truth. My elegantly planned web of lies was about to come tumbling down like a house of cards, and only Comedy Dan would be able to pick up Andy Pond's pieces. In many ways, it was perfect... Although I'd probably have to endure yet another nonsensical, teary monologue. Could I really be arsed? On my birthday? Or would I end up taking the easy way out, yet again?

"Andy, meet my brother, Gareth. Now, I know what you're thinking. Yes: Gareth does bear a *striking* resemblance to my last couple of lovers, and that probably seems a bit weird. The truth is, I don't really have an explanation. I'm just a very perverse individual. My good friend, Dan, on the other hand..."

264

"You don't have to explain." Andy interrupted, his voice sickly sweet. "I once spent an entire summer lusting after my cousin." Why was he always so fucking understanding? "Gareth, tell me what it was like growing up under the same roof as an angel?" Jeff looked terrified. Teeth gritted, I mouthed for him to play along and went to fetch Comedy Dan.

I found him sat at the table, his chair pulled up closely to Big Dougie. They were talking about football. At least, I think that's what they were going on about. Something to do with "hollering out to the players". Tracey was sat on the other side of the table, her arms folded. In front of her was a row of empty glasses. The free booze! I'd only turned my back for a few minutes. She'd drunk at least two-thirds of it. And the majority of my birthday cake was gone. So this was how she'd turned into a house. As soon as she saw me, she started to drone on about her new dress. I said that it was "certainly something", hoping to make a quick getaway, but this just seemed to encourage her.

"I know. It's dead sexy and everything, and I think the Chinese symbols really represent me. They show all my different aspects: strength, beauty, power and fertility. I'm a very fertile woman. It's my second favourite thing to wear." She winked, and paused as though waiting for me to ask what her favourite was. I didn't, but she carried on regardless. "The best's my birthday suit. Maybe I'll give you a sneak preview later." She did a twirl, with all the grace of a ballerina in orthopaedic shoes. And then it was there again. That monstrous tongue. She looked like River Song smugly enjoying her latest double entendre, but it was worse. Much, much worse. Her leg was already snaking towards mine, and *that* troubling thought had reared its head again. I think it had been triggered by the sight of Comedy Dan running his hands over the scar on Big Dougie's bald head. Dan only appeared partway down his first glass of white wine. He couldn't excuse himself with drunkenness. Why wasn't Dougie stopping him? This wasn't right. But I assured myself – Dougie couldn't be gay: he'd been in the army.

My worst fears were confirmed half an hour later, when I walked through to the kitchen and found Dougie and Dan in each others' arms, pushed against the worktop and sharing a passionate kiss.

"Jeff!" I called, my mouth agape. "I've just remembered what it was that was bothering me about Big Dougie. He wasn't in the army. He was in the *navy*." The assorted company let out a collective gasp. Everyone turned to the door, as though Poirot would walk in at any moment. But he didn't. Well, it was time for a cliffhanger anyway.

Pete: Saturday 14th August

Tracey seemed to be the last one left. She kept dragging her heels and throwing her (not inconsiderable) weight around. Eventually, I offered to call her a taxi, but she said she didn't have any money.

"I spent the last of it buying you a birthday present..." She said defiantly, before looking down guiltily. "But then ate it."

"Oh. It was chocolate then?"

"No. A book."

At length, I coerced her out of the door, peering through the letterbox as she reluctantly tottered into a cab. I didn't have any money either, but, as luck would have it, the Scottish driver had just had his 'Pringle' jumper nicked by a hen party and was happy to accept my 'Edinburgh Woollen Mill' voucher.

It was dark when I fell gratefully into bed. I breathed a sigh of relief, relishing the suddenly unfamiliar feeling of being alone (at last!) only to feel an arm slide across my naked torso.

"Ahhhh!" I screamed, leaping to the light switch. Andy Pond lay in my bed, leaning suggestively against my pillow and dressed in nothing but a pair of those awful comic-strip boxer shorts.

"Come back to bed. It's time for your birthday present." He said softly.

"B-But. I'm not... Exactly... And quite tired... Ready." I stuttered. "This is all too much!"

"Oh. It's okay, honey." His facial expression hardly mirrored these words. He looked crestfallen. "I understand." Phew. I'd dodged a bullet there. Except that he didn't get up to leave. I was too tired to argue anymore and fell back into bed fully clothed, trying to force my eyes shut as Andy wriggled closer to me. I began to get the feeling that my one little lie had gone too far, and there was no way I could dig myself safely out now. And so I began my thirty-ninth year in much the same way I'd begun many of the previous ones: embarrassed, uncomfortable, mortified.

Jeff: Sunday 15th August

I was washing up, and as I was putting away the cutlery I realised that I had begun to re-arrange the whole draining board so that each item had its own section. Knives only in the right hand compartment and so on... Christ! I'm turning into Pete! I haven't left the house in days!

Jeff: Monday 16th August

Something's troubling me. I've been thinking about teleportation. Surely it works by taking apart the atoms in your body and reassembling them elsewhere? I can only imagine two methods of doing this. The first is that, in their dispersed state, all the atoms (or molecules, or whatever) are actually transported through space to the new destination. Surely this is quite risky? If just one of them got lost or damaged, then presumably they wouldn't be able to piece you back together again at the other end? Also, if they can find a way to send all of the atoms in your body somewhere simultaneously, then why can't they just send *all* of you in one go?

The second, and far more likely, possibility is that the teleport you leave from takes a kind of genetic scan, beams (emails?) that to the destination teleport and then you are reassembled from the encrypted data. But this creates a fundamental problem – would the teleported you still be you? If it was made from new matter, would it not just be a clone with your memories and genetic make up? And what happens to the atoms that are dispersed in the first place? Are they destroyed? Are you essentially killed and then cloned every time you teleport? And what happens if you keep doing it. Like copying old VHS tapes – the quality gets worse every time. Then, when you're watching a copy of a copy of a copy, you can't see what you're looking at anymore. You can't tell the Cybermen from the people and you end up cheering when Tom Baker gets shot. (Sorry, just thinking of my old 'Revenge of the Cybermen' bootleg there.) Does this mean we'll all be walking around in the future with only one eye and no arms from too much teleportation?

Or... If the atoms are going to simply be recreated, then what's the point in destroying the initial batch? Then there'd be two of you! That way, you could teleport yourself for certain tasks... Like examining soil on alien planets, or paying the gas bill, and then just kill the 'clone' when it's done? Surely it wouldn't mind, knowing that it would still exist out there somewhere anyway? Or would that violate some kind of human rights law? Would the race of teleport clones have to be listed as a new species? Then it'd be like euthanasia – even if your teleport clone wanted to be killed, it would be illegal.

Perhaps we could find some use for all the surplus clones... like terraforming another planet! Who knows... Hundreds of years down the line we could end up having wars with them... Clone Wars!

Jeff: Tuesday 17th August

I awoke feeling positive and energetic. I was going to work on my novel! I shot straight to my desk, fired up the laptop and flexed my fingers. The bed was unmade behind me, but it was still within my line of vision and irritating me. I couldn't be productive with all this clutter around. An untidy desk is an untidy mind!

After I'd made the bed, I was still faced with the problem that the rest of the room was an absolute tip. I couldn't possibly sort through it all, as then I'd have no time for writing! I had a cup of tea, watched a bit of 'The Invasion' and then went straight back to work. I shoved all the clutter into a bin bag (unfortunately this included some clothes and a full ash tray. I'll sort them out later.) It wasn't enough. The carpet had too many bits of fluff on it. I decided to re-locate to the kitchen, as Pete had evidently undertaken one of his frenzied cleaning routines in the small hours.

I was ready! A tidy desk, a tidy mind... All I needed was another cup of tea. And some toast. I was starving. After watching some more of 'The Invasion', I sat down and stared at the blank document. I'd been working on my novel since university. 'The West Bank' – an epic World War II story, recounting the life and times of Captain Dan

Vankerman and his struggle to keep his platoon alive, driving them towards the safety of The West Bank.

Unfortunately, I was yet to write a single word. They say that beginning with Chapter One is a bad idea anyway. Apparently you should just jump in elsewhere and just go with the flow. Okay...

The brown rain lashed at their faces. The sky was a dead colour and it was impossible to tell where it's brutality ended and the grass began. Jenkins was stumbling, still wounded by the attack. The poor soul was delirious, he was calling for Biggins. Biggins had been dead since the 44th squadron fell.

At the helm, Captain Dan Vankerman stood. Steel. They'd been through hell, that much was certain. But if it cost him all his limbs, he would get them to the west bank...

I felt suitably accomplished, so I decided to watch 'The War Games'.

Jeff: Wednesday 18th August

I'm starting to worry that 'The West Bank' doesn't actually have a plot. I mean, Vankerman sounds like a German name. Can my protagonist really be a Nazi? Or is it a coincidence? Perhaps he's a rebel, bringing down the Nazis from within? But then, his team have very British sounding names... I'll put it back on the shelf for now. It definitely has mileage, but I think I should concentrate on 'The Vaporiser'.

Jeff: Friday 20th August

I'm actually going to do it this time. I'm going to break up with Daisy.

Pete: Saturday 21st August

It was sometime in the middle of the night – I couldn't tell when exactly, because the batteries were dying on my digital alarm clock and all the symbols looked Russian – but there were raised voices coming from next door. Jeff and Daisy were having an argument, and I could tell it was getting heated because Daisy's voice seemed to get an octave louder each time she shouted, until she sounded like a whining cat. I don't know how Jeff coped with it. Even the thick Victorian walls of our flats, which had been used as inside-out bomb shelters for inverse-vertigo sufferers during the war, were ineffective. Each angry feline yowl made my head throb a little more, my bed covers sneaking up inch by inch until only a tuft of hair peeped out. It was like when I was little, paranoid about somebody breaking in to steal my home-made Tracey Island. I was convinced the blankets were garish enough to render me totally invisible... Only now I was bigger, and my feet were poking out.

Abruptly, the voices ceased. I heard my door open, then slam shut, and I knew I was no longer alone. I tensed as Daisy's lean body slid under the covers, her bony arms wrapping round my chest and sealing me in a surprisingly tense grip. Fuck. She was naked... Pretty much. Every part of me went stiff and rigid, apart from the bit that was supposed to. By the time she began her teary, largely indecipherable monologue – the words "insensitive bastard", "doesn't understand my needs" and something to do with "a canal barge and an iron leg" were all I could make out – I felt pretty much paralysed. It was as though a horse was stood on my chest, like in that Shakespeare painting. I couldn't even speak, and Daisy refused to relinquish her strangulating grip. (Was this what Jeff had to put up with every night?)

She continued sniffling and whimpering throughout the night, and I knew there was little chance of me getting back to sleep. On balance, I think I preferred having Andy Pond in bed with me. At least he'd had the good grace just to snore.

And why did the whole world suddenly want to jump into bed with me? It'd left me alone for the first 38 years of my life. Why bother me now? Why not when I was 17?

I must have nodded off eventually, at least for a little while, because I was convinced the night had concluded with a vicious tussle against a crazed Ice Warrior, foaming frenziedly at the mouth. They never did that in the programme. What was wrong with me?

I awoke with a gasp, as Daisy released her hold on me to get up. The bed felt unfamiliarly warm, and I was surprised to find myself feeling sad – strangely alone – now that she'd gone. I could trace the outline of her body along the sheets as the now vacant patch, where she'd lay sobbing all night, slowly cooled. The blankets settled into their usual groove, looking as though they'd never been slept in. 'Oh.' I thought. 'So this is what's been missing'.

Daisy returned moments later, placed a cup of tea at my bedside and whispered that she was "sorry". Suddenly my room – where every spare inch of space was stacked with CDs, videos, DVDs, magazines and toys – felt very empty, that single word bouncing off every blank space long after Daisy had gone. 39 years of *this*. The tea was getting cold.

Jeff: Thursday 26th August

I was wandering aimlessly back from the Job Centre when I had a text from Pete, warning me that Andy Pond had turned up unexpectedly and that I was to make myself scarce. But I didn't have anywhere to go! It wasn't like the old days when you could just go to the pub: Pints cost about a tenner now. I'd been delaying this for sometime, but I'd always known it was inevitable. The time had come to return to the nuthutch!

"It's so nice for you to come round here for a change!" Cooed Daisy as she prepared some kind of pink tea. She lived in a huge shared house full of what she called "artists", although this just seemed to be a term for crusties who'd been on the dole since the 80s. The only evidence of any 'art' was all the doodles on the walls in the hall. Something to do with freedom of expression. The words 'I am the carrot of mystery!' were scrawled onto the fridge noticeboard beneath a picture of a tulip in a bowler hat.

"Let's go and sit down." Daisy handed me a mug and I made my way to what I had remembered to be the living room. "No, wait! Someone's moved in there!" Daisy called, too late, as I opened the door. Other than one flickering candle on the mantelpiece, the room was in complete darkness. There was a man with long black hair stood in the centre, naked save a black cowboy hat and a pair of knee high pink socks. In one hand he held a glass of wine and in the other a polystyrene skull.

"Oh, hello!" He said, as I hastily pulled the door shut.

"What the hell?" I whispered.

"Sorry, that's Neville. He moved in last week."

"But... He was... Holding a skull. And naked!"

"He's in a goth band!" She laughed dismissively as we walked through to the back room. "And he's writing a thesis on time travel."

"Why would you let somebody like that into your house?"

"Because he's kooky!"

I drank my peculiar tea as Daisy grilled me about finding a job. "It's about time we put down a deposit on a house Jeffy!" She didn't see the fact that I'd found a vacancy for a stripper particularly constructive, and said she'd put a word in for me with Nancy at Yoga King. I told her she really didn't have to.

Neville came in wearing some kind of black shawl and started showing me Polaroids of his arse, explaining that it was some of the most visceral work he'd ever produced. When Daisy said she was going to feed "Miss Puss Puss Kitty-Kins" I assumed she meant she was going to open a tin of 'Iams', and not spend half an hour steaming tofu and vegetables, which she then drizzled with olive oil and served on a dinner plate. All this time I was left with Neville the goth, who was mumbling about "the transcendency of the human condition" and taking Polaroids of the cobwebs on the ceiling.

This is exactly the kind of house that Daisy wants me to live in! I can't deal with all this existentialism and bizarre food. I just want to be normal! I just want to eat fish custard and try out the new Doctor Who role playing game! I had to be assertive and tell her it was over. I marched into the kitchen.

"Daisy." I looked her right in the eyes. "We can't carry on like this. It's obviously not working."

"I know. I've been thinking the same thing." She sighed. "It's like we're living in different worlds."

"Yes! Right! Exactly!"

"So I think we should move in together as soon as possible! I just don't see enough of you at the moment!" She wrapped her arms around me.

Shit. That hadn't really gone to plan. What had happened to my resolve? I'd been full of resolve! Now I was back to being meek and cowardly as she nestled her head into my shoulder.

"Right then guys..." Neville appeared in the doorway, wearing fishnet tights and a cheer leader outfit with 666 emblazoned across the chest. "I'm off to work."

Pete: Thursday 26th August

Jeff came back and said he needed to "talk about the Daisy situation". Inwardly, I breathed a sigh of relief. Obviously, I'd seen this coming. He'd broken up with her for sure, or at least he was about to. Yeah, that was it. I was about to assure him that it was probably for the best when he caught me off-guard, saying "So it looks as though I'm going to have to move in with her sooner or later." What the hell? Where had this come from? It made no sense. Surely if they ended up living together, then every day would end up like the other night: arguments, torment and hair-tearing punctuated by silent, numb hours of TV watching and increasingly stale bedroom fumblings? Then the inevitable baby would have to come before Daisy got too old and her libido slunk off into anonymous obscurity. After the whole Rachel thing, this was just too much. Why was he always trying to leave me for girls? I hadn't *ever* forced him to make housework schedules or impregnate me. Well, I suppose that was only partially true, but it didn't count. Besides, the last time he lived with a woman – the dreaded Emma - he ended up going mental and smashing up his bookshelf with that axe.

And as if I didn't have enough stress with the microwave thing. I keep trying to turn a blind eye, but it's becoming difficult to ignore the fact that the radioactive glow emanating from underneath my bed is growing in intensity. Jeff's starting to get suspicious. Tonight, he asked what the hell "that creepy green neon thing" was coming through the crack in my door every time I tried to slide discreetly through. I lied and said it was the timer display on my VCR. "Wow. When did it get so powerful? And how do you sleep?"

I suppose I'm going to have to deal with it sooner or later. I can't help thinking that all this stress is going to have a detrimental effect on me. It's a good job I'm so strong-willed – it's not like I'm going to start tripping, having wild hallucinatory fantasies or anything like that!

QUANTUM PETE

After years of watching too much television, and vaguely wondering about travelling within his own timeline, drunken 'Computer Doctor' Pete Ross stepped into the radioactive fallout from his frazzled microwave, only to realise that it had inexplicably transformed into a Quantum Leap accelerator. He abruptly vanished, awakening mystified, to find that he'd time travelled all the way next door, into his flatmate's bedroom. Facing a mirror image that is not his own but that of his best friend, he embarks on what turns out to be a relatively minor quest. His only guide is Dom, a waste of space from his own time who Pete bafflingly continues to hang around with, and who appears in the form of a hologram that only Pete can see and hear. And so, driven by an unknown force – coupled with the desire to make his own life slightly more bearable – Pete sets out to change Jeff's future, hoping that the next leap will be the leap home...

"Oh boy..." Pete sat bolt upright, squinting into the mirror to see the features of Jeff Greene staring bemusedly back at him. "Oh boy..." He said again, thinking that it would probably make a good catchphrase. He was instantly aware that his temporary body seemed to be in slightly better shape than the one he was used to. He tugged at a tuft of unfamiliarly swish hair, marvelled at the feeling of wearing something approximating a set of pyjamas and recoiled when he found himself instinctively reaching for that camp silk bathrobe Daisy had bought. 'Daisy... Of course...' He thought. 'Maybe that's why I'm here!'

Scrambling around for his solar powered science calculator, Ziggy, which had looked rather futuristic in the late 80s but now appeared somewhat clunky, he keyed in a seemingly random sequence of numbers. A bright white rift opened, sliding into existence through a Star Trek-esque electronic door. 'Why would I have Star Trek in my own fantasy when there hasn't been a single Doctor Who reference yet?' Mused Pete. His question was answered seconds later as Dom appeared, wearing a white suit, silver PVC shirt and hideously clashing orange polka-dot tie.

"Oh." Pete let out a sigh of disappointment. "So you're my Al, hell bent on spoiling *my* fantasy by littering it with Star Trek references? Couldn't I have had..." He racked his brains. "...One of my other friends?"

"Heeeyyyy! Easy on the mustard!" Dom quipped irrelevantly, in a weird hybrid accent somewhere between New Orleans and Northern England. "This is no fantasy, Doc."

"Doc?"

"Damn straight. You've been misplaced in time and Gooshie reckons it's up to you to knock some sense into this Daisy chick."

"What? You mean like... Beat her up?"

"Trust you to play the moral boy scout, Doc!" Dom laughed.

"What?! It's like you're not even listening to me. And why the hell do you keep calling me 'Doc'?" He shouted exasperatedly.

"Okay, okay... But just promise you won't go smashing up any Buicks this time!" He folded his arms theatrically as this last comment was met with invisible raucous laughter.

"Is that a laugh track? Quantum Leap *never* had canned laughter. This doesn't make any sense!"

"Precisely! So if you can go round as Jeff and talk some sense in front of Daisy, the whole thing'll be smoothed out in no time. Capiche?"

"Sorry... Are you even hearing a single word I'm saying? You're the one that's supposed to be the hologram. Or am I talking to thin air?"

"Eeeehhhh!" He sounded like a low-budget Fonz. "You want the neighbours throwing you in the nut house? No? Then keep it zipped! Remember, you're the only one that can see me. Now, Jeffy boy keeps all his old letters from Daisy under that stack of pizza boxes. You'll find her address there. Go round... Give her the old Doc Ross charm and make a quick getaway... Speaking of which, I think it's time for me scoot. Pete's gonna wake up any minute."

"But *I'm* Pete!"

"Not today buddy! If you don't get a shift on, you're in for a shock..."

He was right. The last thing Pete wanted was to risk having a conversation with himself. There was too much scope for disaster. But it was too late. There was a sudden banging of cupboard doors, a hasty scrambling of feet and another Pete barged in, looking befuddled. "Jeff, have you seen the ketchup? I want some Frosties, but... We're out of milk..." Wow. This was going to get weird.

It was only when Pete was parking up outside Daisy's a short while later that it occurred to him he couldn't drive. And he hated cars! Everyone knew they were death traps whose only real purpose was to keep the average population down by 0.003% a year. Compared to his sudden blasé attitude with regard to this frightening statistic, the numerous inconsistencies about his hair styling itself into a Scott Bakula side-parting, his car not having passed a single other vehicle, and the fact that he was driving the Bat-Mobile, all seemed immaterial.

Before crossing the street, he took a long, hard look in the wing-mirror to remind himself that he was in

Jeff's body now. Dom had needed to keep reiterating that all the time travel he'd probably been doing would have 'Swiss-cheesed' his brain. That probably explained why he'd spent most of the morning forgetting who he was, and what exactly his mission was. For some reason, every time he tried to do something active or productive, he always found himself back on the sofa, watching kids' TV. It was like he was stuck in a goldfish bowl and time was in a loop. Surely this wasn't how he normally spent his days? He couldn't quite remember. Wasn't he the dynamic and go-getting one? The Roger Moore to Jeff's George Lazenby?

Daisy answered the door and immediately threw her arms around him. Not this again! "Oooh, Jeffy!" She looked close to tears. "I've been going out of my mind twying to phone you all night! It feels like ages and ages since I last saw you."

"But wasn't it, like, 12 hours ago?"

"Exactly!" She twitched her head and flapped her hands about in a cutesy fashion that actually made her look kind of mad. Pete obviously hadn't inherited any of Jeff's emotions because he felt nothing at all towards her, other than a profound sense of impending boredom. Unless this was how Jeff felt *every time* he saw her? When he stepped into the house, he found that any external sounds and voices – which is to say anything happening outside his own head – just turned into a big mush of woolly, indistinct noise. The 'primal scream inner voice workshop' going on in the living room probably didn't help. He knew he was going to have to get on with things quickly and tried desperately to find something optimistic, profound and Sam Beckett-esque to say – 'Just follow the dream?' 'Trust in your heart and it'll get you there?' Daisy probably appreciated that sort of Hallmark Cards bullshit. But it wasn't that appropriate. His mind was still caught up in a mental fog, which only lifted when Daisy started going on about "Something special I've done for you with puss-puss!" Good God... Was this it? Was he about to be accepted into the inner sanctum of woman? As Daisy stood, slipping a thumb beneath her waistband, Pete thought about how Sam Beckett would have a good natured refusal at hand, laughing an advance off and saying 'No thanks, ma'am'. A melancholy look would cross his face, he'd bite his lip, gaze down at his blue collar and whisper 'I'm spoken for'. But surely Pete could rewrite the rules a little, to do good *and* be immoral? Like Bill Clinton. Daisy returned promptly, however, still fully dressed and carrying a prissy looking white cat in her arms. Oh. 'Fair enough – time to get on with business.' He supposed.

"Daisy, I think we need to..."

"Say hello to kitty!" Daisy spoke in a stomach-churning voice.

"But I think there are..."

"Kitty's got a special pink bow in her hair and she's weally pleased to see Jeffy-Weffy. So..." Her voice became more stern. "Say hello." It was an instruction.

"Look, there's something we need to talk about..."

Daisy responded by shaking a furry paw into a waving gesture. It was a close-call between who's hair was going to get torn out first: Jeff's, or the cats. When he didn't say anything for a while, Daisy shot him an admonishing glare.

Pete's resolve was wearing thin. "Hello... Kitty." His voice was heavy with regret.

"Yeeeaaahhhhh! Say it in kitty language!" Daisy clapped the disturbed looking cat's paws together. "Say 'meooooowww!'" She made the noise. Oh, for Christ's sake. Pete had been determined to be sensitive and caring about this, but his patience was stretched to

281

breaking point. He was just going to have to come out with it.

"Daisy, there's not a cat in hell's chance..." Pete knew he could never have thought of pun that good in real life. This was surely a dream? And he was as cool as Kojak! "... No way... That we're moving in together!" She raised her arms in alarm, immediately dropping the cat, which fell squealing to the floor and was instantly forgotten. She practically tripped over it, in fact, as she rushed to smoother Jeff's helpless body in tearful kisses. Pete couldn't get his head round this reaction. Hadn't he just been really horrible and cold to her? Did women like that kind of thing? Dom appeared once more from the white void.

"Heeeyyyy. Easy on the hot sauce there! You gotta get outta here, Doc." But Pete was reluctant to shift. "She's about to unleash her secret weapon. Any minute now, she's gonna drag you to bed and have her wicked way with you." Dom's voice was panicked. "You gotta see things from where I'm standing..."

"Great... Send me a postcard!" That misplaced laugh-track again.

"I'm serious, Pete. You've done what you came here to do. Now we gotta scoot!"

"Then why haven't I leaped yet? Maybe I'm supposed to do this..."

"Gooshie says you got one more job to do."

"Back off, I've got a job on my hands right here. A little room might help!"

"Can it! I'm supposed to be the cocky one. We're not doing that thing where we switch roles again. That was a series 3 exclusive! Now, listen up – you gotta do something about that microwave oven or this whole town's gonna blow!"

Everyone gasped. A title card flashed up, accompanied by a few choice bars of theme music. A string of

cheaply produced commercials advertised debt
repayment schemes and gadgets that no one
particularly needed, and a slick American voice came
out of nowhere to announce that '*We now return to
Quantum Pete*'.

Pete found himself dashing through the corridors
towards his and Jeff's flat, the thrum of radioactive
energy growing louder and more deadly by the second.
Any minute now, the whole building could destabilise!
Running up the staircase, three at a time, he crashed
through the living room door, which swung from its
hinges, and flung himself into the second bedroom
where an inanimate Pete lay inert on the bed covers,
one pale arm draped lifelessly over the edge. He'd
attempted to push the microwave out of range, but the
radiation had got to him. His eyes blinked a few times,
and in a pained voice he whispered "Guess I got to
play the hero after all..."

"Better get moving! We can save him later!" Dom
urged him on. "...If we're not too late! Ziggy says you
gotta stick the microwave in the corner cupboard."

"What? With that broken Hoover and all the other
junk that's too dangerous to use. That's *it*? That'll save
us??!"

"You got it." Fearing little for his own personal
safety, he seized the deadly kitchen item with both
hands. Any normal man would have disintegrated there
and then, but he managed to leap heroically over the
sofa, locking the microwave safely in the cupboard just
in the nick of time. There was a small explosion,
everything went quiet and some reassuring ambient
music started playing.

"You done it, Doc! Let's just hope no one asks too
many questions about this dubious bit of plot!"

"But won't this just kill us, only – you know – a bit
more slowly?"

"Nah. The walls are lined with lead." He produced a cigar, and assumed his 'inappropriately casual' pose. "Didn't you know they used to use this place as a bomb shelter for inverse-vertigo sufferers during the war?"

"Seriously? I thought that was something Pete made up. Hang on... Aren't *I* Pete?"

"See you later, Doc." Winking, Dom chucked the butt of his cigar into mid-air, as though aiming for a dartboard; the white lines appeared around Jeff's glowing outline and Pete leaped back once more into his own body.

Pete: Friday 27th August (10am)

For some reason, I woke up with Mike Post's end credits theme to 'Quantum Leap' in my head, which continued playing as I lolloped sleepily through to the kitchen. I'd been out of it for ages, but I still felt worn out. And to make matters worse, we were out of milk. I hastily scrambled through to Jeff's room and barged in. "Jeff, have you seen the ketchup? I want some Frosties, but... We're out of milk..." Hang on. Why did this feel weirdly familiar? I mean, if I'd been here before, but I was there now, then that meant... Oh boy!

Pete: Sunday 29th August

Mum came round to drop some post off, including 'The Last Will and Testament of Mr. Julian Shirley'. So Julian's last name was Shirley? That explained a lot. I tried very hard to read over it and find out exactly what I was getting, but it didn't seem to make any sense. It was like a foreign language, or a Dickens novel.

Thankfully, there was a plain English solicitor's letter attached, which I scanned with some dismay. They needed me to go and speak to them in person. This was absolutely the worst thing that could happen. If I went outside, people would laugh at me. I'd fall to pieces. I might die! Was a potentially hefty sum of cash really worth putting my personal safety at risk? But there was some important stuff at stake and I didn't think lawyers were in the habit of making house calls. Plus, Jeff kept going on about how our financial woes were becoming woefully substantial. What if we owed a really large sum of money, like £70? Our ill-standing in society would surely force us to go on the game!

If only there was someone brilliant and persuasive enough to go along on my behalf and convince the lawyers to hand the money over without me having to put in a personal appearance... Someone I could trust one-hundred-and-ten percent... Someone that would prevent me from burdening Jeff with another highly demanding responsibility... A master of disguise perhaps, who could assume the alter-ego form of the usually shy and retiring Pete Ross? In short, if only there was someone who could waltz in at this unsociable hour and sort out all my problems.

Then I realised that there was, and felt foolish when I saw that the answer had been in front of my eyes – or at least on my coffee table – all along. The Yellow Pages was still open on the plumbing section, the sacred phone number circled in red. I began to dial, but then realised I'd better fabricate an emergency...

Jeff: Sunday 29th August

I have created a masterpiece!

DOCTOR WHO SAVES CHRISTMAS

SCENE 1

INT NIGHT: LITTLE GIRLS HOUSE

It is Christmas Eve. Twinkly and fuzzy Christmasy music by Murray Gold plays. A little girl wakes up and looks out of the window. It is snowing.

She hears a noise.

She creeps halfway downstairs and peers through the bars. SANTA is piling presents beneath the Christmas Tree.

She gives a loud gasp.

SANTA turns around... IT IS THE DOCTOR!!!

> THE DOCTOR:
> (Grinning)
> 'Ello!... Merry Christmas!

The credits roll.

> THE DOCTOR:
> (Hands the girl a prezzie)
> 'Ere you go! An early one! But now it's straight to bed and no peeking 'till the morning.

The TARDIS is in the far corner of the living room. The door creaks open, and AMY POND walks out dressed in a 'Saucy Miss Santa' outfit.

AMY:
Come on Doctor! We've got four hundred bags of presents left.

THE DOCTOR:
Oh! Only four hundred? That's good!

We hear Rory's voice from inside the TARDIS.

RORY:
Not when the bags are dimensionally transcendental! There are thousands of gifts in here!

He emerges dressed as an elf with pointy ears, a hat, shorts and pointy shoes.

RORY:
And my legs are getting cold!

Everyone laughs! Rory looks annoyed at first, but then joins in. They get in the TARDIS, AMY turns to the little girl.

AMY:
Merry Christmas!

AMY turns to the camera and breaks the forth wall

AMY:
(In a sexy voice)
And that goes for all you lot too!

She blows a kiss.

THE DOCTOR'S head pops out.

THE DOCTOR:
Merry Crimbo!

When I finished typing I was breathless. Not only was this possibly the best Christmas episode of Doctor Who, but possibly the best episode ever!

I had to send it to the BBC immediately! I didn't even want paying! This had to get out there. I went on the BBC homepage. I couldn't find a submissions page, so I cut and pasted the script into one of their comments boxes, with the subject 'Please Forward to Head of Drama'.

I went go make a cup of tea and saw Pete beating seven shades of shit out of our boiler. WTF?

the doctor and jo stepped out of the
tardis where there were some soliders
on a strange planet. "hello said the
doctor where are we? But then one of
the men was KILLED. "Look out!" said jo
it was the DALEKS! They took them
prisoner to the dalek base where they
had to wait to be exterminated. "Dont
worry said the doctor I have a plan!
They had a radio and when the dalek
came in to give them food the doctor
used the sonic screwdriver to make the
radio give out a signal that made all
the daleks explode.

By jeff greeneaged 7

Blair Gets a Taste of His Own Medicine, as Protesters Hurl Shoes & Eggs, Just Like He *Dropped Bombs!*

Skirmishes broke out at the first public signing for Tony Blair's memoirs, when protesters hurled shoes, eggs, bus tickets, tea bags, acorns and a small plastic dinosaur at the former Prime Minister.

Two men, identified only at this stage as 'Lumpy' and 'Mudd', and a woman were arrested and charged with public order offences for their part in the protest. The three, who enjoyed a polygamous relationship during the crusty protest heyday of the early nineties, were released from custody and will appear before Dublin District Court on various dates later this month.

Police had earlier dragged a number of protesters off the street, and during a fracas a male protester in a wheelchair was knocked to the ground. However, it was later revealed that said male, Dave Ross, 67, was not in fact a protester, but merely a holiday maker who had tragically lost the use of his legs in a "near fatal golfing accident".

"I were only gonna tell him he should have wiped all those Pakis out whilst he had the chance!" Commented Mr. Ross. "Then all these bloody hippies came from nowhere! He never should have banned hunting – it made him look soft! No one would protest about war if good old Maggie were back!"

Protesters shouted "Tony Smells!", and other hurtful comments, as they taunted the security staff while Blair remained inside the bookshop. They also sang "Power to the people, 'cause the people got the power" and wiggled their bottoms in a manner described as "bloody 'orrible" by Mr. Ross.

About 400 people were queueing up around the side of the store to meet Blair. They were verbally abused by a number of demonstrators who denounced them as "Just plain daft".

One protester, Faery Dust McKenzie, from Belfast, criticized both the police and the hundreds who had turned out for the book signing: "They are protecting a British terrorist and the people queueing up over there should be ashamed of themselves. Anyone buying the books is a jackeen, a ne'er-do-well, a cad and a traitor".

"Yeah. It's just, like, well wrong." Agreed 'Lumpy'.

Activist Daisy Padbury, from Blackpool, England, attempted to make a citizen's arrest during the signing before Blair's security team dragged her away. "I went up to him and I said 'Mr. Blair, I'm here to make a citizen's arrest for the war crimes that you've committed'," said Miss Padbury, 35, of the group Peace, Awareness, Responsibility and Solidarity for Ongoing Liberation of Feminists (PARASOLF). "And then I sung that Muse song 'Pay! You must pay! You must pay for your crimes against the Earth!'"

The gentleman called 'Mudd' had this to say: "It really is shameful that somebody can be responsible for the death and destruction that he was responsible for in Iraq and Afghanistan and walk away without any accounting for that and become a very wealthy man off the back of it".

Plain-clothes detectives were also deployed as part of the security operation. However, upon discovering that one gentleman in the queue was "a fellow Jethro Tull fan", Detective Inspector Sam Bishop said he "Forgot all about that protest business. We were too busy talking about Little Milton!"

After the signing, Blair was whisked from a side entrance of the store at about 12.40pm for a "hot sweet tea and probably a biscuit or two".

In his memoirs, My Struggle, *Blair defends his decision to go to war with Iraq in 2003. One fan queueing for an autograph supported this decision. Patricia Krauss, 74, commented that Mr. Blair "could not make decisions based on those that shout most. The fact that the youth of today are prepared to take to the streets and criticize the government – who are, let us not forget, the representation of God on Earth – simply goes to show the level of apathy in the younger generations. I blame all these violent videogames. Pacman is the very mask of terrorism."*

12/09/10

Dear Mr Greene,

Thank you for the complaint you registered with CLAIMS! CLAIMS! CLAIMS! We're here FOR YOU! All we need is a no-win-no-fee-not-guaranteed deposit of £2000 and a handling fee of a further £1000 to proceed. This may seem like a steep investment, but just think of all the £POUNDS £POUNDS £POUNDS that will be rolling into your account once we've handled your claim.

Not sure? Read the following success stories!

"My bosses at the crèche were discriminating against me because I have a hook for a hand. Thanks to CLAIMS! CLAIMS! CLAIMS! they're now out of business and I have a vast selection of stainless steel hooks."

"I walked into a bollard once and hurt my balls because I was texting at the time. CLAIMS! CLAIMS! CLAIMS! were unable to sue Vodafone, so they sued my mate Dave, who I was texting at the time. Thank you CLAIMS! CLAIMS! CLAIMS!"

Please send us your bank details to proceed with the claim.

Regards, Mr. Magister

Mr Greene,   12.09.10

How dare you clutter my inbox with this
drivel? I'm a busy woman.

Who are you anyway? I Googled your name,
only to find a French stunt man. As an
unpublished, unsolicited nobody you have
no business using a valuable tool (the BBC
comments box) to abuse it's staff by
suggesting you can do their jobs better.

Quite frankly, I'm baffled as to why you
took it upon yourself to suggest a script
for the Doctor Who Christmas special. Not
only is it our biggest television event of
the year (and therefore only relevant to
experienced, renowned writers), but it has
already *been* written. It has also been
filmed, cut, scored and scheduled for DVD
release.

What were you thinking? I suggest you go
back to cleaning hospital toilets, sewage
maintenance, or whatever dismal profession
you undertake that could drive you to such
desperation as to ask *me* to put *you* in the
same league as this country's lead
writers.

Do not email me again.

Winona Mathews (BBC)

P.S - If you are, in fact, the French
stunt man Jeffoise Greene, I apologise.
Have your agent contact me and we'll
arrange lunch.

Subject: Overpayment

Fylde Borough Council 23rd September 10:43

Dear Mr Greene,

I am writing in regard to the £234.94 you received in **ILLEGAL** benefits. It has come to our attention that you have filed a complaint against us with CLAIMS! CLAIMS! CLAIMS!

The company are disreputable at best, and we also know that their handling fees are a minimum of £3000. The fact that you are willing to spend £3000 rather than settling a rather paltry bill of £234.94 not only suggests you have lied to us about your savings and investments, but that you are a thoroughly troubled and bitter individual.

We demand that the debt be settled immediately, and have also taken the liberty of arranging for you to see a counsellor. Please see attached slip for details.

Regards,
Michael Kilgarif

Overpayments Controller

NEWS IN BRIEF

HOW *BLAIR* YOU?!

Following protests against the Iraq war at a book signing in Dublin by former Prime Minister Tony Blair, a court hearing took place in the city this morning. Of the three arrested protesters, two were sentenced to forty two hours community service, a good wash, and "a long, hard think about what they'd done". The third, 35 year old Daisy Padbury, was absent from the hearing and served with a custodial sentence, the facility to be determined at a separate trial. In an amendment to our previous article, we would like to make the following correction: the title of Mr. Blair's book is actually 'A Journey'.

PANTO BREAKS GENEVA CONVENTION!

Outrage! Occurred in the sleepy English village of Scumby-On-The-Dork, when local players, The Scumby Mummers (or 'Scummers', as they are affectionately known by the Parish Council), were tear-gassed by a crack squad of paramilitary troops.

Rehearsals were under way for this year's Christmas Panto – the humorously titled "Scumby-and-the-Beanstork", when an anonymous tip off alerted the authorities to their somewhat 'less than Christian' behaviour.

Colonel Benton Yates was first on the scene. "I've seen it all." He explained. "Iraq. Afghanistan. 'Nam. I even fought in the Somme in a past life, and I've never seen anything like this."

Full story on page 34.

Pete: Friday 15th October

Wow! What a month! Good thing all that money trouble got sorted. Not without some considerable heroism, a spectacularly cunning plot and the last minute intervention of an unlikely electronics wizard, of course. I'm amazed that whole 'time-shift bomb scare' incident never made it into the papers. I suppose it would have been too complicated and unbelievable to write about. It's just a shame it wasn't entirely without casualty...

Jeff: Friday 15th October

I ran upstairs, the Eleventh Doctor's theme tune pounding in my head, and burst triumphantly through the doors. Pete looked up from his Build-a-TARDIS kit and gave me a bemused look.

"This is it! At last!"

"What?"

"Remember when I went to the Sophie Aldred signing at 'Planet Who'-"

"You swore never to speak of September again!" He gasped like a schoolgirl.

"That bit doesn't count." I said dismissively, before feeling a pronounced pang of guilt. "Anyway, remember I got talking to that guy, Oliver, about 'Mission To The Unknown' for about five hours and he said he'd let me know if they had any jobs going?" I gestured crazily.

"You've got a job at 'Planet Who'?!"

"Yes!"

"Waaaahheeeyyyyy!!!" Pete leapt to his feet, knocking bits of the control room all over the floor. "That's amazing. That's... amazingly amazing!" He looked in awe. "Just think... All the little kids coming to *you* for their Matt Smith action figures!"

"I know!!!" I squealed. "For the first time in my life – a job I'm qualified for!"

"You'll be like Mad Frankie! But less... Astral. You remember? The guy from the sci-fi shop in Preston we used to go to. Ahh, I miss that place..."

"Well, actually, it's-"

"... Poor old Frankie's probably dead by now."

"No, he's-"

"But you'll be cooler!" His mouth opened as the fabulous realisation dawned on him. "You could go to work dressed as the Doctor!"

"I KNOW!"

He caught his breath. "Come on, let's watch 'The Five Doctors' to celebrate!"

"I can't." I checked my watch. "I'm going for a drink with Rachel." I accompanied this with a little dance. Why not? Two triumphs in one day.

"Oh." He said solemnly.

"What?"

"It's just... I mean..."

"Spit it out man!" I did my best Lethbridge-Stewart impression to lighten the mood.

"Jeff, what do you hope to achieve from all this? You don't really want to be *friends* with her, do you? I know you love her, and I know you love spending time with her, but she's getting married. One day the bubble's gonna burst. All I'm saying is... In the long run, aren't you just torturing yourself?" A silence descended. Pete rubbed my arm with a little Adipose teddy to cheer me up.

"Well... No! She might not get married, because she's not entirely happy! Ha! Yeah, and then who'll be there to pick up the pieces? The Jeffmeister!" I did my dance again.

"We've been through this before. What has she *actually* said? Does she actually have doubts about marriage? Or is she just angry because he sometimes leaves the toilet seat up?"

"Yeah, why do they care about that?"

"Another question for another time. What has she *actually* said?"

"Well..." I racked my brain. It was hard to think of anything other than dancing in a quarry with Rachel and some Movellans.

"Yeah?" He motioned for me to continue.

"That..."

"Go on."

"He... Is... Unresponsive to her needs." I nodded triumphantly.

"That's not even a thing. I'm pretty sure one of you just read that in Take a Break magazine."

"How do you know what's in Take a Break?" I snorted. Pete cringed and drew a letter S in the air with his finger. Of course. *Simone*.

"The point is – I don't wanna be the bad guy – but you're going to get yourself hurt."

I started ignoring him at this point. I skipped to the kitchen to get a beer from the fridge and began singing. "I cross the void beyond the mind! The empty space that circles time!"

"Jeff, are you okay? You haven't gone mad or anything have you?" Pete called nervously. I ran back into the living room, still singing. "I see where others stumble blind! To seek a truth they never find!" I leapt onto the sofa."I am... The Doctor!"

I sank down into the cushions and sipped my Budweiser. "Ahh, I had that song on 7" as a kid." I reminisced. "Would I ever have guessed that one day I'd be part of the Whoniverse..."

"You work in a shop." Pete interjected flatly.

"... Women throwing themselves at me!" I sighed at my own brilliance and took another sip of beer.

"Unlimited rice pudding?" Pete scowled.

"Exactly!" I raised my bottle.

"That was *not* a compliment!"

299

My phone beeped. I checked the message. It was Rachel, probably just texting to say how much she was looking forward to seeing me! *'Sorry, my sister can't look after James, so we'll have to make it another time x'.* "Oh."

"Trouble in paradise?" Pete raised an eyebrow.

"I can't believe she's marrying Brutus!" I wailed, and shoved a cushion into my face.

"Well, I did say- Hang on. Brutus? He's called *Brutus*?"

"Of course he is. What did you think he was called?"

"You've always called him Captain Bastard..."

"Well he *is* Captain Bastard." I scowled.

"Sometimes you call him Captain Perfect."

"I do not!"

"I'm sure you were being ironic."

"Brutus Gornall!" I spat. The beer was going to my head. "My arch nemesis! Scourge of the cosmos! He's an unimaginative, no good... Plodder!"

"And a jackanapes to boot!" Grinned Pete. It was the first sensible thing he'd said all day. "Now, how about 'The Five Doctors'?" He held up the Adipose to make it look like it was waving at me.

"Yeah."

"And I'll make us cup o' beans with a sausage for dipping!"

Jeff: Saturday 16th October

A message from Rachel on Facebook!

Hi Jeff,

Sorry about yesterday. Ingrid has had to go back to Spain, so I've got nobody to look after James at the moment. Why don't you come round for a brew? Rach x

It was really bizarre to think that, even after all these years, she didn't live with her parents on Primrose Avenue. I knew she now lived on Weymouth Road, but I didn't actually know where that was. I went straight onto Google Maps to get directions, but before long I was lost in a sea of lines. Then something disastrous happened. I had meant to hit the zoom out button once, but accidentally zoomed out completely! One second I had been in the comforting streets and alleyways of the town I'd lived in all my life, and the next I was staring at a nameless mass of continents surrounded by ocean. I couldn't even see Britain anymore, yet a tiny, insignificant speck was still labelled 'A: St. Annes Avenue'. It may as well have said 'You are here'. And it was the most terrifying thing I'd seen in my life.

I hastily began zooming in, but that just made it worse. As Britain came into view, so did Turkey and Iraq and Iceland. All these places that you hear about on the news and consider to be completely *other*. To be in an entirely different world from Morrisons, Mr Kebab's and Omar's... And here it was, inescapably still labelled 'A: St. Anne's Avenue', but not just between the airport and the zoo – between Poland and Quebec! I was part of the world whether I liked it or not. Every inch of this map was crawling with people... And most of them had never heard of Doctor Who, or eaten a Pot Noodle. I suddenly felt like everything was futile, like I had no place in the world.

I reached shakily for a cigarette and zoomed in on Primrose Avenue to calm myself down. Think of Christmas 1984. The green tissue wrapping paper. 'Do They Know It's Christmas?' on the radio. Nicola Bryant posters and all that fumbling on Rachel's parents' bed. The combination of nostalgia and nicotine seemed to do the trick. I was in the zero room!

I decided it was time I got round to watching the new K9 spin off series, despite its dreadful review on the Clive Banks website. I only managed to watch the first 10 minutes

301

before crying uncontrollably, when K9 exploded after confronting the Jixen. Seeing his shattered, smouldering casing was just too much. Don't they understand that K9 has been my best friend since I was 6 years old? It was one thing having him rebuilt in 'School Reunion', but knowing that he was going to be redesigned was too much. Too symbolic. Thank God it's unlicensed and therefore definitely not cannon: the *real* K9 is here to stay. Regardless of the heartbreak, I thought John Leeson's performance was superb.

Although, now I think about it, it would be possible for both K9s to exist, as the K9 in the spin off series is supposed to be the K9 that was left in E-Space... Don't think about it Jeff: it's not Canon. It's not canon!

Jeff: Sunday 17th October

After much deliberation, I went round to Rachel's yesterday. I didn't like the idea of James being there. It would be like I was sharing her. Brutus was at work of course.

She made us some tea and we walked through to the living room, where I was amazed to see that James was watching K9! The new K9 was flying around and being futuristic. I allowed myself to like it, just so long as we keep the proper one too. I also found myself liking James. So much so that it brought tears to my eyes. He was sat in front of the TV surrounded by toys. In his right hand he held a little model K9. He was flying him around, making "whoosh" noises and crashing him into a Slitheen, who seemed to be gurgling "Hahahaha!" The whole time he'd been ignoring me. I imagine I'd have done the same if there was a strange man in my living room. But when Rachel went to make another drink, I ventured a conversation.

"I used to like K9 when I was little." I said.

James was quiet for a while before turning round and asking me, "Where did K9 come from?"

302

"Well!" I smiled. "He was created by Professor Marius in the 49th century on a space hospital. But he gave him to The Doctor as a present because he wasn't allowed to take him back to Earth."

By the time Rachel came back, we had engaged in a full-on battle. I was holding a couple of Daleks and shouting "EX-TER-MIN-ATE!" whilst K9 was zapping them with his laser. She is now labouring under the false impression that I am good with kids. I'm terrible with kids – I just love playing with Doctor Who toys!

We all went for a walk in Stanley Park. James was running through the fallen leaves with a straw and making whirring sounds.

"What's that?" I asked.

"It's my sonic screwdriver." He said, very matter-of-factly, as he sonic-ed the branch of a tree. If I'd thought about what I was going to do, I may have decided against it. But as it was, it just happened and it was right. I reached into the folds of my jacket.

"Why don't you try this?" I suggested.

"A real one!" He exclaimed, delighted, as I handed him my 'End Of Time' sonic screwdriver. "It makes the noise and everything!" He ran around reversing neutron polarity left right and centre.

It was one of the most heart warming experiences of my life, and had influenced a pretty major decision. I was seeing to it as Pete walked in.

"Whoa! How come you're throwing away your toy- I mean, your authentic collectors' memorabilia?" He cried.

"Because you're right, Pete. They *are* toys. And toys shouldn't just sit around gathering dust. I shouldn't have a shelf full of Target novelisations that I'm never going to read again because I have the DVDs. Limited edition posters shouldn't be kept in oxygen proof plastic wallets, they should be blu-tacked to walls and loved and admired until they fall to bits. There are people out there who need this stuff. I'm not throwing them away. I'm giving them to James."

Pete: Monday 18th October

"Okay, I'll go through it with you again... Although I don't know what was so complicated you could have missed it the first one-hundred times!" I sighed impatiently.

"Sorry." Jeff took a drag. "You know I have to start every day with a cigarette before my brain starts working properly." I cocked my head to one side quizzically.

"Right. Well, that solicitors' letter came through this morning, and my money's gone into the bank. Obviously, it's written in Welsh or Silurian or something, so I still don't know how much exactly, but I was hoping you'd be able to go and draw out the lot?"

"All of it? Seriously? Are you really sure it's going to be safer under your bed? All grown ups have bank accounts now. What if you need one to buy more Clangers DVDs off Amazon?"

"Get with the times, Jeff." I'd never said *that* before. "Rumour has it there's a big recession on the way – a credit *crunch*, if you will. If this copy of The Daily Mail is to be believed, Northern Rock's due to crash any day now, and others will follow like toppling dominoes." I waved the newspaper in his face.

"Pete, have you looked at the date above that headline? It's from September 2007! And journalists are full of bollocks!"

"That's slander, Jeff. Journalists are the gatekeepers of truth – everyone knows that – second in their sincerity only to politicians and police. Are you really suggesting that if this country was run by liars, we'd be the great nation we are today?" I didn't get chance to finish, because a drunken argument had just started up in the street: something about a guy not being able to get benefits for his sick dog. "Anyway, it's as simple as this: I need you to withdraw as much money as possible, placing it in this white sack for ease of storage. And then, after you've been to the bank, and you're sure everything's fine, I want you to get rid of *this* incriminating white sack of papers for me by dumping them into the sea. Now, in order to prevent you getting confused between these two *seemingly* identical white sacks, I've devised a system to distinguish them, which I'm sure you'll agree is foolproof. I was originally intending to mark the money bag with a pound symbol, but I thought that might look a little conspicuous, so I've printed on the American dollar sign instead: $. Whereas, the rubbish bag is clearly identified by the letter 'S' – for sea – with a line running through the middle, in order to indicate that it's rubbish: $."

"I'm sorry..." Jeff stubbed out his cigarette. "Have you completely lost it? You want me to stroll into the bank with a dollar sack in each hand? Why don't I wear a balaclava, stripy jumper and holster, creeping round on tiptoes whilst I'm at it?"

"Oh, I wouldn't do that if I were you. You might look a bit suspect."

Pete: Tuesday 19th October

For the first time in ages, I felt great! I was Jackson Lake, reunited with his son. I was waving to the crowds at the end of 'A New Hope'. I was Christopher Eccleston, waltzing round, beaming and saying 'Just this once, everyone lives!'. I paid Jeff what I owed him – for rent, pot noodles and emotional support – before counting out the rest of my money, which, for some reason, was all in fivers. And it was only 2 months until Christmas! So money really can buy you happiness. We opened a bottle of expensive champagne called 'Lambrusco' to celebrate and I updated my Facebook and Twitter statuses to tell the world of my windfall. It was all going so well...

But then, a few hours later, there was a buzz at the intercom, a vaguely familiar voice asking to be let in. I went down to open the main door, slightly surprised at how wintry it was starting to look outside, and absolutely startled by the sight of the figure before me. She was wearing a fashionable coat over a grey polo-neck jumper, her strangely plain-looking face set grim as she inhaled a last drag of tobacco. Her hair – now presumably its natural colour – was a thin, unexcitingly mousy shade. And she'd put on several stone in the years since I'd last seen her. I gasped, trying to get my head round the strange mixture of excitement and horror which confronted me all at once.

"I bought you a present... To say sorry... I guess." She said, without much emotion.

"It's, erm, a KitKat?" I felt a lump come to my throat.

"KitKat *chunky*." She looked aggravated, kicking the doorstep. "It's cold out 'ere, you know."

"Right. Yes. Of course. I suppose you'd better come in, Simone."

Jeff: Tuesday 19th October

I'd just been checking my messages on Facebook, and was about to sign off when I noticed something in the corner of the page. *'People you might know: Kevin Slater'*. Kevin had a Facebook? I clicked on his picture. Although, it wasn't a picture of him. It was a picture of 'Stone Cold Steve Austin'.

His bio read: '*Im Kevin slater and I love WWF my favourite is the undertaker (realname Mark William Callaway) Undertaker won at smackdown. Suck it! Respect due since day one! He was undefeated at wrestlemania 18-0 too. I also love Princess Di who I do drawings off.*'

Under his interests he had listed 'fishing' and 'wind surfing'. I'm pretty sure he's never done either of those things. I added him as a friend, but had a message from him a few minutes later.

```
I havent added u yet cos I dont now if
there r any cydermen pictures on ur page
can u delete them if there r thanks a lot
kevin
```

What a tragic existence!

Jeff: Wednesday 20th October

The Doctor Who role playing game has arrived!!

Pete: Wednesday 20th October

"WHAT?!" Jeff didn't seem too happy. He slammed a mug onto the draining board, dislodging its handle, which shattered into chips, flew across the room, and ricocheted – rather impressively, I must say – against the fridge.

"I just said the bin was getting a bit full! Don't you think you're getting the whole thing a little out of perspective?"

"Sorry. I didn't mean to fly... Off... The... Handle." **He laughed awkwardly, the double-meaning of his sentence evidently dawning on him. "I'm just struggling to get my head round this whole Simone thing."**

307

"You and me both..."

"You're not actually thinking of giving things another go, are you?"

"I really don't know... To tell you the truth, I can't even work out if I like her anymore. I mean, she's never been that *nice*. I can see that, with hindsight. It's like... I definitely remember being completely infatuated with her... But now I'm not that sure *why*. I think I used to think she was beautiful, or something, I think. But was that really all? And if so, why am I still thinking about her so much? I mean, she's totally let herself go. And I was looking into her eyes last night, trying to work out what it was I used to feel attracted to, and there was nothing. Absolutely nothing. I just felt... Cold. It's like there's no warmth about her."

Jeff turned from the draining board, fixed me with a perplexed stare, and said "A simple 'yes' or 'no' would have done."

I continued regardless. "...Then there's the pregnancy thing..."

"She's *pregnant*?" Jeff interjected. "Oh, you want to steer well clear, Pete. Women only have kids for one reason – to trap men. Do you *want* to end up in prison?"

"I don't want to end up in prison." I whimpered. It was one of my worst fears. "But what about you and James?"

"That's totally different. James is practically a grown up. Did you know he can recite the whole Who theme on his 'Learn 'n' Play Keyboard'?" I seethed inwardly. He'd never given *me* such a good review when I'd learnt it for his birthday. And *I'd* programmed the Imperial Death March on Cubase '90 too. "So who's the father?"

"Rik." I spat contemptuously.

"Which Rik?"

"There's only one Rik."

"Noooo..." He seated himself at the table, and reached for a lighter. "There's Goth Rik, who – as we've established – went out with Simone, and then there's Captain Rik."

"Who?" I scratched my temples.

"You know..." He muttered, increasingly quietly. "The little spaceman dude off the Ricicles box."

"Riiiggghht... And you're honestly telling me you think there's a chance that Captain Rik – who, may I remind you, is a fictional children's breakfast mascot – could actually be the father of Simone's baby?"

"It could happen." He shook the lighter exasperatedly. "He *has* got special powers."

"Well, I suppose there is that." I conceded. "But I don't think he's her type. Hey! That's one thing we've got in common. Ricicles just taste like an inferior version of Sugar Puffs to me."

"They do not!" He slid his chair back confrontationally. "They're *completely* different!"

I shrugged. "I think we may have gone a bit off-topic."

"Oh yeah... So... And maybe I'm missing the point here... But... Remind me again why you're even considering getting back with this cold, unattractive, fundamentally unlikeable, pregnant heffalump of a woman?"

"Unfinished business? I don't know. The more I think about it, the more senseless it seems. But when she's around, it's like she has this strange power over me."

"You can't use that excuse again, Pete. You say that about all women."

"No I don't!"

"Course you do. You used to say it all the time about..." He trailed off guiltily.

"Yeah, but there's something else with Simone. We *definitely* had some good times together. Remember

309

Bridlington '06? I've never really been able to relax around other women. I think that whole thing with Kelly screwed things up for good. I just clam up, talk about barometers... You know? But me and Simone can actually have a conversation. It's like we have this weird connection. So even if we don't actually like each other, that's got to be worth something, hasn't it? And maybe I confused that for love, and maybe that made me do some silly stuff, and maybe she exploited that... But it's the only sort of relationship I've ever known. And that means it's kind of special, no matter how awful it might have been..."

"Well, exactly. That's the whole point, isn't it? You've let a few bad experiences get in the way and now you're resigned to failure, so you're prepared to settle for it. But you've got a lot going for you, Pete. You can... Well, you're... And..."

"See." I shook my head. "You can't think of anything."

"No. Just give me a minute. You're... A-HA... You're nice... And, erm, reliable. Women LOVE reliability. Plus, that thing you do with the washing up? Major pulling power, mate!" He punched me jovially on the shoulder. We both recoiled slightly, me rubbing at my arm and him massaging his knuckles in pain. I felt deflated. If only I'd have taken Dad's advice to 'man up' when I was younger. Obviously, joining a gym or anything of the sort was out of the question now. "You could do so much better, Pete."

"Could I really though? Because I'm nearly 40, and I can't help thinking that maybe... This is it. What if this is all there's ever going to be and she's actually the one? Is it really so unbelievable that, in a quiet moment, she suddenly finds an old photograph and starts to reflect about that nice, not-totally-unattractive man she once had a thing with? That she'd come running back to the Petemeister?"

310

"Be honest... Is that what she said or have you romanticised it just a little bit?" I didn't answer. "Don't you think the money might just have a *little bit* to do with it? Oh, and don't start calling yourself 'the Petemeister'! That's my thing!"

"Can't it be my thing too? Like when we used to wear the same outfits on own clothes day. That was okay, wasn't it?"

"NO! The whole school called us gay. Even the teachers! And when we went away together, all those beardy pensioners seemed to think we were brothers... I mean, why? Did putting on the same shirt instantly forge a blood relation in their day?"

"But it gave us unity... And uniformity... Like..."

"Like a fucking boy band!"

"Alright, calm down!"

"Sorry. This bloody lighter won't work, and you know I get a bit tetchy when I haven't had a fag for a bit." I bit my lip, and was about to ask the obvious question, when the phone rang.

Jeff: Thursday 21st October

The role playing game has been banished to a cupboard beneath the sink. We didn't play in the end as we ended up arguing over who got to be The Doctor. Dom was furious. He said in all his years of being a Games Master he'd never seen such childish behaviour.

I gave Tommy Asbo a call to see when he'd be coming round with those videos, but he was out.

Jeff went to bed, but I knew that if I did the same, my mind would be swirling with Simone. I needed a distraction. So I decided to seize the moment, and begin my new script idea... Right after a little time running round the house, pretending to be Sherlock Holmes. I became a master of deductions. I deduced that the cold tap on our bath needed fixing; that from the crumbs on the sofa, we'd obviously been eating toast; and that the tower of FHMs on the coffee table meant there was no chance whatsoever of Daisy coming round at any point in the immediate future. (But we weren't supposed to talk about that.) Look out Professor Challenger – here comes Pete Ross!

I was surprised – when Jeff re-emerged – to see that it was morning, and I'd lost a whole night. "Ah, Watson!" I clapped my hands. "Be a good chap and ask Mrs. Hudson to fetch us some milk, will you? I've concocted a theorem on The Most Erroneous Case of Doctor Horace Horsefall and I believe it could be just the serum we need to throw a little light on this most dark business!" He squinted, slumping a little to the side and sauntered off without replying. I heard the toilet flushing and, shortly, he was back in bed. I decided I'd probably better do the same. But, as I got under the covers, shafts of daylight were filtering through the curtains, and something began to trouble me. Was it Captain Ric, with a 'C'? Or Captain Rik, with a 'K'? I had to know, or else I'd never sleep again.

I ran a search and found that Kellogg's actually had a remarkably informative Wikipedia page. A little light reading wouldn't do me any harm. It broadened the horizons, expanded the mind. And there was a bit about Banana Bubbles – I'd completely forgotten about them! Ah, 1995! Innocent times. I opened the entry for the year '1995' in a new tab, but got distracted when I saw there was a whole list dedicated to withdrawn cereals! I'd start the script and get some sleep as soon as I'd read it.

But what was that a few entries down the list? C3PO's cereal... How come I'd never come across *that* before? It had been launched in 1984, at the height of 'Star Wars' mania... Or at least a good year after it. Had it ever made it beyond America? Surely I'd have known about it if it had arrived at British shores. My lack of memory on the whole thing was *really* troubling me. Still, that brilliant script idea wasn't going to write itself.

After 20 minutes tossing and turning, I flung the covers off and went straight back to the computer. A Google search unearthed over 25,000 pages about C3PO's Cereal, including a Youtube link for an American commercial. I scratched my head when I saw it. It just looked like a superfluously doubled-up version of 'Cheerios', and they already had a sterling imitator, in the form of Kellogg's 'Honey Loops' range – possibly superior, if just for their amusing cartoon bumble bee logo. Not only that, I still couldn't recall ever seeing the boxes on our local supermarket shelves. What would Sherlock Holmes do? Perhaps I could call Omar? He'd be awake, and would almost certainly have a comprehensive knowledge of retro 1980s groceries. He was like Richard Alpert, but cooler. Ah, but the phone was in Jeff's room. I scanned further down my list of search results and found a website called 'Mr. Breakfast', containing a detailed archive of deleted cereals. Moreover, there was a list of ebay links down the side. I was shocked to see that one box of C3PO's Cereal – still sealed, box in great condition, featuring original puzzles, best before end: March 1987 – was retailing at $175. This was where I drew the line. What geeks! I couldn't believe anyone would be sad

enough to pay that much money for cereal they were never going to eat. The whole thing just defied sense!

Pete: Saturday 22nd October

Yes! He shoots, he scores! My $200 bid's just been accepted as the winner on the C3PO cereal! I'm the Sherlock Holmes of breakfast nostalgia!

Jeff: Friday 22nd October

I took all the Doctor Who stuff for James round to Rachel's today. It was like the end of 'Toy Story 3', although it'd taken me a little bit longer than Andy to realise I should part with my toys.

It was all there: the Target books, a backlog of DWMs, all my old Dapol action figures, all seven Doctors, The Master, Yetis, Ice Warriors and legions of wind up Daleks, Doctor Who top trumps cards, board games, jigsaws, quizzes...

He was over the moon. He told me he's going to be a Cyberman for Halloween. He was rifling through some old magazines and came across an issue from December 2003 with William Hartnell on the cover. "Who's that man?" He asked. It was a beautiful, warm moment. In that instant I realised how exciting it must be for him: to love a TV program, but realise it has a whole history for him to lose himself in. He doesn't know that Tom Baker was a grumpy bugger, or that all of season twenty four was awful! For him it's just excitement. And I was excited too – to know of *his* excitement yet to come. Here was a kid who'd never seen 'The Green Death'. Who probably didn't know that Sarah Jane had been there since 1973!

"That's William Hartnell. The original, you might say!" It seemed like the right thing to say, even if I was *actually* quoting Richard Hurndall. I wanted to sit there with him

314

and watch 'An Unearthly Child', to see his face when that blurred white time vortex pulsed into view and he heard the definitive version of the earth's greatest theme tune for the first time.

It was at that moment that I wished he was my son, that 1990 had never happened and Rachel and I were still together. We'd be married, and live somewhere that wasn't awful. We'd bake things together and put up the Christmas decorations in November because we were so excited. We'd go for walks every Sunday afternoon and play 'Don't Blink' every time we saw a statue. I wouldn't have to lie about liking silly TV programmes because I could legitimately watch them with my kids. No, with my family.

The fantasy burst as the door was slammed open and Brutus Gornall came home. To *his* family.

I bet *he* didn't bake...

"Alright." He nodded at me.

"This is Jeff, an old friend of mine. From school, actually!" Rachel introduced us. It took every ounce of my determination to force a smile. Smile at the man who'd somehow gatecrashed my life. The man who had everything I wanted. "He's brought some toys for James."

"Oh, nice one mate."

"Well, it was either this or Oxfam!" I lied, shrugging. These were some of my most treasured possessions.

"Yeah, or eBay. Everything's online these days." He commented, irrelevantly.

"Yeah." I laughed mirthlessly. What an utterly banal contribution to proceedings. Here we were, two perfect strangers who hated each others' guts, forced into mindless chitchat by the laws of etiquette.

"D'you want a brew?" He asked. He didn't want to make me a brew. He didn't want me to be in his house. *I* didn't want me to be in his house. There was just one single, unspoken thought hovering inescapably in the air between us. *I've seen your wife naked.* Neither of us wanted it to be true. It just was. And we could never be friends.

"Nah, I've got to get back to work." I haven't even started my job yet...

"Late shift, is it?"

"Something like that." I tutted, rolling my eyes theatrically. Actually, it was nothing like that. I was going to drive a safe distance from their house, pull over, listen to 'Vale Decem' on the stereo and cry.

Jeff: Monday 25th October

SPIN-OFF DAY!!!

9am: Auton / 10: Bacon sandwiches / 10:15: Shakedown: Return of the Sontarans / 11:15: Hot chocolate / 11:30: Auton 2: Sentinel / 12:30: Fish fingers & custard! / 12:45: Downtime / 14:00: Corona and lime / 14:05: Mindgame / 15:00: Auton 3 / 16:00: Pot Noodles / 16:15: Daemos Rising (Ring for Chinese takeaway)

Conclude of course by... The Death of The Doctor!! Jo Grant is back!!!!

What a day!

Jeff: Tuesday 26th October

Jo Grant!! (Sorry... *Jones!*) And Matt Smith! Matt FUCKING Smith! It was all too much. We just about held it together until the Third and Fourth Doctor flashbacks... Then we grabbed hold of each other and wailed like babies, until Pete's Mum called and he had to quickly pull himself together and sound like a real man. Well, that was never going to happen... But he tried to sound like less of a pansy.

Meanwhile, I composed a list to explain why I hate River Song:

316

1. She is unable to appear in an episode without using the words "Hello sweetie" or "Spoilers". This has become somewhat contrived.
2. She is incredibly patronising towards The Doctor, despite the fact that the only reason she occasionally has the edge on him is because she learned things *from him* in the future.
3. She is arrogant, egotistical, treats The Doctor like a child, and yet still brags to everyone else (Clerics, Romans etc.) about how he's wonderful.
4. She acts like The Doctor's equal, but constantly ends up needing to be rescued by him.
5. Alex Kingston is hideous. Not only this, she has aged terribly between series' 4 and 5, so the notion that she is supposed to be younger in 'Time of Angels' than 'Silence in the Library' is preposterous.
6. Her jowls are terrifyingly detached, whilst her lips and chins (yes, chins) seem to carry on moving for several seconds after she has ceased speaking. (I refer you to the line "What do you know of the Weeping Angels?")
7. She acts like she's in some kind of dreadful American sci-fi show. "Alpha Meson Burst"?? And the hip holster type thing she wears in 'The Big Bang' is repulsive. This isn't Star Trek.
8. She seems to be intended as a Romana for the 21st century. But Romana (II, at least) was pleasant, well mannered and attractive. If she's based on Romana I, that's fair enough I suppose.
9. & 10. She is AWFUL.

I couldn't help but feel my rage towards River Song had come from somewhere deeper within. I started listening to 'Head Over Heels', an old favourite from the Primrose Avenue days. I shouldn't have done it. I'd had too much to drink. I texted Rachel: '*Funny how time flies x*'. She didn't reply.

Pete: Tuesday 26th October

At 9am precisely, the doorbell began to ring insistently, on and off in strict 5 second intervals, until I traipsed downstairs and answered it. A man in a brown uniform fixed me with an intimidatingly large grin, and tipped his space-age cap. He looked like a beige Captain Scarlett.

"Good day to *you*, sir!" He intoned enthusiastically, producing a clipboard – seemingly from thin air. "Got several packages in your name, if you could just sign for them?"

"Oh..." I blinked several times, flustered. "I don't think I ordered anything. They must be for the guy in the other flat. Want me to go and fetch him for you?"

"No, no. That won't be necessary. You are Pete Ross, aren't you?" How did he have my name? He didn't seem to have looked at my papers.

"Well, yes..." I answered hesitantly. "But I'm not expecting anything. They can't be for me."

"I doubt there'd be an error on the form, sir. Take a look for yourself." He allowed me a fleeting glimpse. The sheet seemed to be covered in 1's and 0's. Did couriers need a knowledge of binary coding as well as a driving license these days? "You see?"

"I'm not sure I do."

"You will, sir, you will." He flashed his pearly white teeth. I found myself signing the paper as he spoke. But what was I agreeing to? Might I have just switched our broadband supplier? Or maybe it was something more sinister. Was I about to find myself subject to some kind of mind probing experiment? "We at Sentinel Services are synchronising the world, don't you know?" I nodded blankly, handing the form back. The courier vanished into his futuristic van, shortly producing three heavy-looking boxes. They weighed a ton but he manoeuvred them upstairs with apparent ease. Was he a robot? It seemed the only likely explanation.

I was perched among several colossal stacks of catalogues and magazines, when Jeff walked in, fixing me with an odd glare, as though something were woefully amiss.

"Pete..." He scanned the room quickly, his face twisting into a worried expression. "I appreciate there's probably a perfectly logical explanation for all of this, but why are you sat on the floor, surrounded by a load of gay porn?"

"It's not gay porn!" I snapped. "It's part of my inheritance – Uncle Julian's photo shoots. Every sodding one of them!"

"It's gay porn." He said, matter-of-factly. "Softcore, but nonetheless..."

"It IS not! They're tastefully done modelling shots, which just happen to feature lots of muscly men parading about in their underwear, and... Posing..."

"Well, what the hell are we going to do with it?"

"I don't know. I'm just going to have to leave it here until I work out how to get rid of it. If it doesn't leave this room, it can't get us into any trouble."

Pete: Wednesday 27th October

The day got off to a good start with a postcard from Berlin. It was from Comedy Dan and Big Dougie, and showed lots of leather clad men cavorting in some kind of nightclub. Those fruity Krauts! A tense phone conversation with Simone, however, left me feeling blunt and honest. So I was almost pleased when Andy Pond texted to invite himself round. Today, for the first time, I was going to be totally straight with him. *Literally*. No more lies. I didn't care how difficult it was going to be. I was going to start from the beginning, tell the truth and extricate myself. And, best of all, I'd worked out a way I could do it without breaking his heart.

As soon as he came round, I marched him straight to the sofa, before taking a statement-making solitary seat in the armchair. "Andy." I wore a serious expression. "I'm afraid what I have to tell you today isn't going to be easy for either of us. But I can no longer live a lie. I'm afraid to say that I, Pete Ross... Am straight." I tensed up, waiting for the floodgates to open. But he didn't respond.

Instead, he ran his eyes along the 26 alphabetical piles I'd made of Julian's underwear catalogues, and then to the postcard propped up against my Sixth Doctor figure. "Yeah, course you are, honey." He rolled his eyes. "I'll go and put the kettle on. I thought we could listen to that new Kylie CD?"

Where had I gone wrong?

Jeff: Wednesday 27th October

Dom rang at 7am to say he'd been abducted by aliens in the night, which he described as being "like penguins with colanders on their heads". I asked him to be honest and tell me what he'd been up to in the evening. I wasn't surprised to hear he'd been watching the X Files and drinking Special Brew. He went on to describe his abductors in more depth, but stopped abruptly in mid sentence.

"Oh. Anyway, I've just remembered that I'm not talking to you. But I suppose you had to be told..."

"What have we done this time?" I sighed.

"Just you! I saw that list about Alex you posted on Gallifrey Base. You're out of line, Jeff! She's a goddess!"

"It wasn't about Alex Kingston, just about River Song. You know how much I-"

"I refer you to point five: 'Alex Kingston is hideous'."

"Yeah, yeah, alright, I'm sorry – I was out of control. I was angry at someone called Brutus and I just took it out on Alex."

"Oh, come on Jeff – if you're going to lie to me, at least make it a credible one. Brutus? Nobody's called Brutus!"

"He *is* called Brutus! Why will nobody believe me?"

"It's just not a very realistic name. There was some crazy Russian girl on Facebook claiming to know a Brutus. And you know how I feel about *Russians* since..."

"...The Event, I know, I know. Look, Dom we've strayed a little off topic. It's early. I'm going back to sleep. Call me back when you're certain this whole alien thing wasn't a dream."

"Fine. Oh wait, no actually, because I'm not speaking to you."

I got up a few hours later to find email from Dad:

```
Dear Jeffrey,

Congratulations once again on your new
job. If I could just clarify something -
you specified you had found employment in
an antiques shop dealing with collectible
memorabilia. A colleague of mine who's
good with computers used the googlenet to
find that it appears to be some kind of
children's toy shop.
  Has there been some confusion on the
matter?

Regards,
Ronald
```

And a message from Dom on Facebook that claimed everyone was 'Inventing Brutuses' with a link to another page. The rest of the message simply read '*Check out her wall! P.S. You still owe me a tenner*'.

I clicked on the link: a page belonging to somebody called Stasiski Polonski. Her latest wall post read '*A night of passion with a tall dark stranger called Brutus! Meeeeow!*' Why was Dom sharing this with me? Then I noticed her photo, and saw the face concealed behind the bottle of Ouzo. Hang on... Stasiski Polonski..? Bond Villain Stacy?!

I checked the rest of her pictures. It was her alright, and they were pretty vile. In one, she was sucking a candle provocatively. The caption read '*Mmmm, wax!*' It brought back painful memories of the tongue piercing...

What if she really *had* had a night of passion with someone called Brutus? What if it was Brutus Gornall? That would be fantastic! Rachel would be heartbroken!!!

If only there was some way I could find out. This was Facebook after all, like the Zygons or the Kraals spying on everyone. If the bank know that I know Dom a tenner, surely I can find out who Stacy slept with?

I looked on her tagged photos. Ha! Sure enough there was a folder labelled with Saturday's date. At a cursory glance, she didn't seem to be in the picture. Just two young people gurning at the camera like that was in some way good. Then I noticed that behind them was an elbow, I hovered the cursor over it and revealed a caption 'Stasiski Polonski'. And there she was with her arms around Brutus! I had him! I'd reversed the polarity of *his* neutron flow!

"What exactly am I supposed to be looking at here?" Pete was clearly puzzled by the pixelated mess before him.

"It's Brutus!" I could barely contain myself. I felt like I was in Coronation Street.

"Forgive me for being objective," he frowned, "but that's just an arm. And possibly an... ear? Or is that a mirror ball?"

"It all adds up!" I said breathlessly.

"But does it really, though? Are you sure you don't just want it to add up?"

"No. It's definitely him."

"It's not definitely him. It's *possibly* someone with the same name. And what if it is? Are you really going to give her a call and destroy her marriage. Do you think she'd thank you for that?"

"But... I'd be there to pick up the pieces... Jeffmeister..." I mumbled pathetically.

"No, you wouldn't. She'd forever think of you as the guy who ruined her marriage! You're being ridiculous. And what if, *what if*..." I noticed he was making an extra effort to pronounce all of his Ts, clearly trying to do a Matt Smith impression to win me over. "...You barge round there to tell her and she says it's definitely not him – that they were out playing bowls on Saturday night..."

"Bowls? You haven't had a girlfriend in a long time, have you?"

"Shut up. They were playing bowls. And then there you are trying to break them up. Do you think she'd ever speak to you again? That would be like sending whatever relationship you currently have to the lunar penal colony for life imprisonment without trial!"

He had a point.

Jeff: Thursday 28th October

We were just settling down to watch 'Human Nature' when there was a frenzied hammering at the door. I opened it to find Dom panting, his parka askew.

"They're back!" He wheezed. "The aliens!"

"Dom, have you gone mental?" I sneered. But he was already inside, pushing past me and pointing out of the window. "There's nothing there..." My dismissal ceased as I saw what he was pointing at: a silver object glowing in the night sky.

"Oh my God..." I stammered. "You're right!"

"I reckon it's hovering over the sea." He said without pausing.

"The Atraxi!" I whispered.

"Lenarians!" Dom snapped back.

"Come on!" I sprung into action.

"Where are you going?" Cried Pete.

"The Roof! No... Hang on! The beach!" I winked.

Half an hour later, we were hauled up in my car, parked by the tram stop at Starr Gate. I suppose if I was going to finally meet some aliens, it may as well be at the aptly named Starr Gate. The otherworldly object was still shimmering in the heavens beyond the sand dunes. Dom was filming it on his phone, whilst I was trying to get some decent quality snaps with a digital camera.

"That's definitely not a plane!" I said in hushed tones, as though the thing hundreds of feet in the air above could actually hear me.

"Nah, it's the wrong shape. And size. It's not moving."

"No, but it's too big and too bright to be a star." I reasoned, reaching for a Dorito. The car was well stocked for a night of surveillance. We had Pot Noodles, flasks of tea and water, crisps, sandwiches and a pizza.

"Maybe it's monitoring us. Scanning us!" Dom hissed in excitement.

"You mean, to scope out our tech?" I gasped.

"Yeah! Seeing if we can fight back!"

"They might blow up the airport!" It was then I remembered. The Christmas present from my Dad that I'd abandoned in the boot, thinking I'd never need it.

"I can't apologise enough!" I yelled, leaping out of the car and running around the back. "I thought you were just a useless gadget. I thought you were just an embarrassing present from a dull Godmother with two heads and bad breath!"

"What are you on about?" Called Dom. Jesus, the guy really needed to brush up on his Doctor Who quotes. What a square!

"My Dad bought me..." I explained, rummaging around in the clutter. "...These!" I exclaimed triumphantly, brandishing a pair of binoculars. "How wrong can a man be?" I chortled, settling myself back into the driver's seat.

"Right then, my friend." I took them from the box. "Let's see just what exactly you are!" There were letters on the side of the craft. Gradually, they slipped into focus. Ah. **'Maxi Gold 26-Hours-a-Day Plumbing Service. We gonna sort you out!'** I zoomed out a little, to find that the spaceship was, in fact, some kind of inflatable zeppelin. It had a sliver hue, and I presume it was glowing as a result of reflected light from Blackpool Tower and The Pleasure Beach lasers.

"What is it? What have you seen?" Dom was clearly beside himself with the thrill of it all. Could I really burst his bubble? Surely I should allow him one moment of magic.

I hastily gunned the ignition. "We have to leave!" I said sternly.

"What? Why?"

"We have to leave right now!" I spun the car around, and fixed him with my most serious glare. "They've seen us!"

I returned Dom, terrified, to his house and then drove home. When I tried the door it only opened a crack and then jammed.

"What the – Pete?" I called.

"Who is it?" Came a muffled cry.

"It's me!"

"How do I know it's really you?"

"What?"

"You might be a Pod Person! Or a Teleport Clone! Answer the secret question!"

"Go on then..."

"What do you get if you cross Douglas Adams, David Fisher and Graham Williams?"

"David Agnew!" I poked my head through the door, to see that the sofa had been pressed up against it as a barricade. Pete emerged from beneath a pile of cushions, wrapped in tin foil, wearing a bicycle helmet and an oven glove whilst brandishing a sonic screwdriver.

"Is it safe?" He demanded.

"Yeah, it's fine." I said, as he pulled the sofa away from the door.

"What happened?"

"You know that secret level on Tomb Raider?"

"Oh yeah..." He sniggered.

"I think I just topped it!"

Jeff: Thursday 28th October

Only four days until I start work!!!

Jeff: Friday 29th October

I was sat in the car park at Morrisons. It had been a dreadful shopping experience. Too many queues and squealing children. I needed to gather myself. I sat there, savouring a cigarette and listening to 'The End of Time' soundtrack. I skipped it straight to 'Gallifrey'.

As I gazed at the stars through the rain speckled windows, I had a text from Rachel: *'Don't take my heart, don't break my heart, don't throw it away x'*.

Jeff: Saturday 30th October

Brutus did sleep with Stacy!!! Rachel's sister, Ingrid, has a friend whose son is in a band called Bad Damage. Stacy is one of the band's friends on Facebook, so she was recommended to Ingrid as 'someone she might know', so Ingrid went on her profile to see who she was, saw the status update about Brutus, and that she lived in Lancashire, and told Rachel! I'm not sure if all that makes sense. Each time I try to read it back I get a headache.

The point is, they weren't playing bowls that night! Brutus was at a Stag Party in *Preston*! That's where Stacy lives! I shudder at the memory. Of course, he's denying it and saying that it could be *anybody's* elbow, but he obviously did it.

Rachel came round to the flat in tears, and who was there to pick up the pieces..? THE JEFFMEISTER!!!

Pete: Saturday 30ᵗʰ October

After many days spent agreeing terms by text, Simone brought a bottle of wine round and said she thought we should spend some time together as a couple. My heart leapt aflutter to the stars, or whatever it's supposed to do according to the law of 80s power ballads. I let Simone go first, partly to avoid any awkwardness if I went into my room and she didn't follow, and partly because she was wearing a short skirt. By the time I got to the living room, however, she'd already parked herself in front of the television and was flicking towards ITV. Oh god. The X-Factor.

During the course of the programme – which mainly consisted of sob stories about supermarket checkout cashiers wanting to 'live their dreams', interspersed with some comically delusional tribute acts, and the occasional bit of 'singing' – Simone went through the entire contents of the wine, without offering to share any, and swigging straight from the bottle. Every time I had the audacity to speak, she pressed her fingers tensely to her lips, exaggeratedly shushing me and shooting a glare that would have ordinarily suggested the accidental murder of a beloved childhood pet. When the adverts came on, and I mentioned that it was all a set up – because they only took the stunningly brilliant or embarrassingly bad acts, and average-looking decent singers didn't make good TV – she snapped and said that I was "*so* uncultural."

After 2 hours of hopping between the main show and 'The Xtra Factor', she asked if we could call for a takeaway and offered to go and pick it up.

"Well... Wow... Yes." I stuttered. I wasn't used to such generosity. Maybe tonight was the night?

"Great. Well, if you could just go and fish out twenty quid, and I'll nip out?" She smiled, suddenly all sweetness and light. My hand wavered hesitantly over my wallet, but she came and leaned over my shoulder as I unzipped the note pouch. The feel of her body against mine made it difficult to resist.

Half an hour later, I got a text, saying there'd been a 'family emergency' and that she wouldn't be coming back after all. Why do I feel a strange sense of history repeating?

Pete: Sunday 31st October

I couldn't help but look on Simone's Facebook page today. It was awash with comments about how great last night had been. One of them was from her sister. Did they have a sick sense of humour, or had the whole 'family emergency' thing merely been a ruse? I felt my hand hesitantly moving towards the 'photos' button. Sure enough, she'd been tagged in several people's photo albums, dressed as a generic looking vampire. Bloody 'Twilight'! One of her friends had commented about how generous she was for buying them all a

round of drinks. I think I know where my takeaway money got to...

1988

Jeff: Wednesday 26th October

Dear Doctor Who Magazine,

What can I say...Wow! For the first time since 1977 I feel like I've just seen a proper episode of Doctor Who! I didn't like Sylvester McCoy at all to begin with but now he's changed my mind. Remembrance of the Daleks is easily the best Dalek story – possibly the best story – since Genesis of the Daleks! It's like the Doctor is mysterious again, with a likable companion (the first since Romana II?). The special effects have come on leaps and bounds, the music is really futuristic! The eerie school, the military, Daleks fighting Daleks – what's not to like!? And all the references to the classic series were fantastic. (Especially Zygons!) I think Ben Aronononovich and Andrew Cartmel are geniuses – long may their reign of Doctor Who Continue! It seems like that little break was just what the show needed. Here's to another 25 years!

Jeff Greene, 17, Blackpool

Jeff: Monday 1st November

My First day at work! I'm being paid to spend my days surrounded by Daleks. Could my life get any better?

Pete: Monday 1st November

There was a bonfire night safety commercial on TV, featuring the helpful advice that it was *inadvisable* to consume lit gunpowder, allow children to handle explosives, or place cats (even the really arrogant, unwanted ones) directly onto fire. It got me thinking about the night I first met Jeff...

Monday 7th November 1983

I can't believe it! Jeff Greene, that really cool kid from my year, was at the Catholic Club community bonfire the other night. And he was wearing an 'Empire Strikes Back' t-shirt! I'd seen him on the schoolyard – showing off in front of girls, playing football with Alex Goss and Matt Riley – but, apart from that time he'd missed the bus and had to come to my after-school chess club, I thought he was in a different league. He always sat at the back of class, making jokes with his cool friends and drawing stupid cartoons. I never in a million years thought he'd talk to me, but he did! Maybe it was because most the other people there were girls, kids from little school or people's parents – not normal grown ups like us.

"Y'alright?" He came over, kicking up bits of gravel.

"S'pose." I cracked my knuckles. What could I say to make me sound cool? "Bit bored."

"Me too. Pretty shit, isn't it?" More gravel kicking.

"Yeah... It is a bit... Crap." I muttered, feeling really guilty. I hadn't sworn since Wat Thompson had

331

pushed me against Mrs. Krunt's wall, saying he'd make me eat soil if I didn't. I'd have to say an extra long prayer later to make sure nothing bad happened. I didn't believe in God much. I was an agnaethist, but we'd just been doing karma in RE, and I didn't fancy coming back as an earwig. "So, you like Star Wars?"

His eyes lit up. "Yeah! It's great! What did you think of the last-" He stopped. Rachel from set 1 walked past with a group of girls in party dresses and waved at us. For some reason, Jeff started to speak a bit like Sylvester Stallone. "Well... It's alright, I guess. The Ewok's were a bit shit." He looked over his shoulder to where the girls stood giggling, singing 'Club Tropicana' and yacking on about how handsome George Michael looked in the video. "Eh..." Jeff poked me, making my arm hurt. I wanted to rub it better, but I didn't. "Why did the Chicken Walker cross the road?" I shrugged. "Because the Ewok forced him to!" He started laughing really loudly, slapping his legs and checking to see if Rachel was paying attention. I tried to join in, but it just wasn't that funny. "You get it? Force?" He swished an invisible light saber.

"Yeah... Great. I know what you mean about 'Return of the Jedi'." (I'm sorry, Ewoks). "You should watch Doctor Who. Doctor Who's waaaayyy better."

"Doctor Who?!" He said it like I'd just told him I was gay or something.

"Yeah." I looked down. "It's... Cool. Peter Davison's so..." I shivered, not sure how to finish the sentence. I'd have to impress him with my encyclopaedic knowledge. "Doctor Who has been on air for 20 years, 129 stories and Five Doctor's. That's more than Batman, James Bond and Flash Gordon!"

"Yeah. Well, it's alright I suppose." He spoke quietly. "I used to like it when I was at primary school. More of a kids' show, isn't it?"

"No! My Uncle Julian watches it, and he's a fully grown man. He's always sending me pictures of him in costume."

"Wow! He sounds cool!" Said Jeff, giving himself away now that Rachel's gang had gone to see the fire being lit. "Hey, I've got loads of toys at home. You could come round to play- I mean, hang out – if you wanted?"

"Cool! Although... I'll have to ask my Dad."

"Your Dad?" He shook his head, smirking. "We're not in first year anymore! I'm a free agent, me. Can do what I want, go where I want. Hey- if I want to go and get some sweets from the shop, I can do it... Just like that." He snapped his fingers. "If I want to go for a game of footie on the park, I can do it. My parents are dead chilled out."

"Jeffrey?!" Just then, a man who looked like a rat in a security guard uniform marched over and Jeff's cheeks went very red. "It is precisely 7pm, and I won't start the fire until I'm sure you're in the peripheral safety zone, keeping firm hold of your mother's hand." He looked at me. "That goes for your little playmate too. No civilians will be placed in danger. Not on my watch."

"Ahhh, Dad!" Jeff stamped his foot.

"Now, Jeffrey. We'll have no more of your lip." He punched him on the shoulder, but not very hard. "Now let's hear the family motto... It's safer with Slater." They said it together, Jeff mumbling and his dad looking proudly to the sky. "That's the spirit. Come on, young man. You'll never make security chief with a sulk on."

We crowded round a row of empty beer crates. There was about 10 foot between us and the bonfire, which was really small looking, so no one could properly see it. Mr. Slater went round to the other side, taking a torch from the pocket of his uniform and shining it in *all our eyes as he made a speech. "I'm well aware" he said "that our primary objective this evening is to have fun. Which is fine." His eye twitched a bit. "There's nothing wrong with fun, so long as it's safe fun. I'm sure we can all have a reasonably enjoyable time if the correct parameters for this aforementioned jollity are upheld. As a prominent figure in your local community and head of security at a leading local shopping establishment..." He removed a badge from his pocket, and passed it round. "...I have elected myself municipal coordinator for this event, and politely request that you observe the following rules. Rule number 1: Please do not leave the pre-marked boundaries, as indicated by the boxes kindly donated by The Serviceman's Club. Rule number 2: In response to complaints last year, from... anonymous sources..." His moustache twitched. "...The bonfire is sized in accordance with British Bonfire Authority restrictions, and we will not be allowing any airborne fireworks. Furthermore, please do not attempt to light sparklers, as these will be seized, by force if necessary. Remember, sparklers can kill! Rule number 3: Should you wish to visit the bathroom, please only do so in one of the allotted time slots. You will see that I have furnished you all with a schedule, featuring an itinerary of events. If anyone is without a schedule, please raise your hand now." No one put their hand up. Jeff's dad grinned. "As I thought. Efficiency is the key to a ship-shape operation, not to mention a happy marriage." He shone his torch on a scowling woman smoking a cigarette, and a few people laughed politely. "Rule Number 4..."*

"Alright, alright." A man with a box stumbled over the beer crates. "This isn't 'ow you're supposed to do it!" Mr. Slater swung his flashlight round and I suddenly felt like I was going to die of embarrassment. "Do you want these kiddies to 'ave a good time? Or do

you want your 'ealth and safety bollocks to turn 'em into a bunch of puffters?" It was my Dad.

"Excuse me, I'd appreciate it if you didn't use prohibited language in front of the youngsters. You will find an 'acceptable language use' section on page 4 of the schedule." Dad advanced, and Mr. Slater took out a walkie-talkie, calling for back-up and shaking it furiously when no one answered.

"You're out o' range, you daft bastard!" Someone shouted from the crowd. My dad snatched it off him, and picked up his box.

"Got a few fireworks of my own here... Expensive ones... From the golf club! With fire power like this..." Oh no, Dad. Not one of your rants. Please. There were third years here! "We could set the air ablaze!" He cackled. "Create explosions of such exquisite power that other local bonfires won't know what's hit them. Oh, how they'll tremble when they see the magnitude and might of my display! We shall reign supreme OVER... THE... SKIES!" No one seemed to know whether to cheer or laugh. Everything went very quiet. As my Mum went over to accost Dad, apologising and saying he'd had too much to drink, Jeff came back over and tugged me on the arm.

"Your Dad's just like Davros!" He whispered.

"Yeah, well your Dad looks like The Marshall!"

"Who?"

"You know? Only one of the best villains of the Pertwee era, from classic story 'The Mutants', penned by Bob Baker and Dave Martin, 1972?"

"Oh, you mean that fat guy?"

"He's not fat. He's really scary! And it's pronounced Dave. Dave Ross." Jeff sniggered.

I went up and said "hi" to him at school today, but I think he must have been playing some kind of joke where he pretended he couldn't hear me.

Of course, I haven't been to a bonfire in years. They're death traps, and I don't want a repeat of the 'Satanic Desecration' incident! But I did miss the magic of seeing all those colours light up a sky that seemed so much blacker just after the clocks had gone back for autumn; being with people you loved; and basking in the sort of warmth you only felt on the coldest November nights, knowing Christmas is just around the corner.

I made my mind up. I was going to plan something special for Simone, and it would be the most romantic night of our lives!

Jeff: Tuesday 2nd November

Dear Jeffrey,

I hope you're settling in well to your new work environment. Remember, do not hesitate to call if any on-site security is needed as I have now severed ties with the indoor shopping centre.

There was a court order. He's not allowed within fifteen feet.

It was an illustrious and fruitful partnership that served me well for 30 years, but as men of the world such as me all know, at the end of the day, everything comes to an end.

Kevin tells me you work at "The Hoo Shop." My googlenet friend says that this is a woman's clothing retail outlet. Could you please clear this up? I don't want anyone thinking you're engaging in transvestitism. The Slater family, and it's various offshoots, have a standard to maintain.

336

```
        Must  go.  Your  mother  needs  the  portable
computer for her poker website.

Regards,
Ronald Slater
```

Offshoots? Was he trying to make a joke about my name being 'Green'. Maybe the pills *were* working. I kept my name as a child because I didn't warm to him for a while. I now realise that, in his own way, he was just trying to be supportive. But as a 5 year old, being held at gun point with a hose pipe whilst he timed how fast I could polish my boots was not an enjoyable experience.

I'd never known my real dad, so my mind naturally filled in the blanks. He was the best guy in the world, who was one day coming to take me away to live in a castle. He was probably the king of some exotic country. Every night I used to go to bed in pyjamas and dressing gown, a pair of shoes at the ready by my bedside in case he came to take me away in the night. For a while, I convinced myself that my dad was The Doctor, and that I was secretly a Time Lord. He'd left me on earth whilst he had to undertake some mission of great galactic importance, but any day I'd wake up to find the TARDIS at the foot of the garden, and we'd run off to Gallifrey together, no doubt getting into all sorts of scrapes along the way!

It was around this time that I got 'Doctor Who and the Auton Invasion', and revised my theory so that my Time Lord Dad's memory had been erased and he had no knowledge of me, and it was my job to get his memory back and fix the TARDIS.

I got into trouble for sneaking into the local garage and trying to find a dematerialisation circuit.

Jeff: Friday 5th November

We had a delivery today – the series 5 soundtrack is here! It's not officially released yet but I got to take one!! It was with shaking hands that I unwrapped the cellophane in the car, and sped home blasting out the Eleventh Doctor's theme!

I put it on the stereo on full volume when I got in. Pete said I'd made his Christmas – and it's only November!

Pete: Friday 5th November

It was the big night, but my confidence had wavered. Simone had been round 4 out of 5 nights this week. That would be great if I thought she actually wanted to see *me*, but every time she arrives, barely a word is spoken before we end up watching telly. What's happened to told old magic? I keep finding myself wondering if there even *was* any old magic. Once or twice, I've tried to wedge my arm between the cushion and her neck, but she always tenses up. Yet, she still maintains that we're giving things another go... Just taking them slowly. So why is it she can't seem to stand the sight of me until I get my wallet out? It just doesn't seem to make any sense. I decided to ask her about it tonight.

"Simone, is your TV broken at home?" She turned round, her face fixed into a warning scowl. I persisted nonetheless. "It's just cause the only reason you seem to come here is to watch television..."

"Yeah, that's what normal couples *do*!" She said, almost confrontationally.

"But it's like we never talk. There's no physical affection or anything."

"You'll be lucky." She laughed mirthlessly, turning up the volume on the television.

338

I was just going to have to come out with it. "Simone... Are you using me for money and Sky TV?"

"Oh, that's a nice thing to say to your pregnant girlfriend, isn't it? Why don't you speak up, so your baby can hear?"

"It *isn't* my baby!" I felt like I'd wandered into one of those nightmare soaps. I suddenly got the point of 'Eastenders'.

"Well, Rik certainly isn't going to take any bloody responsibility for it!" And she began crying. I reached out to touch her arm, but she told me to 'fuck off', running into the bathroom. She returned, moments later, stony faced, and asked for some taxi money.

"But... I had something special planned for later..." I blubbered. "Something... Romantic."

She took a handful of notes from my wallet, and slammed the door. The house resounded with a buzz of static.

When it got a little darker, I made my way up the stairs. The power had been cut at the far end of the corridor, so I had to feel my way along the wood-chip wallpaper. I pictured myself doing this as a child, and thought about how much it would have frightened me, but I felt too sad to be scared.

There'd been no lock on the other flat, since the police had forced entry to arrest Psycho Sharon. The place was mostly a tip, apart from the living room, where I'd spent the day clearing junk. At the far side, some French doors looked out over the rooftops, and there was just enough moonlight flooding in to illuminate a table by the window. It was laid out for two, a glass of wine on each side, a vase of flowers pushed towards one of the place settings – the one that was now empty. I pressed the play button on a battered old cassette deck and a slightly discordant rendition of Simon & Garfunkel's 'Wednesday Morning, 3am' spooled into life, as I sat alone, watching fireworks explode in the night sky. A flickering light show danced on the dirty rooftops of the terraced houses. I knew I was a fool for letting my heart rule my head. I wept silently.

Jeff: Saturday 6th November

We decided to re-appraise 'Time and the Rani'. Despite Sylvester's slightly over-theatrical performance, we had to admit that Richard Gauntlett gave a chilling performance as Urak, the giant bat thing. Who'd have thought the Seventh Doctor would turn out to be one of the best? That reminds me, I must find out if anybody ever made an action figure of the Seventh Doctor in his movie costume... After all, that is what I do now!

Jeff: Monday 8th November

I got an email from Dad asking how 'the lovely Daisy' was. I deleted it. I'll pretend I never got it.

Pete: Monday 8th November

Dom brought round a pirate copy of 'Toy Story 3'. Even though it was the fourth time we'd watched it, me and Jeff spent the duration crying our eyes out, reminiscing about our own forgotten childhood toys and mourning the loss of innocence. Dom had a go at us for taking it too seriously and ended up calling a taxi, going home early because he found us "embarrassing".

Pete: Tuesday 9th November

Dom messaged me this morning to say he didn't want to hang around with us anymore because he found us 'emotionally under-developed, nostalgia obsessed and childish'. But then, *he* watches 'Star Trek'!

On a completely unrelated note, I spent a good deal of the day making a ten point list of why Star Trek's shit (and Doctor Who's better).

1. Dom likes it.
2. The effects in Doctor Who were *way* more cutting edge. I refer any naysayers to the 'making of the giant rat' section from 'Whose Doctor Who' on the 'Talons of Weng-Chiang' DVD. Ground-breaking!
3. The Doctor makes a far more convincing protagonist that Captains Picard (I'm sorry, Patrick Stewart) and Kirk. And he wasn't always trying to get off with the aliens. Well, not in the Classic Series anyway. That scene where David Tennant kissed the giant insect was unforgivable... Or was that 'Red Dwarf'?
4. The Starship Enterprise looks like a microwave hotplate.
5. Whilst wearing a 'Deep Space 9' t-shirt, Dom once spilled ketchup on my prized 'Fury from the Deep' Audiobook... And thought it was funny!
6. None of the Doctors have ever tried to launch a parallel career as a pop singer (Colin Baker's vocal forays and Dalek impressions on 'Doctor in Distress' aside).
7. If anything, Dom's the childish one!
8. I don't even need a 9 and 10. 'Star Trek' just IS shit! Case Closed.

Jeff: Wednesday 10th November

I went on Rachel's Facebook. Her relationship status is still 'engaged'. Why? How can they still be together? He almost definitely probably cheated on her!

I wanted to send her a message, but I had no idea what to write. Pete was right. What do I hope to achieve from all this? Could I really ask her if she wanted 'another drink'? Where was it going? Most people don't just meet for drinks. There's usually a point.

We'd just finished watching the 'scary bit' from 'Fury From The Deep' when Pete rose from the sofa.

"Right, I'm going for a pint." He announced.

"Okay, I'll... What?! You don't go for *pints*."

"Oh... Yeah." He stopped in his tracks. "I said that out loud didn't I? It's at this... Cyber... Bar... Type... Thing..." He mumbled. "Night."

Right, that's it! If people can spend their evenings in, drinking imaginary beer alone with a bunch of strangers (that made sense in my head), then there's nothing weird about going for a real drink, even if there is no agenda. Well, apart from the Jeffmeister's *secret* agenda!

Pete: Wednesday 10th November

It's definitely over between us and Dom. He delivered a carrier bag to Jeff, featuring all our old 'Thunderbirds' toys – models, I mean. (Although I note, on detailed inspection, that Thuderbird 4 is missing from the inside of Thunderbird 2. So he's playing mind games, eh?) He wants his James Bond VHS collection, taped from ITV, back forthwith. The videos are interrupted, at regular intervals, by annoying adverts. And he doesn't even like James Bond that

much anymore! He's so petty. Maybe we should get our lawyer involved.

Pete: Thursday 11th November

Spoke to Jeff about the lawyer thing. It turns out we don't have one. No one does. It's just something people say on American TV. So Jeff drafted a letter, pretending to be a lawyer: Terry McGann of Big Top Solicitors and Co.

Pete: Friday 12th November

Thank god we didn't send the letter! My Mum ran into Dom in Morrisons, bought him a cooked breakfast in the cafe, and had a little chat with him. So he wants to be friends with us again! Thanks Mum! Next year I won't forget your birthday.

Jeff: Friday 12th November

"Everything's shit!" I stormed into the kitchen. "Everything's *so* shit!" I was in such a mood, it didn't occur to me to ask Pete why he was sitting on the sink in his vest and pants, eating cold beans from the tin with a Twix bar.

"Thing's didn't go well with Rachel?" He asked through a mouthful of chocolate and tomato sauce.

"She's giving things another go with Brutus!"

"But he almost definitely probably cheated on her!" He shrieked.

"I know! The dick. She said she believes him, but their argument about it 'brought a lot of things to light'."

"Like the fact he's got a stupid name?"

"Probably. But they've decided to work through their problems *for the sake of James*." I put on a ridiculous, high pitched voice, even though neither of them actually spoke like that.

"I've got a plan!" He held his tin aloft.

"Is it ridiculous?" I shot him a castigating glare.

"We could *kill* James." He ventured.

"We're not going to kill James."

"It would solve a lot of problems though..." He opened another Twix.

"You're not helping!"

"I'm trying! I'm sure David Tennant didn't *want* to kill the Racnoss' children, but you have to admit it *did* save the world..."

"This is all because he works for British Aerospace. If I had a more masculine job, she'd want me!"

"You work with Daleks! They're the butchest things ever!"

"Are they really, though?" I marched to the DVD rack, and held up a copy of 'Dalek'. "It's not the 70s anymore. They've gone gay!" A look of defeat crossed his face.

"The new Daleks aren't gay. They're massive, and they've got really deep voices!" Pete leapt to their defence.

"Yeah, but they're all bright. They look like Teletubbies."

"You know how no one remembered the Daleks, because of the crack?"

"Yeah..."

"Well, now that 'The Big Bang' never happened, and there are no cracks... Does that mean people now *do* remember the Daleks?"

"I don't really know."

"What were we talking about?"

"I'm not sure. Let's get a curry."

After another *gripping* episode of 'Pets Do the Funniest Things', I decided to try and make a move on Simone. After all, what sort of couple were we supposed to be? It didn't go well. Her whole posture stiffened as I leaned over, until she eventually sprung out and forcibly drove me away.

I snapped. "Simone, why the hell are you leading me on when you quite obviously can't stand the sight of me?" She stormed up silently, marched to the bathroom and barricaded herself in. I tried to reason with her but I was drowned out by her theatrical sobbing and talk about "women's things" I "wouldn't understand". I think this was supposed to reduce me to a gibbering wreck, but she wasn't getting herself off the hook that easily this time. Just then, however, there was a scream and she promptly re-emerged, dashing straight into my arms. It was the first physical contact we'd had in all the time since she'd started coming round again.

"Oh, Pete! There's... A..." Her lip was trembling. "...Dead... Body... In the... Bath!" She howled. I froze, as she ran her hands frantically along my back. What if it was Jeff? What if life was imitating art and he really *had* gone into a coma. My whole gambit with Andy Pond would be rendered hideously ironic, that was for sure. But I couldn't cope without Jeff. Who'd deal with the practical stuff like bills and sensible food shopping? Who'd nip down to Omar's to get the toilet paper, and occasionally surprise me with a cheeky scratch card, or copy of Doctor Who Adventures? Who would I argue with about the pointless dance sequences in 'Four to Doomsday'?

With Simone hovering in the doorway, I inched my way onto the damp bathroom tiles, the puddles of water soaking through my socks. The extra bright

345

energy saving lightbulb Daisy had insisted we install a while back *did* add a certain CSI feel to the whole thing. I could just see the outline of a figure behind the shower curtain. Bracing myself, I gripped the flowery material tightly and pulled it so hard that its hooks came loose from the railing. My eyes were screwed up tightly. I couldn't look. I couldn't look. Oh god. Even if it wasn't Jeff, we'd still have the problem of having a dead body on our hands. I didn't want to go to prison. Why were people always trying to make me go to prison? I squinted my eyelids a fraction, and instantly let out a huge sigh of relief, clutching at my chest and falling backwards. I looked at Simone, who was gripping the wall, her face completely drained of colour.

"It's okay." I whispered, smiling. "It's just Mr. Harrison from downstairs." I looked down at him. He lay in the bath, asleep and fully clothed. Ordinarily, it would have been totally unnerving, but I was so relieved. I'd just have to think about the implications later. Simone, however, suddenly seemed to become very angry. She gathered up her possessions, and whacked me across the chest with a copy of 'Top Sante' magazine.

"You think that's okay?" She fumed. "That some guy from downstairs just decides to come and play dead in your house... And that's supposed to be *normal*? I've got to get out of here. Go and get me fifty quid for a taxi!" She was too angry, and I was too panicked to refuse. Although I did shakily ask why the fare had suddenly shot up so much. "Because it's Saturday night, of course!" She snatched the cash straight from my hand, and left.

I chanced a look through the curtains as she fled down the drive, and saw there was already a car waiting for her. As she opened the door to climb in, I thought I recognised the shadowy figure of Goth Rik in the driver's seat. I felt everything knotting up inside of me. I was so angry, I very nearly ventured out after them, but a wizened hand suddenly appeared on my shoulder, squeezing it in a firm but kindly fashion. I turned round to see Mr. Harrison, wearing a plush bathrobe monogrammed with the initials 'PRH', his lengthy white hair tied with a towel into a faintly ridiculous looking turban.

"Much obliged, old chap." He said. "Do appreciate a nice hot bath on a nice cold evening. It's what separates the colonels from the colonials, if you catch my drift?" Then he winked, shook my hand and left.

Pete: Sunday 14th November

I'm not sure which of us heard it first, but there was a prominent jangle of keys, and a good degree of cursing coming from the living room. We walked in simultaneously and were met by a bizarre sight: Lovely Kenny hunched and sweating over an enormous chest-freezer, his builders' backside on show for all to see, accompanied by a man with a spaceship tattooed on his face. They were attempting to direct the freezer through the door, whilst me and Jeff could only exchange horrified glances. I looked at my watch. Christ!

"Kenny... I'm sure there's a perfectly simple explanation for all of this, but... Why are you delivering us a freezer at 6am on a Sunday morning?"

"It's my 'ouse, innit?" He spun round, looking remarkably lithe for all his gaunt, grimyness. "Can do what I want. Just s'appens I want to store this freezer 'ere. Caterin' mate o' mine's just gone outta business. You know 'ow it is..."

"Especially in these recessionary times." The tattooed man finished his sentence for him with surprising eloquence.

"Oh yeah." Kenny snorted. "This is me boy, Tony."

"Your son?"

"Fuck off. Don't talk about 'im. I met Tony inside, didn't I? Why don't you give 'em a twirl, Tone?" To our shared horror, Spaceship Man removed his shirt, and spun round to reveal some medieval looking script that circled his upper torso. At the centre, the largest words read '*Only God can Judge Me: T. Blair*'.

"I don't think Tony Blair ever said that..." Jeff ventured.

"Nah." Tony laughed. "Blair's *my* surname. Can see how it gets confusing, what with Tony Blair being PM and that."

I shot Jeff a puzzled glare. "I thought you said it was that Nick Davids guy now?"

"Let's not get into that again! Kenny, this is very, erm, generous of you. But the fridge-freezer we have does us just fine."

"Nah." He tugged at a straggle of hair. "This one don't actually work. Like I say, just want it storin', but thought you could use it as a table or summit like that..."

In the end, we let them stick it at the end of the sofa after I realised it would make the perfect storage solution for Julian's magazines, and covered it with a surplus Indian throw. When I asked Jeff where the throw had come from, he said he didn't want to talk about it, and instantly reached for the ashtray.

Jeff: Monday 15th November

I've been planning the Christmas display at work. I'm going to put Santa hats on the cardboard Matt Smith and the life sized Dalek!

Maybe we could get one of the Doctors to come in dressed as Father Christmas! We'll do a ghetto, and he can give out Doctor Who themed toys!

Jeff: Tuesday 16th November

Ron says that we can't afford to pay a Doctor or give away stock. He also pointed out that it's 'grotto', and not 'ghetto'. I felt like a bit of an idiot and went back to parcelling up Borg action figures.

I suppose a Doctor (Sylvester, maybe...) dressed as a pimp and holding a boom box whilst dishing out presents would actually be quite funny...

Pete: Tuesday 16th November

Simone texted to say she thought we'd benefit from a little time apart, so she could work out exactly *how* she loved me, and also asked if I'd forward her the extra £130.50 needed to get my 'super crimbo pressie'. It seemed like a remarkably specific amount.

I checked her Facebook status and saw that she was still listed as being 'in a relationship'. What does this mean? Her newest profile comment was from one of her housemates, and read: '*New telly at last. Thanks Rik!*' I had to wonder if this recent acquisition had anything to do with her wanting to see less of me...

Pete: Wednesday 17ᵗʰ November

I happened upon the information today that £130.50 is *exactly* that price of a TV License. Does this mean that Simone is planning to buy me a TV License for Christmas?

Jeff: Wednesday 17ᵗʰ November

We've compromised! Ron says we could get someone to dress as The Doctor dressed as Father Christmas. A costume within a costume? Is that too confusing?

As I was walking through the front door this evening, Pete virtually pinned me up against the wall.

"I've made a brilliant invention!" He yelled. From the size of his eyes, he'd either been drinking caffeine or watching too much 'Quatermass'.

"What?" I asked, wrestling to free myself.

"You see this, right?" He snatched up a can of John Smiths from the coffee table. "Well, I've been thinking... We could brew our own beer... *Matt* Smiths!"

"Well, I -"

"It comes in a pint can, but there are *ten pints* inside!"

"So the can is bigger on the inside?"

"Dimensionally transcendental beer!"

"But... How?" I'd stumbled upon the one flaw in his, otherwise, brilliant plan.

"Shut up!" He snapped. "Y-You dick!"

Jeff: Saturday 20ᵗʰ November

"Jeffrey..." Pete approached me nervously in the kitchen.

"Yes, Peter." I turned to face him. He was wringing his hands. Always a bad sign.

350

"When, exactly, are we going to be allowed to talk about... *The bad thing*?" I hadn't been expecting that. At that moment, the toaster popped, punctuating the shock that was hanging in the air.

"I don't know!" I hurriedly busied myself with buttering. "I'm just not ready to... Admit... Things are okay, you know? I just want things to be *okay* for a while. I think I deserve it."

"Okay."

"Hey, you know what we should do?!"

"What?"

"Let's put up the decorations!"

"But it's November!" He gasped.

"It's the 20th of November, which is *nearly* December!"

"You're right! Let's do it! God, we're such rebels!"

An hour later, the tree was up and dressed in fairy lights, Matt Smith was wearing his Santa hat, the TV and mantelpiece were framed in tinsel and we routed out the various Doctor Who themed Christmas Cards we'd received over the years, hanging them on a line over the television. All whilst listening to the first side of my 'Christmas Mega Mix' tape.

1. Merry Christmas Everybody
2. The Stowaway
3. Song For Ten
4. Love Don't Roam
5. A Victorian Christmas
6. Happy Xmas (War Is Over)
7. A Spaceman Came Travelling
8. A Wombling Merry Christmas
9. Rockin' Around the Christmas Tree
10. Fairytale of New York

We surveyed the masterpiece we had created with pride. In lieu of sherry and mince pies, we had some Export

351

Jurgenbrau larger with a pork pie each and settled down to watch 'The Next Doctor'.

Pete: Saturday 20th November

I was attempting to position the lethal, spring-loaded measuring tape thingy, frantically trying to get the Christmas stockings perfectly symmetrical, when Dom called round. It was a welcome distraction. I decided the time had come to share my epiphany.

He and Jeff looked confused when I insisted we gather on the sofa, telling them only that I was about to share an amazing revelation. I left them in suspense a moment, to survey the spread of food I'd laid out on the table and fully appreciate the immaculate tidiness of the room, joining them only after several minutes. Taking a seat in the middle, a tub of festive popcorn balanced on my knee, I unpaused the DVD player. The Doctor Who theme music started, leading into, of course, 'The Hungry Earth'.

I placed a hand on each of their legs. "Just think..." I paused, largely for dramatic effect. "...This time next year... We *could* be watching Doctor Who."

"Yes, Pete. Yes." Jeff nodded politely. Sympathetically, even. I don't think he'd caught my meaning.

"But... I mean, we could be *watching* Doctor Who."

Dom stared at the screen, and then turned to me, squinting. "But... We're *already* watching Doctor Who."

"A-ha! Yes, we are, but..."

"Pete, what in Piccard's name are you talking about?"

"Elementary, my dear chap. I'm talking, of course, about the mid-season split."

"Oh, hang on..." The penny had just dropped for Jeff. "So, you mean we could be watching *Doctor Who*?"

"*We* could be watching Doctor Who." I nodded excitedly.

"You guys are on another planet." Dom shook his head, dipping a prawn cocktail crisp into a jar of jam.

Jeff: Monday 22nd November

Rachel brought James into the shop today! As usual, she looked effortlessly beautiful. There was some cover story about Christmas presents, but she'd obviously come to see *me*. Ahh, that perfume.

I found myself having more to talk about with James though. He'd been watching series 1 on iPlayer (I guess that's *old* Doctor Who to him!) and thought that the Autons were "cool". I gave him a copy of 'Spearhead From Space' "on the house" and told him to watch it as soon as he got home. Rachel said he had to do his homework first. James and I gave a collective whine of "Awwwww, Mum!" and then we all burst into laughter. It was like being in a parallel universe for a second. There was an awkward look between Rachel and I, and then she left.

I quickly paid for the DVD I'd given James. It would've been cheaper on Amazon...

She text me later to say that James was staying at her Mums for the weekend. I invited her round on Saturday night. I'd better make sure Pete has pants on.

Pete: Monday 22nd November

We had created a sprawling work of art. Our living room looked more festive than 'It's a Wonderful Life'

and 'The Christmas Invasion' combined. Dickens himself could have set his festive masterpiece, 'The Muppet Christmas Carol', here, and even those typically Victorian characters – like Michael Caine and Kermit the Frog – wouldn't have looked out of place. The beauty of it all hadn't hit me when we were dressing the tree yesterday. Only when I sauntered from my room and saw the cumulative effect did I let out an enthusiastic gasp of Christmas-in-November joy. I switched on the radio and was excited to hear Paul McCartney's 'Wonderful Christmas Time'. It was a terrible song, of course, but it was a *Christmas* song, which pretty much rendered it brilliant by default, regardless of musical content. Thank god the local radio station had been spinning their festive playlist since the end of August.

I danced over to the fridge, put some sausages under the grill and got a pan of beans on the go. I looked at the clock and saw that it was early. I planned to surprise Jeff with a Full English before he went to work! It wasn't long before he walked in, however, already dressed but still looking worn out.

"Good morning!" I greeted him cheerily. "Hey- don't look so surprised! I know I'm not normally up this early, but I'm so excited! I was just thinking- only another 33 days until *Christmas* morning! And-"

"It isn't morning, Pete." Jeff interrupted. "It's 6 o'clock!"

"Yeah." I nodded. "6am."

"No. It's 6*pm*. I've been at work all day. You haven't been asleep the whole time, have you?"

I gazed down at my attire, which – it must be said – was mainly of the pyjama variety, and wondered how convincingly I could lie. "No. Of course not." I said, eyes firmly fixed on the ceiling. "I've been doing that exercise video actually. And, even if I had been in bed all day, you needn't be so cranky about it!"

"Sorry. You know I always get like this when I've been too busy for a smoke."

Yet again, I found myself puzzling over such a remark. The time had come to end the mystery. "Do you though? Because..." I chewed my lip in concentration. "...Until a few months ago, I don't really remember you smoking all that much?"

"No? I've always smoked... Now and then. Maybe now more than then. Stress and all that, but..." He shrugged dismissively. "Remember back in fifth year? Mr. Plumber used to call me Smoky Jeff?"

"Yeah, but I'm pretty sure he meant it ironically. You were the only one in his Future Economics class that didn't try to sneak out for a fag every time he went for his regimented toilet break. And even if you did take the odd sneaky drag behind the science block, and he actually meant it seriously, the guy's hardly to be trusted. Didn't he end up teaching the wrong syllabus and getting sacked?"

"Yeah. I don't know he got the job in the first place. But it was the 80s. I suppose all you needed was a rudimentary knowledge of Grange Hill back then. He completely misinterpreted the name of the subject, putting the whole emphasis on the 'future' bit, and pretty much forgot the 'economics'. He used to come in wearing a robot costume most Fridays, and we all failed our exam because when that question came up about 'overcoming the struggle to break even', we all wrote about the practical difficulties of trying to slow a jet powered rocket car. He was convinced we'd be living on the moon in houses made of Bakelite come the year 2000, and that Brian May would be king of the galactic republic. Still, it wasn't all bad. We got to spend 2 years just pissing about and watching that futuristic cartoon. Ah, what was it called?" He tapped at his temples. "You know? It was sort of like a space-age spin on The Flintstones?"

"Hmmm... I honestly can't remember. Apart from retaining all the useful stuff – like... A chronological list of all the lost Troughton episodes – my memory's pretty ropey nowadays. In fact, didn't we start talking about something else?"

"God knows!" Jeff laughed. "I don't know about you, but I've suddenly got a massive urge to watch the Jetsons. How about it?"

Jeff: Tuesday 23rd November

Pete isn't talking to me because I said that 'The Horns of Nimon' "wasn't that bad". I've been searching all over the internet for a toy – I mean *replica* – Of Romana's sonic screwdriver, but to no avail! What was the point in paying £150 for that River Song one in my desperate attempt to have the complete collection?

Jeff: Wednesday 24th November

Pete's still insisting that we never owned a microwave. I flicked back through my diary to the day I got arrested, and I quite clearly stated that I was cooking a microwavable cheeseburger. Have I gone mad?

Kevin came into the shop this morning with 'The Guys'. He was asking me if I would order in some WWF action figures.

"You know the, err, Undertaker? Well he got a new costume. He's lord of the undead now with, err, red on his hat." He went on to tell me the story about the goat in the back of the car. When I checked my watch, I'd somehow lost an hour.

I decided I'm possibly too harsh on Kevin – he can't really help being the way he is – so, on my lunch break, we went and sat by the fountains and I bought us some sausage rolls. The air was cold and crisp in that brilliant early winter way, and by now all the shops in town were covered in tinsel. We actually managed to have a conversation about 'Amy's Choice', but then he strayed back on to wrestling.

"Well, I'd better get back to work." I stood up, brushing pastry from my jeans.

"Oh yeah, Dad asked me to give you this." He handed me a magazine. It was a brochure for a gun supplier. 'Billy Bowie's Shooters – *for a brighter future'*.

Pete: Wednesday 24th November

I may have just got rid of Andy Pond forever! He showed up, saying he had 'devastating' news and insisted I consume a vat of apology 'ice cream' before he told me. After a couple of mouthfuls, however, he gripped my arm and told me he could contain himself no longer.

"I'm afraid I'm going back home... To America." Tightly gripping my thigh, he delivered the news as though he'd only been given a few months to live. "And I may be some time." Naturally, I was thrilled, but there and then I was left in a difficult position. Whilst my initial reaction was to jump up and down, punching the air, shouting 'wahey!', I knew my actual response had to be more sombre and measured. I hugged him with sincere emotion for the first time ever. I was sincerely glad to be rid of him.

"Why, Andy, why?" I asked, adopting a melodramatic tone.

"My therapist's had another breakdown." He sobbed. "He needs me. I have to level with you though. I've got no idea how I'm going to talk him down this time." Oh no. I didn't mean to seem selfish,

357

but this looked in danger of turning into a long conversation.

"Well, I'm sure you'll think of something." I smiled, guiding Andy to the doorway with a hand on his shoulder.

"Thanks Pete. I knew you'd understand. You're a good man. One of the best." He seemed to be leaving, so I went to the toilet. But when I came out, 10 minutes later, he was still there, leaning by the bathroom door and grinning. Oh god- he hadn't been listening, had he? He continued speaking, as though there'd been no interval whatsoever, except that his mood seemed to have changed completely. "Anyway, it's not all bad news!" He enthused: perky, upbeat, chipper even. "My friend Don called – says he's got me an audition for the new 'Star Wars' film. You know the one? They're calling it 'Star Wars 7'."

"Don?" I tilted my head. "Are you sure that's real? I'm pretty sure they're not actually making another 'Star Wars'..."

"No. Green lit. Luke George is directing it and all!"

"Riiiggghht..." The whole thing was almost certainly some kind of practical joke, but if I told him, he might not go. After a moment's thought, I decided to do the honourable thing. "So, what part are you auditioning for?"

"The robot." He beamed with tragic pride.

"I knew it! That part's got your name written all over it."

Pete: Thursday 25th November

Jeff hovered near the receiver, as I replaced the phone.

"Was that..?" He looked surprised.

"Yep." I nodded. "Grandma."

"But didn't she die... Or something?"

358

"Nah, she's more alive than me or you."

"Christ... But she must be ancient?"

"Hardly. She's looking to celebrate her hundredth birthday by marrying hubby number 3."

"We should introduce her to Mr. Harrison. He's got to be at least 200. What did she want anyway?"

"Well, she'd been adding holiday photos on her Facebook, saw that Andy had ended his imaginary relationship with me, and was calling to tell me how sorry she was. I filled her in of course, but that wasn't easy because her short-term memory problem makes her imagine things that haven't really happened. I'd vowed to stop lying myself into awkward situations, but I found myself constructing some pretty elaborate imaginings to make sure Grandma won't imagine the imaginary."

"How did you do that exactly?"

"I used my imagination."

"And now?"

"Well, as things stand, she thinks I'm a bisexual named Barry."

Jeff: Thursday 25th November

In preparation for Rachel coming round, I decided to try and make the flat look presentable and remove anything incriminating. I tidied away a few stray copies of FHM and Nuts into a drawer, and collected some of Pete's toys, which I left in a pile outside his door.

As I was lifting up a stack of 70s Doctor Who annuals, a photograph of me and Daisy fell to the carpet. I picked it up and sighed, a heavy feeling in my heart. It was a picture from the early days, when things had been great between us. We'd been so much more... *Compatible*. Despite everything, despite how she irritated me some times, she really was a great woman. She was lovely, in fact.

She really didn't deserve to be in Hampton Minimum Security Prison...

I'd promised to drive her to the airport for her trial in Dublin after the Tony Blair incident... And it wasn't like I'd *forgotten* ... But when we found out that Sophie Aldred was signing autographs in Blackpool, I just didn't remember to do it.

Sophie Aldred has a *lot* to answer for...

Jeff: Friday 26th November

My head's been teaming with ideas all day. I'm going to get straight to work on 'The West Bank'.

7pm: Okay, this is it. The *definitive* top ten:

The Daemons / The Sea Devils / The Green Death / Tomb of the Cybermen / Spearhead From Space / The Time Warrior / The Terror of the Autons / The Three Doctors / The Brain of Morbius / Genesis of the Daleks / The Android Invasion / The Pyramids of Mars / The Seeds of Doom / City of Death / The Curse of Fenric / Battlefield / Remembrance of the Daleks

OK, that's not exactly ten, but it'll do.

9pm: I forgot 'Terror of the Zygons'! What a moron I am!

9:30pm: I realised there are no new episodes. Even the brilliant ones like 'Human Nature' just don't have quite the same magic about them. Perhaps if the scarecrow's music was a little less camp, then it'd be up there...

10:45pm: After much deliberation, I think that 'The Eleventh Hour' can in fact stand shoulder to shoulder with the likes of 'Caves of Androzani'.

12am : I forgot to include 'Caves of Androzani'! This is hopeless..!

3:09am: 'The Five Doctors'! 'The Invasion'! 'The Dalek Invasion of Earth'..?

Jeff: Saturday 27th November

I'd banished Pete to his room for my evening with Rachel. He was staying put, but playing 'Magical Mystery Tour' too loudly, the bastard! If he thought he could do a Matt Smith and come in here to start rewiring things, he had another thing coming!

I needed to put on something romantic that was loud enough to drown out The Beatles. The best I could come up with was The Chemical Brothers.

We were on the sofa drinking red wine and reminiscing about old times. The time Gitworth caught us smoking behind the maths block, the mix tapes I made her... I was so glad we'd decided to put up the decorations up early. The sparkling baubles on the tree reflected in her green eyes and she looked beautiful. After a couple of glasses, she rested her head on my shoulder. Her face was so close to mine, I wanted to kiss her. I needed to.

But then the subject turned to Brutus.

"It's terrible. He's the father of my child and I love him." She said softly. "But I'm not *in* love with him." *Tell me you love me! Tell me you love me!* "I just don't know what to do."

"Well, if you're not happy..." I mumbled sagely. Nice one, Gandalf.

"I'm not happy." Her eyes fixed on mine. "But I can't see how my life could be any better." She said mournfully. *You could be with me!* "Nobody could ever love me as much as he does." *I could! I could! I would! I do!* I wanted to scream at her, but stupidity and nerves held me back.

"I wish we were young again." She sleepily draped an arm around me and laid her head on my chest. I could hardly breathe with the exhilaration.

I took her into my bedroom and presented her with a vinyl copy of 'Songs From The Big Chair' she had left at my house when she was 15. She said I could keep it. At that moment a look passed between us. It was like everything stopped. A moment of utter realisation. But them she decided she had to go.

I walked her out into the rain soaked night where the taxi waited. Out of the corner of my eye I could just catch the glow of the fairy lights around our kitchen window. It felt like that Christmas so many years ago, except that time it was my mum waiting in the car, come to take me home to eat mince pies and exchange cards with Auntie Linda and Uncle Max. Once they'd gone, I'd rushed upstairs with a little bottle of French beer (a Christmas treat!) and read the letter Rachel had written for me that I wasn't allowed to peek at until I got home. Even the paper smelled of her. I lay there reading and re-reading, feeling that wonderful sensation of teenage love, as though I could burst with all the emotion within. I listened to Tears For Fears as I drafted a reply. The reply she would never receive.

"Rachel..." I began as we neared the end of the drive. "I've always wanted to know... What perfume do you wear?" The rain was beginning to smudge her make up.

"I don't wear perfume, Jeff." She laughed. "Never. The only time I ever wore perfume was when I was 13. It was on our first date."

"The fireworks display at the rugby club."

"Yeah." She smiled, opening the door.

"I'll see you soon." I said, stepping forward and embracing her. She held me more tightly than usual and didn't move. Just like she used to.

I don't know what happened, how it happened, or who started it. One minute we were hugging, just beginning to

362

separate and the next we were kissing. It was like a dream. I had no knowledge of it beginning – I was just there in the middle of it. And it was perfect. The faint sound of 'I Want You/She's So Heavy' sailed from Pete's bedroom window as the rain continued to soak us. I'm not sure how long it lasted, but eventually she slammed the taxi door closed behind her and we ran back inside.

We tore up the stairs and into my bedroom, shedding our drenched clothes. Her unfinished glass of wine was still perched on the bookshelf. She quickly knocked it back before falling onto my bed in her underwear. It was everything I'd ever dreamed of for the last 25 years. 'Because' hummed softly through the wall as I lay beside her, kissing my way down her side. She was old now. The last time my lips touched her skin she was a teenager. Soft and unblemished. Now her contours were framed with slight creases, tiny scars and stretch marks, and I loved every single one of them. I loved her.

I entered her, savouring the moment that had been denied to me for decades, and then buried my face into her neck as we made love. I could just hear 'You Never Give Me Your Money' over the sound of our breathing: '*One sweet dream came true today...*'

I inhaled the scent of her hair as her arms tightened about me. She smelled of Christmas.

Pete: Saturday 27th November

Rachel was coming over, and that meant trouble. I was going to have to at least try and do something. I thought I'd come up with the perfect idea but, strangely, Jeff didn't seem too keen on my suggestion that I sit between them while we all watched the 'Terminator' quadrilogy together. He seemed to be growing increasingly annoyed as I shadowed him round the house, and even had the tenacity to banish me to my room. The bastard! Of course, I did it, because I love him – and deep down we all know he'll never leave me for Rachel – but I made sure to put 'Magical Mystery Tour' on extra loud. Hahaha! My experimental psychedelia would keep them from the bedroom for sure. Not only that, I'd just vacuumed the upholstery and no respectable person would dare canoodle on a clean sofa. Only moments later, he retaliated with The Chemical Brothers and I knew it was all out musical war.

I decided to stick with The Beatles, in the hope that Rachel would find them too unfashionable and decide to leave. And then who'd be there to pick up the pieces? The Petemeister! But it didn't seem to be working. Far be it from me to eavesdrop, but as I stood with a tumbler pressed against the door, taking shorthand notes on their conversation, and whispering my findings to a Dictaphone, they seemed to be moving into worryingly romantic territory. It was such a struggle to resist interrupting. Secretly, I was half-concocting a dastardly plan that involved me going to the bathroom, 'accidentally' leaving the door open, and... Well, that was it actually. Thankfully, I didn't have to take such extreme measures, and breathed a sigh of relief when Rachel reached for her coat. I put 'Abbey Road' on, dropping the needle in at 'Octopus' Garden' as extra incentive for her to leave. I knew it was a dangerous thing to do. Me and Ringo Starr had entered into a dark alliance.

When the track came to an end, I heard Jeff and Rachel vacating the room and drove my swivel chair to the window just to make sure that she was definitely going. I was relieved to see the taxi arrive. Thank god – the evening was ours! I was going to dig out my VHS copy of 'Curse of Fatal Death'. Then it happened. I was horrified to hear them running back into the flat. This could only mean one thing. I don't know why, but

I felt overcome by a strange sense of regret –
something I couldn't define. I put 'Let it Be' on,
playing only the title track and 'Across the Universe'...
over and over again.

Pete: Sunday 28th November

Ha! Not wanting to face Jeff, I spent the majority of the
day locked away playing Pacman. The joke was on
everyone else, because I eventually ended up in the top
5 high scores! Now look who's having a good time in
their bedroom! Who needed a girlfriend? Who needed
love? Watching Pacman wipe out Inky, Blinky, Pinky
and, indeed, Clyde had to be *better than sex.* But
catching sight of myself in the full-length mirror,
sweating from the exertion of a kids' computer game
and looking like Bono gone wrong, my confidence
wavered somewhat.

   I reached shakily for the phone, with the intention of
leaving a heartfelt, but straight-to-the-point, message
for Simone. I stuttered my way through several
beginnings, paused and suddenly found myself saying
"Please. I don't know what to say anymore. I just want
someone to love me. Please."

Monday 29th November

Dear Jeffrey,

I know it's a little early – but
preparation is a virtue – so I thought it
best to plan the Christmas Itinerary.

12pm: You will arrive at our house and
   locate your car in space A. (Cones will
   be displayed on the day.)

12:15 - 12:45: The family will exchange gifts. This year's gift budget is £25 - £30 per person.

12:45: We will toast the birth of our Lord and Saviour with a small glass of white wine. (Prune juice for Kevin. With his condition, alcohol is not advisable.)

13:00: Whilst the women prepare the food, the men will sing a hymn: 'All I Want To Do Is Praise Him'. Then we will watch the Queen's speech.

14:00: We will sit down for Christmas Dinner. This will consist of Turkey, Brussels Sprouts, Boiled Potatoes, Roast Potatoes, Carrots, Mint Sauce, Gravy and Ostrich Pate (a delicacy I discovered whilst posted in South Africa).

15:00: We will retire to the living room and choose from a selection of beverages.

Please let me know this is agreeable ASAP.

Seasonal regards,
Ronald Slater (Your Father)

Pete: Monday 29th November

"I've had some time to think..." Simone sat at the edge of my bed, still wearing a coat and sporting a pair of disproportionately large sunglasses, even though we were indoors and it was winter. "And I *think* that there are *quite a few* things to love about you."

"Right." I nodded despondently, feeling strangely unmoved by the indifference of this admission, and wishing I'd settled on a better choice of clothes for the occasion. I'd decided that all my stuff needed washing wholesale, but the central heating was on the blink,

366

and the only dry thing I had was a free-size white robe. The jury was out on whether it made me look more like an escaped hospital patient or the leader of some obscure cult.

"I mean, you're nice. And you... Try hard. You're very... Trying." She leaned over an stroked my bare arm in a curiously mechanistic way. It was difficult to tell how sincere she was being behind those sunglasses, which seemed to be expanding by the second, threatening to engulf her entire face. It was also difficult to tell which way this was going to go, or know what she was about to suggest. And it was *definitely* difficult to know if I'd actually want whatever it was she was going to suggest. "We've had our differences, but I really feel we can make this work, especially..." She gently moved my wrist onto her body, running it along her breast and down to her stomach. I felt a surge of electricity course through my legs. "Especially with baby on the way." She smiled. Was it just me or were things going unusually well? "So, I guess what I'm saying is, in a way, I *do* love you... And if you'd be able to help me out with some money for the baby..." Suddenly, her words weren't quite sinking in.

"Love?" My body trembled slightly, trying to feel hopeful, but instinctively shrugging itself away.

"Love." Simone nodded. "And money."

"You want some money?" I motioned to the dresser, feeling hazy and detached. All this emotional complexity – or the high bombardment of positive ions – was making me weary. I suppose that bottle of brandy and the bag of sugar mice I'd had for breakfast couldn't have helped.

"You'd really do that for us Pete? Oh, it's so kind of you to offer!" She lifted her sunglasses at last, and I saw that she was wearing pretty eye-liner, just like in the old days.

Still I hesitated, watching her play with the synthetic flower in her hair, and opened my mouth unsure what word would come out. It was a "yes." I saw my reflection rising in a resigned fashion, scrambling under the bed for a brightly coloured sports bag, which had come with a matching shell-suit in 1991. I saw myself handing Simone two big fistfuls of fivers. But it didn't feel like *me* that was doing it. I was completely out of it. Perhaps I had a cold coming on? I knew I shouldn't have sold my soul to Ringo! Simone took the money, and said she had to go to the bathroom.

Just then, her mobile started ringing. I staggered back in horror, coming to my senses the moment I heard the atrocious ring tone: a synthesised version of The Smiths' 'How Soon is Now?', with a cat yowling over its wailing melody. I decided to ignore it, but Simone had disabled her voicemail, so it droned on incessantly, the kitten noises making me want to fling myself out of the window and into the nearest skip. The phone was about 10 years newer than mine, so I couldn't work out which button made it talk, but I did manage to ascertain that the caller was Kitty and the ringtone was called 'How Soon is Meow?'. I eventually shut it up by holding down a big square button next to what I think must have been the 'alert the police' key (it featured something that looked a little like a helmet). The phone had a lot more buttons than mine. One of them had a picture of a butler on it. I pressed it, and raised the speaker to my ear. A man with a Queen's English accent asked if there was anything he could attend to. I got scared and hung up. Where the hell was Simone?

Whilst I'd been playing about with her space-phone, I noticed I'd got a text on my trusty steam-powered model. It was from someone called Kate. But I didn't know anyone called Kate! My contacts list was pretty much a closed book. I certainly thought I would have remembered adding someone I hadn't met, or who didn't exist, because it would be totally irrational just to *invent* a complete person. It all started to slot horribly into place when I read the message, and realised I'd been made a fool of once more: '*Hey Sim! How much did you manage 2 get out of him this time? Doesn't still reckon yor preggers, does he? How's about we spend your winnings at The No. 3 this Fri? K'*. I pressed my clenched fists to my forehead, feeling so totally stupid.

When Simone reappeared, I thrust her bag into her hands, hurled her mobile into the next room and told her to get out. She spluttered a protest, but this time I screamed it: "GET THE HELL OUT!"

I read the message one more time, then took an underarm swing at the mirror with my phone. Both of them smashed and I gleaned great pleasure in jumping on the shattered fragments, mashing them into tiny pieces.

Jeff: Wednesday 1st December

It's time to plan the Doctor Who Christmas Countdown!! A televisual treat to accompany each Adventures in Time advent calendar chocolate...

12th – Listen to William Hartnell wishing us a merry Christmas from 'The Dalek's Master Plan' episode 7.
13th – David Tennant's "I love Christmas" BBC speech.
14th – Nicola Bryant's 2008 Christmas message.
15th – David Tennant flying the TARDIS with reindeer.
16th – The TV Movie (It has Christmas trees in in).
17th – The Dead Ringer's 'Christmas Day at Doctor Who's sketch.
19th – 'The Christmas Invasion'.
20th – 'The Runaway Bride'.

21st – 'Voyage of the Dammed'.
22nd – 'The Next Doctor'.
23rd – 'The End of Time (Part One)'.
24th – 'The End Of Time (Part Two)'.

Pete: Tuesday 30th November

It's fine. It's absolutely fine. I don't actually *need* a mobile phone. If anything, they actually *restrict* social interaction. Perhaps that's where I've been going wrong. Perhaps mobile phones can give you agoraphobia as well as cancer and radiation poisoning. In fact, if you think about it, there's nothing good about them. They're expensive, unreliable and infuriating; they allow unwelcome relatives to get in touch without prior warning; and mean that you're traceable at every moment. It's like having a self-inflicted homing device stashed next to your crotch. I bet that if the police wanted to find me, they'd be able to pinpoint my exact location. Although I must admit, in my case, that probably wouldn't be too difficult anyway. I mean, I don't really do anything and I'm always in the flat. Nevertheless, the point still stands. I certainly won't be missing my mobile phone. MOBILE PHONES ARE THE ENEMY OF FREEDOM!

Pete: Wednesday 1st December

Oh god! I miss my mobile phone! I miss the Matt Smith wallpaper, and the way it made TARDIS landing noises when you put it on charge. I long to update Jeff with my important thoughts and discoveries at any given moment. They were already stacking up: 'Is it possible to break the light speed barrier on a bicycle?' 'Do hedgehogs come from the moon?' And, 'I've accidentally dropped all our teaspoons in the toaster'. It's only been gone for 24 hours, and already it feels like a lifetime. And then a mortifying thought struck me. What if Colin Baker tried to call back?!

I got down on my hands and knees, crawling round and trying to retrieve as many pieces as I could. The only substantial bits I found were a chunk of circuit board, half the screen, and a squashed number 3 key. How ironic! On the plus side, I also found half a 'Marathon' bar, which set the latter part of the day off to a more promising start.

I remembered that it was now officially Advent, and went through to the lounge to open my square on the Doctor Who calender. Seating myself on the sofa, I savoured the chocolate. Christ- it was delicious! But one chocolate was never enough. I suppose I could always eat day 2, and have a day off tomorrow. I did, and returned to my seat, switching the TV on and then promptly off when I saw Anthea Turner's face. Everything seemed so quiet. I drummed a rhythm on my legs, attempting to think of anything other than the appetising contents behind the remaining 22 doors. Picking up a puzzle book, I hummed to myself, feigning contentedness. But it wasn't fooling anyone. I lunged upwards, toppling the sofa and seized the advent calender from the wall with both hands, tearing the cardboard clean off, slashing the foil and shaking it vigorously into my mouth.

Jeff: Friday 3rd December

I'm still reeling from last weekend. My sheets still smell of Rachel. I haven't heard from her since, and I don't really know what to do. I just have this feeling that everything's going to be okay! I decided to be grown up and send her a serious message: '*What happens now?*' Within a few minutes she replied: '*I don't know. I've always loved you, Jeff x*'.

It was time to listen to the series 5 soundtrack and dance around the room like a maniac!

Jeff: Saturday 4th December

On Facebook, Rachel has changed her relationship status to '*It's complicated!*'

I hit the town on my lunch break, dizzy with euphoria and ready to do some Christmas shopping... Bollocks to £25 – £30 per person. I'd put it all on my Mastercard! Everything was gonna be fine!

I bought Dom the complete 'Buffy' box set, a WWF DVD for Kevin and some 'Quantum Leap' novels for Pete, then realised that I needed some normal friends. Which brought me onto Rachel! I bought her a gold and silver diamond locket from Beaverbrooks, some Versace *Crystal Noir* perfume and a copy of 'Songs from the Big Chair' on CD. I got my dad an LED kinetic torch and an air rifle and my mum the 'Midsommer Murders' DVD collection.

I went back to the shop breathless. I felt like the best guy in the world!

Jeff: Sunday 5th December

Pete isn't allowed to go in my room. As well as his 'Quantum Leap' books, I got him about £100 worth of Doctor Who toys from work.

We pinned the Christmas Countdown to the fridge and danced around to 'The Stowaway' whilst playing with our inflatable Doctor Who beach ball. I'd placed a pre-Christmas order with Tesco.com, which arrived just as the song was ending. I'd ordered two crates of Stella, two bottles of sherry, ten boxes of mince pies and more crisps than we could fit in the cupboard.

This was going to be a Christmas to remember!

Pete: Sunday 5th December

Jeff went to wrap some Christmas presents, and I got thinking about Simone – but very differently to how I'd been thinking about her for the last few days... The last few weeks... The last few *years*. In fact, for the first time since I'd met her, I was blissfully indifferent. I didn't care. I'd asserted myself, chucked her out, and I was so proud for doing it that I didn't feel bad about letting her go. It was like taking the bandage off a 3 year old cut and finding that it had actually healed over a long time ago. And it got me thinking... If I wasn't going to let *her* hold me back, then why should I let the rest of the world? I needed to make some kind of statement, if only to prove to myself, that I was getting better. I looked to the dark window, thinking hard and suddenly knew where to start.

"Jeff?!" I all but ran to find him, even though I knew he was only on the other side of the flat.

There was a muffled "Don't come in!" from within his bedroom, a frantic tearing of sticky tape, and the door opened by the tiniest crack so that all I could see was one of his eyes peering through.

"I need to talk to you. I'm going to put the kettle on. 5 minutes?"

"Can't it wait?" He cast a nervous backward glance.

"No." I shook my head vigorously. "I mean, I *need* to *talk*." Instantly, he seemed to understood.

"Okay." He held up four fingers. "5 minutes..."

I went to stock up a tray with tea paraphernalia, watching the steam rising in front of the rainy

373

windowpane as the kettle boiled, thinking I should be bracing myself, but feeling strangely calm. Once I said it, there was no turning back. I had to make a stand.

Jeff was already sat waiting in the living room when I brought the tray through, a teapot, milk cartoon and pair of cups balanced precariously around a packet of biscuits. I'd lingered over the ginger nuts, but had taken an executive decision and plumped for the serious conversation biscuits – rich tea.

"Jeff?" I took the seat opposite. "You know a while ago when we had a chat about me maybe being..." I chewed over the word, until he said it for me.

"Agoraphobic?"

"Yeah. And I went on the defensive, and said it wasn't true?" He looked serious. "And I honestly tried to do the whole signing on thing, but I got a bit... Well, *scared.*" Even now, the memory of Letitia Stevens made me shudder. Jeff placed a sympathetic hand on my leg. "Well, anyway, I think... I think you might have been right. I mean, I'm always having these revelations about completely minor things and fussing around, trying to fix them as though it's become the most important thing in the world. But really it doesn't matter what order my Target books are in, or whether I put HP or Heinz at the front of cupboard..." He looked at me with new admiration, and it only diminished slightly when I added "...So long as they're both in the 'H' section, of course. But I think all that stuff's just a cover up for something bigger, like one part of me knows there's something up, but the other bit won't admit it, so I drown out my *real* thoughts with..." I focussed hard and took a deep breath. This was the tough bit. "...Pointless... Crap."

"Whoa! Whoa!" His hand tensed on my thigh. "Let me just stop you there. By 'crap', surely you don't mean fish custard, sugar puff sandwiches and dancing round the Christmas tree in fezzes?"

374

"No, no... Course not." I smiled. "More like colour coding the towels, and eating the whole Advent Calender in one day."

"*My* Advent calender?!" He affected his rather convincing Nick Courtney impersonation.

"That's not the point." I quickly changed the subject. "The thing is, I think you're right. There's something missing. I'm starting to realise that it's no good hiding from the real world anymore, because you end up living half a life. And, even then, the bad stuff can still get you in your own home. It's like..." I tapped at my jawline frantically. "...Sometimes when I look through a crack in the curtains, I get the same feeling as when I read my old diaries, knowing there's something slipping through my fingers and falling away from me but not knowing what that 'something' is. But I'm *sure* it's important. And I always thought that if I had the right reasons, I'd want to go back out again, but the reasons are never going to just present themselves. I need to go and find them for myself."

Jeff looked at me, nodding in respect. "What're you saying, Pete?"

"I'm saying I've just made my new year's resolution for 2011 – I'm going to go outside."

EPISODE IV:
MONDAY 6TH DECEMBER

A new start. A new hope. I had to clear the decks before I could do it, of course. Thankfully, that didn't exactly take too long. Just one of the many advantages of having no phone and very few friends: no texts, no new emails. Just one Facebook message, but only from Dom – more paranoid crap: *'Aliens back! Area52.com confirmation: Type 2 craft seen in your area. Run for it!'* I didn't bother responding. I knew he'd only be round here later telling us that *this time* it had been a false alarm, but we'd better watch out. I had my own demons to contend with.

Taking a lungful of air, I placed my hands on the windowsill, brushing the curtains open in the middle and allowing just the smallest shaft of light to flood through. I looked back and saw that my room looked surprisingly un-yellow. In fact, it was actually quite colourful when the outside light wasn't filtered through thick layers of net and fabric. That was it. I knew for sure that it was the right thing to do.

The curtains hadn't been fully open for a very long time. Occasionally, I might have peered through, but only to find out what the weather was like; if it was day or night, to stop myself getting totally disorientated; or sometimes if Jeff was late, and I was worried about him. But that was all. No one could see into my room, and I *certainly* hadn't wanted to see out. Not for a very long while, at least. Now, I wanted to see out more than anything. More than I wanted a pizza, more than I wanted a girlfriend, possibly even more than I wanted to see the Doctor Who Christmas special. 'On the count of three', I urged myself on. 'A big deep breath'. 'Today is the first day of the rest of your life'. No, scrap that bullshit. I had it! 'You're Christopher Eccleston, Pete... And a pair o' poncy curtains in't gonna stop yer gettin' out there to kick seven shades of shit outta the Nestene Consciousness!' I yanked them aside, pulling the hooks clean off the rails, and fell backwards onto the bed, laughing in the swirling dust.

Rubbing my eyes when it cleared, I was taken aback at how alive everything looked in my room. It was like I was inside a computer monitor, and someone had just turned the contrast up. Easing myself up, I saw lights coming from outside. Practically every house had a Christmas tree in the window. It looked like a particularly festive *bomb* had gone off in Number 13's garden, where every spare inch of space was filled with inflatable snowmen, candy-cane houses, and plastic reindeer. It was hideously tacky, of course, but I was over the moon. We weren't the only ones who started celebrating Christmas before it was actually Christmas. And surely that meant that, at this time of year, we were just normal people! Imagine that! I looked to the end of the street and saw that even Omar, who didn't celebrate Christmas, had of string of lights around his shop window. Somehow, that made everything right with the world. Okay, so our street was no winter wonderland, but everything was clear and frosty, giving it an extra sparkle. Kids were walking home from school, chattering animatedly to their parents. One of them was even wearing a Doctor Who backpack, with a big picture of Matt Smith's face on it. Why didn't I have one of those?

After we first moved in, I never really paid any attention to this street, but now I found everything about it fantastically intricate and detailed. It was like I could have stood there for ages, watching ordinary human drama unfold, smiling wistfully and muttering 'Takeaway, 2am' to myself. I was about to go and make a brew when I noticed a pretty girl in a Tom Baker scarf looking up to our flats. She might even have been looking at *me*. She did seem to be mouthing something, although it was impossible to tell if she was shouting to get my attention or having a conversation on a mobile phone. Dom had told me some of them were so small they fit right into your ears nowadays. Well, I'd already taken one bold step today – I could manage another. I lifted the latch and pushed against the glass but it didn't budge. It'd been a long time since I'd had it open. So I took a step back and attacked it with a forceful shove. Still, it wouldn't shift. Well, at least I knew I wouldn't be falling out of it any time soon! I gave it one more go, driving all my weight into it. With a reluctant crack, and splintering of paint, it swung open, and a rush of icy air stung my face: it was an unfamiliar sensation – one I would normally only associate with going to the freezer to get an ice lolly.

The girl was just turning away. I could see now that she *was* on her mobile, but, alerted by the noise, she turned and gave me a wave. I felt a warmth shudder through me, spreading outward to my toes and fingers but lingering with a tickling sensation.

The doorbell started ringing. Maybe it was the pretty girl! If so, I had to try and look my best. I didn't have much to work with, so I put on a Santa hat and aimed for cute and charming instead. All but dancing down the staircase, singing 'Spaceman Came Travelling' at the top of my voice, I was overcome with the overwhelming feeling that this was going to be the best Christmas ever! I was even slightly pleased – albeit in a very weird way – when I found out it wasn't the pretty girl calling on me.

"Hello Simone." I smiled. "You know, I'm actually quite glad to see you."

"Oh, thank god." She reached out to touch me, but I pulled away. "I think we need to talk. Can I come in?"

"Can you come in? Let me think about that... Erm... No."

"But I bought you a present... To say sorry." This sounded a lot more genuine than the first time she'd reappeared and said the same thing. Obviously, she was *genuinely* desperate for cash.

"It's a Twix?" I said, shaking my head.

"No..." She held it on her outstretched palm and ran her other hand along it like a saleswoman making a presentation. "It's four Twixes. Twixi? It's..." She grew visibly aggravated. I smiled and tried to look nonchalant, which isn't very easy when you're dressed as Father Christmas. "It's four, okay?!"

"Not really. It's not even a proper Twix. It's supermarket own brand. You can keep it. You may as well eat it on your way home, because you're not coming in."

"But I've got to explain to you. That message you saw... It's not how it looks! I didn't mean to lie to you. I just got a bit *confused*..." Her eyelashes fluttered.

"You got 7-months-pregnant worth of confused? That's pretty mixed up!"

"It was an accident. Honest! It's Rik. He put loads of pressure on me. He's not as good a man as you." Once more she tried to lay a hand on my chest, and once more I pulled away.

"Simone..." I sighed, leaning to block the entrance. "I'm glad you came back into my life, I really am, because – believe it or not – you've helped put things in perspective, and now I *know* I don't need you. In fact, I'm pretty sure that my life would have been a lot better these last few years if you hadn't featured in it. I just wish it hadn't taken you lying and extorting cash to wake me up. I don't want you to apologise. I don't even think there's much point in feeling guilty. Because it's true: out of all evil must come something good, as a certain famous Doctor once said."

"What?" She narrowed her eyes. "Doctor Dre?"

"Merry Christmas, Simone." I chucked her the Santa hat, shut the door, and fell laughing against the wall.

I was trying to gently remove the Hoovian from the cupboard without all the detritus within avalanching down on me, when I spied a familiar shape at the back, lodged beneath the Doctor Who Scene It game. (The most pointless game we ever played: we've literally *scene* everything and we were playing against each other.) The microwave! We did have one! I wasn't going mad! What was it doing in the cupboard? I could use it to make myself a cottage pie. I was feeling pretty hungry.

I looked for somewhere to put it on the kitchen surface, and saw a rectangular gap housing a small piece of cardboard which read '*This bit has always been empty*'. I plugged it in. It seemed to be working fine, if emitting slightly more Dalek mothership "Wum-Wum" noises than usual.

I went to my room to wait for it to heat up when I heard a knock at the door. I hoped Pete would go. I couldn't be arsed – I was in the middle of watching a home made trailer for the return of Adric that someone had posted on Youtube.

I resumed my Christmas medley, punching the air and walked back towards the flat, two steps at a time. I only got part way when the doorbell rang once more. Something uncomfortable throbbed behind my ribs. Not again! Please don't ruin my brief triumph. It had made me feel... *briefly triumphant.* **Surely I was allowed that just once this year? I was relieved when I turned back. The shadow beyond the frosted glass came into focus and I could see that it belonged to somebody short and thin: definitely not Simone then.**

"Ah, good day kind sir! May I come in? I wouldn't wish to appear intrusive, but it's exceedingly cold out here." I stood aside, and an elderly Quentin Crisp lookalike entered, strolling over to the nearest mirror to adjust his cravat and brush a few specks of dust off his

wine-coloured shirt with a fedora. "Thank you. Most generous of you. Small acts of generosity are so often unrewarded. Here..." He handed me an elegant looking box of Belgian chocolates, tied with a satin ribbon. "I'm here to see Jeffrey Greene. Tell him it's about The Doctor..."

"What?" I blinked wildly, wondering if I was stuck in some sort of inverse time loop. "Doctor Dre?"

"Ah, no. I presume you're referring to your general practitioner? You're not sick, are you?"

"Erm, no... I *am* a bit confused... But... That's normal."

"Not to worry. Me and Mr. Greene are good friends. Thomas Asbo at your service!" He placed a manicured hand on my shoulder. "I assure you, there's nothing to be confused about." Except that there was, because the door to the downstairs flat suddenly burst open and Mr. Harrison launched himself upon me, babbling frantically.

I took a deep breath, smiling apologetically to Quentin Crisp. "You'd better go up. First door on the left."

"Most obliged."

"Now then, Mr. Harrison." I decided to play it cool. "What seems to be the problem today?"

"Strange things going on in this building!" He cried, sounding unusually coherent. He mustn't have taken his daily solution of brandy yet. "Weird unearthly sounds coming from your kitchen; a ghostly discord echoing round these very corridors, wailing about travelling spacemen. It's ungodly! Oh, there are aliens here alright. I've just seen one climbing up the drainpipe, right into your bedroom." I was about to laugh this off and escort Mr. Harrison back to his favourite chair, when I remembered Dom's message. Okay- so neither of them made the most reliable witnesses, but it couldn't just be a coincidence. Shit!

What if the man I'd just let in had taken his skin off and was currently sucking Jeff's brains out through a curly straw? I knew he was too polite to be human! It seemed too gruesome to contemplate. But then, it also seemed too *unbelievable*.

"What did these *spacemen* look like?" I ventured. I couldn't believe it: here I was, trying to be normal for a change, and I'd already ended up having a conversation about otherworldly beings with a geriatric pensioner.

"Like P-P-P... Penguins." He stuttered. "With colanders on their heads."

"Okkkaaaaayyyy..." That was kind of weird. "Do you and Dom go on the same websites?"

"Websites?!" He said it the same way my dad said 'immigrants', making a crucifix shape with his shaking fingers. "Websites are the *tool* of the aliens. The powers that be use the internet to spy on us!" He seemed remarkably techno-savvy considering he was several centuries old and completely mad.

"Well, I'm sure there's nothing up there, but why don't you come with me and we'll take a look together?"

I heard movement outside, before a gentle rapping upon my bedroom door.

"Tommy!" I beamed.

"Hello, dear heart." He smiled, patting a large black case. "I've brought the merchandise."

"Fantastic! Have a mince pie!" I grabbed the tray from the coffee table and lead him back into my room. "Sherry?" I offered, brandishing a bottle.

"Why not? I suppose it is Christmas after all! I see you've wasted no time in decking the halls, as it were! I do apologise that it's taken me so long to get round. I've just been so terribly busy. But I was having a route through my

383

chest of treasures at the weekend, and I believe I've found the item you were looking for..." He unzipped the bag and produced a video. My face lit up immediately. The clapper board, Romana, Tom Baker!

"'Shada'! That's brilliant!" I wanted to hug the peculiar little man.

"I thought perhaps this would also be of interest..." He produced another video and my heart skipped a beat as I took it from him, my hands shaking.

"The original 1983 release of 'Revenge of the Cybermen'! The very first one with the incorrect cover! I lusted over this as a kid! I sulked for weeks because my Dad wouldn't buy it for me!"

"Well, I am pleased to unite you at last."

"I don't know what to say! Just... WOW! How much?"

"I do not exchange my merchandise for money. The price will be something entirely... *Other*. The price cannot be made known to you until the time is right." A strange silence fell. "I'm joking, of course, my dear boy! Shall we say 50 pounds?"

"Of course. No problem. That's amazing!" I could barely contain my excitement. I couldn't wait to see Pete's face on Christmas morning.

"There are a few other things in the bag. You can keep them if you like – they're no use to me." He waved a bony hand dismissively.

"Thanks! I don't know what to say, Tommy. You're a star!"

"Oh, not at all. Merely a man with a house full of tat. I must be getting off." He drained the sherry from the glass. "Have a *wonderful* Christmas!"

I saw him out and went to the CD player to put on 'The End Of Time' soundtrack. I couldn't stop looking at the video, the cover of which had excited me so much as a young boy. It was pathetic, but my hand was shaking. I needed to calm my nerves! It was madness, but I reached for the Christmas whiskey. Just a tiny sip, then I'd save the rest. But in my childish, frenzied state I only managed to unscrew the bottle before it slipped from my grasp and shattered on the floor. Not the Christmas whiskey!

I grabbed a tea towel and tried to absorb the puddle that was rapidly spreading across the kitchen floor and poured myself a sherry instead, before opening the black bag and rummaging through its contents: A VHS copy of 'K9 and Company', 'Red Dwarf Smeg Ups', 'The Colin Baker Years'. I noticed some Topps Star Wars trading cards at the bottom: C-3P0, Chewbacca, one with a load of aliens that looked like Yoda. They seemed to be original 70s ones – I could give them to Dom for Christmas! The only other thing in the bag was a tattered old cardboard box. Nothing too exciting, but it was a nice gesture of Tommy to let me have them.

I stormed around the room listening to 'The Master Suite', bursting with seasonal joy. I had another sherry. Why the hell not?

Overcome with curiosity, I opened the box to find a cylindrical metal tin within. I tried to open it but it was really tight, and I got the impression it had been sealed for years. Eventually I succumbed to forcing it with my pen knife and – after some serious prising – levered it open with a satisfying pop. It gave off a faint musty smell and I could see that it contained a film reel. How strange! Perhaps it was an old home movie of Tommy's. I flipped the lid over in my hand. There was a label stuck to the front, but the pencil writing upon it was so faint I could barely make it out.

Holding it under my bedside lamp, I squinted at the letters. I realised what it said immediately, but didn't take it in. I had to read it another five times. Even then it still couldn't be real. There, in immaculately neat, aged handwriting, it read *'The Daleks' Master Plan: Episodes 1 – 13'*.

I felt as though my heart had stopped. I didn't know what to do. I glanced out of the window at snowflakes spiralling down and settling on the ledge. The dark night sky was illuminated by the Christmas lights from Omar's across the street. I took a deep breath and savoured the moment. I knew there and then that this could possibly be the best moment of my entire life.

My phone was buzzing, I looked to see that it was Rachel calling. This was the icing on the cake. My dream girl. My dream job. THE DALEKS' MASTER PLAN. *And* it was Christmas. Any day now I'd be handing the film reel over to the delighted BBC archives department. They'd probably interview me on the featurette of the DVD release! Steven Moffat would take me out to lunch as a personal thank you... Which would inevitably lead to me being cast as the Twelfth Doctor! I answered the phone.

"Hello!" I almost yelled the word.

"Hi Jeff..."

"I love you! I love you! Hello! Sorry... I – What? I love you!"

"Are you okay?" She laughed, slightly taken aback.

"Yes! Oh, better than okay! I've got some great news!"

"Really? Well, me too, actually."

"You first!"

"Jeff..." I heard her take a breath. "I'm pregnant."

We skulked cautiously into the house, listening intently for anything extraterrestrial (however you're supposed to do that.) All I could hear was a droning sound, a little like the Dalek mothership, and Jeff having a conversation with the Quentin Crisp guy. So at least I knew no one's brains were being sucked out. As for the Dalek noise, perhaps it was a hidden track on the series 5 soundtrack? Feeling more confident, I strode over to my room, and eased the door open, letting out a cry of shock and clutching my chest when I saw inside. Oh my god. Someone *had* climbed up the drainpipe. But it wasn't an alien. I only wish it had been.

"There's a strange lady in your bedroom." Our neighbour sidled up to me, whispering matter-of-factly.

"So there is." I muttered angrily. Simone was trying to struggle her way off my windowsill, one leg swung over the edge, wriggling frantically, the other one tangled in the curtains. Tightly gripped in her arms was the neon hold-all containing my money.

"I think she might be trying to steal that bag from you. Stop, thief!" Mr. Harrison commentated, somewhat needlessly. Still, I didn't need telling twice. I dived across the bed, aiming to take advantage of her precarious position and snatch the bag from her hands. But it was more difficult than it seemed. Each time I managed to get a decent hold, she yanked it back, nearly overbalancing numerous times in the process. After several attempts, I managed to dig my hands in behind it and pulled with all my weight, but Simone came with it, and we both toppled backwards onto the bed.

Mr. Harrison remained where he was in the corner, cheering me on with a largely nonsensical diatribe. "Come on boy... That's the stuff... Right in the Aztec gold... Just a swift right hook... No, no- not like that. That's the way the enemies won the empire!" Etc. Until, suddenly – god only knows how it happened – *he* was the one holding the bag. For a fraction of a second, everything paused. I was on my feet, by the far side of the bed. Mr. Harrison stood routed to the spot, open mouthed and unmoving. And Simone was partway towards getting up, looking – more than anyone else – like she'd frozen in time. She was the first to snap out of it, leaping forwards to apprehend the bag and make good her escape. And what could Mr. Harrison do to stop her? He looked dazed, and even if he was fully conscious, surely he wouldn't have the strength to resist her.

Just then, there was a loud bang in the kitchen. What the hell? Mr. Harrison came to, leaping to one side away from Simone.

"Look out, old boy – catch!" He slung the bag from behind his shoulder. It all happened in slow motion. Simone fell. The bag sauntered gracefully through the air towards me. Somehow, Mr. Harrison had saved the day. Everything really *was* going to be okay! If I hadn't been so caught up in euphoria of the moment, perhaps I would have felt the bag hit me. I lost my footing as it collided with my arms and watched it fall outside. I couldn't work out why the swirl of five pound notes seemed to be raining upwards until I realised I was looking at it upside down. Skidding backwards on the curtain fabric, I felt a jolt of terror shoot through my body as I edged head first over the window ledge. I was going outside alright. I was falling to my death!

I prepared myself for impact, and cried out with the only words I could. "No! Nooooo! Noooooooooo!" I felt no pain. I just saw a black shape hovering over my inanimate figure. And then I was gone.

Everything stopped. The elation was cut dead and everything was black. It was just me and the phone. I had lost the ability to speak – the ability to be rational or comprehend a single thing. I was snapped back into reality by the clattering the tin made as it fell from my hand, the reel inside dropping onto the kitchen surface. A strange humming noise from the far side of the room caught my attention. Oh, no! The cottage pie!

It was at this point that the microwave exploded, coating the walls and ceiling in sauce. But more disconcertingly, it burst into flame. In my mad panic, I dropped the phone and reached for a nearby tea towel to smother it. I hurled it over the remains of the microwave, realising too late that it was the tea towel soaked in whiskey. It was immediately ablaze and, before I could react, the fire had spread to the curtains. The little plastic Daleks on the windowsill began to melt, and within seconds the entire kitchen was on fire. Noxious fumes from the smouldering curtain rail filled my lungs as I fell to my knees. A blazing stool collapsed, blocking my exit and setting alight the door frame.

I couldn't breathe and fell helplessly onto my back. My eyes began to cloud, and the last thing I saw was the 16mm film of 'The Dalek's Master Plan' bubbling in the heat.

"No!   NO!
NOOOOOOOOOOOOOOOOOOOOOOOOOO!"

Jeff: Wednesday 6th December

I'm really worried. When the credits rolled on part three of Survival the announcer didn't say when it would return. They always say when the next episode is, even when it's the end of a season. I feel like the whole world's falling apart. Doctor Who was what I always loved when I was a child. No matter what happened, moving house or changing school – you always knew that every Saturday night that wonderful man would be there to take you away in his magical blue box.

It's weird that, now I've turned 18, Doctor Who has finished. It's like I'm not a child anymore so I'm not allowed to have it. School's over, everyone's getting jobs. Even Dianna Langton, the girl I sat next to in physics, has had a baby now. And now I'm leaving home to go to university. I always thought I could come back and my childhood would still be there, preserved somehow. I'd come home for the holidays, or for the weekend, and my room would be there with all my Target books on the shelf. My mum would be cooking hotpot downstairs and that weird, scary, brilliant but comforting bass line would be throbbing through the ceiling because Doctor Who was on TV. But it's like everything's just gone.

When I was younger I thought that you grew up gradually, you slotted comfortably into whatever age you were supposed to be. I didn't think it would be like this. I feel like the rug has been pulled from under my feet. I was a child, but now I'm not. I don't know when it happened, or how it happened, I just know I wish it hadn't.

The stories usually end with the TARDIS dematerialising, and you feel like you're going with them. You know there'll be another adventure next week. But tonight there was no TARDIS, just Sylvester and Sophie walking away from the camera and it was like they were leaving me behind. The Doctor's gone. I'm not a little boy anymore and the Doctor's left me.

Jeff: Thursday 7th December

Pete rang me in tears last night. All he could say for about ten minutes was "the tea's getting cold" through bouts of hysterical sobbing, although at one point I think he said it was "all Christopher H Fucking Bidmead's fault". Eventually I heard his Dad yelling in the background about how it was one thing "crying like a nancy" but something else to be "running up a bloody great phone bill". So we went for a pint at Pig & Whistle.

We ended up staying until closing and I was really drunk when I got in. I slumped on my bed feeling like the world was ending. Even Rachel was gone. I reached for a book: Doctor Who and the Daemons. This was just what I needed. I could rely on Barry Letts to cheer me up!

I read the first sentence. "Doctor Who was a happy man." And burst uncontrollably into tears. I don't remember when it ended, I just remembered waking up fully clothed on top of the covers. My head was pounding and the book had fallen to the floor.

Acknowledgements

Many thanks to Dr. Who, and his wacky pals; William Troughtnall, Paddy McHart, Joe McGann, Jonny Gummidge and David Smith.

Charlie Marxworth, The Parasolf boys from Witherbottom Working Men's Club, Penelope Cheapskate, Claudia Farmgate and nobody but Fred (a popular individual!)

Russell 'The Rod' Davies, Grand Moff Steven, Dicky Terry and the famous Cartmell sticky toffee pudding.

Big it up for Eileen (the silver nemesis!) and not forgetting Chris McEccles. If ever there was doubt in our hearts, he'd be there with a reassuring "F*** off, you daft C****!" Chris, you old charmer!

And, last but not least, thanks to Tim Hirst for lending us this type-writer. (They're made of electric these days!)

All proceeds from this book will be donated to 'Who Gives a Toss' – campaigning to get Doctor Who off the air since 2008.

We'll write a proper book next time. Promise.

The authors and publisher would also like to thank the following people for their support:

Gemma Arnold
Carl Bayliss
Suzanne Boothman
Roisin Brennan
Steve Caldwell
Brian Charlesworth
Martin Cook
Mike Cook
Paul Engelberg
Neil Fawcett
Ian Greenfield
Carol Hands
Mark Humphrey
Louise Leddington-Hill
James McFetridge
Jennifer Mckears
Nicholas Mellish
Camilla Neill
Cathie Newton
Charles Northrop
Alister Pearson
Paul Roche
Tim Small
Nigel Terry
Robert Turner
Stephen Walker
Robert Watson
Martin Wiggins
David Zachritz

Doctor Who Titles for 2011!
from www.hirstpublishing.com

1. Life Begins at 40 (Mark Charlesworth & Chris Newton
2. Single White Who Fan (Jackie Jenkins)
3. Gallimaufry (Colin Baker)
4. Shooty Dog Thing: 2th and Claw (Paul Castle & Jon Arnold)
5. Script Doctor (Andrew Cartmel)
6. Through Time (Andrew Cartmel)
7. Planet of the Fans (Darren Floyd & Steve O'Brien)
8. Who's Playing Who (Barnaby Eaton-Jones)
9. Patrick Troughton (Michael Troughton)
10. Dead Woman Laughing (Daphne Ashbrook)

Plus further titles to be announced.

Why not save money and guarantee a regular fix of new books by taking out our Doctor Who subscription?
Please see our website for details